GREEN FIRES

GREEN FIRES

Assault on Eden:
a Novel of the Ecuadorian Rainforest

by
Marnie Mueller

curbstone press

Copyright © 1994 by Marnie Mueller
Originally published 1994 in a cloth edition by Curbstone Press
First paperback edition, 1999
ALL RIGHTS RESERVED

Printed in the U.S. by BookCrafters
cover design: Les Kanturek

Curbstone Press is a 501(c)(3) nonprofit literary arts organization
whose operations are supported in part by individual donations
and by grants from private foundations and government agencies.
This book was published with the support of the Connecticut
Commission on the Arts, National Endowment for the Arts, the
Plumsock Fund, and donations from many individuals. We are
very grateful for this support.

Library of Congress Cataloging-in-Publication Data

Mueller, Marnie.
        Green fires : assault on Eden : a novel of the Ecuadorian rainforest/
by Marnie Mueller
        p.   cm.
        ISBN 1-880684-16-0 (cloth)   ISBN 1-880684-59-4 (paperback)
        1. Indians of South America—Ecuador—History—20th century—
Fiction. 2. Rain forests—Ecuador—Fiction. 3. Americans—
Ecuador—Fiction. 4. Germans—Ecuador—Fiction. I. Title.
PS3563.U354G73   1994
813'.54—dc20

CURBSTONE PRESS
321 Jackson Street
Willimantic, CT 06226
www.curbstone.org

To F.M.

I thank the Virginia Center for the Creative Arts, the Duxbury Colony, the Gordon family of Bromica, and Hermine Ford and Bob Moskowitz for providing me with marvelous retreats at which to do my writing. I am indebted to Janice Eidus, Carol Ascher, and Lorrie Bodger for the time spent going over various versions of my novel; and to Antonio Burr for his assistance with the Spanish. Also, I am grateful to Jane Blanshard for her meticulous copy-editing. My warm appreciation goes to Rhoda Weyr, my agent, for her dedicated work on my behalf. *Abrazos* to my publishers, Sandy Taylor and Judy Doyle, and to Michael Schwartz and Lisa London who have made my first publishing experience what every writer wishes for: artistic support, deadlines met, attention to detail, enthusiasm, and inventive marketing. And lovingly, to Ruth Elberson, who supplied technical assistance by buying me my first computer and FAX, invaluable instruments for any writer. If only she could have lived to hold the book in her hands.

CHAPTER ONE

It was dark by the time our bus lumbered down a dirt street past narrow, dimly lit windows that Kai said looked more like the burrows of bank swallows than human constructions. At the end of the block we turned left and were again engulfed by the pitch-black night. The bus stopped and the driver killed the motor. "Puerto Napo, *la última parada*," he called in a weary voice.

This settlement was the last one on the map of Ecuador before the jungle took over. We'd been traveling more than twelve hours on the bus to get here. The trip should have taken only eight, but just outside of Puyo, on the eastern slope of the Andes, we drove off the road into a ditch. The usual. It took hours of conferences, laughter, arguments, and muscle power before the bus was finally pushed out. Kai and I sat covered with muddy weariness, too exhausted now that we'd reached our destination to get up out of our torn, spring-pierced seats to lift our backpacks down from the overhead rack and descend, undoubtedly into more mud. Add to that the loneliness that I always felt when arriving anywhere.

The Indians we'd been traveling with shuffled silently through the dark bus, dragging their burlap bags stuffed with possessions along the floor, hitting against me as they passed, wrapping me in their smells of wet wool, *aguardiente*, and dirt. A damp breeze blew across the bus from window to window, carrying with it the sweet, funky odor of pig feces I knew so well from my years of living in this country, causing me to sigh as I lifted myself out of the seat.

"I'll get the packs," Kai said. His German accent was magnified by his fatigue, so the sentence came out, "I'll get ze pahks." He raised himself up and hit his head loudly on the rack. "*Verdammte Scheisse!*"

I laughed. "Sorry," I said, and finding his head, I rubbed my hand through his hair, which was like the pelt of some wild species of cat, thick and tawny. Who got more comfort from this, I wondered: he being patted, or I feeling his lush fur between my fingers?

Kai had been hitting his head on bus roofs and door jambs for the entire week of our trip up from Guayaquil where I had been a Peace Corps volunteer six years earlier, on to Quito, then across the mountains, and over into the jungle of the *Oriente*. I had the slight satisfaction of his seeing how difficult it had been for me in 1963, an average-sized woman getting used to towering over the population like some giant being, clumsy and too obvious.

The bus driver had said to wait outside by the vehicle while he found someone to help us. I didn't know where he'd gone, though as we stood beside the bus with our heavy backpacks on, I made out the sound of men's voices to our right, barely audible above the rush of a river. The sky was dense with stars, and the moon was beginning to rise up over the trees to our left. Otherwise, it was completely dark. Even the headlights of the bus had been put out.

In the cool dampness of the tropical night, my loneliness began to overwhelm me. I surmised from what little I'd seen of this place as we drove through that it could be a pretty rough spot. I'd stayed in frightening locales in my years of living here, but I'd never much liked it. Even though I'd always put on a brave face, I'd never stopped longing for comfort, for lights that were electric and over forty watts, for my surroundings to be free of huge, crawling cockroaches and darting lizards. For cold running water. Warm was out of the question. For a toilet. Some would say this had to do with a spoiled North American's need for comfort. Not so. Just the opposite. Throughout my childhood, I'd lived a nomadic life of relative discomfort, and I craved security. After a day or two I could accustom myself to anything, or almost anything, but the first hours of the unknown were terribly hard for me. It wasn't the same for Kai. He could adjust immediately to any situation. Kai had lived through a world war, but even when he had sat in a bunker as a child with bombs falling outside, he'd had the comfort of his family, a mother who protected him.

Where was that damn bus driver, I worried as I shivered in my shirtsleeves. The roar of the river was beginning to grate on me. I started to resent being here. It had been Kai's choice to come this far. I would have preferred to stay in Baños, a town known for its sulfur baths and perfect spring-like weather, but I'd been ashamed to say I wanted such luxury. Now here I was, a wife following her husband on his adventure. I'd resisted Kai when he'd first proposed marriage, but he'd finally worn me down, and, as of this moment, we had been husband and wife for exactly eight days. Being a wife didn't hold much appeal for me. Lovers, yes, which we'd been to my satisfaction for three years. But a wife—well, I was even more uncomfortable with that notion than with the prospect of being without a room for the night.

"I hope they have a *pensión* at least," I grumbled.

"Just keep calm, Annie. I'm sure there is something."

"What you have to learn in this country," I continued, "is that you must always be ready for the worst."

"Annie, cut it off."

"Cut it out is the correct term."

"Cut it off, cut it out, what's the difference?"

"There's a big difference between the two."

The driver appeared all of a sudden, seemingly out of nowhere, saving us from further escalation. "*Señorita, señor, tienen habitación, es muy bueno!*"

"*Me alegro,*" I said. "I'm sure we'll be very happy there."

"This is not *los Estados Unidos, señorita.*"

"I don't need it to be the United States," I laughed, already feeling better being able to banter in my second language. "All I want is a bed, some quiet, and the morning to be many hours away."

"And your man beside you," he said, insinuating more with his tone.

"Yes, my wonderful husband of many years who may not speak fluently but he does understand some of the language."

With that he stopped. At least being married had the advantage of squelching suggestive innuendo, I thought, as we followed the driver up the slippery stairs dug into the steep rise of the river bank.

The Hotel Jaguar was a series of cubicle sized rooms that opened off a cement outer-walkway. The structure was of thin, ill-fitting wood planks. We could see the lights from the other rooms through the cracks as we passed by.

The minute we closed the door to our own narrow box the electricity went out.

We both burst out laughing.

"We had our ration, I guess," Kai said. "Now where is the goddamn lantern?"

"I saw it on the crate between the beds," I said, groping my way along the two cots, whispering for no other reason than that it was dark. "Do you know where your flashlight is?"

"I'm looking." I heard him fumbling in his backpack.

I felt around the top of the crate and found the box of matches. I was so relieved to be there that even being without electricity was fun. I was in a room with a padlock for safety and a roof for comfort. I had a bed, such as it was. Not exactly a honeymoon suite, but then this had never been planned as a conventional honeymoon trip. Our intention had been to fly into Guayaquil so that I could take Kai to my old *barrio* to meet the people I had lived and worked with, and then we would go off to the mountains for a romantic week before heading into the *Oriente* so Kai, an inveterate birdwatcher, could fulfill an old desire to see rainforest species. As it turned out, I couldn't bring myself to stay in Guayaquil. I wasn't able to visit my *barrio*. We were ahead of schedule.

The flashlight went on. Kai shone it first on me and then over to the sign on the door.

"*Electricidad.*" he read. "*Siete a ocho.*" He looked at his watch. "Right on time. It's five after eight."

The tiny room was filled with light and the strong smell of kerosene when we got the lamp to catch. I opened the window beside my cot, letting in the sweet damp air of the rainforest.

"Mmm, I wish I had some flowers," I said, heaving my backpack onto the foot of my bed. "Then it would be just like home."

Kai stretched his slender body the full length of the cot, his heels hanging over the metal rest at the end. He folded his densely freckled arms across his chest and grinned at me. Kai's deep blue eyes—with their Tartar cast—are reduced to mere slits whenever he smiles or laughs, elongated above his high cheek bones. I love his eyes. "Glad to hear you cheerful again," he said.

I sank down on my bed. As though in defiance of his statement, when I should have been savoring my relief, a vacuum descended on me, sucking me into its silence. I felt it invade with a quietness that I knew too well. I had kept it at bay all week, since abruptly leaving Guayaquil, but it had found me again. I curled onto the bed, laying my head on the muslin-covered pillow, pulling my legs to my chest.

Kai sensed immediately what I'd thought of.

"You want to come over here, my big hero," he said. "Just have a minute of warmth and then try to find some food?"

Without answering I got up and crawled in beside him on his cot, letting him wrap himself around me, tucking his knees up into the backs of my legs. His hands came in under my arms and gently held my breasts.

"It's Gala and the baby, right?"

I nodded.

"Maybe I should have insisted that we stay in Guayaquil a few days. To visit the grave at least."

"Will I ever be free of this?"

"I can't answer that, Annie."

Lying safely in his arms I replayed, as I had innumerable times, that morning in 1965 in the *barrio* of Cerro Santa Ana when the child Gladys had appeared at the community center, coming through the high metal green gate with her brown features blanched to beige.

"My mother wants you," she had said in her gruff, too adult, voice.

I had followed her up the *barrio* stairs, climbing the hill to our yellow-washed cane-and-wood apartment house, through our main door that had been garlanded with white satin and pink plastic flowers, to enter the small dark room where two adults, five girls, and an infant boy lived. The wooden chairs were in a circle. *Doña* Marta, *Señora* Citrón, and the others sat in silence. The tiny coffin was under the picture of the Christ child as were the altar of candles and offerings of water.

Gala had seen me the minute I entered. "Aaiiee!" she screamed, her brown arms stretching out, her breasts rising beneath the fabric of her white mourning dress. "Ana, help me. God has taken my only son."

"Why couldn't I have saved her baby?" I said angrily to Kai. "What good was I to anyone if I couldn't even save Ladito?"

"You suffer from an American malady," he sighed. "You think you truly have the power to change the world. You did the best you could."

We had been over this many times, trying to conquer the memories that had caused me night terrors, sudden rages, depression, and the inability to speak of my experience in the Peace Corps. Except to Kai. Though even with him I didn't open up entirely. In my most private thoughts there were realms of recollection I couldn't yet enter. Perhaps I had chosen this trip to face once and for all what had happened in the seaport city of Guayaquil and to put it to rest.

"At the time you couldn't have done better," Kai continued.

"I'm ashamed of acting this way."

"There's nothing to be ashamed of," he said, wrapping me closer. "Nothing at all."

CHAPTER TWO

From the moment Kai and I met at a mutual friend's dinner party I gave myself over to him as I never had before with another person. It was strange, considering all I knew about him was that he was German and a chemist with Bell Labs. I was suspicious of Germans.

One afternoon, during our first balmy, erotic days of infatuation, we were lying in the dusky twilight of my apartment, spent from lovemaking, when I said, "I'm Jewish."

He reached across me and flipped on the bedside lamp, bathing me in full light as he settled back to his elbow. He stared at me in silence before saying, "My father was a Nazi. He joined to protect the family."

I closed my eyes against the severity of his gaze. "How do you know?"

"I don't. My father died before I could ask him about it." His voice was flat.

"What does your mother say?"

"One doesn't ask such questions in Germany. I put two and two together. It's what I came up with myself. But I'd rather not talk about it now." He lay down and rolled away.

I violently yanked him around by the shoulder, my fingers digging into his flesh. "What would you have done in your father's place?"

His face was sad and pinched when he said, "I can't answer that. What you Americans don't understand is that for children like I was, war was what was normal. Peace, when it came, was the aberration. That permanently affects your thinking. All I know is that I loved my father. And then he died. In peacetime. But not before he was de-Nazified by the Americans."

Soon after, I told him my own secrets, concealments so deeply embedded in me that I'd never confided them to anyone. I told him that my father had been a

conscientious objector during World War Two and that
he'd been imprisoned for three long years, when I was
between one and four. I had visited my father a couple of
times, or so my mother had said. I didn't remember. What I
did know was that I had recurring dreams of prisons all my
life and that they'd intensified on my return from
Guayaquil. In these dreams steel clanked against steel, but
my terror was not of being locked inside, rather I was afraid
of being kept out by the high chain-link fences and the
bars on the windows, while on the other side, standing on a
long concrete ramp, a woman in a beautiful red dress
beckoned to me. When I called out, tears formed on her
face, but she wouldn't speak. Instead she turned away and
vanished. It was at that point that I would begin to cry
inconsolably, gasping for breath like a baby, crying so
violently that I started to choke on my own fluid. Kai woke
me from such a dream on the night I'd confided in him.
"Annie, please," he pleaded. "I'm here beside you. You're
dreaming, *Liebchen.*"

He held me in his arms as though I were his baby,
rocking me while I told him the dream. When I'd finished
and he put his palm to my cheek in a gesture of further
comfort, I experienced a sensation akin to erotic pleasure
on the surface of my skin. It was so intense with feelings
both foreign and known that I began to weep again. "My
mother was Jewish," I said softly, leaning harder into his
chest. "My father was Christian. She was my prison, not
my father."

"How did she hurt you?" he whispered.

"I can't tell you."

"Why not?"

"I'm too afraid."

"She can't hear us," he said.

"No, she can't. She's dead."

"Annie, I'm sorry. How old were you?"

I squeezed my eyes shut and plugged my ears with my
fists to be able to tell him. "I was seven when she
committed suicide."

He responded in the kindest way possible, by clasping his hands over my fists and not saying a word.

We lived in Winooski, Vermont. It was winter. I was already in the third grade, having progressed much faster than the French Canadian children who had not yet learned English because their parents had recently emigrated for factory jobs. Winooski was a mill town, across the river from Burlington where the university was located. My father was traveling the state, organizing farmers into fuel cooperatives. We lived in soot-blackened brick factory housing because it was cheap, and because he had a friend who had found it for us when we moved up from southern Ohio.

My mother had been very unhappy in Ohio. My father was always out working, and she never liked our neighbors in any of the small farm communities where we relocated. She told me they were narrow-minded and bigoted; that I was her only friend there. Things became worse once we moved to Winooski. When she and I were alone, she stared off into space for hours. I chattered to her, but she didn't hear me. I sang songs the way we used to do as we drove together across the country from California to Ohio to Vermont, following after my father, but she didn't sing back. Even though her eyes were open, she disappeared behind them. I thought, "Mommy's gone far away. She can't see me," and tried harder to get her to return.

On a bitter February noon I came home for lunch and wasn't allowed in the house. I stood on our outdoor second floor landing among the frozen clothes that my mother had hung to dry in the early morning. It was windy and they hit against me like razors, slicing against my face until someone gathered me away. Whispers of "she hung herself" filtered about me. For a long time I was confused, thinking it had something to do with the clothes on the line.

My father and I moved across the river to Burlington, where I kept secret the nature of my mother's death and that she had been Jewish. In my new classroom, I witnessed two girls hold their noses as they walked by another girl's desk saying, "Peeuwy, Jews sure stink." I was terrified they would learn I was related to that awful, smelly breed called Jews. It never occurred to me to confide my fear to my grieving father.

All through high school, college, and the Peace Corps, I concealed my background by saying my mother had died of pneumonia, by passing as gentile under the cover of my father's last name of Saunders and my own bleached blond hair, and by never revealing that my father had been imprisoned. It wasn't until I returned to the States and to New York City where my father was living and working on the lower east side, that I admitted to a new friend that I was half Jewish. Soon after that I moved to my own apartment in the East Village, dyed my hair back to its natural brown, and began reading whatever literature I could find on Jewish history. I became preternaturally aware of Jews with numbers branded on their wrists: the man at the spa fountain who made the egg creams, the woman behind the appetizing counter at Ratner's. On Yom Kippur of the fall of 1966, I attended services. I had never been in the company of so many Jewish people. I glanced around the synagogue and recognized my mother's face reflected in theirs, saw my grandparents whom I knew only by photo, and the visage of my mother's sister from California. When the dead of the holocaust were remembered and Kaddish was intoned and the setting sun entered the temple and the shofar filled the room with its plaintive cry, I wept along with all the rest, openly and without shame. I felt all Jewish in that moment.

Two months later I met Kai.

CHAPTER THREE

We walked along the street toward a golden light coming from one of the distant buildings. I could still hear the river to our right, but now it sounded romantic, as though it were a special effect adding to the exquisite beauty of the night, along with the sweet smell of frangipani and the white explosion of stars in the black sky. The three-quarter moon had come up and was hanging in the east, just above the ridge of trees, and though it was blindingly bright, it did little to dim the stars. The only discomfort on our walk was how wet my feet were getting as mud seeped into my sneakers and socks. There was no one else out, but as we neared the building, the murmur of voices reached the road.

We passed through swinging doors like those I'd only seen on saloons in the western movies I loved as a child. The room was as wide as it was long, about thirty by thirty feet, with ceilings so low that Kai wisely stooped when he stepped inside.

The golden light was from a few kerosene lanterns set on tables and on a bar in back. Shadows loomed and flickered on the walls. All talk stopped as we stood in the doorway. *Mestizos* and full Indians looked up from their beers and stared, not saying a word while we crossed the expanse of packed dirt floor over to a table by the bar.

I'd not experienced such staring since my early days in this country. I suspected that even now not many *gringos* had traveled this far into the *Oriente*.

I glanced at Kai. He looked too pale, his freckles absurdly splotchy, and his body too long and thin. I knew he wouldn't be feeling the least bit self-conscious. Kai had almost no vanity when it came to this sort of thing. All he was interested in was seeing what was new to see. I, on the other hand, had to control myself to keep from asking him how I looked.

I made a mental note to practice the Guayaquil sway in our room. It was the particular hip-rolling action that all women in my coastal city were known for. And with that thought, the side of me that loved this country and felt a certain prowess in dealing comfortably within its borders returned.

The waitress was standing by the bar, staring straight ahead, not making any move to come over to us. Once we were seated, I clapped my hands to get her attention.

"*¿Qué quiere?*" She mumbled when she arrived at our table with her head down. She was a *mestizo*, with dark ruddy skin and her straight black hair pulled away from her face into a pony tail. She had tied it with red yarn. She wore a faded pink cotton dress, low-cut and tight around her waist and hips, the style Guayaquil was famous for. She turned to look over her shoulder at the men, who continued to watch us silently.

"Is there anything to eat?" I asked.

"Nothing." Her head was down again. The nervous smirk I'd seen cross her lips was gone. She may wear a Guayaquil dress, I thought, but she still has the inhibitions of an Indian when faced with white people. I softened my voice.

"Nothing? No soup, no yucca?"

"Yes, there's soup." Her mouth pursed against the returning smile.

"And bread?"

"Yes, *señorita*, some bread."

"The soup and bread for two is fine," I said. "And anything else you may have."

"There is nothing else, *señorita*." Her eyes met mine for a split-second.

"Then two beers."

"Large or small?" For the first time her gaze held. I knew what she was thinking. Who is this *gringa* who drinks beer? What is she doing here? Is she here to sleep with men?

"Two small Pilsners for my husband and me," I said.
Fuck it, I thought, I'll do what I want. But I let her know I
was married, just in case.

Once again, I saw that being married was going to have
its advantages. I had told myself before I came down here
that I wasn't going to fall into being overly sensitive to the
cultural ways. It had been one of the many soul-grinding
paradoxes during my Peace Corps time. I was a community
organizer and as such I was supposed to ferret out the felt
needs of the community. I was supposed to get each person
to be genuine with me about what they wanted, and, I, in
turn, would act natural with them. My father had always
told me, "Don't try to become 'the people.' It's always seen
through. Remain yourself, be respectful of others' ways in
the community, but keep your own counsel." But what he
hadn't told me was that when working in a culture very
different from one's own, as the organizer, you can only
pretend to be yourself. Can only pretend to be relaxed and
open. To go all the way, to make explicit the enormous
gulf between you and others, would make it impossible to
accomplish anything. Having hidden the truth of my
mother's suicide and her religion for so many years, I was
well-practiced in not letting on who I was. In the barrio the
talent served me in getting the work done, but, as it had
been throughout my childhood, such constant duplicity
was exhausting.

As we finished our soup of broth and yucca, a young
man entered and stood at the doorway looking around. He
was Indian, though not Sierra Quechua. The men at the
table glanced up. One man raised his hand in greeting, but
then they all went back to their beers. No one called him
over. I watched him as he walked across the dirt floor. He
wore a light-colored, short-sleeved shirt open to his smooth
mid chest. The shirttails hung out over his white pressed
pants. On his feet were sneakers. He had a modern hipness
to him, from the way he carried his large canvas bag over
his shoulder with his thumb hooked into the strap to the
latest shag cut of his straight black hair. I couldn't help

noticing how handsome he was with high cheekbones, wide-set eyes, full mouth, and a long, prominent nose. His skin, in the lantern light, was a deep coppery color. At the bar he stood with his back to the room and talked to the waitress. She smiled flirtatiously as she went behind the bar. He turned, glanced over at us, and nodded.

"*Buenas noches*," Kai said, surprising me.

"*Buenas, patrones*," he said.

For all his up-to-date look, he was still addressing us as his bosses.

The waitress returned then with a whiskey bottle and shot glass which the young man picked up in his free hand; he came toward us. He smiled, revealing perfect white teeth. He was smaller up close than from the distance at the bar. His face was rounder and, despite his fine bones, more flat-cheeked than the faces of Indians in the mountains, and he wore a single strand of tiny red and turquoise beads around his neck. I wondered if he was from this area.

"May I join you, *patrones?*" He asked in Spanish.

I glanced at Kai and saw that he was eager to have the conversation, though I knew what drinking with an Ecuadorian, particularly an Indian, could lead to. They weren't known for holding liquor well. But I said, " *¿Cómo no? Siéntese, por favor*."

"*Gracias, señores*," he said, dropping the *patrón* business. He shoved his bag onto a chair and pulled another out and sat down. "Oh, that feels good."

"Have you come a long way?" I said, for lack of anything better.

"*Sí, señorita*," he smiled accommodatingly. "From down the river, all day from down the river."

"Ask him what he does downriver." Kai sat forward, ever curious.

Before I could ask, the man beckoned to the waitress. "What do you drink?"

"No, no," I said. "We're doing fine." I indicated our half-filled bottles.

But he insisted that we drink whiskey with him and sent the girl behind the bar for extra glasses.

Once the whiskey was poured, we toasted each other with *salud, pesetas, y amor*. The young man then told us his name was Mingo Mincha. "Mingo, short for Domingo."

He looked startled when I told him Kai's name, but in the next moment he was smiling broadly.

"Kai Schmidt," he said. "Are you two German?" He reclined in his chair, letting the front legs rise.

"My husband is," I said. "I'm North American."

"Where do you live?" he asked.

"In the United States. In New York City."

And you have a cousin in New York, I anticipated.

But no, to my surprise he didn't say that, only nodded and stared at me, not smiling.

Kai asked again, in pigeon but decipherable Spanish, what Mingo did downriver.

"I sell things to the Indians," he said directly to Kai.

"What things?" Kai kept it up.

Pretty good, I thought, beginning to feel superfluous.

"Oh, what they need." Mingo waved his hand through the air. He gave me another long look. He seemed to decide what he would say next as he inspected my face. "I am Shuar, or Jívaro as you may call my tribe. They trust me."

Kai had understood. Our eyes met. Was this true? Were we actually meeting a Jívaro, those who practiced the rite of shrinking heads? In New York, I worked for an alternative, listener-sponsored, radio station. I'd brought a tape-recorder with me to document bird songs, but also perhaps to do interviews. This Mingo could be the perfect subject.

"That's interesting," I said. "I didn't know any of the Shuar had left the forest."

"Some of us were fortunate to be rescued by the Salesian priests. And educated so that we could carry on business with the outside world." He grimaced, self-consciously brushing his hair back over his ears, first on one side, then on the other.

"Where is the school?" Kai asked.

"In Macas, beside the Rio Upano. Close to a hundred kilometers from here."

Mingo pulled the chair with his bag on it closer to him. "I continue the process of bringing my people civilization," he said, unzipping the canvas carry-all and laying on the table tee shirts, cotton skirts, children's socks and shoes. "It's a service I provide. They have a desire to dress themselves now in western clothing. It's important that we become civilized, don't you agree?" He looked from Kai to me.

I knew where Kai stood on this. Besides wanting to see the birds of the area, he'd come to learn about the indigenous population. He had strong feelings about tampering with people's traditional ways.

But Kai merely shrugged. "It depends," he said.

Voices rose over where the men were sitting and as quickly subsided into a murmur.

"Depends on what, my friend?" Mingo poured more whiskey into our glasses.

A memory intruded of how we volunteers used to escape our *barrios* to spend evenings on the *Nueve de Octubre*, drinking at outdoor cafes while armless beggars wove among the tables, pushing stumps into our faces until we had to give money. The jukeboxes blared *cumbias*, and the hot humid winds off the river Guayas swirled sensually around us. After we'd been in-country for a year we began making cynical jokes—about the beggars, about the spoiled rich boys who cruised the avenue in Mercedes, even about the poor of our *barrios*, especially those who stole from us on a regular basis until we had nothing left to take. The joke was that after each visit from a neighbor one did inventory. "One wrist watch for the Ekkies," as we derisively called Ecuadorians, "one camera saved from thieving hands. A good night for the *gringos*." I was ashamed of such talk, knowing how luxurious my simplest possessions— ballpoint pens, books, extra underwear—seemed to my impoverished neighbors, but still I entered into it, sometimes with my own stories, sometimes with appreciative laughter. Those nights I caught the last bus back to my *barrio*, the Cerro Santa Ana, distinguished by cane houses built up the side of a hill, where by ten everything had closed down—the *tienda*, the shutters on the apartment windows, the army yard across the plaza. At six the next morning the sound of young recruits goose-stepping in their black shiny boots would enter my apartment, a daily reminder that our host government was a military *junta*. But late at night the cement stairs rising to my building were empty and silent except for the drug dealers who sat at the bottom of the hill, calling double entendres after me about the cow who gave milk, the *gringa* who loved bananas and who had come to bring aid to the poor.

"Depends on who does the civilizing and to what end," I heard myself saying. "Depends on the alternatives."

A fleeting reaction passed over Mingo's face, as though he had sensed my implication.

"Did you know that there is another German living down the Napo, very far in?" he said.

"No," Kai said. And to me he said, "Perhaps we could travel with him if he is going back downriver. This is a great opportunity, Annie."

I would have been as enthusiastic as he at this point, but for Mingo's mention of the German. What was a German doing in the jungle? But I asked him for Kai's sake.

"Are you planning on going downriver in the next few days? If so, my husband wonders if we can accompany you. He wishes to see birds."

"To shoot?"

"No, no," I said.

"No, to see. *A ver*." Kai raised his hands and made circles with his fingers in front of his eyes. "*Nur* to see," he said confusing German and English as he often did when he was overly eager to communicate in a third language.

"Ah, to see," Mingo nodded. "*Tienes lentes*," he said, speaking in the familiar. He used his hands to indicate binoculars as Kai had.

"Yes," Kai nodded.

"Ah." Mingo said. "How much are these binoculars in America or in Germany? How much in dollars?"

"Quite a few dollars," I said.

"*Sí, señora. Pero cuánto?*"

He wasn't to be played with. Like most Ecuadorians, he wanted to know the worth of every expensive First World item.

"Around a hundred dollars," I said.

He whistled and looked admiringly at us. "But they are wonderful," he said. "They make the world come close. I've seen it for myself." He made the hair-brushing gesture again. I guessed he was twenty-two, older by a year than I'd been when I'd arrived six years earlier. What would it have been like if I'd met such a boy when I'd worked here. I thought of César, my boyfriend back then, *mestizo*, handsome, and completely assimilated. He had the same color skin and the same black straight hair.

"I am going tomorrow morning. I can take you as far as the German if you wish. I think you would like to visit the German. I believe he would like to meet you. Perhaps." He was watching us very closely again.

"Who is the German?" I asked, forcing myself out of the memory of César and the dangerous thoughts of Guayaquil that were threatening to take me over. "How long has he lived here?"

Mingo wagged a finger back and forth in the air. His fingers were long. César's hands had been slender, and his fingers long, the skin on them dark, and heavily etched with lines for a young man.

"I don't know. They say he has been here for twenty years. Though who can say? I only know him for the last three since I have come to the area. There are many stories about him, and our government, well, the government in Quito, doesn't..."

He stopped in mid-sentence. His attention moved over my right shoulder and his expression hardened.

CHAPTER FOUR

Following Mingo's gaze, I saw an enormous man filling the entire arc of the two swinging sections of the door. His largeness was more in girth than in height. He didn't have to stoop. But what was most curious was that he appeared to be a Franciscan monk, dressed as he was in rough brown hopsacking tied by a rope at the waist. From this a huge wooden cross hung. On his feet he wore the rubber tire sandals of the highland Indians. He stood scratching his thick black unruly hair and then scrabbled in his beard with his fingers.

Mingo spat on the floor, a common practice in Ecuador, but in this case it seemed a display of disgust. Perhaps the monk is one of the Salesians, I thought. Whoever he was, he was taking in the room. His eyes moved slowly around with seeming nonchalance. He looked at the Indians sitting in the far corner. They appeared to keep their heads even lower toward their glasses under his scrutiny, their conversation to a steady hum. The waitress remained leaning over the bar, her chin on her hands, staring blankly at him.

"¡Cholita!" the man roared, and walked directly across the room to her, ignoring us, though I was certain he'd studied us as well. We were the only other people in the room, and Mingo was glaring at him.

"Who is that?" I asked.

Kai leaned closer to hear.

"The *padre*." Mingo's face aged so in the candlelight on our table as he spoke that I thought I had miscalculated. He could have been thirty, judging by the line that ran down from the sides of his nose to the corners of his mouth.

"Is he Salesian?" I kept my voice low.

Kai shook his head and said before Mingo could answer, "He looks more itinerant to me. Sort of self-made."

"No, he isn't Salesian," Mingo sneered.

The *padre*, who had been conferring with the girl who kept looking over his shoulder at us, turned and roared, "¡Mingo Mincha! *Los años, que no nos hemos visto!*" He came toward us, beer bottle and glass in hand. "Who are these nice people I find you with? This beautiful young woman, and this gentleman. *Americanos?*" He stood grinning at us, emitting the smell of perspiration, hopsacking, and garlic breath. It was a pretty powerful combination. He hadn't spoken with an Ecuadorian accent, but in high Spanish, though I couldn't quite pinpoint from where I knew it. "*Padre* Roberto Báez Chamino, *a sus órdenes, señores.*" He bowed extravagantly. When he raised his head I looked into eyes so pale blue as to be almost transparent.

Kai stood and bowed slightly, as was the German way when shaking hands. "Kai Schmidt," he said and indicating me, "Anne Schmidt."

I almost corrected Kai to say my name was Saunders, but I let it pass.

"*¿Alemanes? ¿No son americanos?*" His grin left. "So this is it, Mingo? More Germans for you."

"*Soy norte americana,*" I said, when Mingo didn't answer. He was sitting glowering over his whiskey.

"*Así es,*" the *padre* said. So that's it. "*Y habla español también.*"

"*Sí, un poquito,*" I said.

"Not so little, it appears. You wouldn't be sitting here speaking with my friend Mingo if you only spoke a little, unless you speak Quichua."

One quick glance told me how much Mingo hated this guy. I didn't know what to do. The *padre* wasn't about to leave, but I didn't feel like inviting him to sit down. My loyalty had already lodged with Mingo. Admittedly, he reminded me of César. But even without that, I attach to people quickly if I like them and sense them to be trustworthy, attach to their roots and have a hard time disengaging. It's a problem I have, or some would say an attribute, a survival skill picked up in childhood.

"No, only Spanish."

"And very good Spanish, too." The *padre* said. "Peace Corps?"

"Right on the first guess, but not for four years."

"*Señorita*." He said this with a certain finality.

"Yes?"

"May I join you and your party?" He looked from Mingo to Kai who had remained standing.

"Of course," Kai said.

Once seated, he drank heartily from his beer while the rest of us sat silently. He pounded the empty glass on the table. With proximity his smell grew more pungent and his grisly looks more intense.

"I want to know more about this Peace Corps business. I could tell immediately that you were Peace Corps. You are neither tourist nor native. You are Peace Corps!" he roared. "Tell me where did you do your good works?"

"In Guayaquil."

"Aha, *La Perla del Pacífico*!"

I laughed, remembering how we would call it the shit hole of the Pacific.

"So I see, the ex-Peace Corps volunteer recalls her contempt for the country." He put his head down and scratched his neck under his long curly hair, all the time keeping his gaze on me.

"What's going on?" Kai asked.

"Nothing," I said, though sensing for the first time that I was dealing with a crafty man, despite the bumbling manner he affected.

"You misunderstand," I said. "I am so fond of this country that I brought my new husband back on our honeymoon."

"Well, well." The father clapped his hands twice. "This calls for a round of drinks."

"Not for me," Mingo said, scowling. But to me he said, "Congratulations, *señora*," and lifted his shot glass. "And to you, *señor*."

Kai seemed to have slipped into the phase of not understanding a word of the foreign language. He raised his glass and smiled faintly, tired of making the effort.

The waitress brought a round of beers for the four of us. Mingo still declined, even when the man continued to insist in his unbearably robust manner. I wondered why Mingo remained at our table, if he disliked him so.

"So you are not *amigos* of my *amigo* here." The father continued, this time speaking slowly so that Kai could understand.

"New friends," Kai said, perking up. He smiled and nodded to Mingo.

"So have you been telling *Herr* Schmidt here about his countryman?"

"I spoke of him," Mingo said.

"I'm certain you did. I suppose he told you what a fine fellow he is," the father said, his voice searing with sarcasm. When Mingo wouldn't look up from the table, he continued. "I suppose he told you how he has been living, I won't say hiding, in the most remote region of our jungle for many, many years, since the end of the Great War? And has he told you how our fine German took a black woman, an Ecuadorian no less, as his wife, and how she is willing, it seems, to live out there alone in that wilderness, with only the indigenous as her friends? Not that the indigenous are not the finest people, but most of them, as you know, have not been civilized as our friend here has, and as a result do not exactly welcome visitors. Though lately they seem to have been kinder and more accepting of our German than of other outsiders. Many of us have wondered about that."

Mingo clutched his glass. If it had been any more fragile it would have broken between his fingers. I heard him mumble something.

Kai nudged me under the table with his knee. I shook my head slightly.

Who was this German they spoke of and what was the father insinuating? The more that was revealed, the more it appeared that there was something suspicious about the German. Or was I being manipulated into wondering about him? As much as I disliked the allusive racism the father was evincing about Indians, I didn't want to challenge him yet. My curiosity had been piqued enough to want him to continue about this German. Recently at the radio station, I had interviewed two men from the Simon Wiesenthal organization. They spent most of the time on-air discussing their latest hunts for Joseph Mengele and Klaus Barbie in the jungles of Bolivia and Argentina. Though I had no desire to meet a Nazi face to face, the challenge of such a discovery was beginning to compete with my disinclination, and my desire for a romantic honeymoon. What if this was one of the Nazis the Wiesenthal people were looking for? Perhaps we could spot him, spend a little time, then be off and report him as soon as we reached a shortwave radio in Quito. At the same time, I worried about what such an encounter would evoke in Kai.

"C'mon, Annie, tell me what's going on," Kai said. I knew he'd be angry with me for assuming the man was a Nazi in hiding. He would say I was being intolerant in my presumption of a Nazi around every corner. This assumption of German guilt was still a problem for us. We'd had some terrible fights whenever I had suggested he ask his mother about what his father did during the war. I said he was afraid to know. I said that it would be good for him—that without knowing the truth, how did he expect to live a fully realized life? When he went silent, I didn't stop. I became relentless in my attacks. Once I grabbed his hair as we were driving and he almost swerved into an oncoming car. It was then that I realized how violent my feelings were, and perhaps he saw how dangerous his silence was before them, because after that we were more circumspect when it came to issues of German and Jewish and worked hard to remain rational in our discussions.

"He's talking about the German," I said, "how he's lived back in the jungle with a black wife among the Indians for many years, in the remotest of areas."

"I know what you're thinking." He gave me a chilly look.

"So, my friend." The friar was speaking to Mingo who still avoided his eyes. "Have you invited our friends to meet your illustrious hermit?" He turned to us then. "Sometimes Mingo does that. He invites people and they come out of the forest with all sorts of tales. Isn't that so, Mingo?"

"They come with truth," Mingo spoke distinctly but softly.

"What is that truth? What is truth? I ask you, *señorita*, is truth so easy these days?"

Why was Mingo remaining here, enduring this public ridicule? He seemed to grow smaller as the father lit into him. The father's behavior was most unbecoming a man of the cloth. In all my time in-country, I'd met quite a few morally unfit clergy, but this seemed extreme behavior. As though hearing my thoughts, the father suddenly changed his stance.

"Forgive me, please," he said in an unctuous tone. "I've traveled all day under the hot sun. I believe it's gotten to me, and add to it this beer. I am not being myself. My good friend, *don* Mingo, you know I don't like to carry on this way. Even about the German."

But I'd already witnessed the vein of cruelty in this man.

"Don't worry," I said in my sweetest voice. "We're not interested in the German. My husband is a birdwatcher and a naturalist. We asked Mingo to take us down the Napo so my husband can see birds. Isn't that right, Mingo?"

Mingo looked up, a shy grin spreading across his face. "Certainly, *señora*, that is what we decided. The first thing in the morning I will go to Misahuallí and get the boat ready. You will come in the bus and meet me there. That is how we planned it, no?"

The *padre* who had been watching us as though seeking the lie in what we said, slapped his hands from on high onto his knees and said, "In that case, I will join you. I must return to my village tomorrow. I need a boat. I was wondering how I was going to get there. What do you say, *Señora* Schmidt, if I accompany you?"

"What's going on?" Kai leaned close to me.

"The father wants to go with us with Mingo tomorrow."

"We're going for sure?"

"Yes. You look like hell."

"I feel like hell, I can't wait to hit the bag."

"Sack," I laughed. "Hit the sack is the saying."

"Oh." He yawned.

"So, *señora?*" The *padre* still waited for my answer.

"It depends on Mingo, no?" I said, hoping Mingo would refuse him.

Mingo shrugged and said, "If he must, he must." He zipped his satchel. "Until tomorrow then."

I stood when he did. "We're going too," I said, giving Kai a nudge.

"Do you stay at the Jaguar?" The *padre* got up as well.

I said yes.

"So do I, so do I. What good fortune. We can walk there in the moonlight together."

In the corner, the Indian men were conversing, those that were still awake, that is. The others slept with their faces flat on the table as though they'd passed out and would stay that way until morning. After we'd paid and begun to walk toward the door, Mingo broke from us and went over to their table. One of the men rose when he approached and the two stood close to each other talking.

The silence of the night was like a physical presence. Only the faintest hint of the river came through the motionless, soundless outdoors. Looking up it was as though we were inside an enormous paperweight and the stars were snowflakes pouring down. Great white splashes against the black, moving dizzyingly nearer as I stared.

"Glorious," Kai whispered.

"It's God's way," The father bellowed, breaking the spell. "God provides beauty even to the downtrodden."

I didn't think it necessary to answer him, and instead began walking toward the Jaguar. It had rained while we'd been inside, judging by the puddles we had to skirt. The mud was denser and more slippery than before. The father lumbered along beside me grunting with each step. However did he manage in the jungle?

"Do you work in an Indian village?" I asked.

"I do, child, I do," he wheezed.

"What work do you do?"

"Why, I bring the word of God, my child."

With that we reached the Hotel Jaguar.

"Goodnight. Until tomorrow, my children." And he turned left toward the river, his large hand held high in the air as he shambled on, walking to the last door of the hotel.

CHAPTER FIVE

"I hope we can go deep in, perhaps stay with the German. Spend a few days. I'd love that." Kai lay on the cot in his underpants, with Schauensee's *Birds of Colombia* open on his chest.

I sat on my cot watching him. There were aspects of Kai that would remain mysterious to me, such as why he had no suspicions about this German. Because he is a German himself, is what I told myself. But Kai was a jumble of contradictions. He didn't want to live in Germany, and at the same time he balked at becoming an American citizen. He chose to make his home in the city with the largest Jewish population and yet he was furious when someone Jewish said, "You don't seem German," or "You're the one good German we know." And he married a Jewish woman who challenged him to talk about exactly what he wanted to avoid, the guilt his country carried.

Once when we were going through some of his old drawings and we came across a collage with the announcement of the deaths of Goodman, Schwerner, and Chaney painted over with violent black and red, he told me he had wept when they'd been killed. Above the collage section was a painting of a burned-out building with gaping holes that had been windows, smeared with raw sulfur-colored paint. He didn't want to talk further about it, but I insisted as I always did. I was intrigued by the newspaper material and the violence of the applied paint. When he did begin to talk, he said his first job in this country had been in South Carolina, where he'd been shocked by signs: "For Whites Only." It had been in the summer of 1964 when the boys had disappeared. He told me how each night he sat by his radio listening for the news. He knew from the start that they'd been killed. Still he hoped, not wanting to be right. On the night the fatal announcement came, he stayed up painting the picture of the burning building. The next day he cut up the newspapers and pasted them down and painted over them. He took his time telling me the story, and for once I didn't push. I could see how moved he was. When he finished, I only asked, "Why the burning building?" And that was when he told me a story from the war.

When he was eight years old, in the last year of the war, the Allies had begun to carry out night-time bombings of the cities. During the day, the Americans bombed the plants, but at night the English targeted the cities. Often his two sisters and he were wakened from a deep sleep and bundled down into the basement, carrying pillows and feather *plumeau*. But one night his mother woke them and in an anxious voice told them to put their clothes over their pajamas and to rush. Instead of carrying their bedclothes, they put jackets on, went out to the garage for their bicycles and pedaled through the February night toward the main bunker that was dug into the wooded hill behind the Rosenauberg beer hall. Reaching the bunker, they only had time to throw their bicycles against a tree and run to the gate. Inside they followed dimly-lit, earthen corridors lined with low wooden benches until they found a place among the silent people already sitting there. He told me how he sat huddled against his mother and felt the tremors of the earth as the bombs did their destruction. He watched in terror as the sand dribbled down the walls. His mother held them all three against her breast. He could still remember the acrid odor of her sweat. He didn't know at the time that it was evidence of her own fear. When the all-clear signal came, they climbed out into what was supposed to be morning, but was more like dusk, with cinders and ash and smoke obscuring the sun. The beer garden was gone. The trees were gone. But a miracle had occurred. Their four bicycles were the only ones that had survived the bombs. While others had to walk, his family rode home through the streets, slowly this time, taking in what was left of their city. He told me the snow was black where it had been crystalline the day before, and the sky was a most sickening sulfur. That, he said, was the sulfur of the painting. A color he would never forget. But it was the standing buildings, black against the sky, burned out completely, and the window frames that stood alone without walls, that struck him as the most sorrowful. It was those burning, free-standing, individual window frames that he still dreamed of regularly.

In the days following his revelations, I couldn't get any other discussion of the war from him, not even an answer to the question, "Where was your father during the bombings?" He acted as though he hadn't heard. I felt too much sympathy to insist that time.

"That *padre* doesn't seem to think too highly of the German," I said to Kai who was now immersed in leafing through his bird book and making copious notes in his journal.

"And this makes him a war criminal to you?" He didn't look up.

"Maybe."

"Then we'll find out." He met my eyes.

"Could you at least allow it as a possibility?"

"Why that any more than some other reason? Why not that the guy hated civilization and wanted to get as far away from it as possible? Why not that he may be a Swabian and stricken from birth with *Wanderlust*? Why not that he began trading, was a merchant of some kind, like Mingo there, and ended up out with the Indians and decided to stay?"

"Maybe so," I said, beginning to feel like an alarmist. "But you admit there is some reason the *padre* doesn't like him."

"This friar isn't the most savory character," Kai laughed.

"People can get pretty run down after a while out here." As soon as I said it, I wondered why I was defending a man who seemed proof enough himself that the German was an okay guy. "Let's stop," I said, sighing. I undid my skirt and stood, letting it fall to the floor.

"Then I won?" He laughed again.

"Nobody won, asshole." I undid my bra and slipped out of the straps, pulling them through the sleeves of my tee shirt.

"You know something?" he said.

I could tell from the way he was looking at me that it was going to be a compliment. "What?"

"*Mit dir kann man Pferde stehlen.*"

"So what does that mean?"

"If you'd learn a little German, you'd know."

"We just avoided one fight, Kai. Don't push your luck."

"Translated it means, 'with you I can steal horses.'"

A river of pleasure pulsed through me. "My God, you love me for all the right reasons, don't you?"

"*Ja*, and then some."

"Can I join you?" I said, trying to get in beside Kai on his cot.

He shifted over. "They get an inch, they want a million."

"You give them an inch, they take a mile." I said smugly.

He got his arm around my shoulder, and I shifted down so that my head was on his chest, my eyes close to a page of multicolored birds.

At our wedding, one of Kai's ornithologist colleagues said we looked like a couple of tropical birds. I wore a bright red knit mini dress and though Kai gave in to his mother and put on a gray suit from his Munich days, his tie was a wide swirl of psychedelic greens, yellows, and oranges over a gentian blue shirt. His mother, who had just flown in from Augsburg, was still shocked. But perhaps it prepared her for the man my father had found to marry us, a black Baptist minister with whom he worked at Mobilization for Youth. The ceremony before the lighted fireplace in the apartment we'd been living in for the past two years was an amalgam of political speech, Baptist rousing, and a ritual breaking of the marriage glass, by both of us. I wanted to do that much in my mother's memory. Everyone cried—my father, Lucy Albright who was my best friend from the Peace Corps, Kai's associates from the lab, my scruffy friends from the radio station who refused to change out of their blue jeans for the occasion, and various neighborhood people and co-workers from my stint organizing in the South Bronx after I got back from Ecuador. They, of course, were all dressed in wedding finery. Even Kai's mother loosened up after drinking a bottle of champagne. Kai had bought the best German *Sekt* he could find. "What the hell," he'd said when the liquor store man handed him a bill for three hundred dollars. We had enough for twice the number of people. We drank it all. The party started at two in the afternoon, but we danced into the night. People had arrived with armfuls of records. John Smith, a Black Panther organizer from Tompkins Square Park came with the hit of the evening, the new Jackson Five album. At three a.m. when everyone had gone home and Kai was taking out the sacks of empty champagne bottles, Lucy and I sat on the floor in front of the fire. She was pretty tanked on pot and was smoking yet more. Lucy was stoned most of the time those days and when she wasn't, she was loaded on bad jug wine. "Annie, sweetie, I love Kai. Even though he's a little straight." She giggled and then gave me one of her wide-eyed haunted looks, the smile now a grimace. "I'm going to miss you, guy," she said.

"Lucy, I'll still be here."

She reached over and combed her hand clumsily through my hair. "You going to come back safe from that place? You sure you want to go back to Ekkie land?"

I took a toke off her joint. I didn't answer. We both just sat and stared into the fire until Kai finished with the garbage.

Lying beside Kai in the Hotel Jaguar, I imagined Lucy before she'd fallen apart down here. She would have gotten a kick out of the hotel and Puerto Napo, made some cynical jokes, but would have been intensely curious about the mystery of the German in the forest, would have thought Mingo cute and sexy, and probably would have followed him into the jungle, if only for sensual reasons. But not anymore.

I must have sighed because Kai, who had continued to make field notes in his journal, asked, "What are you thinking?"

"About our wedding."

"It was nice."

"You think Lucy's ever going to be okay?"

"I hope so."

He turned the page with the arm holding me so it went across my face.

I sighed again.

"What now?"

"I was wondering about Mingo and the Salesian business."

"What about it?"

"Who are the Salesians? I can't remember."

"They're terrible. Racists. Deracinators more like it." His voice turned cold and angry. "From what I've read, they go in and so called "recruit" the young boys from the indigenous settlements, sometimes deep inside the most primitive areas. Better said, they kidnap the children, take them to the schools and teach them Spanish and won't let them speak their native tongues. They make them into monotheists, Catholic monotheists. It would be interesting to know if Mingo even speaks Quichua anymore and what his religion is. I'll bet he has nothing left of his past if they got to him young."

I imagined Mingo as a boy, being kidnapped from his jungle village. Tiny with an oversized belly, naked, with husky little thighs. I imagined him playing on the edge of the forest when the white men came with Indian guides from another tribe and snatched him away, perhaps with two or three other boys, making them cry, unbeknownst to the elders. That would be enough to explain the animosity between the two men. Mingo's hatred of white clergy could have riled the *padre*, who in return had a minor vendetta against the Shuar.

I smelled Kai, his sweat, that particular odor that was his. It had a tinge of the acrid scent that he said his mother had during those nights in the bunker. Perhaps it was his way of keeping her with him, even when he'd left her to come to America. There were stranger means of sustaining a memory. I played my hands through the pale hair on his chest. His thickly freckled skin was soft as a woman's beneath the hair, and on the sides of his torso where his arms gave shade so that the skin was perfectly white, he was as soft as a rose petal. I kissed him there, in the white area.

"What's going on?

I looked up to see him grinning at me.

"Oh, nothing much."

He put his book on the orange crate, followed by his journal and pen. I shifted up and then over on top of him and found that he was already hard. I sat up and looked down on him and thought how beautiful he was, especially in the golden light filling the room. Outside it was silent except for the dripping of water from leaf to leaf.

"Do you think you can be quiet, or do you plan to wake Puerto Napo?" he said, smiling at me, but immediately the smile left his face as desire took over.

"I can't promise," I said as he slowly lifted my tee shirt over my head and I let myself down until my breasts slipped like silk against his chest.

I lay on my own cot in the complete blackness of night. It was darker than any New England countryside. The rain played delicately on the corrugated tin roof. What a sound that was. How visceral the sensations it stirred in me, of lying on my bed in Guayaquil, while the rain teemed down on the tin roof so loudly that I'd have to shout at the top of my voice if anyone were there with me. It is such a sound of the tropics, that pounding of the *aguacero* on thin metal, and the feeling of being barely protected from the onslaught. But, in a way, I was most protected at those times because I could stay in my apartment until it let up. I didn't have to go out and about the neighborhood, up and down the hill, visiting, organizing people to go to this or that meeting, having to drink the proffered beverage in each home, *kwaker*, an oat-based drink mixed with nectar of the *naranjilla* fruit and unboiled water. There were times in my second year when I liked nothing better than the protection of the downpour. By then, by that third and last rainy season, even a visit from Gala was a burden. My nerves were so frayed and my beliefs so shattered that it took all my energy to get through the most minor encounters.

What had happened to me? That was the question I asked myself all the time. Kai said it was criminal of my government to send us down there, twenty-year-olds without training into a foreign culture to do the work even experts could expect to fail at. Kai was very good at accusing my government. When he said that to me, I would secretly think, but I *was* an expert. I knew from childhood how to organize people. I had learned it at my father's knee the way most children hear stories or learn the family business. My earliest memories are of a smiling adult face bending down into mine and saying, "Aren't you proud of your daddy?" "Yes," I'd answer this stranger, thrilled by the attention, jealous that they knew him so well, frightened by the intensity of their admiration of him. "Well, you should be, young lady. He's a fine, fine man. Smart man your father is, and sure as dickens knows how to get us moving." This encounter could happen anyplace: in a union hall, in a farmer's field, in a grange, outside a factory, or at a church supper, all over the United States, wherever my father had gone to corral people into doing what they themselves felt needed to be done. Or that's the way he would put it when I would ask him what he did. "I sit around and wait until they let me know what it is they want to do and then I help them to do it," he'd say, throwing his head back and letting loose with his unmistakable laugh. "You've got to get to their 'felt needs' we call them, chicken. People won't budge until you attach to what they most desire." In private homes, in schoolhouses, out on open lawns under elm trees, I'd see him sitting in a circle—my 'father believed in circles because "no one's better than anyone else in a circle, chicken"—and I'd watch how through probing silence, through questions and arguments, he drew people out of themselves in ways they'd never "been done before," or so they said afterward. So when I went down to Ecuador as a community organizer, I knew exactly what to do. I knew how to involve people in constructing a community center. I knew how to get them into it once it was built, and how to guide them toward deciding what activities they wanted to fill it with. When the center's monthly subsidy provided by a Guayaquil businessmen's club ceased, I even figured out how to make the *Centro Comunal de Cerro Santa Ana* self-sufficient.

I wasn't like the majority of volunteers, I kept telling myself, novices, from privileged backgrounds, with their liberal arts educations, who were either overwhelmed after a few months and left their neighborhoods to become English teachers of middle class boys and girls, or retreated deeply into their neighborhoods and settled into a pattern of drinking and smoking dope, sleeping through the day, and locking themselves off from their communities. But then there was my friend Jody who drank herself into a stupor most nights out in *Barrio* El Cisne, the furthest and poorest neighborhood. It was under water half the year and a dust bowl for the rest. On our first Christmas at a volunteer party we found her lying weeping on the bathroom floor in the Peace Corp director's house. For four hours we tried to stem the flow of tears with tepid washcloths to her face while she screamed, "I hate it here, hate the stealing, the filth, the stench, the men grabbing my butt! I can't stand the hypocrisy!" The Peace Corps doctor sent her state-side the next week, saying she was to be treated for resistant parasites. She never returned. Jody wasn't a pampered girl. Though Anglo, she'd been

Pachuco, bearing the tattoo on her hand of a L. A. gang she had hung with in high school.

And dear Lucy. She was stationed in an Indian village outside of Cuenca in the southern Andes. The villagers became worried when they didn't see her for over a week, when they knocked on her door and no one answered even though they were certain someone was inside. A contingent journeyed to the Peace Corps office in Cuenca, bringing the Peace Corps representative back with them to the village. When he got there, he broke the door down and found her sitting in her own excrement, chanting mantras, in the middle of her darkened living room. But Lucy hadn't been prepared by life, I told myself. She had attended fashionable private schools and then gone to Antioch. She was from Sausalito, California, straight from her parents' luxurious redwood house overlooking San Francisco Bay. I wasn't the same. I was more like Jody, except for her streak of wildness that could have been a cover for fragility. As far as I could fathom, nothing accounted for how devastated I'd been by the experience in Ecuador, for my inability to return to my *barrio*, even with my new husband, and for the way I was periodically overcome by paroxysms of paranoia. It didn't explain either, why I couldn't think of Gala and the death of baby Ladito without being consumed by guilt.

CHAPTER SIX

I spent the night in a peaceful, dreamless state. When I woke up, the narrow room was filled with morning light coming directly in the window. I looked out onto a tangle of green, wet with the night's rain, inspiring in its morning freshness. I slowly turned over and saw that Kai wasn't in the other bed. The white muslin sheets were rumpled, sticking up in folds. The indentation was still in the pillow where his head had been. He must have gone out birdwatching when I was in my deepest morning sleep. The travel clock on the box between our beds said it was eight-fifteen. He'd be back soon. The equatorial sun always rose at six. By now it would be too hot and bright for good watching. I listened. There were virtually no bird sounds. Rather, I could hear the squawking of metal against metal in the distance, and a slight hum of river. The sun was too hot on my bare skin as it flowed through the open window. I got up and went over to Kai's bed and lay down again.

I actually felt joy, and I wondered how it would be at this hour in Guayaquil. I imagined the cement stairs rising up the Cerro Santa Ana with pastel houses on either side, pink, turquoise, yellow, bathed in morning light. Just above the community center was my yellow building and my second-story windows decorated with filigreed maroon ironwork and louvered shutters. I could walk down to Gala's. She would already be in the patio washing clothes, scrubbing them under the water spigot, on the wooden scrub board. She would look up as I came out, her mocha face, with its deep punctuating dimples, taking me in. She'd make a caustic remark, "The *gringa* princess finally decided to start her day," and then laugh, exposing her toothless mouth. At twenty-five she had five girls, and a baby on its way, and no front teeth.

It had shocked me in the beginning that half the adults were missing their teeth. Missing limbs were worse, of course, and there were uncounted numbers of people without arms and legs, many of them children. But seeing a woman as beautiful and young as Gala with shiny black hair, liquid black eyes, mauve lips, whose loveliness was profoundly diminished by not having teeth, was still shocking. Once I got to know her and others like her, I failed to notice that they had no teeth. It was only after I'd returned home and showed photographs to my father, and he'd said, "Hell, almost nobody's got his teeth," that I saw it again. When I did, I saw, too, how poor they were, how their clothes were worn thin and patched, and their skin was marked with white splotches from the sewage mixing with the drinking water, and how most children either had no shoes or wore broken-down jellies, and that their houses were mere hovels of cane and tin, surrounded by rubble. I looked at the photos of the kindergarten we had started in the center, and I saw that the children I knew as five year olds were the size of two year olds in the states. I had grown as accustomed to the conditions as my neighbors.

Putting the pictures down, my father said, "What I wouldn't give to do what you did. What an opportunity."

"I just made matters worse."

"Annie, don't always denigrate yourself. You're wrong. Of course you had an impact."

I sat up abruptly in bed, then stood on the cot and flung my arms back and forth to physically shed the thoughts I'd allowed, bringing me precariously close to worse ones. No thoughts of that sort, I admonished myself. No such thoughts on this beautiful day.

"Get up, the sun is shining!" Kai's voice sang out from beyond the wall.

"I'm awake," I called.

I heard him scrape the mud off his shoes on the landing outside. The door opened, and Kai stood with glaring light and green and reflecting water in the distance behind him.

"*Donnerwetter*, is this a stunning sight! A naked brown-haired, tawny tit-tit, with a dark-brown furry underbelly."

He came over to the bed where I still stood. I wrapped my arms and legs around him and clung there.

"Or is it a marsupial? But wrong continent. Perhaps a classic case of convergent evolution," he said before sinking into the kiss I was really after.

I reveled in that kiss. I let my happiness play around and around inside of me. I thought, someday this joy will last. Someday my entire life will be like this.

"This is going to be a great trip," Kai said, letting me slowly down to the floor. He stepped back and clapped his hands. "A great, great trip. Put your clothes on and come outside and see how spectacular it is."

I slipped into my skirt and a clean tee shirt and followed him out onto the walkway. The air was already heavy with humidity. Only at daybreak is the air in the tropics what one would call fresh, and even this is relative, a sense you come to after having lived in the climate for years. As soon as the sun is inches above the horizon, the air feels tramped down, used up. It becomes full of rotting sweetness and the tiredness of the universe, as though everything living has only four feet of vertical space to move around in, squashed between the mud and the atmospheric heat.

It must have rained a lot throughout the night, because the dark-red dirt road was more a series of small ponds than a thoroughfare. The grass and *palmitos* glistened in the sun. The river was a swollen, thick, reddish brown. From where we stood, I could see a pulley-ferry stretched across. There were a few mountain Indians, dressed in their heavy wool ponchos, waiting on the dock for the coffin-sized box to return from the opposite side of the river. I could make out one structure on the far shore. It appeared to be a large aqua two-story building with a wide, wraparound porch.

"Do you believe this?" Kai gestured toward the forest that began to the right of the aqua building. "For thousands of miles there is nothing but wilderness. I remember when I came to America on the Rotterdam, I stood on the deck and thought, I can only see ocean, miles and miles of Atlantic Ocean. I thought, America is at the end of my journey. America. Now if I were to travel to the other side of this enormous forest, it would be ocean that I'd find. The Atlantic Ocean." He squatted down on his haunches and bobbed up and down like a young boy.

He was silent a moment. I walked a step to him and put my hand on his head. He turned and looked up at me.

"I'm sort of a fool, aren't I? Getting so excited by this. A regular romantic German. I'd better watch it. A dangerous trait in us."

Several times in the years we'd known each other he'd referred to not wanting to be a romantic German. I'd always thought a romantic view of the world was a nice quality and told him so. He had answered, "It's not something a German can afford to be anymore." Though I didn't entirely understand what he meant, what I did know as I looked out over the wilderness through his eyes was that I envied his endless capacity for embracing life.

We bought our breakfast at a tiny *tienda* with a counter, just up the slope from the ferry platform. Three Indians, a woman in the elaborate dress of an Otavalón, with ruffly blouse and dozens of strands of gold-painted beads climbing her neck, and two men with the Otavalón's trademark of a single long thick black braid down the back and white trousers and shirts, stepped aside as we approached, and looked at the ground. Otavalóns were the true Jews of Ecuador, I'd always thought. Discriminated against, publicly humiliated, but rising up as a merchant class in the face of it, aggressive and ingratiating where trade was concerned. They sold their weaving around the country, outside tourist hotels, in every marketplace. I'd heard that they had begun appropriating the designs of other tribes, weaving them and selling them along with their own. When the Salasacas, the finest, most original weavers in Ecuador, grew angry with them, a deal was worked out whereby Otavalóns took the Salasacas' merchandise on consignment and sold it, turning back a sum on each sold item to the Salasaca community. Yet despite the power they were garnering, they retreated deferentially when we came near.

The coffee was delicious. *Esencia* from a small pitcher, which a glum, round-faced woman behind the counter slid over to us, was what we poured into the warm milk.

"*Bien rico,*" I said for her benefit.

"*¿Le gusta?*" Her face came alive with her gold-toothed, glinting smile. "Do you get coffee as good over there?" she asked, meaning whatever was farthest away to her, Guayaquil or the United States.

"Never as good as here," I said sincerely.

She ducked under the high counter and when she appeared again, her hands were full of sweet rolls. "They came on the morning bus. This is the only place to find fresh sweet rolls."

Kai was delighted, and kept repeating over and over *riquísimo, riquísimo.* The woman laughed full out, and said to me that my man spoke good Spanish, too.

Four young *mestizos* arrived, freeing us to move down the counter beside the glassed-in food-holder. We ate in silence as the men, dressed in high rubber boots, unpatched, mud-streaked pants and short-sleeved shirts open to their belts, joked and flirted with the *dueña.*

I breathed in the hot wet air rising off the river and off the pools of muddy water on the roadway. That and the taste of the *café con leche* mixing with the slightly rancid butter scraped from a banana leaf onto the small soft sweet rolls brought back my early morning breakfasts in Guayaquil. I was in the Cerro Santa Ana in the moments just before dawn when the gray light was tinged with red and the hawkers began their daily ascent, calling their wares into the relative silence, carrying bread on their heads on huge rough-hewn wooden trays or milk cans on their shoulders, climbing laboriously up to the top of the hill where there are no *tiendas* for people to buy goods. "*Leche, leche de vaca, pan dulce, pan de sal, como quieras,*" their dull flat voices intoned. And as though to mark time

for the hawkers' rhythms, the army recruits grunted their
uno, dos, tres, uno, dos, tres marching back and forth on the
parade ground at the foot of our hill. It was rumored that
they learned the straight-legged strut watching old Nazi
footage. At that time I barely understood the implications.

I would sit in my window drinking coffee from my
enameled tin cup, eating the sweet roll I'd just bought in
the *tienda* below. The view from my floor-to-ceiling
window reached out to the pastel city in the distance and
the mile wide Rio Guayas to our left. By that hour, this
river of floating flotsam, vegetation, and balsa canoes was
crowded with banana boats, heavy with cargo, muddy water
lapping almost to their decks, and as they made their slow
progress I would think that these boats were the only bodies
in Guayaquil that grew lighter as the day went on. They
were traveling to the piers a few blocks upriver along the
Malecón, the main piers of Guayaquil, where the
cargadores raced along the gangplanks with huge stems of
bananas on their backs to deposit them on the sidewalk at
the feet of the merchants or the United Fruit buyers. If you
stood and watched, as I sometimes did, you saw that, as the
men, always Indians, strained under their burden, the boats
lifted inches and then feet out of the water, until the
names painted in corroding color appeared, and you could
read *La Reina*, *La Perla del Pacífico*, or *La Angelita*, in red
and green and yellow or blue curlicues and sweeping lines.

"*Buenos días, mis niños. ¡No podía encontrarles!*" The
unmistakable roar of the *padre* hit us from behind, breaking
into my reverie. Good morning, children. I couldn't find
you.

He shuffled, legs splayed, down the side of the hill,
lifting the skirt of his rough brown robe which was already
spattered waist-high with red mud.

"My God, my God. What a filthy mess." He shook his
curls as though they too had become plastered with muck.

A look of disgust contorted the face of the woman in the
tienda before it reformed into a stiff smile. "*Buenos, padre.
¿Café, té o ron?*" Coffee, tea, or rum.

"Ah ha, listen to her. As though I would drink rum this early in the morning." He gave us an exaggerated wink. "A man of the cloth."

"I didn't know that drink was a sin," I said.

"Not a sin, my dear. *Café con leche, por favor, cholita,*" he said to the woman. "But when you've taken an oath of poverty as I have, such luxuries can only be received, not paid for, and our dear little enterprising *dueña* here is not known for her charity, is she now?"

She smiled, but the moment he had his back to her a glowering expression replaced it.

"Did you sleep well?" Kai asked in not such bad Spanish.

"I did, my German, I did at that." He picked up his coffee cup and drained it. "So tell me, have you not changed your mind in the night? You were up early this morning looking at your birds. Perhaps you've seen all of them in this area and will be leaving us?"

I wondered how he knew Kai was birdwatching, and then answered for the two of us. "No, sir, in fact we're more excited than ever about our trip. My husband has only seen the tip of the iceberg, if you'll excuse the silly comparison in this heat. He looks forward to more and richer varieties."

The *padre* took a soiled handkerchief from a fold of his costume and wiped the sweat that was accumulating on his brow and running down his temples into his beard. "He knows, of course, that the forest for hundreds of miles from here has been heavily hunted by the indigenous. They are using guns these days. They kill everything in sight. They don't care if it is for food any longer, what they want are feathers for the tourists. You know what tourists wish, those beautiful *collares*, or necklaces, I believe you call them." He shook his head and a look of sadness crossed his face. "Such a shame. Saint Francis would weep to see what is happening. The result of unplanned civilization invading the jungle. They cannot adapt to new machines and new ways without the help of people who know these things better. Know the repercussions. I don't believe you would like what is out there. Perhaps it is better to keep one's illusions?" This line rose in a question, as though he'd known all along how his rambling statement was to end.

"No, I want to see," Kai answered. "How do you say, I take my chances?" he asked me.

I translated for him.

"Well, if you must, then you will stay with me in my humble community. I have a Peace Corps volunteer with me. Bringing civilization to the region. A very interesting project he is involved in. Making certain that the Indians acquire land they can call their own. And what is this, madam?" He pointed to the black box hanging from my shoulder.

"A tape-recorder," I answered.

"Of course. Of course. I haven't been back here in the jungle for that long, not to know the machine." He mopped his face. "But what for? What do you plan to record with it?"

"Birds. Bird songs."

"Aha. And nothing more."

I shrugged. "I work for a radio station back in New York. Perhaps an interview with a dedicated pastor living with the Indians?"

"You know we must be on our way if we're to be there for the bus," he said, clearly avoiding my question. "There is only one bus to Misahuallí. It is ten kilometers to Misahuallí. I would not want to have to walk. So if you must come, let us step on it, as you Americans are fond of saying, I believe."

The young men who ran the ferry were dressed in tee shirts with English messages printed on them. Apparently, some tourists or Peace Corps volunteers had passed through. 'Peace' was written on one under a large peace symbol. The man who wore it was medium height, skinny, and *mestizo*. His partner, shorter and purer mountain Indian, sported a Peter Max design of psychedelic sky and stars which turned into a woman's long streaming hair.

"*Señores*, who rides next?" the man with the peace sign said. He smiled, revealing his lack of front teeth.

The box arrived, swinging, and bumped down onto the landing.

"You two go first," the friar said. "*Señorita?*"

"Yes, if the cable breaks, *por lo menos* our *gringos* will be on the other side," the toothless man said.

His partner smirked in satisfaction before he turned away to prepare the pulley system.

"Always jokes at my expense. No respect from any corner," the *padre* answered in jest, but there was an edge to his voice.

"*Listo*," I called out when I was settled in the narrow box.

With that the ferry operators both reached high and dragged with all their weight on the rope hoist and I shot up, bucking forward and then back. I grabbed the sides of the box. The screech of metal cables filled the air as I was whipped up a few more feet. My fear was quickly replaced by exhilaration at rising suddenly over the furious rush of water below. I was filled with a feeling of freedom, a sense of finally beginning our adventure. A breeze came off the river, and I was high in the air now. It was like being on a ferris wheel with the land disappearing, the people growing smaller. The same thrill of abandon. Ferris wheels were one of the constants in my nomadic life with my parents, and later my father alone. In each town where we lived, in summer or fall, a traveling amusement park would appear, usually as the seedy side of the county fair. The ferris wheel was my favorite. It was protected freedom, soaring out over the world, held in by the rod that the man on the ground had snapped closed. Up, up above whatever town we lived in, looking over the hills in the distance, just as now I saw where the river cut deep, deep into the jungle. I had a clear view across the tops of the trees, and as Kai had rejoiced, these trees went farther than any human could sensibly fathom. The brown water sparkled in the light. The sky was blue. The heat was bearable. Blue, green, brown, and sunshine! This was the way to live.

Then the box finished its arc, dropping suddenly, the cable squawking as the box hit and thudded to a stop on the new dock, and I was on the other side of the river.

CHAPTER SEVEN

This side of the river was even rougher than the other, with mud that looked as though we would sink to our calves, so we stayed on clay-coated planks that served as sidewalks. They ran the distance from the ferry dock to the building I'd seen from our hotel. There was another structure opposite us where planks were also laid down to give access. Judging by the seal of Ecuador over the wide-open door entry, it was a government office. A simple interior courtyard was filled with potted plants. When I inquired about it of the friar, who hobbled along in front of us at a turtle's pace, he wheezed back that it was where papers could be stamped. Ecuadorian officials liked nothing better than to "*fijar el sello*," to documents. But as we had no papers that needed attending to, we continued on our way toward the aqua building which I now knew contained a general store.

Our packs were making us top-heavy, and our progress that much more difficult on the slippery boards. We were passed by a few motley, straining burros slogging through mud that reached to their knees. Their riders dismounted and began to pull them along, clucking in soft tones to the exhausted animals. These men looked as though they'd been out in the jungle for weeks by the appearance of their beards and the scraggly length of their hair. They were Latino, not *mestizo* or Indian, as everyone else we'd met was, save the friar. He stopped for a moment, letting the men and their animals move by.

"Gold miners," he said conspiratorially.

"Where is there gold?" Kai asked.

"Wherever," The *padre* waved his hand. "All along the river. There isn't much. But enough to make it worth their while. It takes time to extract, but if you have patience, you can pan out a couple of hundred *sucres* worth." He resumed walking.

I calculated. A hundred could vary anywhere from five to ten dollars. A good week's salary for some people.

He stopped again. "It is what gives the shamans of the Canelos Indians their power among the other tribes, including the Shuar. They call their shamanistic power *panjü*, or *banco* in *Castellano*, for the power of the gold in the rocks of their river. I hear it said that our Mingo trades in that power. Yes, I hear it said that our Mingo trades the magical darts, the *tsentsak* from the Canelos shamans, to the shamans of his own people." He shook his head. "Like trading the bones of Christ, some would say." He met my eye as though to see my reaction.

"I know nothing of it," I said. "My husband is more conversant in this area."

Without reply, he continued his slow way along the boards.

The store was a well-stocked trading post of the western American style. The room was cavernous, with a high vaulted ceiling sustained by huge tree-trunk posts and beams and completely encircled by glassless, screened-in windows. The floor was of rough, mud-caked wood, and the walls, too, were of uncured, unpainted lumber. We stopped in similar places, I remembered, when my mother and I traveled across the country. I would be enthralled with the drugstore Indian statues outside, with the piles of blankets, canned goods, hardware, rifles, and cowboy boots inside. She would have a hard time coaxing me back to the car.

By the time Kai and I had purchased our supplies, tins of sardines, some hard cheese that looked suspiciously like CARE food provisions, and cans of condensed milk, the friar had gone out and returned to announce that the bus hadn't arrived yet.

"*Pero ya mismo viene,*" he assured us. "You should get out there and watch for the bus if you don't want to miss it. That is if perhaps you haven't changed your mind. Sometimes the bus never arrives. One can't know for certain." He frowned darkly and went out the door.

I looked at Kai and shrugged. "He really doesn't want us to go downriver." I said. "Why do you suppose that's so?"

"I don't know, but I'm beginning to wonder myself. Maybe I'm catching your paranoia about people. It could be nothing more than that he thinks it's wrong for tourists to be traveling back there. Perhaps he doesn't want any more birds killed for tourist trinkets."

"Could be," I said. "But I think it's something else." I told him what the friar had just said, seemingly trying to discredit Mingo.

"It's a serious accusation," Kai said.

"Why so serious?"

"Shamanistic power should only be passed between shamans themselves. If Mingo were interceding, unless he's a shaman, which is possible as a trader, he would be betraying the beliefs of his people. Because if the metaphoric darts aren't passed between shamans, their power is lost. They cannot possibly be curative."

"What you're saying is that Mingo is also sort of sleazy."

"Why do you always have to assume the worst about everything, Annie?"

"Then what's your scenario?"

"That it's not true. That our friend the friar is lying."

"You're right," I said, shuddering involuntarily. "That's possible. But why?"

"I don't know, but it seems a pretty elaborate lie to come up with just to keep a birdwatcher away."

I laughed. "From my experience it takes more than a big lie to stop you."

We paid our bill, and Kai and I went out to the story-high wraparound porch of the store. We looked up the road in the direction the bus was to come. We could see for a mile, out across land that had been cleared for cattle, an activity that was one of the newest scourges of the jungle. Virgin forest was being felled so that a couple of head of cattle could graze.

"Why don't we walk," I said, knowing that this would appeal to Kai.

"Wonderful idea." He put his arm around me. "More than one way to skin a cat, right?"

"Absolutely right," I said, nudging my head into his shoulder, savoring his nearness, glad to be going off with him alone for a while. "I'm sure Mingo will be there whether the bus comes or not. It's only ten kilometers. We can easily make that even if the bus doesn't come along. But the big question is, should we tell our pal, the friar?"

"If the bus doesn't come, he's still not going to walk. I'm willing to place everything on Mingo and the German."

I lifted my backpack into position, but I wasn't feeling completely sanguine. I slipped my tape-recorder over my shoulder. The thought of the German didn't bother me right now as much as the mystery of the friar's reluctance to have us travel into the forest. I wanted to know why.

We climbed down the steep stairs from the porch. I looked around and didn't see the friar anyplace. There were three men, the usual guys who hung out, standing in the shadow of the porch drinking beer. Whenever anyone drank beer outside as they were, there had to be a *tienda* nearby. In Ecuador, you couldn't carry bottles away from the store unless you lived close by and went there regularly with an empty bottle to replace the full one you were buying.

"Excuse me," I said. "Have you seen a man in brown robes?"

"The *padre*, you mean." An older man who was squatting near an open doorway spoke. He pointed with his thumb over his shoulder, his expression slightly glazed from drink.

Kai followed me into the shadow of the overhang. My vision was dimmed after the strong daylight. I peered in through the doorless portal, into a dark, dirt-floored establishment. There was a battered and dented Coca-Cola cooler just inside and a line of about ten coke bottles on a narrow shelf behind a dirty wooden counter. I heard voices, and then noticed three men toward the back in further darkness. One, by his shape, appeared to be the friar, but I thought I heard English words.

"*Permiso*," I said.

The conversation stopped abruptly.

"*Señorita, mi hermosa gringuita*." The friar sounded strained in spite of his attempt at jolliness. "Would you like a Coca Cola?" He lumbered toward us over to the cooler and lifted the lid. "Let me see what I can find."

When I looked again to the back of the room, the men were no longer there.

"*Que pena*, there are no more cold drinks in this pitiful *tienda*." He slammed the cover closed. "Come, let us step outside. It's a little dark and stuffy in here."

"Your friends seem to have left you," I said.

"My friends?" He looked around as though no one had ever been in the room with us. "Oh yes, the owner and his son. They're in the back."

A *tienda* owner who speaks English? I wanted to ask.

Once outside, and at a distance from the overhang where the men were still drinking their beer, we explained our plan. In a turnabout, he seemed relieved, telling us to do as we wished.

The friar started to describe which road to take, but Kai said he assumed there could be only one road, that which ran east alongside the river we'd crossed. The friar complimented him on his good sense and then heartily bade us "*hasta la vista*."

The mud was already beginning to dry in the intense sun, forming deep ragged ruts down the center of the road. It was rough going for a hundred yards, but once we got past the last shacks in the town, it smoothed out. From there on it became only the two tire ridges where the daily bus drove. We stayed on the banks of the road, Kai starting out on ahead to catch the birds.

"He seems to have changed his tune," I called after him.

He slowed to wait for me.

"I don't know, maybe he just gave up. Figured that you were more persistent than he." Kai grinned at me as we began to walk side by side. "You know I love you."

"Thanks. That feels nice. Maybe it will be okay being married to you."

He stopped and put his hand to my cheek. As always a powerful sensuality entered at that spot as though a window had been opened into my innermost self.

"It's hard to hug you with these damn packs on," he said. "But know I want to."

I nodded, leaning my face farther into his palm.

After a few moments we began to walk again, Kai staying by my side, which was unusual when birds were about.

"You know, my father and I used to go out together bird-watching during the war. Before it became too dangerous."

Startled to hear him speak unbidden of his father, I kept quiet, didn't even glance over at him for fear of squelching what he had started.

"Even on snowy days we went along the Vertach. When only drab birds foraged for food." He sighed. "Much like humans during that time. Last night Mingo said the thing about the glasses bringing things close. You remember?"

"Yes."

"My father gave me my first binoculars. On Christmas Eve of '43. I carried them to midnight service and sat the whole time in the cold, candle-lit church with my hand in my overcoat pocket fingering each detail of my new possession, knowing I now had my very own ability to bring the birds close."

I couldn't help it, but an image came to me of the freezing *Lager* of Dachau not thirty kilometers from their city.

"After Pappi died, I would sneak out of the house at three and four in the morning to walk in the forest. He had taught me to band birds. That first spring I recaptured previously banded birds in the hope I would find his mark." He took my hand. "I lived for those hours alone with him."

"Oh, Kai, I'm sorry."

"*Macht nichts,*" he answered.

We continued in silence for a few minutes until he said he'd like to go ahead to reach the birds before we disturbed them. I watched him make his way down the road. Not until he'd gained a good thirty yards did I follow.

I was lost in thoughts of how much easier it was to hold a memory of a good father than of one who was suspected of evil behavior when I heard someone coming up behind and turned to find two of the men who had been hanging around the *tienda*. They wore high rubber boots that sucked and squished through the thick drying mud. They carried rifles over their shoulders.

"*Hola,*" I said, twisting back around to see Kai continuing on.

"*Hola, señorita.*" They said in unison, stopping. I could smell their beer breath and days' worth of old perspiration wafting off their soiled shirts.

"Did you wish something?" I asked.

"Just to make certain that you found your way, *señorita,*" the smaller, older man said. He could have been in his forties. The other one might have been his son. I noted that they both wore hunting knives in their belts. It took everything I had not to yell for Kai.

"I think we will have no trouble," I said. "We're only walking toward Misahuallí. To meet Mingo Mincha. I understand there is no possibility of losing our way."

They smiled and nodded and moved closer. I told myself that Latin Americans like to stand closer than North Americans do when conversing. Lesson number one, Cultural Differences, State Department Manual.

"We know Mingo Mincha. We know him well," the younger man said. He smiled some more. Silence.

"Are you friends of his?" My body began to vibrate with fear.

They looked at each other. "Of course we are, why not?" The younger man shrugged.

Again we stood not saying anything. What did they want?

"Your man is getting far ahead, *señorita*. You don't want to lose him." The older man spoke. "We can walk with you."

And with that I felt the complete fool. I had done it again, suspected the worst. Certain that they meant me harm, these two men who were only being cordial. I had stopped, so they stopped. I had spoken to them, so they had spoken to me. It was all courtesy. I had them pegged as murderers.

We walked. They were going to hunt, they told me. They had only said the thing about making certain we found our way out of politeness, they said. They hoped the *señorita* liked their country. Then they fell silent. As we continued along companionably I realized how far inside the aura of my paranoia I had just been. It was as though I had no emotional rudder out here, veering wildly from passionate concern one moment to terrified suspicion the next. I had to get hold of myself.

There was no breeze anymore; the wet heat closed in on me, and sweat began to slip down between my breasts. Up ahead, Kai stopped to look with his binoculars into a tree and then continued on. We kept walking, the two men in the roadbed and I on the bank.

The older man spoke first. "We have many *norte americanos* come through these days for the oil. Is that why you and your husband are here, *patrona*?"

"No. Only traveling," I said. But with that I got an idea. "Were those oil men in the *tienda*, talking with the friar?"

"*Pues, no sé.* Did you see, Xavier?" the older man asked the younger.

"It could be," Xavier said. "The friar often talks with the oil men. *Los gringos y los paisanos.*"

"Is he special friends with them?"

"The friar is friends with many people, *señorita*. Who is to question the motives of the friar?" Xavier shrugged.

I changed my tack slightly. "Is there so very much oil in this region?"

"That's what they say." The older man spoke with great solemnity. "The American company, Somaxo, it does exploration with the blessing of the *gobierno*, and word has it that there is a richness of oil deep in the forest. *Pues*, they will build a road, they say. We all are hoping this is true. That's why we've come, for the *oro negro*, the black gold, and the work, even if it is a sacrifice. But without trying, nothing is won. We are poor people, *señorita*, as you can see, so poor we must hunt to eat."

His voice had begun to take on that self-deprecating singsong rhythm what we volunteers used to call the whine of the poor. In the beginning my neighbors begged, "We are poor, *niña*, give us a little gift from America. You are a rich *gringa*. Be a good *gringuita* and give us a little favor, *una caridad*. Don't be a bad *niña*." They pulled on me, stroked my arm, looked sorrowfully into my eyes, until it took every bit of my self-control not to yell, "Damn it stop begging, have some respect for yourselves!" Instead I said, "I have no money to give, only my time. I can give nothing more than myself." Gradually the concept took hold, and we began to work together and the pleading subsided. But now the play of these men's voices, the cadences brought the worst of it back, and I felt as though there were hands all over me, beseeching, trying to take a piece of me.

"I know this is a poor country," I said, fighting against my disgust, concentrating instead on the sunshine and the sound of their boots slogging through mud. "I lived here for two years. Let us hope that finding oil will bring some prosperity to you. And to the nation."

"*Ojalá*, what you say is true, *señorita*. *Gracias a Dios* that it is true." The older man stopped then. "We leave you here, *dueña*," he said pointing to a barely visible path into the forest. "We try our luck." He touched the muzzle of this gun.

"And good luck in your future endeavors," I said.

"*Igualmente, patrona*," the older man said, starting in. They waved their guns and then they were gone, disappeared into the green. Hard as I strained, I couldn't follow their progress.

When I reached Kai, he was stopped on the side of the road looking up.

"Wait until you hear what I learned," I said.

"Shh," he motioned me with one hand to be quiet and approach slowly. "My God, nature has no shame," he whispered. "It's a red and black tanager, a spectacular tanager."

He handed me his binoculars.

"You see, there, a foot over the orchids. Look for red, crimson. It has a glorious crimson belly."

I moved the glasses up and down, but all I could see was dense variegated green, light and shadow. "I can't," I said. I could never seem to find the birds that he saw so easily.

"It's in the cecropia tree, higher." He moved the binoculars up.

"I don't know what a cecropia tree is," I said, irritated.

"You don't? You lived here for two years and you don't know what a cecropia tree, the most common side-of-the-road, waste-area tree, looks like?" He stood back, giving me one of his incredulous stares, his eyes narrowing.

"I told you, damn it. I don't know," I said, turning away.

"It has leaves like hands. See, there. The leaves look like fingers and if the wind blows they have whitish undersides."

Then, in spite of myself, I saw the bird. Bright velvety red amongst the green. Its beak, black and silvery. "My God."

"Isn't it spectacular? One of the most beautiful things you've ever seen? Here, give them here."

He took the glasses from me and was immediately engrossed in watching the bird, his vision trained on the spot high in the cecropia. I thought how like my father he was in this. My father was also thin and tall, but he was dark, his hair almost black and his skin like mine, able to tan to a golden brown in hours, the legacy of being a quarter French Huguenot, he would say. The stunning similarity, though, was not in physical appearance, but in this kind of concentration, the ability to cut out everything and everyone extraneous to the task.

I saw my tiny family unit—mother, father, and me—that April when I'd just turned seven, entering the grounds of a horse weight-pulling contest. We had left the car on the road, somewhere in northern Vermont. It was another of those weekend outings, supposedly for pleasure, but in truth all business for my father. We walked through the muddy spring field, toward the area where the horses were being yoked for the pull and attached to the sledges stacked with sandbag poundage. One minute we were three and then we were two, my father striding ahead of us, in the direction of a group of farmers who stood by the split-rail fence, and my mother and I were on our own. I looked to my mother to tell me where we should go first, and saw her face, tight with anger, her mouth trembling with rage, and her skin turned sallow under the harsh April sun. My father was standing now in the group of men, laughing, backslapping, working his charm. Probably he was set on getting these men to attend some meeting or perhaps he was just accustoming them to his presence. "Get them used to having a city slicker around, honey," he would explain to me. "You do that by having them see you so much they don't see you anymore." I wanted to be with my father, having fun, basking in the attention he got, not with sour-faced mommy, trying to make her happy again.

But as I stood watching my new husband, I felt my mother's unhappiness around my own mouth, pulling my chin down, tightening my brow. I turned and started down the road. I didn't want Kai to see my mother's sad face on mine.

I walked at a good pace, knowing Kai would eventually run to catch up with me, excitedly describing what he'd seen. My pack was heavy and sweat built up beneath it as the sun burned down from straight overhead. A slight breeze was stirred by the speed of my walking, refreshing my face and arms, bringing relief.

I breathed in deeply, telling myself to stop feeling sorry, and smelled the sweet frangipani, and the wet mud where the sun hadn't reached it under the dense plants and fallen leaves. Hummingbirds whirred beside the path, and parrots with their hammer heads and pointed tails streaked straight across the now white sky.

Farther on, butterflies skittered and flitted along my way, landing on a pile of dung a few yards ahead in the middle of the road. From a distance they looked like a mosaic of color, turquoise, red, a vibrant orange, a pale yellow, shimmering in the equatorial midmorning light. I walked closer, slowly, tiptoeing, not wanting to disturb them, when suddenly they sensed my approach, and I sent up a storm of flickering color into the air. They lifted like bits of confetti, caught in a draft, swirling about me as I walked through their universe, feeling the kiss of frail wings against my cheeks and arms. I wished my mother could have experienced such joy.

The noise of an engine came up behind. I moved off to the side of the road as the bus came jiggling and sliding and bouncing toward me. It was the usual Mercedes front followed by a wide wooden frame, almost as broad as the road, built on top of a flat bed. The bus was open-sided like a merry-go-round and painted the usual carousel colors of blue and white and yellow and red and green, with swirls and filigrees around the lettering. *Mi corazón* was the name painted on the front and side. The bus lumbered by me and stopped just beyond where I stood. As Kai leaned his head out the side, his hair red-gold in the sunlight, he looked like a figure head on a Viking ship.

"Come on," he called. "I think we'd better grab this one."

I laughed and trotted to where he held his hand out.

The ticket-taker jumped out of the front of the bus and came running back. I hoisted myself up before he got to me so as not to have my bottom fondled on the lift up. The memory of helpful hands lingering in places I didn't want

them was still vivid. I grinned down at him triumphantly.
He smiled back and shrugged.

"*Para ayudarte, señorita, nada más*," he said. To help you,
miss, nothing else.

"I paid for her," Kai said, and made a gesture of money
with his fingers.

The man gave him the high sign, his hand to his
forehead and trotted ahead to his position, the bus already
beginning to move forward. He swung himself in through
the front door to stand in place beside the driver.

The seats were like long wooden pews running the width
of the bus. The friar sat a row in front of us, a little over to
our left. He turned, smiled, and nodded to me. The driver
ground the gears into the next position and we picked up
speed.

Kai put his arm around me.

"Where did you meet the bus?" I asked.

"About a mile down the road. Not much beyond where
you fell off the handle."

I laughed. "Do you do that on purpose?"

"Do what?" He laughed.

"Screw up your clichés."

The friar leaned back and spoke to us over his shoulder,
his face in profile. I noted that when one looked past his
unruly appearance and his rough clothing, a rather
aristocratic man could be found, with his aquiline nose,
high forehead, and gray-blue eyes. His skin, where it
showed, was quite fair. Then I realized what his accent was.
He was Chilean, probably from Santiago. When the
opportunity arose, I would ask him.

"You are emerging as quite an independent adventuress,
señorita," he said.

"Yes, I always have been," I said, intentionally in
English. I scrutinized his face. There wasn't a hint of
recognition of the words. "I was brought up to do whatever
a man can do, and..."

"In Spanish," Kai interrupted.

"What?" I looked at him.

"You're speaking in English, not in Spanish."

"Oh," I laughed. "*¡Que boba! Lo siento, señor padre. Me olvidé.*"

He bowed his head with grace toward us. "No bother. If I were so fortunate to have the benefit of two idioms, I would certainly use them and confuse them." He turned his back to us again and, crossing his arms over his large belly, he let his head fall forward in a seeming doze.

He hadn't given anything away, but he also hadn't asked me to translate my reply to him. But why, I wondered if he did speak English, wouldn't he want me to know?

"What was it you wanted to tell me when I shut you up back there on the road?" Kai asked, pulling me closer.

"It was nothing," I said. "It can wait."

Up in the front of the bus, the driver and the ticket-taker were shouting back and forth to each other. Otherwise, no one else was talking. The four young workers we'd seen at breakfast sat in the back napping, their heads lolling from side to side. An Indian couple sat just ahead of them, ramrod straight and silent. They looked to be from the area, with the same round flat faces I'd seen in photos and on Mingo. They had black patterns either tattooed or painted on their cheeks and foreheads. He wore his hair cut in a bowl shape and she wore her long black tresses clipped away from her face with red and blue barrettes.

The jungle gradually closed in on us, giant leaves hit and swished through the open sides of the bus. We had to shift toward the center to keep from being struck. The driver was using a great deal of strength against the motion of the steering wheel. His ticket-taker held onto the bar overhead and laughed. The fringe around the window was dancing like a hula skirt and the saint in the center of the dashboard altar looked about to fall over, when ahead of us, through the windshield, I saw a wider opening and a shimmer of water. At last, the Rio Napo.

CHAPTER EIGHT

We pulled onto a broad stony beach and the bus stopped. Only then was I aware of how noisy the ride had been. There was complete silence now. Not even the sound of wind or water lapping, nothing. I looked out but couldn't see anyone waiting for us. No Mingo, no boat.

"Do you think he's coming?" I said to Kai.

"I sure hope he is." His face showed his disappointment, as well as the beginning of a sunburn. "I counted on this. I was so certain of him. But if he doesn't come, we'll find another way. I mean to take this trip." He brought his pack to standing on the seat beside him.

"*Senõres*," The friar turned. "There is nothing to worry. Mingo, for all his failings, never breaks a promise."

Had he understood, or simply intuited our *gringo* distress?

"Why there he is now, my friends."

In the distance came the sound of a motor. It grew louder as we listened. The bus driver, who had already stepped down onto the beach, started shouting and waving in the direction of the buzzing engine.

I slid across the seat after Kai, dragging my pack behind me. Remembering, I turned to reach for my tape-recorder at the moment that the friar had his arm across the seat and was about to pick it up. Our eyes met.

"Your listening device, *señorita*. You mustn't leave it unattended. Any machines are attractive to the natives. At the least they can trade them for more useful items from people like our friend Mingo." He smiled widely, showing startlingly perfect teeth.

"Thank you," I said. "I'll be more careful from now on." I slipped it over my shoulder and continued along the seat toward where Kai waited to help me down.

The sun baked the beach, but a slight breeze had picked up off the river, which spread out brown and wide before us. A few hundred yards to our left was an area that had been cut from the dense green forest. There was a soccer field ringed by various graying two-storied, split-cane buildings. So this was Misahuallí, the last actual settlement we would reach before venturing onto the river and into wilderness. Misahuallí wasn't on any map I'd ever seen, and at this point didn't seem to be occupied. There was no one out on the field, no one standing around the houses, and no smoke rising from any of them. I was about to ask about it when the bus driver called to us from the beach.

"Mingo waits, senõres. The Jívaro waits for his customers," he laughed, stumbling on the pebbles in mock drunkenness.

The ticket-taker came out from behind a tree, hitching up his pants.

"Be careful, señorita," the ticket-taker said. "You know what those Jívaro like?" He made a motion as though cutting his neck with a knife. "They make shrunken heads. You know that, señorita? Does your man know they especially like blond hair?" He tucked his striped shirt into his well-worn pants as the friar shuffled past him to go behind the tree.

Mingo waited stoically beside his boat. I didn't know what to say, not wanting to insult him as a Shuar. Head-shrinking was a violent act, the taking of heads as the spoils of war, but I knew there was a powerful ritualistic aspect to it for the community. I also didn't want to be in the position of the righteous gringa lecturing the ticket-taker.

"What do you say, señorita? Are you afraid of the Jívaro, afraid he'll take your head?"

"He's our friend, no?" I said. "And what are you to us, friend or enemy, amigo o enemigo? Can you prove your friendship by helping a gringa woman with her heavy pack?"

As I knelt to put my arms into the straps, I caught Mingo's look of pleasure.

The two busmen laughed and shook their hands in front of their chests, letting their forefingers snap against the next. "*Pues*, help the *señorita*, man," Mingo called. "Are you going to insult the first *gringuita* to come your way in months?"

"Very good," Kai whispered to me in German. "*Sehr gut, Fräulein.*"

Another boat, a long canoe riding low in the water, moved quietly into the landing area. An Indian man and woman sat in the bow and stern, the man doing the paddling. He wore a yellowing white cotton shirt, and she, a faded print dress. When they drew close, I observed a ribbon of black dashes and circles across the woman's forehead and down her cheeks. They sat waiting, not smiling, their backs as straight as his uplifted paddle. The two Indians who had been in the rear of the bus appeared with giant striped flour sacks on their heads. They ran under the weight, their legs bent by it, and without greeting the other two, they loaded the bags into the center of the boat. They ran back to the shadow side of the bus and emerged with bark baskets decorated with fine line painting, similar to the design on the woman's face. Before I could inspect the patterns more closely, they were in the boat themselves and the four moved out silently across the water.

"Phew," the bus driver squeezed his nose. "Thank God the smell is gone of those lazy stupid ones."

Just like the children in my third-grade class. I was surprised. Most *mestizos* remained quite decent about the tribal Indians. They wouldn't intervene when an Indian was being mistreated, but I'd never seen them express such open contempt. I had always felt a kinship with *mestizos* in those public situations when an Indian was being denigrated. It was not so far from my own days of silence in the face of anti-Semitic remarks. Those times at college when I'd been with people who didn't know I was half Jewish, when I endured their talk about how Jews always think they are so special, or jokes about how tasteless certain Jewish students from New York were. I suffered my shame in silence and I suffered my guilt alone afterward for not speaking up. Even though I didn't believe in God or a heaven, at those times I imagined my mother judging me from on high, hurt and angry at my betrayal of her people.

Mingo muttered something under his breath. He looked furious. "We must go," he said aloud.

As our belongings were being loaded into the dugout, it came to me that the remark had been made because these were Indians of the *Oriente* and not of the Sierra, and as such were deemed by all to be the absolute bottom of the heap.

"Is this a taping machine?" Mingo asked when I handed him the black box.

"Yes," I answered as I watched the friar's slow progress across the beach, back from relieving himself. "I work for a radio station."

The information registered in Mingo's eyes. "All the better," he said in a quiet voice as he carefully wedged it between a large metal tool chest and Kai's pack.

With Kai and me in the bow and the friar in dead center, Mingo pushed the boat off the shore and jumped in. He revved the motor on the first try, and we took off, leaving the shouts of the driver and his ticket-taker to disappear behind us.

The river was as wide as three city blocks, flat and brown, slow moving with clumps of tangled vegetation floating by. As we worked our way down the center of the Rio Napo, the sun even felt oppressive through my straw hat, and a hot dampness closed in around me. The omnipresent smell was of wet mud: gone was any scent of flowers or trees. Far away on the banks, thick brush and trees grew right down to the shore line. But the trees looked dwarfed, seemingly only inches of greenery between the brown water and the flat horizon of hazy white sky. We could hear nothing but the roar of our motor. The wake, as brown as the water itself, fanned out, setting up surface crosscurrents on the dark turgid plain of river. We began to move faster. Looking back I saw Mingo sitting high on the rear rim of the boat, his hand on the throttle and his shaggy hair blowing straight off his face. He didn't smile, and when the friar yelled something unintelligible to him, he merely nodded.

As for Kai, he kept his glasses trained on the banks.

"See anything?" I shouted to him.

"Not much. A gray tanager just as we started out. I wish I could ask him to slow down."

As we passed the four Indians in the boat, I saw them having trouble with the waves we stirred up. After that we just moved along through the water. A few birds came by to interest Kai. But that was it. The friar had given up on his attempts at conversation with Mingo. As for me, there was nothing much to look at except for the patterns our boat's movement conducted on the water's surface. It could get pretty boring traveling for days downriver. I hadn't considered that. The longest trip I had ever taken was on the Guayas, from Guayaquil across to Durán to catch the *autoferro* to Quito. It was on my day of departure from my *barrio*, on my way to Quito for debriefing before leaving the country. It was well before dawn. I'd been up most of the night at the ritual *despedida*, or goodby party, drinking *aguardiente* my neighbors insisted on toasting me with. I was fragile to an extreme from the booze, from my two years of work, from my sense of defeat, from the apparent love being lavished on me—love I didn't understand—and from a sadness I couldn't let myself feel about leaving this place. My only desire was to get out of there, escape finally from the responsibility, from the complicated ties. I had been counting the days till my departure for months. So when Rina Alvarez, the community center's treasurer, hung on me, weeping, begging, "Don't go, Ana, don't leave us," the journey across the Guayas became as interminable as today's promised to be. I wanted none of her sorrow, none of the memories of our time working together. I didn't want the weight of my debt to her as she now clung to my dampened shirt and pushed her weeping face into my breast. The others, girls from the neighborhood, who were accompanying me, tried to pull her off. She only clung more furiously and cried louder. "Don't worry, Ana," they assured me over her sobs, "she will get over this. It will pass. She grew to love you. We all grew to love you, Ana. You must come back to us." At that, Rina stiffened and abruptly pulled away from me. Her Indian face, framed by thick black straight hair, collapsed in on itself with grief and fury. "You'll never come back. You came here, pretended to be poor like us, and now you leave. We stay where you found us, living the filthy life you'll only remember." When she said that, searing as it was with cruel truth, all I wanted was to be free of them. I didn't even want to have to say the last good-byes. If I could have flown of my own accord from the deck of the boat into the approaching mountains, I would have gone with no competing remorse, no conflict in my heart. Or so I thought.

Later, as we stood at the back railing, a longing did arise. Rina had her arm in mine and her head on my shoulder as we watched the hill of Cerro Santa Ana grow smaller and take on a pink glow in the dawning light. But my heart strained not for my parting from Rina; rather I imagined that I could see Gala by the *tienda* at the foot of the hill, buying the day's bread and milk, as she tried to find the dot of our boat on the river. I imagined her hands clasped at her belly and her head tilted slightly to one side as she, in all her dignity, wept silently.

"How do you like our river, *señorita?*" The friar had reached past Kai to tap me on the shoulder, startling me out of my thoughts.

"It's beautiful."

"It's kindly, too," he said. "There aren't any man-eating fish they speak of in your movies, only fish to be eaten by man. You'll see. We all go swimming in the river at the settlement."

"And nothing ever happens to anyone?" I asked, thinking that I was not about to venture into the murky substance.

"Never. Even the *gringo* volunteer takes his daily bath in the river." He yelped with laughter. "First he got pretty foul, bathing out of bowls. Then he made himself a shower. But one day, too tired from his work in the forest to haul the water needed for his little shower, he came back and dove directly into the river. He shot out like a rocket when something brushed his ankle." The friar disintegrated into helpless laughter.

I smiled.

"But don't you worry, *señorita*, you will love it." He gasped as he regained control. "You will never want to leave. I am hoping that anyway. Hoping that we will entertain you so well that you won't want to go on to visit *don* Jorge."

"*Don* Jorge?"

"Yes, *don* Jorge, the German. That's how he's called out here. I don't know what his name is in German." He pulled on his beard and scratched in deeply with his fingers. He thought a moment, then spoke. "He has a brother, the name of Max. He lives in Quito, I hear. I've only seen him a couple of times. He comes for his vacations. I hear he's visiting now. They say he came to Ecuador after *don* Jorge arrived. They say he went to Argentina first, and lived in Bariloche before he worked his way up here."

Bariloche? Bariloche was a hot bed of Nazi activity, according to the Wiesenthal people.

Suddenly the water we were going through became rougher. I'd been looking toward the stern of the boat so I hadn't see it coming. We began to move erratically.

"*Tienen que ayudarme*,"—You must help me—Mingo called out. "We must pole through the white water to maintain control."

What he called white was now churning up pale tan. There was a sand bank to our right where the water rushed around and twisted back, flowing against the current we'd been riding.

"What can I do?" Kai asked, distracted from his birdwatching by this commotion.

"Tell your husband," the friar shouted over the increasingly loud noise of the water, "he will have to help Mingo pole. I am too old and fat to be of much assistance."

We were getting soaked. The boat began to lose its course, turning under the onslaught. Mingo handed a pole to the friar who gave it to Kai, but not without hitting me on the head.

"What am I supposed to do?" Kai shouted, trying to stand.

"Dig it down deep into the water," Mingo called.

"Put the pole down deep into the water," I yelled to Kai and pantomimed the action. "Deep, he says."

In the moments while the instructions were being given the boat had turned a hundred and eighty degrees. Kai's pole touched bottom. He fell with all his weight and pushed until the dugout began to veer back in the direction we had been going.

"*Bueno*. Tell your husband to keep doing that. Keep picking it up and putting it down," Mingo shouted. It was getting so noisy I could hardly make out his orders. He had thrust the boat's throttle even higher. His muscles strained to keep control of the motor. "Keep doing it. Go forward. Go forward. Stay ahead of the current."

"This isn't easy," Kai called. "The water is powerful."

"I've seen boats go over here, in this very spot," the friar shouted.

"What should we do?" I shouted.

"Pray," he shouted back.

In lieu of that, I added my weight to Kai's pole and as I did its tip knocked my hat off. The Panama disappeared like a leaf beneath the fiercely churning water.

And then we were through the rapids and floating in silence on placid water. It was as though the heat of the sun and the humidity had sucked all sound from the universe.

Kai's chest rose and fell as he caught his breath. His blue shirt was flattened to his body. Speechless, he smiled at me. His freckles stood out large and dark at his hairline, and his skin beneath them was ashen.

Mingo mopped his face with a red tee shirt while the friar fussed noisily about how wet he was.

Our clothes dried quickly and the heat soon became unbearable. It was close to two o'clock and the sun had begun to slant slightly from the west, hitting more area of our bodies than when directly overhead. The breeze had died completely, even in the middle of the river where we slowly made our way. I dug my long-sleeved white shirt from the outside pocket of my pack and soaked it in the water before slipping into it. I also soaked my canvas hiking hat, but it wasn't much protection against the low angle of the sun.

"Take my hat," Kai said. "You look hot."

I told him I was fine, that he needed it more with his fair skin. He dunked his bandanna and gave me that to drape down the back of my neck.

The green of the foliage on the eastern shore had deepened in color and was beginning to take on some contour. The water remained as brown and opaque as before. Birds passed from west to east and Kai shifted behind me to follow their flight. I dragged my hat through the water until it was completely saturated. Again, relief, when I put the cool, dripping fabric back on my head.

It could have been two hours later, judging by how low the sun was, when Mingo turned the boat sharply to the left and headed for the shore. I had been drifting in and out of fantasies, mostly of what we would find as we traveled farther down the river. Not frightening images this time of treachery and intrigue, but more of walking through the cool forest. I longed for the respite of shade. I was much too hot, and I had a bad headache.

"Are we at your settlement?" I asked the friar.

"No, we are not, *señorita*," he answered brusquely. "And I don't know why we are stopping here. Perhaps *don* Mingo has some supplies he is dropping off. Is that true, my friend?" He shifted around in his seat, causing the canoe to shudder precariously. I grabbed the sides.

Mingo didn't answer.

"This looks like a fairly big settlement," Kai said, training his glasses in the direction we were heading. "Here, take a look."

Through his glasses, what appeared to be tree stumps with the bare eye, was a row of people, adults and children. The children were entirely naked; the adult men wore cut-off pants and the women skirts. Most of the women were bare-breasted, but a few were wearing cotton shirts. The adults all seemed to be of the same height, brown-skinned, with black hair long to their shoulders and cut in straight thick bangs across their foreheads.

"This is quite something," I said, handing back the binoculars. We had come close enough so that even with my piercing headache and the intense sun in my face, I could discern human bodies without the glasses. Two men broke from the line and ran down the bank and into a canoe.

"Only the beginning," the friar said, as though in answer to my statement. A bullet of awareness shot through me. "Here we see the last remnants of a civilization, thanks to our friend Mingo, who brings them clothing from the cities, the clothing of the white man. He tries to do the same in our little settlement, but we will hear nothing of it." He spoke with his head turned so that Mingo couldn't escape his comments. "Later you will see the indigenous population in their purest form. These are Cofán, moved down recently from the Lago Agrio region. Their language is unrelated to any other in the region, but now they know a little Quichua. Perhaps to better confer with our friend, Mingo. My Indians are Quijos Quichua, with a few Canelos Quichua, *Runa* to themselves. Some Canelos have journeyed up to me from Chapana in the south. They make the designed pottery you may know of. But more of that later. Now we must greet our friends."

The men paddled rapidly out to us. They weren't smiling. Their expressions were neither forbidding nor welcoming. They simply stared straight at us out of brown faces a shade darker than the reddish brown of the river this close to shore. Their shoulders and upper arms were banded with black designs.

When their canoe reached ours, the man in front greeted Mingo in what I took to be Quichua, while the Indian in back spent his efforts keeping the canoe in place by executing a J stroke with his intricately painted paddle.

"*Buenas tardes*, my children," the friar shouted.

Neither man looked his way. Instead they turned the dugout about and began to paddle to shore. We followed by motor.

"Where are we going, *don* Mingo?" The friar's voice rose accusingly at the end of the question.

Still Mingo didn't answer.

When we reached the beach, we pulled up beside the escort canoe. The Indian men remained seated, gazing straight ahead as though we weren't there. Nothing happened for several minutes, and then I noticed that the group of people who had been on higher land were gradually moving en masse down toward us. They circled our boat, half of them standing in the water, silently staring at us.

"I'm getting out," the friar said. "I don't know what you're up to, Mingo, but I'm going to stretch my legs. *Senōres*, will you join me?" Without waiting for a reply, he grabbed his satchel and climbed out. "My children, please let me pass," he said to the assembled, who, whether they understood him or not, made way.

He was a different man as he spoke to them and rudely pushed by, even physically bumping a young boy. All blustering pretense was dropped. I wondered that he didn't even bother to maintain a modicum of geniality, however false, with these people.

Meanwhile the men had risen from their canoe and came to stand by ours. The crowd squeezed closer. Their ripe odors of breath and body bloomed in the concentrated space. To actually be in their presence, to be surrounded by a people so foreign was overwhelming for me. I didn't even notice that Mingo had climbed out of the canoe until I saw him standing next to where Kai sat. He reached inside his shirt and pulled out a packet tied in cloth the size of a stack of bills, saying a few words before handing it to the man who had sat in the bow of the canoe. This man, who wore only shorts, was old with a loose-skinned chest sagging around his breasts, though he was as thin as an athlete and his legs were powerfully muscled. His dark-brown face was tattooed with the same delicate geometric designs I'd seen on ceramic pots from this region. Where he wasn't ornamented with drawings, the lines of age were carved as though by a leather gouge. His hands were large, thickly jointed, and stiff, judging from the way he moved them, his fingers straight and wagging, pointing but not bending as he gestured. Then he held his arms out at near right angles to his body and began to move his torso from side to side as though imitating a bird or a plane. The people shrank back to make room for his pantomime. He made a sound that was an unmistakable hum of a motor. That went on for a few seconds; then he abruptly stopped, dropping his arms. His face became pensive. Mingo asked something in angry tones. The old man didn't answer. Mingo asked again. This time the old man began to make a gushing, hissing noise followed by a prolonged silence that he repeated over and over, again with his arms extended, at which Mingo's expression turned dark. Mingo spoke harshly. The old man made high yipping yelps that were not returned in kind by Mingo. Instead Mingo spoke in a quiet, sad voice. Whatever the old man had said greatly disturbed him.

It was then I saw the friar standing on higher ground, at the top of the steep bank, watching us. I sensed cold calculation in his posture as though he understood what he was observing and was storing it for later use. But moments later, when he made a show of clamoring that it was time to go, waddling foolishly down the bank, I began to doubt my perception, thinking perhaps I was only suffering from paranoia again.

It wasn't until we were on our way and had lost sight of the settlement that I thought of my tape-recorder. I couldn't see it by the toolbox where Mingo had secured it earlier. I asked the friar to look as he sat closer.

"¡Aiyee, Dios mío! I told you, señorita, to be careful. I told you that these people want nothing better than machines. Now that our friend here has taught them to appreciate the items of civilization."

"Cállete, padre ladrón." Mingo growled.

I was surprised to hear him tell the padre to shut up and also to call him a thief.

"He dares to call me a thief. I saw that money pass his hands. I saw it, Mingo. I know what that was for."

I assumed he meant money for trading in the magic of shamans' darts.

"You will never know what passes between the indigenous, padre Báez, nunca." Mingo spoke with venom. He revved the engine to its loudest level and succeeded in silencing the friar.

Kai moved cautiously up to share my seat in the bow. We had to sit very close to both fit on it, which was fine with me.

"Now I don't have a tape-recorder," I said.

"It doesn't matter. Everybody speaks a different language anyway," he said, sounding unusually despondent.

"I hate to be stolen from."

The sun was behind us as the river had turned slightly toward the east. It hit our backs with a late afternoon vehemence. Kai began to hum a Mozart tune as he methodically polished the lenses of his field glasses.

"What do you think happened to it?" I spoke in a voice low enough not to be heard by the friar if he indeed understood English.

Kai shrugged.

"What do you think Mingo's exchange with the Indian was about?"

He stopped humming. "Bombs," he said. He picked up where he had left off in the melody.

"What? Why do you say that?"

He turned to me, his slit-eyes meeting mine. I'd forgotten how dark-blue they were. In the shade of his hat they looked like the New York sky just after dusk. "I know bombs. Their sounds and silences as translated by humans. We children used to imitate them." No emotion was betrayed on his face.

"What do you think it means?" My breath grew shallow.

"I don't even want to think about it, Annie. So let's drop the ball, please."

I didn't correct him this time. And I had enough sense not to try to continue the conversation here. But it didn't stop me from trying to understand on my own. There was a memory, like my headache, nagging at me.

Chapter Nine

Rina Alvarez had been my best friend in Guayaquil and certainly in the *barrio* of Cerro Santa Ana. Gala was family, but Rina was a colleague and a friend. I never knew how old she was, as she would never divulge it. She was unmarried, probably because of her intelligence and independent character, though I wondered if it had to do with what she might project sexually. Rina had a way of acting as though you and she were close, but one could never, ever penetrate her entirely. Perhaps that metaphor held for sex as well.

She was attractive, not pretty, with her blunt Indian features, brown skin, straight black hair. She lived high on the hill in the poorest area, where there was no electricity and no running water. In spite of that, her clothes, cotton dresses in a rainbow of pastel shades, were always washed and pressed. She did have the smell of poverty on her, a combination of old cooking grease and sweat and the foul water from the hill that had a way of getting mixed with raw sewage. But her telltale smell of poverty couldn't have deterred any men on the hill. We all suffered from it.

Rina didn't work at a paying job, but instead helped out the center as a volunteer and the treasurer of the accounts. She spent day and night, seven days a week, working with me, and because we passed so much time together, we talked a good deal. We would often stand out on the narrow porch of the *centro comunal*, leaning against the raw splintery wood of the railing, watching the kindergarten children playing games in the rubble-strewn front yard. Or we would sit talking in an empty classroom, next door to the children's room, after having worked with their mothers to mix the dried CARE milk with water for the children's free breakfast. Rina never talked of herself, but only about her mother and the Indians of the Sierra. Her mother had come from Riobamba, had worn a poncho through girlhood, had braided her hair into two long plaits, and lived in a mud house. The stories were her mother's tales, told to Rina. Rina would also sing the haunting songs of the Sierra, flat tunes, in her dark, deep voice. She taught the children those songs and often as we sat, their voices entered our room with their sad tales of mountain life.

As Mingo's boat carried us through the afternoon river heat, I recalled the morning that Rina had a different story to tell, this one of Indians living on the eastern slope of the Andes, and to the west of the Cordillera Cutucú, in the *selva*, or the rainforest of the *Oriente*.

"They're called Shuar, or Jívaro," Rina said. She sat in one of the school desks that were used by the women for their classes in cake decorating and sewing, and in the evening by the men for mechanics class. I had just finished drying the huge aluminum pot we made the milk in. The room still smelled of the kerosene from the stove and the leftover milk that was already souring in the morning heat. I came over and sat in the desk beside her.

"They are a tribe that is still wild, living in the jungle where they cannot be found. They are warriors. The most warlike of all the indigenous. But it is said that they only fight to protect themselves, to protect their families and their gardens. What I do know, too, is that they cut the heads off the people they kill and boil them down until they are shrunken like a wool sweater to the size of a rat's head. I know this because I have one of those heads, bought by my father from a trader. They are the Indians the Incas could never subdue and the *conquistadores* also couldn't. It's said they are the only Indians that fought and won against the *conquistadores*. And when they won, they retreated back into the forest and weren't heard from again by white people until recently, five years ago in 1958 when they killed three gringo missionaries. When the missionaries had disappeared for too long, the *guardia civil* were sent to look for them, and all they found were bodies, without heads. And it was understood that the Shuar had shrunk their heads."

I expressed coy distaste at this point. It was the way I played with people in the *barrio*, masking my true self, acting as though certain things were just too awful for a *gringa* to endure. They would usually laugh and the game would go on with their chiding and kidding me. But with Rina it wasn't the right tack and as soon as I'd pretended to be squeamish, I felt foolish in front of her.

"It's serious, Ana. It serves the missionaries right if they go in there where they're not wanted, trying to bring their religion to these people. The Shuar take the heads for their own religious reasons, as important as the Christians'. They take the heads to make certain they have control over the avenging spirit, the *muisak*, of the man they've killed. They perform rituals, many rituals with the *tsantsas*, as the heads are called, to protect themselves and their families from harm. But this time the rituals didn't work, not against the avenging *gringos*." She said this last with particular contempt. "No, it's told that the relatives' *musiak* revenge or the revenge of the church came in the form of the air force dropping bombs into the forest. And if they didn't actually kill the Shuar, I'm certain they caused them fear and destroyed their peace, which is as bad."

After hearing that story, I tried to check on its veracity. I asked our vice consul general, a decent man in his thirties, but he said that he'd only heard of the beheadings, and that the other business of the bombings was ridiculous. "You know how these stories grow from nothing. Particularly in primitive populations."

As I sat in the bow of the boat, feeling my headache return in full force, I tried to recall if Rina and I had had other discussions about the bombing of the Shuar. Probably I'd been too busy with my work at the community center, too overwrought with the pressures that were beginning to intensify in the *barrio* shortly after that conversation with Rina, too preoccupied to pursue it further. And even now, trying to remember, I was drifting again too far into the past, back into those pockets I kept safely closed, and it seemed more like a dream than a real exchange between two friends.

Mingo turned the boat toward shore. Beside me Kai was watching intently in the direction we were headed. The sun was low and a deep yellow, slanting from our right, turning the brown water to an almost golden green. My headache was intolerable. I realized that we hadn't eaten in hours, and that the constant heat and sunshine were making me feel shaky and nauseated.

"We're arriving," the friar, who jolted awake, said. "This is my home." His voice was still hoarse as he cupped water with his hand and splashed some over his face and with another handful, dabbed his neck. "And not a moment too soon, isn't that right, *señorita*?"

I nodded weakly.

"You don't look good." Kai put his glasses down for a moment.

"I'm too hot."

Then we entered the long afternoon shade of the shore trees. With the sudden change of temperature I began to shiver.

"Are you sick?" Kai looked at me with concern.

"I'll be fine. I'm just not used to the heat anymore."

Kai dipped the bandanna in the water and swathed my neck. But it made me feel worse.

Mingo cut the motor and began to pole along the shore under the shade. We passed through the greenest green I'd ever known, and from that into golden sunshine and back into green. Green shadows. Golden light, green shadows, golden light and on and on. The water here was amber, thick and murky with motes of dense, dusty light shooting through it. I felt myself following those lights, deep down to the muddy bottom. From the forest, the sounds of the birds became cacophonous to my ear. Kai had his arm around me, but even so, he had his binoculars trained. I looked and thought I saw people in the forest, skittering by, peeking out, moving along with us. Black-haired, brown-skinned people. Bare-skinned.

"Do you see the Indians?" I said to Kai.

"Yes," he whispered back. "They've been following us."

The friar had replaced his hat over his face and appeared to be sleeping soundly. Mingo was in his own world, setting up a rhythm with his poling, placing the long stick in the water and letting his body weight go onto it, down and down until his shoulder touched the amber-brown water. Then he lifted the pole over his head and the water drops became golden specks in the sunlight, and down on the other side, until his body skimmed the surface and up with the pole, and this time the water droplets were emerald green. A face appeared in the foliage not three feet from us. My eyes met jet eyes. The face disappeared.

I began to worry about what was in store for us. How could we have been so foolish simply to come there solely on faith. What if Mingo and the friar were in some sort of conspiracy together? What if their animosity was feigned for our benefit? My tape-recorder had disappeared. They both knew I worked for a radio station. Perhaps they wanted to keep any evidence of their plans from leaving with us. It wasn't the first time I had been fooled by people in this country. The man in Guayaquil who had given me money every month for the community center, Fernando Calderón, the president of the local chapter of the Kiwanis Club in Ecuador, unbeknownst to me was the chief in-country operative for the CIA. By the time I learned that piece of information, the damage had been done. I had made the contact through the Peace Corps representative in Guayaquil. I had trusted Calderón, joked with him, even gone to the country club with him and drunk gin and tonics by the pool, thinking I was so clever at getting money from this man. And all the time he had been prying into my background and into the activities of certain people in the hill, Angel Castro in particular. Angel, who was making it out of the *barrio* by going to the university. Angel, who had been my friend, who had been as skilled an organizer as my father.

I began to shake. Kai held me more tightly. "We've got to get some water and food into you."

"I'll be fine," I said, but my voice shook and my teeth chattered uncontrollably.

"Are we almost there?" Kai asked Mingo in patched together Spanish. "My wife is ill."

"Right away, señor. We are almost there."

The friar woke with a start. "She needs potable water. You mustn't worry, señorita. We will take care of you."

I made myself look at the shore, not think of what had happened. Then a memory filtered in, of hearing that Angel had been mistreated in prison. "They said he's a communist." Rina again, her deep accusing voice. Had she known that I'd made light of Angel's political affiliations to Fernando Calderón? Like a schoolgirl, thinking it was simply university politics. Playing at being tough and savvy with this man. I'd had no inkling how serious the matter was.

I, of all people, should have known better. Three years after my mother died, my father was forced out of Vermont when the Burlington *Free Press* called him a communist on their front page. I hadn't understood at the time what had happened. When my schoolfriends were no longer allowed to visit me, I was devastated, believing it was because we had moved to a yet cheaper apartment in a rougher section of town, and because I didn't have a mother to oversee our activities, only a babysitter. It wasn't until years later that I understood, when my father confessed to me he'd been fired from his job with the Farm Bureau as a result of the accusation and had been blackballed throughout the state, making it impossible to get work in Vermont. Even though it was "damn Joe McCarthy's fault," my father was palpably ashamed that he somehow hadn't been able to master the obstacle, win people over again, and re-establish himself. I saw his pain, the way he couldn't meet my eyes as he told me, the way his mouth and chin went slack in the telling. I saw a man humiliated, almost ruined, by lies about his politics and yet, when it came to Angel

Castro, I'd played the innocent American girl, joking
about his leanings, laughing when Calderón had said,
"Angel Castro is a communist, Ana. Why do you associate
with him?" I'd replied, "What does it matter? It doesn't
make a difference to me." Then with charming bravado,
"What so frightens you about a communist? As long as he
helps the people to organize?" Of all the people in the
Peace Corps, I should have understood the ramifications of
that luxurious afternoon by the country club pool,
surrounded by green lawns, with waiters hovering, and
Fernando Calderón, with his coifed gray hair, his compact
body in fancy tennis clothes, staring intently into my eyes
as though he found me the most charming *gringa* he'd ever
come upon. He had been so adept at covering up his rage
at me, his virulent anticommunist rage.

I must have been shaking again, because Kai now had
both arms around me.

The light had become an aura. I couldn't look into it.
The green shadows were tangled and full of snakes, the
water thick with piranhas. Any moment an arm would
reach up from the muddy bottom and pull us all under.

Then we were there. A large gringo was guiding our
boat over to a small dock. He had waded out to meet us. He
was talking to me in English, saying what a great surprise
this was for him.

"I'm Annie Schmidt,"

"I'm Jon Dunham."

"Annie feels pretty sick," Kai said. "Kai Schmidt."

"The girl needs water," the friar said in very slow
Spanish to Jon Dunham who looked back at him slightly
confused. "*Agua, agua, agua.*" The friar made motions as
though drinking from a glass. "*Agua hervida.*" He made
circles with his hands to indicate boiled water.

"I'm not even thirsty anymore," I said as Kai helped me
out of the boat into the water.

"That proves you're dehydrated," Kai said. "Do you have
any sterilized water?"

"Sure we do. Sorry, my Spanish isn't the best. Quichua is as much as I can handle," Jon Dunham said, rubbing his big hand through his light-brown curly hair. I marveled at how big *gringos* look when they are big.

Massive is what some of us were. Too large boned, too fleshy, too many long wide bulging muscles. Too much expanse of white skin. This gringo had skin that was sunburned in raw patches. He wore cut off jeans. Ragged, with strings hanging over his bulky legs.

The men found me a place to sit under a small leafy tree on the otherwise bare muddy bank. I sat on the dirt, not caring if my skirt got filthy. Mingo pulled the canoe up onto the beach and tied it to a hand hewn block of wood. A group of Indian men in loincloths came out of the forest on the far end of the beach and stood together and stared in our direction.

"I will be back, *señorita*," the friar said, lugging his woven bag up the rise of wooden stairs set into the bank. "I will see to your water. Make certain it is sterile. And you, Mingo Mincha, don't you sell your corrupting goods to my Indians."

Mingo spat. The friar disappeared over the rise.

"*His* Indians." Mingo's fist rose in the air.

My thoughts kept spinning in and out of the present, back to the past, and into some sort of visionary state, where for a moment I thought I knew the Indians, that I had known them for years, that we had met and talked in their language, and then the image left again, and I was back in the real time of the late afternoon, and I didn't feel as though I'd ever been here before.

Kai and Mingo were conversing. They stood down by the shore. They spoke in words the sounds of which filtered up to me, but they also spoke with their hands and by stooping to the earth and drawing pictures. The Indians had disappeared again and the friar and the Peace Corps volunteer hadn't yet returned. I must have dozed because the light was more filled with color than I'd remembered. It was late, late afternoon, going into evening. The birds, too, had begun their feeding noise. Whatever it was that Mingo and Kai were speaking of, it must have been captivating to keep Kai from his birdwatching at this hour.

"What are you talking about?" I called to them.

"In a minute, Annie. How are you?"

"Better." I did feel cooler, but now terribly thirsty.

"I come. I come." It was our friar. He appeared on the bank with a ceramic water jug held close to his chest, his fingers in four ceramic cups.

I drank the water greedily. My veins felt like parched riverbeds that soften at the first touch of rain. The relief was almost instantaneous. My headache hurt less, my eyes could embrace the beauty, my thoughts cleared.

The friar looked down on me, fretting. He, too, stood in the shade of the tree which was now casting its shadow almost to the spot where Kai and Mingo still talked in low tones. Then they shook hands and Kai walked up to where I sat. His expression was one of concentration and concern. I thought how fine he looked. Even thinner than usual after close to ten hours since our last meal. His jeans hung low on his hips. He had unbuttoned his light-blue shirt exposing his chest and belly.

"Did you get enough water?" He hunkered down beside me.

"I think so. I can feel the difference already. What were you talking about?"

He shook his head as he began drawing circles in the dirt with a twig. "*Wir reden später.*" We'll talk later, is what he said.

"So, so. You speak a third language as well, my brilliant *señorita.*" The friar poured another cup of water. "If I may?"

"Certainly."

As he drank, he turned to see that Mingo was unhitching his boat.

"You don't stay the night, my friend?"

"But I thought..." I started to say, but was interrupted by Kai squeezing my shoulder.

"I must go, *don Padre* Báez. If my friends are not well, it's better that they don't travel now. I'll come by in a day or two for them. If they still wish to continue. *Pues*, we'll see then."

"Good. We'll look forward to your return. That is much better, *señorita*, *señor*. You will much prefer it here. Even though *don* Jorge is a countryman of your husband, you would not be satisfied with your visit."

I couldn't get any explanation from Kai. No hint. I got up on slightly shaky legs and went down to Mingo. He was already out to his mid calves in the water.

"I hope you do return," I said in a low voice.

His skin was red brown in the lowering sunlight, the same color as the lapping water. He squinted into the light, but didn't shade his eyes. Deep lines ran down either side of his face, from the edges of his eyes through his cheeks. Again I was reminded of my old boyfriend, César, but even more so of Angel Castro. While not alike in features—Angel had close-cropped curly hair and a light-tan complexion and wore wire-rimmed glasses—there was a similarity in their seriousness of expression. Yes, something that passed between Mingo and me recalled my neighbor Castro.

"I will, *señorita*. You can be certain of me."

I watched as he poled out toward the middle of the river. I felt the quiet of the shore, of the slipping water and the delicate sounds of birds as they scavenged for their meal. I waited until Mingo had started the motor and I watched the churned-up water of the wake catch the red of the sun. I watched until he had disappeared into the distance, and, all the while, Angel Castro remained with me.

CHAPTER TEN

It had to do with our being in the dry season that on a mid-August morning in 1965, four months before the end of my tour, a putrid, green-brown slimy substance erupted out of the drainage holes at the top of the *barrio* steps and began to spread out and down the hill, reaching from one line of houses across to the other, leaving only a thin strip of concrete on each side where a modified curb rose a step higher. It was on this curb that people had to balance their way up and down the hill, hugging the houses not to fall into the horrifying filth. It went on for days without stop, the stench filling our nostrils until we could smell nothing else.

I went to the *municipio* to report it after four days, and had to wait hours even to get into an assistant's office, and then all he wanted to do was flirt. After another hour of charming back-and-forths, he put his hand on my knee and said, "Come back tomorrow, beautiful *señorita gringuita*, and we can begin to fill out the forms."

When I returned to the center late that afternoon, there was a congregation waiting to see me. They included Rina Alvarez and Angel Castro who had apparently been talking around the community and had arranged for people to meet at the center to discuss the overflowing sewage. From the anguished faces I could see these men and women meant business. Even Gala and her husband Eladio had come, something that wasn't common. Gala usually had no time; with the five girls and now with the baby Ladito barely reaching his first birthday, she was completely occupied. But it was the baby Ladito who had brought her to this meeting, she said when we were seated, all twenty of us in the room that served as the *jardín de infantes* in the mornings. The baby had taken sick, she said, "since the *basura* began to flow. It is the stinking garbage that has given *mi negrito* the diarrhea and fever. *Pues,*

otherwise it is the bananas I've begun to feed him. Who
knows?" I was about to say, for heaven's sake, Gala, don't
you know by now that bananas don't give diarrhea or
amoebas. Instead, I sat silently as other people began to
voice their preoccupations about their health, and how
sickening it was to live with the stench. When Angel and
Rina said that we had to do something, take some action,
the rest of the group turned to me and said, "You go, *niña*
Ana. Go to your Peace Corps director, go to your
embajador, go to the *junta militar*. Use your power as a
beautiful *gringuita* to get the sewage to stop."

I explained to them that I had already been at the
municipio that morning and afternoon. "But," I said, "it
wasn't a smart thing for me to do. I shouldn't have gone
alone. I should have gone with the community. *Con la
gente del barrio.*" I saw Angel nodding approvingly and
Rina watching me with intense concentration.

"But you are more powerful," *doña* Citron said. This was
a woman who lived directly across the stairs from me. I
could look into her windows, watch her life go on, as
certainly she could mine. "They will say only that we are
poor people, and not pay us any honor."

"And I did better this morning, with the *señor asistente*
feeling my knee? Perhaps if I offered him something
more," I laughed.

"Nooo, no, no, *niña*," a chorus of indignation greeted the
last, though I wondered if they would have minded such a
solution.

I saw Angel smirk. Then he spoke. "We must organize,"
he said. "There is no alternative to the power of the *pueblo*.
If we are enough, they must listen. We can go together to
the *municipio*. We can get hundreds of the people of the
barrio and march on the *municipio*."

And so after more discussion it was decided. Our
assembled group, minus Gala, who said she didn't have the
time, would go up and down the hill talking to people,
telling them that we would gather here in the center in

two nights for a meeting to decide when to march on the Department of Public Works.

"For the children, we do it for the children, don't we, niña Ana?" Gala's husband, said, and I noted that he was more than a little drunk.

Throughout the next two days we walked the hill, Angel and Rina and Eladio and I and the others. We sat on the tiny porches of people living in shacks high up on the hill, drinking their proffered liquid refreshments, saying that even though they didn't have running water, they would someday and didn't they want to set a precedent for the municipio helping the poorest in the barrio. And didn't they have to walk each day down the hill through the filth and even if they didn't, weren't their children required to in order to go to school or go down to buy from the tienda? The people nodded that yes, all that was true, and yes, they would be there in two days for the meeting.

"Do you think we'll see them?" I asked Angel as we walked together up the steep, rocky dirt path to the next shack.

"It's not a question we can ask, Ana. We just keep on," he answered.

I thought of how my father would love him, as we entered a tilting structure with no floor and almost no walls. A piece of corrugated metal full of holes was placed precariously across beams to serve as a roof. With me sitting on the sole chair, after the woman of the house would hear of nothing less, we were offered glasses of water with two squeezes of orange in it, and we began again.

When I arrived home the evening of the first full day, I was greeted by Gala's worried face.

"Ladito, mi negrito, burns with a fire, Ana. What must I do? Please tell me."

I found the baby soiled and reeking of diarrhea, lying listlessly in the hammock. "He must drink boiled water, Gala, with sugar in it. You must keep him drinking. And I'll give you a piece of aspirina for the fever. Try to get it down him." I said, desperately trying to remember what they taught us during training about infant diarrhea.

The night of the meeting arrived. Angel and Rina and I stood on the porch of the *centro comunal*, leaning over the railing, watching the sky change abruptly from what I called mango sky to a startling peacock blue. One minute the sky was on fire with color, the next it was cool night.

"Like a revolution," Angel said, when I commented on it.

I laughed. "Always the radical."

His rounded features were in profile with the small metal framed glasses he wore reflecting the last strains of orange in the otherwise dark-blue sky. When I saw how serious he was, I felt again that I'd been too light, too much the silly American girl.

But then people began to enter the yard. First they dribbled in. After fifteen minutes they arrived by the dozens. We'd never had such a turnout.

"Look at this," I said to Angel, still standing beside him, greeting people who slowly climbed the steep wooden stairs to the porch and entered the meeting room. "Look at what we've done!" He said nothing, only reached over, and clasped my hand. Before we entered the jam packed room, Rina put her arms around me from behind and held on, her head on my back. No words. Just the warmth of her large body for the moment against mine.

The meeting was an easy one. None of my father's techniques for drawing people out were necessary. No manipulation, no waiting. The room was vibrating with energy. All that was needed was Angel leading them into the channels of action. In this way it was decided, by an almost unanimous vote, that we would gather in three days time, early in the morning and march on the *municipio* and demand a meeting with the minister of health, who was an old army man, brother to one of the five who ran the military government.

I remember the room so well at the moment of the vote. There must have been a hundred and fifty of my neighbors, many squashed two and three at the children's desks and the rest standing around the edges of the room and out on the porch with their heads straining in through the open windows. I remember the lights swaying in the breeze off the river, sending active shadows onto the twelve-foot-high, aqua-washed, cement wall that was the back of the center. I remember thinking, these are such smart people, so able to do what is necessary, given half a chance. Mrs. Rios was suckling her baby in the front row. *Don* Alonzo, the old man, stood regally beside the front door. The four Citrón children gathered around their mother, leaning into her from sleepiness, against her freshly washed and ironed blue print blouse. I felt so proud of them. So proud of myself, of Rina, and, most of all, of Angel.

On the day after the meeting, I went to the Peace Corps representative to inform him of our plans and hoping he could apply pressure on the city government, possibly opening doors.

It was so hot in Paul Halliday's office that the air felt like pressure on my skin. The little fan on the floor only served to push the heat from one side of the room to the other. He leaned back, his feet against the top of his desk, and bobbed continuously in his spring-back chair as we talked.

"I wish you'd told me about this before jumping in, Saunders," he said. "You know we don't want you fooling around in the politics of this country."

"It's not politics," I said, joking. "It's my work."

"Your work is to take care of things *within* your community." He didn't look at me.

It was then I sensed the seriousness of this matter in his terms. He was afraid to ruffle feathers. Even so I thought I could convince him to see things my way.

"But this is happening inside my community." I shifted my chair around so he would have to look at me, but he didn't. "The sewage is overflowing *inside* my community. I'm trying to get it remedied."

"There are other remedies besides marching on city hall."

"Such as?"

"Such as getting a *minga* of men together, young lady, and going to work. I'm certain there are enough hardy men in the community to see to the problem."

"This isn't a village. It's a city," I said, by now incredulous. "Cities have services. In training they always told us to utilize the municipal services."

"Utilize them," he said sharply. "But that doesn't mean to push them around."

"We organized people. It was their felt need," I said, giving back some of the words from our community development courses. "They decided to march on the *municipio*."

"Did they decide, or did the local rabble rouser Angel Castro decide for them? Be honest, Saunders." There was a hardness in his clear blue eyes that I'd never encountered before, and a distinct dislike either for me, or Angel, or for both of us.

"Angel is the best organizer I know. He never tells people what they should do." I laughed. "Anyway, we probably will fail. So there's nothing to worry about." I stood. I could see that for both of us the conversation had ended.

Where the Peace Corps office had been hot, outside, in the noon sun it was hellish. I walked, unprotected by trees across an open dusty field to the nearest bus stop. The August sun blasted down out of a flat blue sky. I was a young woman walking across that expanse, small and desperate, though I reminded myself that I didn't need that man's help, didn't need his okay on anything, didn't need his admiration. I had the community. I had Angel and Rina. That was all that counted. My father would have called Halliday an ignoramus. "What a hell of an ignoramus that guy was," he would shout when some bureaucrat wouldn't see things his way. I smiled to myself, hearing his familiar voice in this foreign place as I scuffed along, the fine white dust covering my sneakers.

I woke on the morning of the demonstration to the usual overcast predawn sky and the counting-off of the recruits. It was so cold in my apartment those nights of the dry season, with the wind blowing fiercely off the river and up the hill, that I had to sleep in sweat clothes under a blanket. But the wind and cool air mercifully kept the stench of sewage from our nostrils during the night. Though now the wind had died down and the fumes of raw excrement wafted up. I got out of bed and went to the flank of floor-to-ceiling louvered windows that looked out over the stairs. Children in school uniforms hugged the walls across the way, holding their noses, as they sidestepped down the steep incline. Rina arrived at the center, unlocked the large gate and walked across the yard. She wore a new dress of pale lavender, probably specially made for the occasion. A perfect color with her black hair.

When I went out, I passed Gala's door and looked in. "Gala, *don* Eladio?" I called.

"Ana." Gala came to the door, distraught, still in her nightgown. "I can't come to the march. He's not better. He cried all night and vomited. Did you hear him? *Aiie Dios mío*, the smell outside! I'm going to vomit myself. The girls are ill and don't want to get up."

Stepping into the room I saw all five girls in their one bed in the sleeping alcove, their heads just visible above the soiled blue cotton. Next to them in the other bed lay Lalo. He waved.

"I'll still come, Ana, don't you worry." He slurred his words either from hangover or fatigue.

"I hope so," I said. "We count on you, *don* Eladio.

The baby was nothing more than a tiny bundle of dirty cloth in the middle of the hammock. I touched his head. He was burning.

"Gala, you must bathe him. Take him out of swaddling and put him in cool water with a little warm in it."

Gala picked up the listless child and began to untie the cloth that bound him.

"Ana," a voice sounded sharply at the door. I turned to see Angel. He was dressed in a crisp white *guayabera* and light-blue trousers. "People are starting to gather."

"Gala, I must go," I said, reaching out to touch her. "Give him more aspirin."

"I know," she whispered, stroking her baby's naked puffed up belly. His twig thin arms lay limply on her own sturdy ones. His skin was purple with fever. I wanted to help, to start the bath.

"Ana, we must go."

"Go, *niña* Ana, I'll do what you've told me." Her usually coffee-brown skin was gray, her sad lips a raw purple as though in sympathy with her child.

"I'll come up as soon as we get back."

By nine o'clock over a hundred and fifty people had massed in the yard and were spilling out to the street. They had come early. I sat with Rina on the steps of the storage room surveying our success. Angel was circulating among the people, giving instructions, deciding who the leaders were to be. I had relinquished all authority to him.

Rina sat close beside me with her arm linked in mine and her head on my shoulder. "So now we will know," she said in her hard, sarcastic voice. "If the people will succeed as the *gringa* likes to believe. The always optimistic *gringa*."

"Am I so optimistic?" I laughed.

"Oh yes, you Americans are all optimistic. You believe that the world will go the way you want it to. And it usually does, doesn't it? Especially when it concerns controlling the poor." She wasn't smiling.

"That's not completely fair." I said.

"Oh, is the world fair?" She smiled, not pleasantly.

I looked away from her out to the people in the yard. Many had combed their hair back with water. I noted the shy stance of some with their hands folded across their waists, and others who fussed with their children, spitting and rubbing any indication of dirt off cheeks and chins.

They were in their best clothes, children and adults. Though most skirts and pants had patches, they were clean and pressed. Like Rina they had dressed for the occasion. Like Rina, did their care in dressing belie their skepticism?

The trouble began at ten-fifteen. Angel had just said that it was time to be leaving. By then we had two hundred people, including children. I had begun to make my way to the front gate behind Angel. Rina stayed at my side, still holding onto my arm. I was greeting *Señora* Citrón and a groggy Eladio when I heard it.

"*¡Viene el ejército!*" The army is coming!

Angel turned with a question on his face. Before I could answer that I didn't know what it meant, men and women began to surge back through the front gate, into the yard. They jammed up against the people who were moving out to the street through the same door.

"Be careful, the children."

"Don't trample the children."

"Be careful you fool."

"*Puta de Madre.*"

Dust rose as everyone scrambled up the slight incline back into the yard. *Señora* Citrón fell. I saw the old man, *don* Alonzo, begin to go down, but his godson Contelisio caught him before he hit the ground.

Angel pushed his way through the crowd toward the door. He asked one of the teenage boys to hoist him up to the top of the wall. Once on top he scrambled up and over the rampart. As his white *guayabera* disappeared over the wall, I saw the last glint of his glasses where the sun caught them. I saw his tawny brown hand as it clutched the top just before he released his hold. I heard screams beyond the wall. Women's shrieks. Men swearing.

"They are grabbing *la gente*," Alma Aponte shouted. She was a skinny woman with long cords of muscles on her forearms that she raised threateningly close to my face to illustrate what the soldiers were doing. "They are striking the boys. Striking them with clubs."

"Lift me over," I said. "Lift me over your heads so that I can see." I wanted to follow Angel.

"No, niña, no," was called back to me. "It is too dangerous. You mustn't go out there. You will be killed."

"Rina, help me."

"Let me go ahead," she said, her face twisted in disgust.

I pushed against the sweating, clawing bodies. The people who now forced their way in through the door had blood down the front of their clothes. Out beyond the wall I could hear the thuds of hard objects hitting against flesh and muffled moans. Rina had finally cleared the path and we were at the door, and then we were on the street, and the air was suddenly cooler, thinner, the sight before me horrifying. Men and women and children lay dazed on the ground, blood all over them, as others crawled on all fours away from the source of their injury. The soldiers, mostly Indians, the same recruits who marched each morning training to do the dirty work of the *junta militar*, swung their sticks in the air, coming down on whatever was in their path. They wore helmets over their shaved heads, and dark-green uniforms, and the high, black boots they goose-stepped in, and they were coming toward me.

"Don't you hit her. She's an *americana*," Rina screamed, throwing her body between me and them.

"Stop it!" I yelled, my throat like flames from the force of my rage. "Stop hurting these people." I looked around for Angel. He wasn't anywhere. I checked the bodies on the ground for his *guayabera*, his glasses, his short wavy hair. His slight physique. No Angel.

The recruit who had advanced on me with raised club backed off. As he did, over his right shoulder I saw a battered, black Chevrolet pull away.

"Please," I cried. "Can't you see that people only want what is their right."

Rina grabbed me. "Don't beg them," she hissed. She turned and walked to the line of men who had stopped their battering and stood at semi-attention with their legs spread.

For the moment nothing happened. A profound silence lay in the plaza. Then the crowd from the center began to surge out into the street, led by some young ruffians of the neighborhood, carrying rocks from the rubble of the courtyard. "Stop it!" I yelled at them. "Don't make it worse!" But they didn't hear me, and when I turned to find Rina again, I saw her, too, on the ground with the others, holding her head, the blood spreading down the side of her lavender cotton dress. I saw the recruits raise their guns and I heard the pop of their fire and then I couldn't see because my eyes were burning and the air was filled with smoke and I was coughing and weeping uncontrollably. I stumbled toward the stairs that led up the hill, carried along by the crowd that had risen from the ground and was doing their best to get away. I could only see the people closest to me. I couldn't find Rina. I made my way by instinct away from what I later learned was tear gas. I ran past my own building because the gas was still following us there.

After we reached safety, high on the hill, and water was brought up in buckets, and we drank and washed our faces and bathed our eyes and sat breathing deeply in the hot noon air, and smelled the lingering traces of tear gas mixed with raw sewage, Alma Aponte began to taunt me. "*Mentirosa*. Liar." She sneered. "You said we could help ourselves and look what has happened." The grumbling passed through the crowd who stood by the buckets. People began to laugh. "Did you do this to make us look foolish?" "Did you do it so that the *ejército* could capture us in one place?" Dried blood caked the sides of mouths. Hair was matted with dirt and blood. Clothes were ripped. "Ha. You waste our time, *gringa*. You come here to waste our time."

"Ana." It was Rina, climbing the hill to me. "Come, get away from them." She made me stand. "*Basura*," she growled at her neighbors. "You are nothing but garbage to treat her this way."

They began to taunt Rina as well, ridiculing her for taking my side. She put her arm in mine and led me down the steep rocky path. Once my back was to them, the stones began. They picked them from the ground and threw them at me and at Rina. A large rock struck me in the middle of the back. Rina pulled me closer to her and held firm. "Keep walking," she said.

A rock hit Rina on the head, but she didn't stop. Then we were out of their range and on the silent, sun-blasted, stinking stairs, hugging the wall as the children had in the early morning. Next we were slipping into the door of my apartment house, into the dark hall, and Gala was at her door.

"Ana," she called after me. "Ana."

But I was up the stairs with Rina. I unlocked the padlock that held my door closed and we were inside.

Rina threw the latch behind us. She had me sit on the couch while she went to the window and, opening a slat, looked out.

"The *ejército* is in the center's yard," she said.

It was dark in the room with the doors closed and only narrow slits of sunlight entered between the slats. I couldn't see her expression, only the solid, stubborn set of her thick body. The room was stinking of trapped fumes from both the sewage and the tear gas, and stifling, too, as we cooked beneath my sun-heated corrugated tin roof.

After a while Rina came over and sat beside me on the couch. She leaned her head on my shoulder and put her arm around my waist. Blood was drying on the bodice of her dress, dark-red against the pastel lavender. Her hair was stiff with blood against my cheek. I smelled its unmistakable metallic odor.

What would my father say about this? He had never told me how badly I could fail. I thought of how humiliated he'd looked when he'd confessed to being run out of town after he was labeled a communist. He'd never spoken of his life in prison. What had he protected me from in the stories he didn't tell? What had his relentless optimism masked?

In the afternoon I went back to the Peace Corps office. Halliday, who was on the phone, looked up startled and motioned me to sit.

"I have to talk to you," I said.

Clearly irritated, he told the person he was talking to in English that he had to go.

"Who did you talk to about our demonstration? Who did you report it to in the *junta*?"

"Saunders, stop this. You're out of control. You're a mess. Your clothes are filthy."

He got up from the desk and went over to the fan and adjusted it to high speed. It did nothing to change the temperature in the room. His shirt stuck to him and his pants were stained with sweat. At least he was suffering a little, too. He came back to the desk and sat down slowly. "Now tell me in a more controlled manner, what is going on?"

He's not innocent, I thought. His voice had the sound of someone speaking with a wad of cardboard in his mouth.

"You know very well," I said. "We didn't even get out of the plaza. Half the people didn't get out of the center's yard."

"I heard there was some trouble in your *barrio*. I'd hoped you would come and talk with me about it. But with a little more humility, perhaps." The nerve jumped under his right eye. He nervously brushed at his crew cut.

"Humility? They could have killed someone this morning. Did you tell anyone what we'd planned? Tell me."

"You are screaming, young lady." His thin neck shrank to scrawny. I watched the pulse in the hollow of his collar bone, and thought how fragile human life is.

"Tell me where Angel Castro is. Where was he taken? I want to know that."

"Young lady, don't you go accusing me. You're lucky this didn't happen in the center of town, and that this debacle wasn't worse and more public." He rose from his chair.

He walked a wide circle around me to the door of his office and looked out. The typewriter began to clatter once again. María Elena, the secretary had been listening.

"Where is Angel Castro?" I asked again in a low, furious voice.

"I don't know where your communist friend is," he said, his lips tightly set. His blue eyes bored into me as he indicated the door.

I walked across the same dusty field of the day before. I stopped. Suddenly I understood. Fernando Calderón. He had called Angel a communist. Halliday had told Calderón about the demonstration. I had led them to Angel. I turned in place. The sun was hot, but I saw no color. The world had been washed of every hue, leaving only gradations of gray. A trembling overtook me. This lack of color. I'd heard somewhere that it indicated craziness. I had to have it out with Halliday about Angel. I turned to walk back but I found I couldn't take a step in the direction of the Peace Corps office.

In the middle of the night I heard Gala knocking on my door, calling my name, but I didn't answer. When I went to work the next morning their door was closed. I didn't knock, even though I suspected something. I was so afraid of what was to greet me at the center when I opened up for the kindergarten children that I ignored the sign. Instead I went on with my tasks, trying to hold myself and the community center together, until the child Gladys appeared at the tall green metal gate to say in her gruff, too adult voice, "My mother wants you."

CHAPTER ELEVEN

Kai climbed the ladder propped against the split-cane building that was to be our sleeping quarters. It was his second trip up, this time with my backpack. I followed him, grateful for his help. Though I was considerably better, I still felt weak.

The structure was a twelve-foot-by-twelve-foot room, with the east wall completely open to the outside. Benches were piled to one side. On the back wall was a blackboard and over it a large, garishly painted picture of Jesus on the cross. On the north wall was a saint's picture with a shelf beneath it holding burned-down candle offerings and glasses half-filled with water. The altar in Gala's room had held those same gifts to God, I thought, as I sat on my pack looking out to the trees that began twenty feet beyond our shelter. I had to stop remembering every little detail or I would certainly spoil our trip. The memories were rushing in on me as they never had before. I had strenuously kept them at bay after my return from Ecuador when I couldn't speak of what I'd been through, when I would go to visit old friends for a dinner in my honor and close down completely in a dark, vengeful rage, despising everyone at the table for their privilege, for their obliviousness to the way most of the other people in the world lived. Some months later the incapacitating anger abated, but I was left with an edgy amnesia, where the memories I most feared stayed hidden from me. All except the death of the baby Ladito. But here they were again, like hordes of bodies trying to get in, clamoring for attention. To my surprise, not all were frightening. There was a relief in making their acquaintance again, even those related to Angel and the riot.

"We have to decide what to do," Kai said, sitting beside me on my pack. He took my hand in both of his.

"About going on? What did Mingo say?"

Outside all color was leaving the sky. In a moment it would be night.

"You remember what I surmised about the bombing?" He glanced at me.

"You mean someone really is bombing?"

He cleared his throat. "I'm not sure. I was at a disadvantage with the language. But he mentioned Somaxo."

"Those men I met on the road said Somaxo was beginning exploration out here. But what bombings? Of the Indians?"

"I don't know, Annie. I couldn't understand everything. But he said, bombs from the sky. He drew houses, and stick figures of people, so I supposed he meant civilians."

He sat in silence, the pressure of his hands around mine telling me how upset he was.

"Could it be true?"

"I don't know." He snapped at me.

"You don't have to get mad at me," I said.

"Why ask such a question? How can I know the answer?" He dropped my hand and stood up. He grabbed hold of the wall beam, his elongated body silhouetted against the purple sky.

"What does Mingo want of us?" I asked after a long silence.

Kai started speaking in such a quiet voice that I had to strain to hear him against the rising tide of cicadas.

"He says he's coming back for us. He wants us to go to *don* Jorge's with him, without telling the friar and the Peace Corps fellow. He says they will stop us if they know."

"Why?"

"Again, Annie, I don't know. I can only say he was adamant about our not telling." His voice was sad and defeated coming through the darkness of the night and the din of insects.

I stood and joined him at the open wall. Beyond the trees was a clearing. I saw a small fire burning out there and smelled the faint odor of food.

"Do you still want to go?" I asked.

"Of course, I want to go. It's the only way that I can figure to get deep enough in for the birds I'm after, birds I'll never be able to see anywhere else. You know how much that would mean to me. But this other." He stopped. "*Um Gottes Willen*, I don't know what to think."

"What about the German? What does he have to do with this?"

"Mingo insisted he's a good man. He kept saying over and over *que bueno es el alemán*."

I had a sudden vision of a benevolent, patriarchal dictator, one who plays the saint so that others will adore him and be beholden to him, but is all the while using them and keeping them subjugated for his own purposes.

"I don't think I want to go, Kai."

"Let's feel it out," he said, reaching over and smoothing my hair. "I would like to leave it open. This is an opportunity of a lifetime for me."

"And the danger? The possibility of being someplace where bombs are dropped."

"I suppose it doesn't seem as dangerous to me," he laughed softly.

Either that or you're denying your terror, I thought.

When Kai reminisced about his university days in Munich, it was always about drinking in beer gardens, weekend ski trips, and girls they would pick up in après ski bars. When I questioned him about more serious activities, he said, "We wanted fun and nothing to do with politics." In the three years I'd known him, as the Vietnam demonstrations were growing, though he was against the war, he participated reluctantly, complaining about their chaotic style and lack of dignity. It seemed paradoxical, considering he had chosen an activist in me, one who worked for a radio station that was a hub for the movement.

Then one day he went with me on a march to support some Black Panthers who had been arrested in New York City. We had walked over the Queensboro Bridge and were standing in the parking lot of the Queens House of Detention when a speaker began to exhort us with cries of

"Power to the People!" and "Black Power!" until the thousands assembled raised their fists and punched them into the air. Kai stood perfectly still, his arms at his sides. His face went pasty and he began to sweat. "I've got to get out of here," he said. He fought his way through the crowd. When we were finally free of the people, Kai walked rapidly from me. I caught up with him when he stopped a block away at a tiny triangle of green in the middle of an intersection. He collapsed on the bench, his head in his hands. Hard as I tried to get him to talk about what the raised fists had reminded him of, he maintained a complete and resolute silence.

As we stood together looking out from our tree-top house into the darkness of the jungle night, I thought his denial of the danger in this situation was just the other side of the silent terror that had overcome him.

"It frightens me a lot, Kai. I mean, I'm not exactly used to bombs. You know I can't tolerate any kind of violence."

"Don't worry. I promise we'll talk more about it. I don't want to get hurt either."

We joined the friar and Jon Dunham for dinner. The friar had changed his brown robes for what could be called summer garb, a bleached-muslin version of the darker hopsacking, though it was definitely a mistake, because whatever filth the darker material had camouflaged, this stuff didn't. There were grease spots and food drippings all down the front, and from the hem up to knee level it was splattered many times over with mud. Behind, when he turned, smudges of brown and black, grass stains, and more grease indicated the various substances he'd sat in. Jon, at the other end of the spectrum, wore a fresh, blue, oxford cloth, button down collar shirt with the sleeves rolled and a spanking clean though wrinkled pair of khaki Bermuda shorts. Even his sneakers were washed. I recalled what the friar had said about his fashioning a shower for himself. I wondered how the two of them could tolerate each other.

"Sit, sit, my friends." The friar indicated a long rough hewn table in the middle of the dirt-floored, screened-in room. Bamboo posts connected the floor-to-ceiling screens at the four corners and held up the thatched roof. It was a primitive structure but functional, shading those inside from the sun and keeping out the bugs while letting in breezes, sweet forest odors, and sounds.

Kai and I sat down on opposite sides of the table.

"This is some pleasure, I'll tell you," Jon said, remaining standing. "It's not often we get visitors."

A Coleman lamp hung from the center of the ceiling. His skin didn't look as mottled in its light. Harsh as the buzzing white lantern was, it wasn't as merciless as the tropical sun.

"How long have you been here?" I asked.

"Nine months." There was none of the sigh that I remembered punctuating any recital of service time beyond six months. Instead he still seemed eager, fresh.

"Roberto tells me you used to be a PCV, too, back in the early days. I'm impressed."

"Nothing to be impressed about."

"I hear it was pretty rough then. Some people didn't come through at all. Had to be shipped back home." His hands dug into his pockets, he rocked back and forth on his feet.

"It was ridiculous," Kai said.

"What was?" Jon's face was completely innocent and young.

"Criminal really, to send young, untrained people down to do a job they knew nothing about. They were just kids."

Though I appreciated Kai's taking my side, I felt diminished by it. Particularly because Jon was the same age I had been, and he didn't seem to be suffering.

The friar walked over to the door of the kitchen annex. He stood with his large dirty back to us, looking out, but I felt he was listening to our conversation.

"Yeah, in training they told us some pretty grim stories about those first groups. They made sure we were better trained, had some skills. I'm a civil engineer." He shrugged, his lower lip went forward. "I just do what I was

trained to do. What was your job, community organizer?"
He laughed.

"As a matter of fact, yes."

"Sorry." He scratched his head and looked sheepish.
"But from what I hear it was the dumbest. People just got
drunk with the natives and set up a few credit unions that
the natives stole from."

Though I would rather have called him an asshole, I
laughed and said, "Yeah, that's the way some of us got
through."

I was certain now that the friar was listening. He had
no other reason to be standing at the threshold, except to
position himself to eavesdrop. There was movement in the
other room. A pot hit against wood, but there was no
exchange of words.

Jon had gone on to describe his project. "Land reform
you might call it. I'm here to survey land plots for the
Indians."

"Plots?" Kai said.

"So that they can have their own land when the oil
companies come in here and begin doing exploration. This
way, there are officially demarcated places and there won't
be any disputes."

"But aren't the indigenous in this region nomadic?
Don't they need to move from place to place to sustain
themselves with hunting and fishing?" Kai said.

Jon pulled over a roughly made chair and sat in it at the
head of the table. He ruffled his hand through his hair.

"Hey, you sound like some other people I know." He
looked over at the friar and then back to us. "These folks
have to change with the times. It's not going to be easy
getting them to adjust to a new life, but there's no choice."

"Why no choice?" Kai asked.

"It's progress." He lifted his big hands in the air and let
them drop on the table top with a loud smack. "Simple as
that. If this country wants to go forward, they have to
exploit their oil potential. Otherwise they stay in the
middle ages."

"Or back in the stone age where these people exist," Kai said.

"That's exactly correct," Jon said, missing Kai's sarcasm. "It's the best for them really. Peru just expropriated all foreign-owned oil companies, and Venezuela is about to place their oil industry under state control. So the market's going to break wide-open. Venezuela's oil is "soup," you know, filled with sulfur, whereas Ecuador's is "sweet," and real easy to process. Sooner or later it's going to happen here, and better if the Indians are settled peacefully. It could get pretty dirty otherwise. It got real ugly recently up on the Aguarico, by Santa Cecilia. They're having trouble deeper in, too, farther downriver, I hear. Don't know what sort, but I hear rumors that it's on the verge of getting pretty messy. That's not good for anyone."

"So, so, my friends. It is time to eat," the friar interrupted. "A *comer, a comer*," he said very precisely, apparently for Jon's sake.

"Oh, *a comer*," Jon repeated, laughing. "I know what that means. Not that the food's much to write home about."

"You look like you're surviving," I said, aware that the friar had picked a crucial moment to interrupt.

"I'm trying to pack in as much as I can. I've seen some guys get stick-thin. Hey, how is it, that the guys in the Corps get thin on this food and the girls blow up? Did that happen with your group?"

"It did. I gained fifteen pounds right away, but then I got worms and amoebas, and in two weeks' time I dropped twenty-five pounds." I smiled.

"Ewww," he screwed his face up. "Haven't had the pleasure of them yet. Boil that water, boil that milk, cook the meat 'til it dies," he laughed.

Dinner was a small piece of tough meat, cooked dead as promised, a heaping serving of rice, and a platter of yucca. When the yucca was passed I took only a tiny portion. Yucca can be succulent in a soup when it absorbs the juices of a fatty chicken broth, but when boiled in plain water as this pile had been, it's deadly, sort of like swallowing damp papier-mâché.

"You might not want that much," I said in a low voice to Kai as he began to load the tuber onto his enameled tin plate. "It's yucca." I hoped my intonation would explain all.

"Yucca's good," he said cheerfully.

So be it, I thought.

Even when I'm not ravenous, rice prepared the Ecuadorian way, with lots of oil and garlic, is irresistible. The meat was tougher than it looked, and the yucca was beyond redemption.

"Delicious," I said. "*Muy rico.*"

"*Sí,*" a muffled voice came from Kai. "*Rico.*"

Looking at him across the table, I had to clench my jaw not to laugh. As he would probably say, he'd bitten off more than he could swallow, and he'd be correct this time. His cheeks were full and his face strained as he attempted to get the dry root out of his mouth and down his throat.

The friar got up at one point to go into the kitchen, and Kai tried to fork some yucca onto my plate.

"No thanks," I smiled. "I'm full. But it's delicious, isn't it?"

When Jon wasn't looking, Kai gave me the finger.

The cook cleared the table. She was from the mountains, her hair in two long graying braids. Her ankle-length, gathered skirt was of a cotton floral print, and her blouse, though soiled and patched, was ornately embroidered. She kept her head down as she stacked the dishes and didn't say a word even when the friar asked her for *café tinto* with sugar.

"A little coffee and then I will let our guests retire," he said. He'd been quiet all through the dinner while Jon did most of the talking. Now he returned to his boisterous old self.

"Tomorrow perhaps you would like to accompany Jonathan into the forest. He goes to survey the land. He is helping to divide the land so that the Runa can live their lives in peace and comfort. An admirable occupation, don't you think?" He spoke directly to me.

"Jon told us before dinner," I said. Had he really not understood our conversation? Or was he an expert actor? "But isn't it distressing for the Indians to have to settle down in one spot after the kind of life they've always led?" I said repeating Kai's earlier question.

"Not a good way to look at it, *señorita*." He shook his curls vigorously. "You know better than that. What did you call your work in this country? Development, no? We need development in our hemisphere, development *and* protection of the cultures. What do you think I'm doing, *señorita*? I'm trying to preserve this fine Indian culture. Protect it from the men who will soon be encroaching looking for work. I must protect the culture from people like your Jívaro trader friend. At the same time I'm trying to curtail the use of firearms in hunting and dynamite in fishing. And to make certain these poor Indians have land to live on in the future." His face became long and morose, like a tortured dog's, as though the pain of these Indians' destinies was his own.

"How much land is allotted for each Indian?" Kai asked in his improving Spanish.

"That you will have to ask my colleague." He pointed his massive hand toward Jon, who had faded out of the conversation.

Before Kai could ask the question again, I said to Jon, "How do you two get along without language?"

A look of distress passed over the young man's face. He covered it with a laugh. "We stumble through. But we don't see each other that much. I'm either out in the forest or falling asleep over my meal, and he's usually going around ministering to folks." He nodded over toward the friar.

The friar was smiling benignly, appearing not to comprehend.

Kai asked the question again about the land.

"One half acre per family," Jon answered.

"That's all?"

"Yes, but these fellows don't think the way we do. They don't get the idea yet of private property, hard as we try. We map it out, give them papers, and then they all go together and plow it and plant and build those extended-family houses like before. It's something. I'd think they would love to have their own land, unpaid for, but they don't. It's a cultural difference, you know. Practically a communistic thing. Also, the shamans give us some trouble. They get real obstreperous when all we want to do is co-operate with them. But I guess we have our own strange ways of being if we were looked at from outside. Probably we'd find any kind of imposition a threat to our way of life. What do you think?"

"Yes," I said, holding back, "probably so."

"But you know, these people might have the right idea. They get more land, in a way, by going together. So it all works out for everybody. They get their land and we have to parcel out smaller tracts. By the time we get done, I think everybody'll be happy."

"Who's *we?*" Kai asked. He, too, was restraining his anger.

"What is going on, *amigos?*" the friar interrupted. "Let me in on your good conversation, if I may."

"My husband just asked who *we* is," I said.

"*Nosotros.* What do you mean by *nosotros?*" He hit the palms of his hands in a loud insinuating rhythm on the table. "*Nosotros!* For what? Let's not have such serious talk here tonight. We have more nights for serious talk. Why don't we relax a little. I have a surprise." He looked from one to the other of the three of us sitting around the table. His gray-blue eyes were opaque in the dim light. He smiled conspiratorially. "I have a stash of cognac that even my friend here knows nothing about. So what do you say that you wait one moment while I go outside and bring it in. Juan, *ven conmigo.*"

Jon, looking slightly bewildered, got up and followed friar Roberto Báez out the screen door into the night.

The woman knocked dishes around in the kitchen. Otherwise it was silent, the cicadas having ceased. On two sides I could see forest impinging on the clearing, and beyond the screen door where the two men had exited, light shone out across open space. Nothing moved out there. The friar must have gone around back someplace. I wished I'd been more alert when we'd arrived and had surveyed the settlement.

"Naive guy, this Jon," Kai said. "But he seems to know about the oil industry. That business about "sweet" oil. I've heard that Venezuelan oil is filled with impurities and a mess to refine. Even so they're the main suppliers of the eastern United States."

"So if Venezuela nationalizes, the U. S. will be looking for another major source."

"I'm sure they've been looking for some time."

"And our friend the father doesn't want us to know who 'we' are."

"Maybe he's just the buffoon he appears to be."

"I think he's more devious than that."

"Of course you would." He grinned, but his face was clouded with thought.

The friar returned some five minutes later, alone. "*Voilá*," he said, brandishing a bottle of Armagnac.

"Where's Jon?" I said.

Without answering me, he called to the woman in the kitchen to bring the coffee and four glasses for the cognac. I heard a mumbled *sí, señor patrón* and then the clatter of tinware.

"Jon will be back with us soon, if he finishes the business he must attend to. He is checking the plans for tomorrow. If you are to accompany him, the women need to know to prepare lunch for you as well. They meet the men in the forest at midday with lunch and *chicha*. Do you know *chicha, señores?*" He remained standing, holding the bottle he'd brought with him.

"I do," I said. I had had the corn drink once before, but knowing that the women masticated the corn before spitting it into a bowl to ferment gave me trouble. "It was tasty," I lied.

"Good, most *gringas* aren't very partial to it. Good, good, good." He walked impatiently to the door of the kitchen just as the woman came out.

She brought a tray with a bottle of *esencia* and a steaming pan of water and the four glasses. She placed them in the center of the table and retreated soundlessly.

"Very fancy," Kai said, picking up the bottle of Armagnac. "*¿De dónde es?*"

"Ah, that you should ask. To be honest, it came from the infamous *don* Jorge, in the days when we were on speaking terms, when *don* Jorge still cared some for the finer trappings of life. One day I visited him downriver, oh, a year ago, two years." He spoke very slowly and distinctly for Kai's benefit. "We had a charming visit. I was new to the area. He kindly gave me this bottle as a welcome gift to me. The generous present has lasted longer than the friendship." He handed the full glasses to us.

"*Salud,*" he said.

"*Prosit,*" Kai offered.

We drank. It went down like smooth fire.

"What brought you to this area," I asked after we'd admired the Armagnac sufficiently.

"Much the same as what brought you here, *señorita*. Am I presumptuous to believe that you came out of a desire to do good for the people? As for me, I have my debt to pay to the indigenous, to the poorest of this continent. I come from a wealthy family in Santiago, Chile."

"I know Chile," I said. "I thought perhaps that's where you were from," I said, remaining breezy, charming.

"Aha, even beneath my humble robes and full wild beard, are you saying you saw a Chilean? You are a clairvoyant if that's so, or an astute observer, *señorita*. Most people can't tell what my origins are." He lifted his glass to drink, watching me over the rim as he did.

"Astute perhaps," I said. "Special powers, no. I'm as often wrong as I am correct in my guesses."

"I doubt that," he said. "I rather doubt that, my *señorita*."
He turned his pale gaze on Kai.

"Jesuit, or Franciscan, or perhaps Salesian?" Kai asked.

Good going, I thought.

"My, my. Franciscan of course. Not Jesuit, God bless me.
I could never be a Jesuit. Too much discipline. Too much
high thought. And the Salesians. No. They're a special lot.
I'm not that special, I fear. No, much simpler for a rich
boy, to be a Franciscan. No demands really to the calling.
I'm left to my own devices. It's much better for me. I'm
perhaps what you might call an iconoclast. Or at least
that's what my dear father used to accuse me of. 'My no-
good iconoclast son.' My father was a manufacturer. His
father brought the first cars to Chile, God bless him, and
my father built the first factory. But his son, I am sorry to
report, was more comfortable in the robes of monastic
simplicity than in a three-piece suit. My loyalty is with
the simple people. I wish the best for them in all of this,
señorita, *señor*. Please believe me." He got up and walked
over to the area with an oversized roll top desk and a
lounge chair of bent bamboo, made more comfortable with
two large filthy pillows. "You'll excuse me, but this old
body is too stiff and creaky to be sitting without proper
back support." He stretched out, emitting a series of
extravagant grunts and puffs, the length of the chaise.

"And what is 'all of this'?" I asked.

"All of this, *señorita*?"

"Yes, *padre*. You said you wish them the best in all of
this. Could it have anything to do with the bombings?"

Báez squinted at me. Kai kicked me under the table. I
knew he wouldn't want me to be so direct.

"So you've already heard those nasty rumors. Now who
could have told you about that? Ah, let me guess. Mingo.
Yes, of course. I've heard those stories myself, *señorita*, and I
can assure you there is nothing to them, only the dementia
of a war crazy German living in the jungle. Please beg my
pardon of your husband, as I know it's impolite to defame
one's countryman to one's face, but please assure him that

what I say is true. The man is insane, and for his own purposes he is stirring the population up. He is starting harmful rumors, even leading attacks on innocent people. Trying for some sort of insurrection that can only harm these humble Indians in the end."

His cheeks and forehead turned red while he talked. His demeanor and his speech patterns lost all of their false joviality as he reverted to the man who had stomped out of our canoe this afternoon and stood high on the bank of the river.

Báez poured more Armagnac for himself and drank it, throwing his head back. His demeanor changed again, this time reverting to his overly affable self. He smiled at us in the light of the lamp that flickered and sputtered, spreading illumination out of our screened-in room and onto the cleared areas and forest beyond us. It was as though our circle of light was a separate universe in this far-off place, with the friar in control of our destiny, the one who completely determined the direction of our conversation, of our thoughts.

"I take the liberty of warning you, my friendly senõres, to stay away from the German, don Jorge. No matter if Mingo returns in the next few days for you. Only miserable misfortune can be the outcome, as it is for anyone who has contact with him." He closed his eyes. "Good heaven, I am exhausted, and the American boy doesn't seem to be returning." He yawned, clasped his hands over his barrel chest, and began to breathe deeply in apparent sleep.

CHAPTER TWELVE

The night was more silent than it had been back in Puerto Napo, where I'd thought I'd never heard such quiet. Now I felt as though I was on the other side of silence as I walked across the packed, swept earth of the clearing outside the friar's room. It was as though it would take light years of travel to reach the place where silence began and then an eternity to find where sound started again. That was how still the night was. I turned back when we'd reached the middle of the area to see the Indian woman shuffling around the table, picking up cups and glasses. Either her feet didn't really touch the floor, or stillness begets stillness, but she made no noise.

"C'mon, Annie," Kai hissed.

The friar raised his head and spoke to the woman, and I heard the soft sibilant murmur of her answer. After that a squawk came from a place to the left of the screened-in room. It sounded like the signal of a short-wave radio. The friar lay down again, and the woman disappeared through the kitchen door.

I joined Kai in the shadows, just beyond the light that shone from the room. I brought my face close to his, smelling his familiar odor of sun-baked skin, and wished that we could curl up together in some comfortable double bed and make love. But I had other ideas of what our next hour would entail. I whispered almost noiselessly into his ear.

"Did you hear that sound?"

He nodded. "Short-wave."

"I want to see," I said, my voice barely more than my breath, a fine ribbon going from me to him. "Do me a favor. Go with your flashlight to the schoolroom. Light a candle. Leave it. Come back *ohne licht.*" Come back without light, I'd said in German, surprised at finding the words which I usually avoided coming from me.

"Don't go anywhere without me."

I nodded.

Waiting for him, I breathed in the sweetness of the forest. The rising moon was beginning to create a skim of silver over the trees to the east. I imagined it throwing shadows and light wherever it could penetrate the forest or wherever campsites and other tiny communities had been cut into the jungle.

Kai had reached the schoolhouse and was climbing the ladder, letting the flashlight swing around, making himself as conspicuous as possible. He was "good to steal horses with," as well, I thought with a rush of affection. I watched as he surveyed the room with the light. Then the flashlight was replaced by the faint shimmering of a candle flame coming through the open spaces of the split-bamboo walls. The flashlight went on again. I heard some scurrying and throwing around of soft objects. What was he doing? As I was about to go and find out, the flashlight was extinguished, and I saw a dark shadow coming down the ladder. I turned to check that the friar was in his chair. He was, but he sat now with his arm thrown over his forehead and some papers in his hand held close to his face.

Kai was beside me. "Bastards," he said.

"What?"

"The camera's gone."

"Are you sure?"

"I know where I packed it."

Glancing over to the house I saw that the friar remained engrossed in his papers. Nonetheless, I motioned Kai away from the clearing toward the trees to the right, closer to where the squawking sound continued. It would camouflage our voices.

"Was the place ransacked?" I asked when we were safely in the shadow of the trees.

"No, it was very methodically done. The bag was closed up again. I wouldn't have noticed if I hadn't looked for the candle. I want to ask that bastard in there if he set this one up."

"You know what he'll tell you."

"What?"

"That it's all Mingo's fault for raising the aspirations of these poor indigenous people." I let my voice singsong in the sanctimonious rhythms of the friar. I knew full well why the camera had been taken. Not for resale, or perhaps only as a secondary gain. No, I was certain, no matter who did it, they'd stolen our camera so we wouldn't take incriminating photos, just as my tape-recorder had disappeared. Perhaps Mingo had returned and sneaked up to our bedroom while we were eating. But I didn't think so. My suspicions had shifted again onto the friar. Away from his provocative personality, his denunciations of the German seemed too determined, designed more for effect than based on truth. I found myself asking the question: Why was he so hell-bent on our not meeting this mysterious man?

I heard Jon's voice through the increasingly loud squawks of what I was now certain was a short-wave radio.

"Let's go take a look," I said to Kai. "Before we do anything rash."

"You're right. We're never going to see that camera again."

I reached for his hand. It was warm and brought comfort. We made our way around the screened-in structure, past the lean-to that held the kitchen with its charcoal stove and smoldering coals. The Indian woman methodically dipped a gourd bowl into a barrel of water, transferring the liquid to a smaller tin washbasin. We skirted far enough around that she couldn't see us if she looked up, which she didn't, but we could see her clearly in the rich yellow light of the kerosene lantern set on the ground. Her shadow loomed dark and stooped against the back wall separating her from the friar.

My body was highly tuned from the adrenaline that was coursing through me in throbs, like heartbeats. I felt an exhilaration beyond fear. I sensed wrongdoing and, to my surprise, I wanted to follow it to the end, to the truth, no matter what it was.

We rounded the corner of the house to find another small structure, this one enclosed with walls of split-bamboo into which windows had been cut. The windows had no covering, no shutters, no screening. Crouching to one side, a distance away, we could look directly into the bedroom-office of Jon. He sat with his back to us, but his head turned a quarter into our view. In front of him, on his desk, was the radio, and above it, a contour map with certain areas plotted out. Paul Halliday had a map of Guayaquil with each street in the minutest of detail. Suddenly I recalled that on his map there were pins indicating where volunteers lived and pins showing community centers, and even the homes of community leaders. I remembered with a harsh clarity that my house had a blue pin in it, and, until it was removed, Angel Castro's mother's shack held a black pin.

"Jon-Jon here in Napo. Three hundred, over." Jon was saying.

All we could hear in return was the squawking. No words, only the irritating noise.

"Who's he talking to?" Kai breathed into my ear.

I shrugged, and then indicated the earphones that Jon wore.

As we waited to hear what he would say next, I remembered talking to my father on the short-wave after the riot. I had to go into Halliday's office and use his radio. How distraught and destroyed I'd been as I'd yelled through the static to my father in New York. Trying to make contact with a sane, reasonable person, I suppose. What had I expected, that he would make everything all right? That he would tell me I was doing the best I could do, that I'd been correct in the decisions I'd made. But he couldn't tell me any of that because I could barely hear him and he could not reasonably hear me and Halliday was in the next room. Instead I heard him call me chicken and sweetheart, and say he missed me and was proud of me, as I sat crying helplessly, the tears streaming down my cheeks over my chin and down my neck, catching in the pocket made by my collarbone. That was the last attempt I made to speak of Angel Castro's disappearance to anyone besides Rina.

"That's right, sir. We'll do our best, sir. I don't think it will create a problem. Over."

The friar appeared in the room. How he'd entered I didn't know, but there he was standing beside the desk, then he was bending close to Jon and had lifted one of the earphones away from Jon's head so that he, too, could listen. He nodded at what was being said, making eye contact with Jon. His demeanor was now serious, in complete control, professional.

"They'll stay here with us. You can count on that. Don't think they'll want to go on. They seem to like it here. Over," Jon said into the microphone.

I waited in anticipation of the moment he and the friar would begin to converse in English.

I was straightening out of my crouched position when a hand touched my shoulder. I thought it was Kai until I saw him with his arms crossed before him a few inches from me. I leapt back. A hand went over my mouth. I struggled against the body that held me close. "Shhh," he whispered in my ear. "*Soy yo*, Mingo." His voice like ours barely louder than a baby's breath.

Kai lunged toward us. I put my hand to his mouth. We stood like that, paralyzed, listening to hear if the two men in the room had noticed anything of our sudden commotion. I could feel the heaving of Mingo's chest as he held me against him. He was all muscle. He smelled of garlic and sweat. Kai's eyes were wide, staring at me. I felt the softness of his lips under my hand. The moon had risen over the crest of trees and we were now illuminated by it. I knew we had to move quickly. If the friar or Jon should turn and look out the window, they would see our forms that were becoming silver in the light.

I dropped my hand from Kai's mouth.

"Have you heard enough?" Mingo whispered into my ear.

I nodded.

We made our decision easily to go with Mingo. "We don't have much of a choice," Kai said as we stood under the shadow of the schoolroom. "I don't want to stay around here. I'm furious that they lied to us. Stole my camera. If I weren't afraid of them, I'd go in and demand it back."

I held onto his hands that were balled into fists. I'd never seen him angry in this way.

With everything ready and packed carefully into our bags, Kai swept the room with the flashlight, over the blackboard, the picture of Jesus, the shelf with the candle and water glass offerings. What baby had died, I wondered, to warrant these offerings?

Kai snapped off the flashlight.

"We should wait before going down," he said. He walked carefully over to the candle at the open end of the room and knelt to blow it out. I stayed in the back and could only see the sky now lit by the moon to a shimmering slate. We sat down to wait and listen. The moonlight was so bright it brought out the turquoise of the tee shirt Kai had changed into. He sat on one leg with the other pulled up so his knee was under his chin. His back was to me. I watched him and thought how good it was that he was here, and wondered how much better everything would have been if he'd been with me five years earlier. Maybe he would have known how to get the fever down, would have wakened in the night when Gala had come for help, or gone with her to the clinic the day before. And if in the end Ladito had died, Kai would have gone with me that next morning before dawn on the long walk behind the tiny white casket, behind the neighbors, the family, the *compadres* and the keening Gala. We would have walked together in the rear of the procession with *don* Alonzo, along the street from the *barrio* to the cemetery. If Kai had been with me, he would have put his arm around me as we walked through the cemetery's ornate iron gate and along the black and white checkered terrazzo floor, lined with royal palms, past the mausoleums and castles of the rich, and up the hill past smaller and smaller headstones until they turned to small white wooden crosses and then to nothing more than fresh plots of earth with a few plastic flowers on top. How would it have been to have someone holding me in the moment when the young men of the neighborhood began to dig the earth under the intense heat of the just-risen sun, when Gala screamed out more like an animal than a human, "aaaiieeee," and fell to the ground and began rolling down the hill, tumbling her full body over graves until the boys ran to grab her and brought her clawing and thrashing back to the grave of her only son.

"Let's go," Kai said. "If anyone was watching they'll think we've gone to sleep by now."

I was calm when Kai said this, but as soon as I began to descend the ladder my legs shook violently. I looked across, over to the screened-in room, and realized how close we were. If the friar stepped outside for a breath of the night air, he would easily spot me in the intense natural light.

"Annie," Kai hissed.

I looked up to him but couldn't answer.

"What is it? Get going."

I began again, my legs still trembling. But once on firm earth, in the shadow of the trees, my fear transferred to Kai.

Kneeling beside Mingo in the brush, completely hidden in shadow, I worked to keep my breathing under control as Kai came down the ladder. My heart was beating erratically, stopping every five beats as though to gather its own courage. I imagined the friar appearing suddenly and demanding to know where we were going. What if they tried to forcibly keep us here?

Kai walked toward us, exposed by the moonlight.

"Come on, *please*," I said aloud.

"*Señorita, cállese.*" *Señorita*, shut up, Mingo said.

His anger succeeded in calming me down. Kai, warm by my side, accomplished the same.

Beckoning us to follow him, Mingo led us to a slight opening in the forest and we were on a well-worn narrow path leading away from the friar's settlement.

The only sounds were the whooshing of branches as they hit against our packs, the soft thud of our feet, and the inhale and exhale of my own breathing. The way was lighted by the moon that had climbed high over the trees in the time we'd waited. The sky was clear overhead, but I hardly looked up, keeping my eyes on the path to watch for roots or holes. When we came to another clearing, we didn't stop, but instead Mingo skirted it on the side farthest from the river. I could see houses of an Indian settlement. Beyond them was the glitter of river. There was no movement here, not even the barking of dogs as we rushed by. Everyone must have been long asleep.

"Ssst." The tiniest hiss came from Mingo as he motioned us to turn right and we were again in the underbrush. We slowed to a walk now as this section was not clearly cut, and I had to pace myself far enough behind Mingo not to be slapped in the face by branches. We went on and on, until I wondered where we could be going. When I'd seen the river before, I'd assumed we were almost at the spot where he'd moored his boat. It became darker, and I looked up to see that the branches had closed over our heads so there were only patches of luminescence. Mingo sped up again, even though it was, if anything, denser than before. I kept my hands in front of me to protect my face as I ran. My breathing became labored and my backpack bounced uncomfortably on my spine. Why had he started to run? Had Mingo heard something that I hadn't? I tried to listen but all I could hear was Kai's loud breathing behind me. Where could Mingo be leading us? Maybe this was all a terrible mistake. Suddenly, Mingo's arm shot across the path. Kai came crashing into me from behind. Mingo had stopped us just short of the water.

"Are you okay?" Kai asked in a slightly out of breath voice.

"Fine," I giggled nervously.

Mingo had gone over to the side and was dragging his boat out of the underbrush.

"I'll help you," Kai said in Spanish.

"*Gracias*," Mingo said distinctly in the night.

The two of them pulled the boat along the sandy beach and then shoved it into the shining water where it bobbed gently. The water lapped and slipped and splattered against the boat, setting up a hollow irregular beat. I thought of the friar beating time with his fingers against the table top, and imagined his irritation when he discovered we were gone. When would he know? In the morning when he called us for breakfast, or in the night when he would send someone to check on us, perhaps the person who had stolen our camera? I shivered at the thought and hoped that if he did, it wouldn't be for many hours. Because if he were discovering our absence now, we were in trouble.

I waded out to the boat where Mingo helped me off with my pack and piled it in on top of Kai's.

"We push the boat out," Mingo said.

I stayed back at the stern, with Mingo and Kai farther up on either side, as we slipped the boat first along the shore and then out toward the center of the river. The water rose up to my thighs. We couldn't see the other shore. The river was particularly broad here, I recalled from the afternoon. A white sheen of moonlight coated its surface. The sky was abundant with stars, despite the intensity of the moon. I didn't recognize any of the constellations, but it was enough to be beneath its dazzling beauty. There were huge clusters and masses of whiteness against a steel-black. Any fear I'd been feeling was completely eradicated by my joy at such loveliness. I had to be safe in this perfection, and if I wasn't, what did it matter? If harm were done us and even if we were killed, we would certainly be one with the universe in a place like this.

"Climb in," Mingo said. "*Señora*, now."

I moved forward along the side of the dugout and hoisted myself up and tumbled in onto the floor.

"*Señor*, now you."

Kai rocked the canoe as he thudded in.

Hand over hand, Mingo worked his way to the back of the boat and slipped over and in, though more lithely than either of us had. He handed a wooden paddle to Kai and one up to me. Mine had a grooved handle, curved along the top, perfectly fitted to my hand.

"I will tell you who should paddle when," he said. "*Señor*, you first."

Kai pulled his through the water, leaning into it with his entire weight, causing the boat to turn toward the center of the river.

I dug mine in as far as I could, determined to keep the boat as close to course as possible by exerting all my strength. The canoe shifted easily toward the shore.

We proceeded like that, first Kai, then I, then Kai, than I, quietly pulling our way along the river. The only sound besides the splash as wood hit water was the creaking of the side panels, Mingo's hushed directions, and an occasional splash of a fish surfacing and sucking at air.

Only once did I look back, but I merely saw the shape of trees and the luster of the river. There was no indication of a settlement, or of a lantern dangling from a hand as the person searched the night, nor a glint of binoculars, or, my secret fear, a gunstock. It appeared that we had gotten away without their suspicions being aroused. I wondered if Jon was still communicating on the short-wave with the friar standing over him. I wished I could have questioned Jon further. With more time, I could have worked my wiles on him. He had to feel some comradeship with me as an ex Peace Corps volunteer. But maybe that was wishful thinking. We had most likely joined for entirely different reasons, for loyalty to a different sort of vision. My president had asked me to serve my country, not to take it for granted. Then shortly before we'd arrived in-country, he'd been killed. We had walked through Quito still stunned by the events, by the newness of this land, and the effects of altitude, our eyes squinting against the glare of mountain sun on the white-washed walls of stone colonial buildings. We blinked away tears as *Latinos* and *mestizos* alike came up to us with their own sorrow flooding their cheeks, expressing their condolences for the dead *presidente católico.*" Jon's President Nixon could never elicit such passion from either Peace Corps volunteers or the people of this country.

As we moved down the river, the moon rose directly over our heads. It was as though we were in broad daylight. The stars now were somewhat muted. I still couldn't see to the other side of the river, it was so very wide.

CHAPTER THIRTEEN

"Now you can stop," Mingo said, when we'd been traveling for an hour.

Kai and I pulled in our paddles. The boat began to turn with the current.

Mingo yanked the motor cord three times before the engine caught and a roar was set up.

"It's awful," I said, covering my ears. "Do we have to?"

Mingo laughed for the first time. "If we want to get there before the week is gone, we need the motor. We're beyond any settlements now. We can take a chance with the noise."

"It's like a *pecado*, this noise," Kai called over the din.

"You're right," Mingo yelled back. "It is a sin, but this is nothing compared to what sins I will show you."

Mingo, who had been sitting up on the back ridge of the boat, moved down to the seat and began to steer from there. With the sound of the motor behind him, he was easier to hear.

"It should take the night to reach *don* Jorge's camp. If you like, you can sleep. Though there isn't much room."

I didn't feel the least bit tired. I was relishing the movement of the rocking boat, and the cool wind on my face, bringing with it little particles of water and the fresh, muddy fragrance of the river. Despite my trepidation about what was to come, I felt a certain happiness and wanted to savor the thrill of being on this unsettled, lonely river in the middle of the night.

"How long have you lived here?" I asked Mingo after a while. I sat in the center of the canoe between the two men.

"I don't live here," Mingo said. "I travel back and forth between here and Macas. Often I go to Quito to buy more merchandise. That's when I'm gone for a long time. It's a very arduous trip from Macas to Quito."

I'd almost forgotten his salesman's bag of merchandise.
And the friar's accusation about the shaman's darts.

"It's been my life for three, four years. Only in the last
year have I gone regularly to don Jorge and María."

"María?" I said.

He self-consciously brushed his hair back from his face.
He looked cute in the moonlight. He smiled at me.

"María is the wife of don Jorge, the black woman we
spoke of. The Black María, if you wish." He smiled again.
"She's una negra from Esmeraldas. Pues, now she lives with
a white man among the Indians. A good woman, María.
No children, but a good woman."

I was about to ask him why and how he'd first gone to
see don Jorge, when Kai asked, "Do you know the bird, pico
negro? It's a toucan, black with a yellow breast, white rump
and a yellow beak?" He indicated with his hands what he
was speaking of, saying the colors in Spanish.

"Aha," Mingo laughed in recognition when Kai
mimicked the song. "Dios te dé, we call them. 'May God
give you.' For their song, we give them that name." and he
began to sing, "Dios te dé, Dios te dé."

"Dios te dé," Kai laughed repeating the term. "Very
good. Dios te dé, much better than in English. Black
mandibled toucan." He laughed again.

"How was it you called the bird in Spanish?" Mingo
asked.

"Pico negro."

Mingo thought a moment, before shaking his head. "No,
I've never heard it called by that name. But all the Indians
know Dios te dé. It has good feathers." He laughed
maliciously.

"Sorry to hear that," Kai said.

Mingo smiled, but the smile left quickly, and I noted
that he watched Kai for many moments before turning his
gaze out across the water.

"Did you meet don Jorge through trading?" I asked.

"No." Mingo slowly shook his head.

"Then how did you meet him?"

I thought he wasn't going to answer, he took so long to speak, but then, "Through *Padre* Báez. I first had the honor of meeting the *padre*." He sneered. "He had such powers that I believed in the beginning that he had sympathy with the plight of the Indians, and he flattered me that I could work with him to protect these tribes. He can be a man who convinces, perhaps you noticed that, *señora?* He knows our weaknesses. He knows if he takes us into his confidence, tells us fine words about ourselves that never, ever come from a *blanco's* mouth, that we believe he is on our side. We're foolish in this way."

I hadn't expected him to be so direct. I told myself not to be coy with him, not to make the mistakes of my past.

"How did this foolishness show itself?" I asked.

He revved the throttle. Behind him the wake was white in the moonlight. I could see his face as clearly as though it were the middle of the day.

"I went to talk to the *don* Jorge as a spy of the *padre*. I was sent as an *indigena*, one of the peoples of the *Oriente*, to persuade him to adopt the program that the *padre* and his friends were pushing. I believed he was correct. But I had my conversations with *don* Jorge, and I changed my way of thinking. Don't get me wrong, *señora*, I'm not a man to be swayed this way and that. What I saw was that *Padre* Báez didn't want the best for us and our customs, no matter what he said to me."

"I'm not understanding," Kai said behind me.

I quickly translated.

"Roberto Báez accuses me of what he calls cultural genocide because I trade the goods of the white people with my people." Mingo spat into the water to his right. "I've heard that word spoken by many whites who come back here, the ones who come to study our ways. But what they don't understand is that we can have both, the clothes of the westerners and our own customs. But we can't survive the real killing they do to us. Or the religion they force on us. I've had my arguments with *don* Jorge even."

"About the religion?" I asked.

"No. No. About the thing they call cultural genocide. He too thinks I shouldn't trade in these items."

"Which items? The clothes or something else?" I asked, afraid to be more direct.

"But he forgives me because I try to help him otherwise," he said avoiding my question. He smiled. "I bring witnesses."

"Have you brought many witnesses?" I decided not to pursue the question of what he sold, though it disturbed me that he hadn't answered.

He shrugged. "A few, but nothing came of it. I believe that no matter what you people see, you forget it when you arrive at your home. Is that so?"

I was startled by his question. I had a sudden memory of Rina writing me letter upon letter after I'd left, begging me to help in finding Angel, and to help her gain passage to the United States. "I'm unwelcome among the people of the *barrio*," she had implored me. "I am afraid the army will come for me as they did Angel. Please, Ana, help me as I helped you." After awhile I threw the letters out unopened. I could no longer bear the sight of her tiny, formal script, squashed onto the blue airmail stationery.

Mingo continued to speak, not noticing my silence. "I've brought the others back to meet *don* Jorge, but nothing ever comes of it. Even when *don* Jorge writes to them afterward, their answers never arrive."

Kai responded to Mingo as I remained silent. I heard him saying that with the disappearance of my tape-recorder and his camera, we too would have trouble conveying information.

"But you can speak," Mingo said. "The *señora* can speak on the radio herself. People will believe her. She is an American. She is white."

"*Don* Jorge is white," Kai said.

"But no one believes *don* Jorge. He is not an American."

Kai put his hand on my back. I was both relieved and made more ashamed by his touch. He knew nothing of the contents of Rina's letters. I had never told him about not answering them, about the seriousness of her requests. I had never told him about Angel, nor about my few feeble attempts to find my colleague and how I'd given up the search. How I'd been too fatigued. How the world had gone gray. How I had been met with blank stares or insinuations of paranoia. Fernando Calderón's secretary had looked at me with contempt and said her boss wasn't in after I'd made a scene in the office. I had tried for awhile, but not hard enough. I'd wanted to go home. I'd wanted to leave it all behind me.

The motor hummed. The light of the moon made it easy to see the expression on Mingo's face. He looked more like an Indian out here on the river in the middle of the tropical night.

"*Don* Jorge lives among the Roani. Or Auca as you may know them. *Pues*, the Roani come and go from *don* Jorge's area. The Roani live on a reserve set up last year by the government and the *evangelistas*. They moved the Roani out of areas where Somaxo wanted to do oil exploration into the protectorate," Mingo said, sneering at this last. "But now Somaxo has found oil in the Roani protectorate. Hundreds of barrels a day are pumped from Lago Agrio to the north, but I hear they think there will be millions of barrels a day from the Roani territory. They are building a pipeline to Esmeraldas for refining. The government closes its eyes to the violations of the reserve agreement, and so do the missionaries."

I translated for Kai. I was amazed for the moment by Mingo's casual mention of the Aucas. I didn't think any contact had been made with them. They were known as the most remote known tribe in Ecuador and were reputed to be ferocious. But then again, so were the Shuar.

"Does the friar work for Somaxo?" Kai asked.

Mingo shrugged. "Who can know?"

"There must be some way to find out," I said.

"For Somaxo, or because of his desire to make his own cultural genocide? Who can say for certain? Or as the *padre* asked in the bar, 'What is truth? Is truth so easy?'

Strange sentiments for a religious man, no, *señorita?*"
Mingo didn't smile now. His head tilted back and he stared
at me.

"Does he try to bring Christianity to the Roani?" I
asked, glancing back toward Kai.

Kai moved himself down to my seat and I shifted over.
I felt his body warm against my own.

"Not since he lost me as his messenger." Mingo smiled.
"The competition with the *evangelistas* is difficult for one
man."

"And the Peace Corps volunteer?" Kai asked.

"I don't know this man well. He has been here for less
than a year and he can almost not speak Spanish and he
doesn't speak Quichua."

"He said he spoke Quichua," Kai said.

"Not that I could understand. But he does know how
to cut up the forest and make people live on little pieces
of land. The Roani will die if they have to live on those
white man's squares. They will kill before they will give in
to such a thing. Those engineer men and Christian men
harmed my tribe the same way, making us live on their
idea of land, in their idea of houses."

Again I helped Kai with the Spanish.

"I've heard that many of the Shuar still live in the
forest," Kai said.

"Some do and some don't," Mingo said. And then he
was silent.

The wind at my back was cooler and carried more force.
I lowered my hand into the current trying to keep it in
place against the pressure. I had many questions to ask of
Mingo. About the Roani reserve to be sure, but I also
wanted to know more about how he reconciled selling the
Indians western items so deeply down the Napo with his
objections to the friar bringing Christianity and Jon
plotting out settlements for them to live in permanently.
Particularly if he were indeed falsely bartering the magic
of shaman's darts. Where did he draw the line between
doing good and doing harm to a culture, to a way of life?

And what exactly was the friar's plan for the Roani that he had carried to *don* Jorge?

"My father followed me out of the forest when they took me to the Salesian school as a young boy." As Mingo began speaking again, his voice was tinged with a regret I hadn't heard before. "He brought his two wives and his other children by them. He wanted to know where they had taken his son. My father had a reason to exist when he lived in the *selva*. He hunted monkeys, tapir, *agutes*, and he fished. He helped move the community every four years and he rebuilt his family's house each time. He carried out the rituals and he went on warring parties. That is what he tells when he is drunk, and he is very often drunk. My mother doesn't drink. Wife number two drinks to drunkenness with him. But they have their *casitas* and their surveyed land, and their private gardens. My father dreams aloud when awake, of the forest. I don't know what his night dreams are anymore. He doesn't tell their stories as he did in early days. Perhaps those night dreams are the only place he lives like a man anymore. Maybe he is afraid if he speaks them in the awake world that they will also be snatched from him."

Only the purring of the motor broke the silence in our boat.

"Yes, some of the Shuar still live in the forest," he said. "To the east of the Cutucú mountains there is a place where it is very difficult to penetrate, and so far no one wants oil or gold from there. For now they are safe. Even I can't reach them with my suitcase of clothes." A smile creased his face, and I saw the charming, skilled salesman in him.

The Cutucú range was where Rina had told me the Shuar were bombed in 1958. If I ever did the radio program, Mingo could corroborate Rina's story.

"And the bombings?" Kai asked.

"That is the present tactic," Mingo answered. "I have only experienced one, to clear for the road, they said. It is not to be forgotten."

"Are they bombing where we're going?" I asked, thinking, perhaps that was the explanation; it was a crude, brutal form of defoliation. It made sense.

"No, not at *don* Jorge's. They don't dare bomb the house of a white man, even if he isn't an American. You'll be safe, *señora*. I wouldn't bring you anyplace unsafe."

Sometime in the night I drifted asleep with my head against Kai's chest, feeling his voice vibrate as he spoke to Mingo in fractured Spanish of the birds and animals in the forest. Beneath me the boat moved swiftly and smoothly through the water and I felt comforted to be in a gliding boat hearing the hushed tones of these two men.

I woke to find that the moon had completed its track across the sky and was slipping behind the tree line.

"Morning," Kai said, rubbing his eyes and the auburn growth of beard that had appeared in the night.

"*Buenos días*," I said to Mingo, who still sat in the same spot, alert and not seeming at all tired.

"*Buenos, senõres.*"

The birds were chirping on the riverside we skirted. Kai found his binoculars in the backpack.

"Always prepared," I said.

"*Natürlich*," he laughed, slipping the strap over his head. "Always ready for the first light."

The dome of sky turned green, and then purple grading to blue. Shortly, a pink glow washed the horizon directly before us. All but the brightest planets had faded from the sky when the pink deepened to magenta. The river became the same purple-red. Mingo returned my smile. It felt as though we had spent much longer than one day and night on the water together. When he shifted the motor slightly higher, and stood to see where we were headed, I thought, it was right to come with him.

Kai was examining the shore through his glasses.

"What do you see?" Mingo asked.

"It's the black mandibled toucan. *Pico negro*," Kai said.

"*Dios te dé*," Mingo sang.

"Yes, *Dios te dé*. Beautiful! Black with a sulfur yellow breast, white rump," Kai continued, pointing to his chest, saying, "*amarillo. Es un milagro, señor, de la naturaleza.* A miracle of nature." With that he handed the binoculars to Mingo.

Mingo motioned him to come back and monitor the motor stick. He let go when Kai reached him, and made his way up to where I sat. I felt the warmth of Mingo's body as he settled beside me, noted how smooth his skin was, how slender his wrists were, and then I turned away. Being this near him made me uncomfortable.

"*Dónde, señor?*" he said, holding the glasses to his eyes.

Kai helped him find the bird while I admired the intensifying color of the horizon and the river's surface.

"There she is," Mingo shouted. "I have her in my hand. *¡Dios mío!*"

"No, no," Kai admonished, laughing. "*Dios te dé*. It is called, 'May God give you.'"

Mingo joined him in enjoying the little joke.

Just then I saw a shot of red metallic light, a flash like a tiny acetylene flame shooting up from the curve of the earth.

"*Mira*," I said. "She has arrived."

And the three of us watched in awe as the huge sun lifted her scarlet heft up and up, out of the highway of water we were traveling down.

CHAPTER FOURTEEN

When the sun was well up in the sky and burning down on us, Mingo killed the motor and said, "We're here."

This shore was lush, unlike the settlements we'd seen yesterday with their bare muddy banks denuded of vegetation.

"There's nothing but trees," I said to Kai.

"That's what you wanted, wasn't it?" he said. He was thrilled, but I wasn't so sure, faced with the reality of absolute wilderness.

"Please hand me the paddles, *señora*. I don't want to disturb the *naturaleza* if your husband wishes to observe." With that Mingo propped the motor up out of the water.

"I can help," Kai said, not making a move to put down his glasses.

"I'll do it," I said.

The current was strong and I had to pull deeply and steadily to keep on course. When I let up for one moment the boat veered wildly toward the east.

Mingo moved again to the seat beside me. I glanced over and saw that he was grinning, his teeth very white against his skin. His arm brushed mine as he picked up the other paddle.

"I love the river," he said. "I love how quiet it is out here, how uninhabited. Your turn, *señora*."

We had already drifted many yards with the current. Quickly, I dug in.

He continued speaking in a soft, intimate voice as Kai sat with his back to us watching birds.

"My river, the Rio Upano, is rushing, fast moving, with many rocks brought down from the Andes and many little places where the current catches and makes whirlpools. It is the one reason I forgive the Salesians for bringing me out of the deep jungle to Macas. I became acquainted with the great and powerful Rio Upano. You must go there one day yourself, *señora*. You would like its power, I believe. You would find it exciting."

His arm moved against mine, as though accidentally with each stroke of the paddle.

I thought of César, with his skin the same bronze shade as Mingo's and his mouth wide and so soft. One night when we'd been kissing in the darkened hall of my building, up the stairs from Gala's, I'd been overwhelmed with wanting him. I could feel him grow hard against me, but instead of continuing, he held me away and opened my door with my key and sent me inside without following. He later said it wouldn't have been right; I was a girl to be married, not slept with.

"A little stronger, *señora*. *Más fuerte*. Pull a little stronger if you can."

I did. I concentrated and plunged the paddle in as deeply as I could, doing my part to get to shore.

Angel Castro always chided me about dating the naval officer, César. A military man. He made fun of the fact that when I went out publicly with *Teniente* César, it would invariably end up in the gossip column of *El Universo*. I wondered now if it wasn't only on political grounds that Angel ribbed me. Had he been interested in me as well? I recalled a night when we'd been up in the apartment talking strategy for the community center. I had left all the windows open so that the neighbors could see what was going on. To keep them from talking, as though they didn't anyway. We were standing by the floor-to-ceiling front windows, looking out over the lights of Guayaquil, letting the wind off the river cool us.

"Why did you come down here?" he asked. "What made you come?"

"Because President Kennedy asked me to," I said in jest and then to my surprise I went from laughter to crying.

Angel moved closer to where I leaned against the window's waist-high railing and our arms touched.

"I can't imagine having a leader of a country inspire me enough to do anything," he said, "unless perhaps if we had a Castro here."

I smiled at that, my tears stopping. "We do have a Castro here."

"Not quite, *chica*, not quite." He looked at me. I could sense his gaze, though I was turned in profile to him.

He didn't move any closer to me, but he didn't shift away. His arm remained touching mine. If I'd leaned toward him, I was certain he'd kiss me, but I didn't. Instead, frightened by the feelings he had stirred in me, I turned around and stood with my back to the city, looking into my room with its bare light bulb and my bookshelf made of boards and cinder blocks, scavenged from the rubble in the community center yard. My books from the Peace Corps footlocker were lined up, the Hemingways, the Fitzgeralds, the Twains. They seemed so foreign, so incongruous here.

"Why did I come? Why do I stay? That's what you asked, wasn't it?" I looked over my shoulder at him.

He moved back and leaned against the window frame. I saw raw passion on his face. "Did you come to subdue us, Ana? Is it a new kind of power over us? Or is it a new kind of help? True help?"

"And what do you answer?" I said, feeling that for the moment I did hold a certain power over him.

"What I answer is, I don't think you *norte americanos* know. I think in your *gringo* naiveté you have faith but no knowledge. Though with you, Ana, I amend it slightly. You seem to know a bit more than the ordinary *gringo*, male or female. You seem to know the principle of organizing. From your father, you say, you learned it. That may be so." He reached out then, and ran his finger down my cheek and around my collarbone. "I work with you because if there is anything to be gained, I want to use it." His face crinkled into a smile, but his eyes were obscured by the reflection of my light bulb in his wire-frame glasses. "Are you agreeable, *chica?*"

It was now my turn to be choked to silence with passion. I could only nod.

He left moments later, gathering his schoolbooks from the chair by the door and going directly out without pausing, giving no chance for an embrace. Two weeks later he had disappeared.

When we reached the shore, in under the cool shade of the trees, Mingo jumped out and I felt strangely deserted by him. Then Kai was climbing over the side and reaching out his hand for me to follow. The moment I touched down in the tepid water, I let myself go under, sinking beneath the surface, relishing the river's embrace. I opened my eyes and saw brown murk, shot through with golden spears of light. I had a desire to stay under there indefinitely, suspended, cool, not responsible for anything, not afraid, not haunted by my memories. Finally my breath gave out and I broke through to the air. I shook myself, sending water flying. Both men were smiling at me.

"That felt good," I said.

"You look like a pig in mud," Kai said.

"In shit. A pig in shit."

"*Señorita, disculpe la molestia.* But we must get this boat in," Mingo said. "I have to find the trail that leads to *don* Jorge's. I haven't been here in a week and it closes up rapidly." He spoke over his shoulder as he made his way through the water, pulling the dugout behind him.

Kai helped Mingo.

"Hey, wait for me," I called as the two of them heaved the boat up onto the bank, settling it under the branch of a low leaning tree.

"Stay here, *senõres*," Mingo said. "Perhaps unload the canoe. I'll be back." And he disappeared into the green.

Together Kai and I lifted out our belongings. I took everything but the large toolbox. It was very heavy when I went to pick it up, and I decided to leave it until Mingo came and said whether or not he wanted it. I couldn't imagine carrying such weight on our trek through the jungle.

Kai and I leaned against our backpacks in the tiny area that served as a beach. Stretched out, our feet would have touched the water. We sat instead with our knees up and our heads back, looking up into the suntipped foliage. It was refreshing to be soaking wet sitting in the shade.

"I doubt that I could ever get enough of this beauty," Kai said. "So, so *schön*. I'm happy," he said turning to me.

I felt momentarily guilty about the memories of César and Angel and my reaction to Mingo's arm brushing mine. But when Kai kissed me on my neck and down my collarbone, I felt the scratch of his beard, and I remembered that César's skin had been as soft as a woman's. César had always smelled of soap and his lips were so full that I'd felt as though I were being enveloped by them. I recalled again how I had wanted him.

Kai must have felt my resistance because he pulled back.

"What's the matter?"

"Nothing." I let him settle in closer.

He put his hands over my breasts, but instead of making me feel sensual, I was irritated, nervous, wanting him to stop.

"All this green and fragrance makes me feel sexy," he said, once again kissing me on the neck.

How could this be happening? I'd always responded to him physically. Even in our most difficult times, when I'd raged at him about his family and about how unpolitical he was, we'd always resolved our anger with lovemaking. It was often better after a fight, more physical, more dangerous. But now, all I wanted was to be away from him, alone, intact, unto myself.

"We can't now," I said, "Mingo will be back in a minute."

"You nipples are getting hard." His hand was up under my tee shirt and inside my bra.

I did begin to feel something. I kissed him now, breathed his smell, liked it again, thought of our lovemaking in Puerto Napo. "Shit, we can't do this. It's embarrassing."

"I know." He took his hand out and slowly eased it in between my river-soaked legs. "My how wet you are," he laughed. But he stopped abruptly. "What's that?" He sat up, looking into the canopy. "My glasses." He reached behind himself, not taking his eyes off the treetops where something screeched.

Kai stood, pushing down his erection with one hand as he walked to the forest's edge. I followed until he motioned urgently to stop. The branches overhead swayed and the leaves rustled as though a strong wind had moved through.

A flash of red shot from one high branch to another.

"There," I pointed.

"Shhh." His glasses raised, he searched. "*Um Gottes Willen*," Kai whispered. "I've never seen anything like this, so close."

"What is it?"

"Howler monkeys. *Coto mono*. They're up there snuggling into each other. You must see this." He gave me the glasses and helped direct me to the splotch of red.

"Oh my." Two large, black, naked faces surrounded by red-orange hair and beards filled the lenses.

"I hope they stay so Mingo can get a look," Kai said.

Soon I tired of craning to see. But Kai remained motionless, his arms akimbo, holding the glasses, whispering characteristics to himself to imprint them on his mind until the time he recorded them in his fieldbook.

I walked out to the canoe, deciding that I should get the toolbox after all. I tried to lift it and finding it much too heavy, I opened the clasp that held the top to the bottom and looked in. It took a moment to fully comprehend what I was seeing. My tape-recorder. Kai's camera. How could I have been so stupid? It was Mingo who had stolen them. When they had disappeared, he hadn't responded. I had interpreted his silence as disgust with the friar, as his own assumption of the culpability of the friar. But the friar was innocent. I'd been wrong. Once again I'd been pitifully naive in this country. I felt no anger, only fear. He meant to harm us. Perhaps we could get away in the canoe before Mingo returned. We could make our way to the friar, apologize, get help from him and Jon. Just as I turned to get Kai, a rustling came through the brush.

"Kai," I called as Mingo emerged from the dense green, walking toward me, smiling.

"Kai." I tried again, but my mouth had gone so dry, it came out a whisper.

"*Señora*, I have found the way."

"*Bueno*," I said, edging down the beach. "*Mi esposo esta cerca*." My husband is near.

He walked past me to the canoe and looked in. Now he knew.

He turned, not smiling any more, but instead of the sinister gloating I expected, he was frightened.

"I was going to show you, *señora*, *de veras*. I swear to your God and to mine. Please. I didn't steal them." His hands were in prayer position at his bare chest. His brown complexion had gone gray. He appeared to be sick with unhappiness, but I wasn't willing to believe him.

Kai came out of the forest. He stopped and looked from Mingo to me. "What's going on? Has something happened here?"

"Look in the canoe," I said.

"What do you mean?"

"Just look in, damn it."

"*Señor*, please, I meant to tell you," Mingo begged.

Kai went over. He slowly turned back to us. "I trusted him." His eyes questioned me. "I can't believe this. Why would he take our things?"

"We had confidence in you," I said to Mingo. "Why did you lie to us? What do you want from us? *Pues, ¿que quieres, hombre?*"

"I don't wish to lie, *señora*. Believe in me, please." He bent from the waist as he spoke.

"How can I? You made me fear the friar, but now I fear you."

"No, you have nothing to fear from me. I promise."

"But we do, *señor*," Kai said. "The loss of the camera made us come. We thought the friar and the Peace Corps volunteer stole it." He didn't have the word for 'stole,' and made the fanning motion for thief that I had taught him.

"That is what I planned, *patrones*," he implored us, subjugating himself yet more. "I took them so that you would suspect the friar. I was afraid he would use his ways to make you decide not to come with me. I thought only if you believed him a thief would you come with me. That way you would have to trust me over him. Why wouldn't you more trust a white man over an Indian? A rich white man, even in his poor robes is better to you than an Indian. He told you he is rich, no? He tells the same to everyone. Is it the truth he tells? It doesn't matter. He is a white man. Isn't that so?"

I didn't answer, nor did Kai. Kai looked at me but I could read nothing on his face.

"Isn't that so, *pues*? You would trust a rich man more than a poor one?"

"Tell him I trusted what Mingo offered," Kai said. His features were pinched with distress. "Tell him, Annie, that I trusted what he said about the animals and the birds. That's why I came with him. I wasn't interested in staying with the friar. And tell him that I worried about those bombs and I wanted to see for myself."

"You never said that to me," I said.

He sighed and looked tired and paler now. Sweat stood out on his brow. "No, I never did. But it doesn't mean I wasn't thinking about it." He took his bandanna from his front pocket and mopped his face.

"What did your husband say?"

"He said he was concerned about the bombing you told him of. Or have you lied about that, too?" I waited. Please let us have trusted the right person, I pleaded to myself.

His eyes shifted from me to Kai. I didn't feel heartened. I thought of how he'd seemed to flirt with me. Had that been part of the manipulation?

"Yes, there have been many bombings lately. Nearby the settlement of *don* Jorge. I lied to you about the danger. They bomb with liquid fire that suffocates and sticks to the skin and burns it off." He turned his eyes to the ground.

"Shit," I said.

Without my translating, Kai said, "It sounds just like napalm."

All around us it was so green, so tranquil, the air beckoningly sweet. I thought of Vietnam and how I had heard there were similar forests there, as beautiful, as full of life. I'd had to sit one day with a black Vietnam vet outside the recording studio while a talk show was going on. He'd been too stoned on heroin to participate. While nodding out, he told me of the "green, green, green of the forest in Nam, so beautiful, man, not like the projects, like a heavenly place, like I'd never seen. Like in the a.m.'s you'd sit there toking up and you'd watch the mist like it was God's breath blowing through those green valleys, like green pussy it was, so goddamn gorgeous. Then we'd go down in there and power it out, we'd burn the fucking shit out of it."

"I promise you, *señora*, that I was going to give back your items when we arrived at *don* Jorge's. I haven't harmed them, not in any way. I wasn't stealing. I promise. I only wanted you to come with me. *Solamente venir conmigo*. It is very necessary that you see what is happening, that you meet *don* Jorge and María. Also, there is the brother Max. He is a little..." He put his finger to his head in such a way as to indicate madness. "I want to tell you all, so there will be no surprises. This Max comes from time to time to stay with his brother and to fish." He was all humbleness now, too solicitous.

"To fish? Why are you telling me this?"

"Because this Max, he doesn't speak. They say he was damaged by their war, that's what *don* Jorge says. That's what María says. And now with the bombing he is more crazy. I want you to know everything before going with me, if you will. I lied to you before because I didn't want you to be frightened and decide not to accompany me. Please, *señora, señor*. I tell you I am not a thief and I don't wish to harm you."

"I still don't understand why you are telling us this about this Max. Do you understand, Kai?"

"Maybe I do," Kai said. He began polishing the lenses of his glasses with the tip of his bandanna. He looked intently at Mingo. "Is this man in hiding from anything?"

"Who can know?" Mingo didn't look at him.

So it was as I had feared, not only were we entering a civilian bombing zone, we had a damn Nazi hiding in the jungle. We were going to stay, that is if we didn't go back right now, in the home of a killer of Jews. Fine, that was just fine. I turned and walked as far down the strip of sand as possible and looked out to the river. How simple the way it kept moving along. I thought again of the Guayas, of how I would sit for hours in my window watching the boats and the vegetation float downstream. I used to wish I were one of those vines lying passively in the water, letting the current do all the work. I heard the conversation resuming behind me.

Mingo spoke slowly for Kai's sake. "People have said he is hiding. The people from Europe want to leave when they see him. The Americans think he is *loco*. But those from Europe say he did bad things in a bad war. I know nothing of it. *Pues*, but *don* Jorge is a fine man, *lo mejor*. He could never do harm, I know it. I ask only that you come with me for one day. Talk to *don* Jorge. We will protect you. If you don't wish to help I will take you back the next day. No questions. Nothing, *señor*. I would not ask this if it didn't mean so much to the indigenous people. To the forest. To our life. These are not people of my tribe, but they are my people. It has become a very grave situation. *Muy serio*."

"But why us," I heard Kai ask. "Why haven't the other Americans and Europeans been enough?"

"I told you, I don't know, but I've not heard from them after they leave here. Perhaps they helped. I don't know. What I know is, I have not heard from them."

"Maybe their letters got lost," I said, angrily. "Maybe they did try and got nowhere." I kept my back to him.

"Maybe you are right, *señora*. But no help has come. No one believes. We are alone and desperate in this. No one has heard outside of this area what is happening here. Did you hear of the bombs before coming here?"

"I heard once of bombs," I said turning to them. "I had a friend in Guayaquil, she told me of bombs long ago, bombs in retaliation for the killing of gringo missionaries. She said the air force sent planes into an area where few could penetrate by foot." I felt Rina's presence as I spoke.

"Aha," his voice came in a whisper. His face relaxed, became soft in recognition. "That's good you came to hear of that. Perhaps then it's possible that this other information can reach other ears."

"Now that I have my tape-recorder back," I snapped.

"Yes, *señora*," he said. "That will help."

I watched this young man in his washed-out jeans and white shirt open to his waist. His shag haircut was as incongruous as we were out here. He self-consciously hooked his thumbs into the belt loops of his pants.

Kai nodded to me.

"You're willing to go, aren't you?" I said. "I can see that."

"I believe him," he said.

"Even with a Nazi out there," I said, not attempting to disguise the bitterness in my voice. "Even with napalm."

"I've told you, that part doesn't worry me," he said. "There are ways to protect oneself. And about the Nazi, I'm used to them." His voice was as harsh as mine was bitter.

"But you weren't Jewish then and you aren't now."

"I know that, Annie." He looked sadly at me. "But the person I love most and am now married to is."

Tears brimmed my eyes. "And still you are willing to go?"

He took a deep breath. "Yes. I feel I must."

"Not just for your damn birds?"

"I feel I have to see what is happening. Sure I want to see my birds. But believe it or not, they've become secondary."

I laughed, but I was moved by what he said. "Praise be. All it took was bombs and ex-Nazis to pull him away from his birds. Okay," I said. "Let's go. I can be as brave as you are. I guess."

CHAPTER FIFTEEN

It's correct what you are doing," Mingo said. "I promise you, *senõres*. You will be glad for it."

Before we set off we shared two bananas from his sack and three beef jerkies, Made in the USA, written on the plastic wrap. We ate them greedily and only then did I realize how hungry I was. We hadn't eaten since the night before at the friar's. Now even boiled yucca sounded delicious.

Mingo led the way, hacking through the dense foliage with his machete. He said that this was the path, but I didn't see a trace of one. I kept a safe distance between us, cautious of the flashing blade. Then we were out of the underbrush and in magnificent high forest. Here the floor was free of low-growing bushes. It was carpeted instead with fallen leaves rotting in the damp shadows of hundred foot tall, liana entwined trees. The blue sky seemed miles above, peeking through the latticework of canopy. It was as cool and damp inside as a stone cathedral, with only narrow streaks of sunlight sifting down to where we walked.

Suddenly I realized that Mingo wasn't in front of me. I rotated completely around, or so I thought. But by now I was disoriented, no longer sure which way we'd been going. I saw clear floor in all directions, and everywhere the light was green, and vines fell from every giant tree, one after another, all looking the same.

"Where is he?" Kai came from my left. His voice resounded through the forest as though indeed we were in a real stone cathedral.

"I don't know. He was just there." I pointed in the direction I thought I'd been walking.

"You've got to keep him in sight every minute, Annie. It's deceiving. Everything looks alike in here."

"I noticed," I said, beginning to giggle.

Then I stopped laughing. Was Mingo always planning to leave us? Was this why he'd gotten us out here? Just ten minutes into the forest was all that was needed, and the *gringos* would be irretrievably lost. But Kai would get us out, I assured myself. He had a perfect sense of direction. I glanced at him. He looked as worried as I felt.

"We'll be fine," he said. "He'll be back for us."

A whistle called to my left. Another whistle, longer and lower, followed it.

"That's him," Kai said. "That's Mingo."

Kai whistled back, three short followed by an extended low note. The whistle to our left moved closer. Kai repeated his call and it was returned again. Then Mingo appeared like a ghost through a transparent wall of green.

"There you are," he said. "You must stay close. If for one moment you lose me, call out and I'll stop. The forest plays tricks unless you know it. Your new eyes can't see what I know from childhood."

We proceeded apace despite the heaviness of our packs, and the necessity of intense concentration on the ground so as not to trip over vines or roots. The humidity won out over the shade and soon I was sweating profusely. I tried to reach back into the pocket of my pack for a barrette to get my hair off my neck. But we moved too fast and I gave up. I felt my lack of sleep. My bag was now weighing all its thirty-five pounds. One foot in front of the other, I ordered myself. Don't question why you're here. Keep walking. Get your mind on something else.

I thought of three girls walking through a forest half-drunk, laughing, and singing.

During training Lucy, Jody, and I were sent out on a four-day survival trek into the rainforest mountains of Puerto Rico above Arecibo. Pass this test, the instructors said, and you get to serve your country and the people of the Third World. Fail it and you are a coward and will be sent home a reject from training.

On our fourth day out, just when I thought I couldn't make it up one more root lined, rock strewn slippery farmer's trail in the heat and humidity, Lucy stopped dead in the middle of the track. "Annie. The time has come. Reach into my pack and see what you find." She backed into me. I felt around until I discovered three oranges and a bottle of rum. "We shouldn't," I said. Lucy and Jody hooted. "They said to survive. What else is this but survival?" Using an army-issue pocketknife, Lucy made a circular cut in the top of the orange, removed the skin and a cone of pulp, leaving an indentation into which she poured the rum. "You've got to be flexible, Annie," Lucy laughed, parodying the anthem of the Peace Corps trainers of 'strength, flexibility, and courage in the face of adversity.' For the rest of the afternoon we sucked rum, marching along, giddy as thirteen-year-olds, Lucy's white blonde hair in the lead, followed by Jody's wild black curls. Jody sang *La Llorona* and other Mexican songs through the afternoon, her full contralto rising up into the trees, lifting us with it as we made our way.

At dusk we swaggered down the last stretch of rocky trail leading to Tomacito's *tienda* where the volunteers gathered each night for beer. We were full of ourselves, anticipating our hero's welcome. As we rounded the last bend, Jody said, "What the hell kind of music is this?" A dirge played where always jangling Latin tunes blasted into the woods.

"They killed Kennedy," someone said, when we got to the group sitting on the ground in front of Tomacito's shack. "Some fucker shot him in the head in Dallas."

I lay on my back beside a narrow tumbling river, my pack as a pillow, looking into the tops of the trees. The water beside me was gray-green where the sun hit and a darker mossy brown-green where it moved into and through shady spots. The bank was of polished pebbles. The sun came through here as white light, from directly overhead, and even the shade was brighter, part yellow, part green, than we had found deep inside the forest. But cool air off the rushing stream brought relief, which my body gratefully accepted.

Kai had removed his pack but remained standing, inspecting the area through his glasses. Beside me Mingo sat throwing pebbles into the water. He was in profile. I noted the straightness of his nose and the sensual thrust of his mouth. He seemed younger, more innocent as he sat like any young man, easily tossing stones.

"The brother of *don* Jorge, Max, comes to this river often," Mingo volunteered, not looking my way. "Up there." He pointed upstream to his right.

"Are we that close?" Kai asked.

"An hour more. Less without heavy packs. There's a path from there on, because of the brother."

"Is the fishing that good right here?" I asked.

Mingo shrugged. "He never catches any. All the fish they eat come from the Roani. But he is so *loco*, the Max, *loco, loco*." Mingo shook his head, chuckling.

"I hope he's not like my uncle who lived up in the north of Germany in a small town." Kai spoke rather expressive Spanish now. Original, slangy, patched together, but definitely understandable. I listened carefully. I'd never heard of an uncle who lived in northern Germany. "He humiliated his wife by dressing in his old Nazi uniform with all his medals and marching through the town square with his right arm lifted saying 'Heil Hitler.'" Kai laughed.

"That's not funny," I said.

"Annie, the man was insane."

"Or his madness was a cover for sheer evil."

"Believe me," Kai said angrily. "I've met this man. He was an idiot and completely nuts."

I stopped myself from replying when I saw that Mingo was watching us. We'd shifted to English and though he couldn't understand a word, I was sure he could read our anger.

"So this Max," I said to Mingo. "How is he crazy? How does it show?"

"He is as though deaf and dumb. *Sordo y mudo*. He eats. He walks around. He fishes fruitlessly from the first light to the last. But he never speaks." He shook his head. "Every village in our country has them. But I thought white men were born with words in their mouths and never stopped tossing them out until they breathed their last." He glanced over for my reaction, then away.

I was about to work my way into a conversation about the shaman's darts, feeling that the time might be opportune. Now that he was so forthcoming with his opinions of white men, perhaps I could venture an inquiry about the sacred ways of his people. I also thought such a discussion might smooth over my argument with Kai. I was ashamed of my hostile outburst. But just as I'd formulated a question, Mingo stood up abruptly with his hand to his ear.

"What is it?" Kai asked. "I heard it, too, a moment ago."

Mingo motioned him to be quiet.

Through the quiet of the forest, over the burbling of the stream, came the faint sound of a motor. It could have been a boat with an outboard except that it didn't come from the direction of the Napo, but rather from where we were heading, though slightly more to the right.

"That's a plane," Kai whispered.

"Sí," Mingo hissed. "It comes this way. Get your packs on," he said, moving quickly to his satchel.

I scrambled my arms into my straps. Kai helped me to my feet. His eyes were fear-filled. I was surprised to see that he was afraid. I felt nothing.

The sound of the motor was closer. It was moving our way.

"Come," Mingo motioned us to follow along the river's edge. He walked rapidly and then he asked, "Can you run, señora?"

"Yes," I said, following directly behind him.

We ran downstream along the stones, slipping and sliding back with every third step. Mingo kept checking that we were with him. The plane kept moving toward us. Its engine became so loud I thought any moment it would come crashing through the trees. Then it veered and lifted in the opposite direction, moving upriver, away from us. Mingo stopped. We stood listening, breathing heavily. The plane turned. It was coming back, and then as panic rose to my throat, it retreated.

"It's circling," Kai said, making the motion of a circle.

I watched his freckled hand, with its thick gold hair like a field of wheat. I wanted to hold it to my cheek, feel the safety of it. My heart was beating raggedly.

Mingo again said, "Come," and he climbed up the river bank, slipping to his knees on rocks and muck. So he was frightened too. "In here." He disappeared into the underbrush.

We found him hunkered down under cover of small second growth trees. It looked as though a camp had once been here.

Kai and I squatted beside him.

"*Señora*, take that thing off your hair." He pointed to the barrette that I'd finally gotten from my bag and used to clip my hair off my neck. "Put it away. The sun catches it. They may get suspicious if they sight it."

I did what he said. We waited in silence. In moments the plane was roaring toward us, and this time it didn't turn back. Before we could run for deeper cover it appeared in the sky directly above us. It was a small plane, a crop duster, like those I'd seen many times in the west when driving across country with my mother. It was old, squarish, and painted with camouflage. It dipped so low over us that I could see a man's head against the sky. He wore a helmet. The plane veered and was gone, wheeling swiftly up, just avoiding the immense trees of the old forest. I was certain he hadn't seen us. I started to chatter my relief when Mingo's hand shot out and covered my mouth. His hand was rough and warm, like when he'd grabbed me from behind while I'd listened to the squawking short-wave radio the night before at the friar's. I nodded. He dropped his hand. Kai was like a statue beside me, still squatting, balancing himself with one hand, with the other to his ear.

From the distance came a whistling sound, followed by a whirring, hurtling noise and seconds later an explosion and another.

Kai threw one arm over his head as though ducking from an onslaught. He began to shake. He was propped up by his other hand, but it was white with the strain of controlling his trembling body.

I wrapped my arms around his shoulders. I felt the power of each jerk his body made.

"It's okay," I hummed. "Please, Kai, we can leave."

"They're bombing. The bastards are bombing," squeezed out of him. "We can't leave. We can't ever leave."

"No, Kai, no."

"What is it?" Mingo asked. "Is he afraid?"

"I'm sorry, so sorry," Kai kept saying.

"Shhh, shhhh." I tried to comfort him and keep him quiet. "When he was a child, they bombed his city," I explained to Mingo.

Mingo stared at Kai.

"*Lo siento*," Kai said. He looked up, grimacing. In his eyes I saw a young boy consumed by terror. Then as though he knew again where he was, he put his arms around me. "Just hold me, Annie. I'll be fine if only you'll hold me."

CHAPTER SIXTEEN

When we arrived at the clearing a huge brush fire was raging at the far end, with flames leaping into the air, licking at the tops of trees and consuming a large thatched structure. So far the fire hadn't penetrated the forest. Mingo broke from us, leaving Kai and me to stand and gape helplessly, our breathing still labored, as he ran toward a group of about ten people who were working frantically to put it out.

"Let's go too," Kai said.

We dropped our bags and followed after Mingo.

A black woman in a black dress looked up from where she was beating at the resistant flames with a burlap grain-bag. One minute the fires were extinguished in a spot, the next they flared in the same place. The woman's exhausted face was smeared with soot, her hair covered with dust and twigs.

"Ah Mingo, *por fin*. Get water. *Necesitamos agua*."

"The containers?"

"Under our house." She motioned with her chin at a thatch-roofed house built on stilts across the clearing from the burning building.

"Come," he said to us. "You must help."

Beneath it in the cool darkness the chickens were huddled and squawking and a dog cowered in the far corner. We scrambled bent-backed to where the dog was and grabbed large tin buckets from under the stairway that led up one side of the house. I glanced at Kai as we emerged again into the sunshine and heat and saw that he was now all determination and anger.

The buckets hit against my legs as I ran to keep up with the two men. We raced along the path toward the river, the same one we'd just arrived on. As we met the river again, the sun pressed down on us and the heat of the fire stayed at our backs. My eyes began to burn from some sort of chemical in the air. We waded in and laid our buckets on their sides to catch the amber water.

"Fill them only halfway," Mingo instructed. "You'll lose too much otherwise. And they'll be too heavy for you."

We could hear the crackling of the fire as we knelt in the cool water. Then a hollow roar rose to the sky, followed by repeated crashing and breaking and a blast of flames that visually penetrated all the way to the river through the openings between the green, shooting red against the green, until you didn't know which was the fire, the green or the red.

"That was the building going," Kai said. "I know the sound."

Our eyes met. I saw only bitterness, not fear. The young boy had been replaced by the man who knew the explanations for such things.

"¡Vámonos!" Mingo said. "There's no time. We must hurry."

We half-ran, half-shuffled, with our knees slightly bent, straining not to hit the buckets on the ground, tip them, or knock them against our legs, not daring to lose a drop of the precious water. I'd never carried anything so heavy. I counted my steps in Spanish. Uno, dos, tres, cuatro. When I got to ten, I started again to keep my mind off how my arms strained, how my back felt as though it would break in half. The heat had become like a storm sucking the oxygen from the air, drying my throat beyond tolerance. But we reached the fire fighters: the black woman, a white man, and about seven Indians, both men and women. The building had indeed collapsed, spewing burning detritus of a palm-frond roof and walls. The children were standing out of the way, beside the house on stilts, where the brush was still green, and where the flames and sparks weren't headed if the wind stayed down. As we hefted the water over to the black woman, I saw the children step out from their protection under the shade of the trees to stare at us better.

One of the Indian men noticed them too and yelled, motioning them angrily back, causing the children to giggle. He yelled and started toward them, walking directly into one of the paths of flames. The children ran back into the trees.

The black woman pointed with her long thin arms this way and that at the various rivulets of fire, and we heaved the contents of our buckets. In moments, all the large pails were empty and the fire, if anything, was burning with more intensity. The chemical smell in this area was horrible. It burned into my nostrils, down my dried-out throat, into my chest, as though the flames had entered my body. I put my hand to my face.

"Here," Kai said, reaching into his pocket and bringing out a bandanna. "Tie it over your mouth. This stuff is lethal."

"And you?"

He took off his shirt. "I'll use this."

Before we could get our masks on, Mingo had picked up his empty buckets and mine and was starting back. We ran to catch up with him. I felt an immediate relief as we distanced ourselves from the center of the poisonous fire.

At the river, dropping panting to the water, Kai dipped his shirt and took his bandanna back and did the same with it.

"Mingo, do you have a bandanna?" Kai asked, holding his up.

"*No importa*," Mingo grimaced.

"It is important," Kai said.

"These aren't so bad," Mingo said.

"Well, it's bad enough to damage a person's lungs," Kai said. "Tell him, Annie, that fumes are poisons, and can harm as much or more than the fire when breathed."

I told Mingo. He shrugged, but took a cloth from his back pocket and wrapped it around his face.

"These are not the worst," Mingo's muffled voice came through the dark-blue handkerchief. "These are only fire bombs. What I told you before about the other bombs, those are the ones that suffocate and burn the skin off of people."

"For sure he's talking about napalm," I said to Kai as we struggled along. My arms felt as though they were going to give out before we reached the clearing. I didn't think I could withstand much more.

"Those shits," Kai said, and then pulled out ahead of me and started a slow, even trot toward the clearing.

For the next few hours Kai and Mingo ran back and forth from the river to the fires. I kept up until I could barely handle quarter-filled buckets and was assigned to beating the flames. The fire grew as the wind picked up and turned in new directions. More people arrived to help, Indians who must have lived deeper in the interior judging by their lack of clothing save a narrow cotton waistband, the inch diameter plugs of wood in their ear lobes, and ritual red and black designs that covered the bodies of a few. I barely comprehended that these were actually Roani, people who had rarely been seen by the outside world. They were rougher of feature than Mingo, stockier. The men's hair was cut in a bowl shape, the women's with bangs in front and long in back. We labored intensively side by side, but even with all of our effort we couldn't contain the fire. Finally, the black woman stopped working. She stood in the midst of the flames and smoke, her arms dangling by her sides. I continued to beat futilely and with dwindling energy at a newly erupted blaze as I observed her. Her hair, covered with gray ash, stood stiffly around her head. Sweat poured from her body, her face shiny brown-black where the liquid ran through the cinder dust, and her black dress soaked blacker.

"More water. We can only fight this with more water," the woman said. "Nyawadae, Tedikawae, Naenkemo, Kemonka." She went on to call a long list of men and women. "Join the *blanco* and the Shuar Mingo. Carry water. It is our only hope." She looked at me. "You remain with me. Jorge, *geh' mit ihnen,*" she said to the older white man who had come up on us from the far end. Black soot

streaked his deeply tanned face and slender naked torso.
He wore only a black bikini and brown workboots.

"*Ja, Liebchen. Ich gehe.*"

I continued working but watched the man as he ran to
catch the others. This was *don* Jorge, the man we'd come to
see.

That was how we conquered the fires. *Ollas* and jugs
appeared and were carried by the men and two strong
women down to the river. From there they formed a
continuous cordon, passing the water-laden receptacles to
us. Directed by the black woman, we tossed and tossed until
finally there was nothing more than steam rising into the
air, and she called out, "*Ya estamos terminados. Ya hombres*,
now we can rest."

We staggered a few hundred feet away to the edge of
the forest, where nothing had been touched, and collapsed
onto the ground and lay there not moving in exhaustion.
Around me the breathing was labored and rasping. We
smelled of sweat and smoke. If I breathed too deeply the
noxious acrid fumes seared my nasal passages and throat.
The most I could do was to stare up into the intensely blue
sky. I couldn't close my eyes, my fatigue was so great that
even sleep would have required too much effort.

We lay there for a long time, not speaking, as the light
changed from the flat white of afternoon to a deeper
warmer yellow. It grew hotter as the sun moved across its
path, but none of us seemed to care enough to rise and
settle in a more protected area. I listened as birds shrieked
in the surrounding forest. There was one shockingly loud
ringing call, unsettling in its constant repetition as though
it were signaling distress. It was not melodious, more like
an amplified continuous striking of a hard object on metal.

I wondered if Kai was listening, but I was still too weary
to lift myself to see. The voices of children playing nearby
diverted my attention. What did it mean to them to see
the area they lived in set on fire by something dropped
from a plane? What would these children take into
adulthood of this? I thought of Kai reliving his original

terror. It had been inside him all this time. I thought of the children in the *barrio* taking up the taunts of their parents, "*mentirosa gringa*, lying *gringa*," and pelting me with stones, laying blame for the betrayal.

People began to rise and I turned toward the sound of voices to see an elderly woman with long, flat pendulums to her waist, and a girl with plump breasts resting on a very pregnant belly. They walked over and spoke to the black woman who remained lying on her back, before they went off down the path to the river carrying large *ollas* on their heads.

A fly was buzzing around and landing intermittently on my face. With enormous effort I lifted my hand to shoo it away. After a while I gave up and let it do its business.

I was awakened by the older Indian woman prodding my arm. "*Agua*," she said in the harsh voice of someone unaccustomed to speaking the word. She pointed to a gourd bowl beside me.

"*Sí, por favor*," I said, trying to raise myself. She held my head, and I let myself fall gratefully back onto her strong arm. I drank the delicious cool water, becoming greedy once I realized my thirst, and gulped at the edge of the bowl, causing much of it to dribble over my cheeks and chin.

Immediately refreshed, I looked around for Kai and found him sitting up a few feet away. His cheeks and nose were raw with sunburn where they weren't smudged with soot. His hair, now turned brown with dirt and sweat, stood up around his head like a crazy sort of crown.

"How are you?" I called.

"Not great," he answered, looking over the wreckage.

"What was that horrible call before, the repetitive one?"

"A screaming piha. Sort of said it all, no?"

Beyond him the white man was doing sit-ups and attempting to touch his toes. He looked naked, his black bikini hidden in the bend of his lap. None of the Indians nearby, who were rising slowly, seemed to notice anything peculiar in his doing calisthenics. After a few more minutes of the toe touching he turned over to lift himself push-up style from the ground. Once standing, he stretched his taut torso, first to one side and then the other. He followed these with a couple of deep knee bends with his arms straight out before him in a perfect right angle to his body. I continued to watch incredulously, while the others moved around him unperturbed, gathering buckets and *ollas* and making their way across the steaming yard, over to the house. The man finished by rubbing his hands vigorously over his face and chest as though taking an invisible shower.

"*Hola*," he called out in greeting to Kai.

"*Grüss Gott*," Kai answered in the traditional south German greeting. He got up and walked toward the man with his hand extended.

"*Grüss Gott*? Are you German?"

"*Ja*, I'm from Augsburg."

"And I, too, Georg Häberle, am from Augsburg," the man shouted, throwing his head back and howling in disbelief.

"Schmidt here," Kai said. "Kai Schmidt, the son of Karl Schmidt."

"Karl Schmidt!" The man stood staring at Kai, squinting his eyes as though he were trying to see deeper into Kai's, trying to bring some memory back. "I know him! That is, he is known to me. Karl Schmidt, the Chemical Director after Steinhardt the Jew left," Georg Häberle said. "María!"

My spine tightened at his way of describing Otto Steinhardt. I'd never met *Herr* Steinhardt, but I knew his son.

María, the black woman in charge, stood alone at the edge of the forest, wetting herself down from the large gourd bowl. Her dress was soaked to black again, her skin glistened where the water poured over.

"Here is someone from my hometown," he said excitedly in German to her.

"*Muy bien,*" she answered. She didn't smile and barely moved her head to look over. I wondered if there were trouble between them or was it merely exhaustion on her part?

He didn't seem to notice her lack of response. After another exchange with Kai, some laughter and a slap on his own knee, Georg Häberle walked over to a group of Indians who were gathering jugs and *ollas* from the ground and appeared to be ready to leave. In his bikini bathing suit and ankle high workboots, Häberle stood chatting with them as naturally as he would have with proper Augsburger *Bürger* at the gate of his *schrebergarten.*

Another group continued working with hoes, scraping at the hissing earth. They must have lived in the settlement as they wore various minimal pieces of machine made clothing. Probably sold to them by Mingo. I looked around for Mingo and didn't find him anywhere. Kai had joined Häberle and the Indians who huddled so close around the man that they seemed to be breathing in each other's mouths. Suspicion overwhelmed me. I thought of what the sorely discredited Báez had said about *don* Jorge leading attacks on people. Was it possible this was some sort of retaliatory strike? What was he doing here? What did he want with these men and women?

Kai turned and smiled at me. When I didn't return his smile, he looked confused. He beckoned me over, but I shook my head. Seeing him standing there beside this German made me see Kai as a German, too—the son of the man who took over the factory from Steinhardt the Jew.

Kai came to me. "What is it, Annie?"

I shook my head. I couldn't speak.

"Why are you being like this?" he said, looking confused.

Just then the group of Indians dispersed and began walking around the clearing toward the forest on the far side. Häberle looked toward us and pointed to the smoldering pile that had been a building. It stood a hundred feet from an undamaged long low structure. His face was hard, cruel-looking to my eye.

"The ball-breakers have destroyed the cookhouse. The bastards are just like our Nazis." He glanced at Kai, but didn't look directly at him. "They are committing the genocide of these peoples just as our Nazis did to the Jewish ones. *Schrecklich!*" Terrible! he had said. "These new criminals are just as filthy, have the same genocidal blood of the innocent on their hands."

He moved a few feet in the direction of the house on stilts and stopped, turning back to us. His face had softened. "We will start rebuilding it tomorrow. I hope you can stay to help. We can use extra hands." He twisted in a full circle. "Where is Mingo? Mingo!"

"*Aquí estoy.*" Mingo came trotting out of the forest.

"*Vente,*" the German Häberle said, walking again, raising his arm in the air over his head and waving us forward. "Come, all of you, to my house. María, come. Let's feed our guests."

The large house had a set of broad wooden plank stairs that rose up outside and which earlier we'd ducked beneath for the buckets. Now we climbed them, following after Georg Häberle.

"This is my home, my own very best home," he said, stopping halfway up the staircase, running his hands along the wood of the railing. "It is all made from the sides of old used well-weathered canoes." He laughed, continuing to speak in German. "Weathered like their owner."

"How long have you lived here, *Herr* Häberle?" Kai asked.

"*Ach, vergess' den 'Herr,' mein Freund.* Call me Georg, or as the people here say, Jorge. We aren't any longer in the country of formal titles, though pardon me, I don't know your preference. But when in Roma, as they say. But this Kai, isn't that a Northern German name? Not Swabian." He ran his thick callused hand through his thinning gray hair.

"*Ja,* my mother is Westphalian," Kai said.

"Ah, Westphalian." Häberle nodded as though the explanation were somehow profound, and started up the stairs again.

Mingo lagged behind with María. They had their heads down and appeared to be speaking.

"María-le, *por favor*, why don't you come inside and rest?" Häberle called from the landing.

She separated herself from Mingo, saying something in a low voice, and began her ascent. Her exhaustion showed in the effort of each step. Her expression was flat, close to sullen.

"I will see to our visitors, María-le, *mi corazón*."

She passed by me. I saw her nod, unsmilingly, at him. She didn't even respond when he reached out the back of his hand and with the slightest of touches, brushed it against her cheek. He watched her wearily take the last step to the landing and disappear into the house. He held up his finger, telling us to wait. The slanting light of afternoon illuminated his face, showing deep lines etched with soot. His eyes were a faded blue with puffy bags beneath.

"María is grieving. It is more than this afternoon. It is of a personal nature." He had returned to German. "Her baby brother was killed in a bar fight in her town of Esmeraldas on the coast. He died two months ago, but she only just received word of it when the missionaries boatman brought the mail in. So María mourns. Usually María laughs. Ask Mingo. He can tell you."

Mingo had remained at the bottom of the stairs. I repeated in Spanish what Häberle had said.

"*Tiene razón*. María is a happy woman. Even with these bombings she has held onto her spirit. I have never seen her like this."

"You see," Häberle said, bending forward, staring into my eyes. "What I told you is the truth. In case you've heard that I tell lies." He straightened up. "You speak a fine colloquial Spanish, *señorita*. I suspected as much."

"I do my best," I said to him in Spanish, thinking, so you were testing me. But what for? I realized, also, that he hadn't answered Kai's question of how long he had lived here. Was that an oversight, lost in discussion of *Herr* versus first name etiquette, or was the omission intentional?

CHAPTER SEVENTEEN

The main room of the house was astonishing. It was both wide and deep, perhaps four hundred square feet. Though open to the air on three sides with only waist-high walls, it was as dark as the shade beneath a stand of trees. The encircling veranda and low hanging eaves of a sharply pitched thatched roof protected the room from both light and heat, making it degrees cooler inside. The floorboards were of wide-planked, dark-brown wood, polished to a soft sheen. "From canoes, too," Häberle said proudly. Beyond the low exterior walls on one side was the forest and the green aura it gave off. The other two sides were open to the burned clearing. The forest end was a sitting area with a wooden couch and chairs holding bright blue and yellow fabric cushions. But to my left, on the only inside wall of the house, was the biggest surprise. Over a long, dark wooden table with benches for seating, was a SANE poster, with a peace symbol in black on pale blue and a white dove flying across the emblem. There were no slogans on the face of the poster, but otherwise it was identical to ones sold at the Vietnam anti-war demonstrations.

Häberle motioned for us to take seats around the table. "*Fräulein*, perhaps you would like to shower first."

I answered him in not much better than pigeon German, that I could wait.

His eyebrows rose. "You are not German?"

"*Nein*," I said.

"*Italienisch* then. That explains why you are so dark and beautiful, too beautiful to be German." He laughed to reveal crooked, tobacco-stained teeth. He nodded admiringly to Kai.

"*Meine Frau ist Amerikanerin*," Kai said. "We live together in New York City. Like you, I've traveled away, like a true Swabian." Kai was watching me as he spoke.

He knew that I was suspicious of Häberle's question. This had happened before in Germany, people taking me for Italian. He knew I was waiting for the deeper, more inquiring look. Why *is* she so dark, so exotic, the look would invariably ask when I would say I wasn't Italian. He knew this waiting for the question that probed, but stayed on a safe surface, the question I was certain they asked to discover if I was Jewish. Sometimes, as now, I simply let the unasked question pass with a pregnant pause.

"So," Häberle said. He walked around the table and settled himself at the end under the poster. "*Señora, por favor*, go out through that door and find María and tell her you wish to be rid of some of the dirt we have inhospitably covered you with. And I will sit here with your husband and question him." He looked from Kai to me. Kai had remained standing as had Mingo, though Mingo hung back, leaning against the outside banister.

I would rather have stayed and asked my own questions about the bombing, but Häberle began to drum his thick-knuckled brown fingers on the table top, ratta, tatta, tat, tat, tat. I was reminded of the friar.

"Come, children. Let us proceed with this afternoon."

Lifting the bright blue cloth that covered the door Häberle had indicated, I found myself in a tiny darkened bedroom. I walked through and out an opposite door to a kitchen area on the wraparound porch. A man sat at a table near the railing. He was a plumper, younger version of Georg Häberle. María leaned over him, her arm around his shoulder. He jumped up when he saw me and began backing his way down the length of porch. He wore trousers, high rubber boots, and a light-blue shirt buttoned to the collar. His eyes didn't make contact with mine, but instead darted and shifted rapidly. Then he was gone around the corner and I heard him clopping down the stairs.

A plate of fish was left at his place. I wondered whether he'd been having a conversation with María, if this was the brother Max who reportedly didn't speak.

"*Señorita*," María said. She took a comb from the railing and started to fight it through her dusty, matted hair. "What can I do to be of help to you?"

"*Don* Jorge sent me to shower, *señora*. I hope I haven't disturbed you. I can return to the others."

"No, no," she said wearily, returning the comb to the railing. She had a wide mouth and a prominent nose and flat, sagging cheeks. She seemed only notable in her extreme plainness. But then she smiled, and I saw a face that could be loved by most anyone. "You have frightened Max a bit." She came closer and said, "But almost anything gives my brother-in-law fear. You must forgive him." Then in a normal voice, "*Ven, nena,* let me show you to the shower." She led me around the back corner of the porch to where a rudimentary shower had been set up. There was no protection for privacy, only a showerhead hanging from a hose that disappeared into the thatched roof.

"There is plenty of water, *señorita*," María said. "It will be warm from the sun. You have nothing to dry yourself?"

"No," I said. "But I can use my clothes. I don't want to bother you."

"Phht," she said, giving me a look as though I were crazy, like Gala getting pleasure out of scolding the *gringa* for her stupidity. "Look at your clothes, *chica*."

Of course she was right. I was filthy. I smelled and my tee shirt and skirt were coated with smoke, soot, mud, and poisonous fumes.

"I have other things in my backpack."

She gave another of her rebuking frowns and left me.

When she returned, she held a ragged but clean towel over one arm and a faded blue and yellow print dress on the other.

"This is mine," she said. "I won't have need of it now." I knew she meant that she would be dressed in mourning for the year. She put the items down on the handrail and left before I could find the proper words of sympathy.

The shower was deliciously warm. I wet down and then turned it off while I soaped my head and body. It felt good to make contact with myself. I'd grown very thin. My hip bones jutted out. When I opened the tap again and let the water play over me, I realized that every muscle ached. The raging fire and fumes felt illusory as I dried myself on María's threadbare towel, looking out to virginal green spotted only with the waxy red of heliconia flowers.

When I returned to the kitchen area, María was cooking at a charcoal stove which stood against the smoke blackened wall. Her back was to me.

"May I help you?" I asked.

She turned, startled by my voice. "Oh, *Dios*, I forgot you were there. No, please go in with the men."

Her face was puffy, swollen under her eyes. It could have been fatigue or the fire from the afternoon, but I suspected she had been crying.

"You shouldn't have to work more because of us."

"Oh, *niña*, please. Go." Her voice was harsh and she turned her back to me.

As I walked toward the door, she said, "Leave your clothes here, *niña*."

"Please, *señora*, I can wash my own clothes. I can't have you working any harder."

Now her face warmed. "Don't worry so," she said quietly. She put down the spoon she'd been stirring with and came over to me. She patted my shoulder and then my right hip. "My dress fits you. *Muy bien*. Go now. We can talk some other time." I noted that her eyes were hazel, more gold than green. Like the forest light by the river.

I entered the main room to find the men talking animatedly in Spanish and German.

"*Señora* Schmidt," Häberle said.

"*Sí, señor*."

"Your husband tells me that you work for a radio station."

"I do."

"Mingo has done well to find you young people."

Mingo fingered the beads around his neck. I felt as though he were appraising me anew.

"*Señora*, before you join us at the table, why don't you get your tape-recorder and camera." He waved his finger in front of his face. "But don't waste photos on me. Take that out there." He pointed in the direction of the clearing. "Take photos of the Indians who have been burned. The children who have been maimed by their bombs. The frightened faces of gentle people who want nothing else but to live in their forest, but are routed out."

"Maybe I could photograph you as well."

"No, no, nobody wants to see this old German face." He paused. "An old Nazi, some would say." His voice was low and disgusted.

"What do you mean?" I said. I was surprised he would be so forthright. From my experience in the two times I'd visited Germany with Kai, no one mentioned the war, much less uttered the word Nazi in even close company. What Kai had first said to me, 'we don't ask those questions in Germany' had turned out to be shockingly correct, especially in the bourgeois circles of Munich and Augsburg.

"Nothing, nothing, *señora*. You're too young to understand."

"Not too young to read," I said. I looked at Kai. He was listening, observing Häberle.

Häberle turned his bloodshot pale-blue eyes on me. He began to tap his signature rhythm on the table top.

"You, my dear, can decide if you believe me or not, believe what I have to say about the destruction they're causing. Before you leave here, you must decide if Georg Häberle is a villain or a saint. Are you willing?"

"I'll get the tape-recorder and the camera," I said in answer.

I was halfway down the outside staircase when I realized that Mingo was following me.

"I know where the tape machine is, *señora*," he said.

"It's in Kai's backpack under the house."

"No." He smiled and trotted down the stairs ahead of me.

"Mingo, what do you mean?"

"Follow me," he called over his shoulder as he strode rapidly around the vast, still-steaming, charred clearing. The combined smell of smoke and poisonous sweetness sickened me as I moved along behind him. He headed for the long house at the far side. I thought he was planning to go inside, but he went past and followed a narrow path into the forest. We were in fresh green again, and cool damp air. He stopped a few feet in.

"There," he said, pointing to a mound of newly packed dirt. "I buried them."

"You mean you went into Kai's backpack?"

"Yes."

"You can't do that. It's not right."

He shrugged and gave me a half-grin. "By your rules it's not right. By mine, there are times when I can do that."

"But it's my tape-recorder."

"And it's my hope that it will be safe for *don* Jorge's words. I buried it in case there was another bombing before you could use it." He knelt down, took his knife from his belt, and began to stab the trampled earth. Sitting back on his heels he stared up at me. "Please help me," he said. His expression was part pleading, part seduction. I resisted the excitement it stirred in me.

But when I knelt beside him and our shoulders and arms touched as we dug, I didn't pull away. We scraped and scooped until we uncovered another metal box like the one in his canoe. We dug more and brought it up. He opened the latch and inside were my tape-recorder and camera. I felt inordinately grateful to him for hiding them but still had enough sense to keep my enthusiasm to myself.

"What took so long?" Kai said when we appeared at the top of the stairs.

"Mingo hid the recorder for safekeeping."

"That was a good idea," Kai said, not seeming the least bit suspicious. He changed to German. "So, are you ready, Georg?"

"*Ja, meine Herren und Damen. Ja wohl.*" He bowed his head slightly as he sat with his hands clasped on the table, waiting.

Mingo slid into the bench after me.

"I hope this works," I said. I pressed the record button. Nothing. "There's no power."

"I'm afraid we have no generator here, *Fräulein.*"

"I'm so upset," I said, trying again and again to get the tape to move. Absolutely dead. "It must have gotten wet."

Häberle ran his gnarled hand down and over his face, and when it reappeared, his visage was older and more tired than before, his jowls exaggerated, the bags under his eyes seeming to sag from extra weight.

"I hear you met *Padre* Roberto Báez Chamino, the rich boy from Chile. What do you think of his Peace Corps volunteer? Do you think he does more than give the Indians their little pittances of land?" he asked.

"He seems relatively innocent," I answered, still trying to get my machine working. "But that doesn't mean he isn't being used for ill purposes."

"She knows what she's talking about," Kai ventured. "She was also in the Peace Corps from 1963 to 1965."

"Ah, an idealist." Häberle looked at me with more interest. "And this radio station, *Fräulein*, is it an extension of your idealism or merely a job?"

"Of my idealism, I'm afraid," I said, taking the batteries out. Then, realizing I had no way to test them, I snapped them in and gave up on the possibility of recording him. "It's a left wing station. We're interested in covering issues in ways that other stations don't. Like the American involvement in the Vietnam war. We give what we call alternative coverage."

"Ah, more interesting yet. Would you say possibly a pacifist opinion, my dear?"

"Perhaps, though often we give voice to a more militant stance. We have people who appear on our air who give credence to the struggle of the Viet Cong."

"I see," he said.

"*Que bien*," Mingo said.

I noted disapproval in Häberle's eyes after Mingo's "*que bien.*"

"We are pacifists here, my dear *Fräulein.*" He indicated the peace poster on the wall. "Like your late departed Martin Luther King. Even when violence is done to us, we passively resist."

"Annie's father was a pacifist," Kai said. "He went to prison for those beliefs during World War Two."

Kai's unusually eager and pride-filled description of my father irritated me. It was as though he wanted to impress Häberle and was using me as bait. Nor did I like my father equated with this man.

"Sooo, so. This becomes even more interesting and complicated. Your father, an American, didn't fight the Nazis."

"Yes, but I'm a Jew," I blurted out in German. *Ich bin Jüdin.*

"My, my, my." Georg Häberle reached out his old hand and covered mine with it. His palm was thick, rough, and scratchy on my skin. "We have so much to speak of. So much, my dear." He lifted his hand and shifted his gaze to Mingo. "You have done me a fine favor in bringing these two to my forest home. These are two fine young people, Mingo."

Kai and I lay in hammocks in the back corner of the side porch. Farther to the front, the veranda overlooked the burned clearing, but here the trees were dense, overhanging the high railing, shutting out the strong afternoon light. The birds and animals were quiet in the late-day heat. The only sound was the murmuring of the voices of a man and a woman from the far side of the house. Mingo had lain down to nap on one of the table benches. Häberle brought him a piece of foam rubber from a back room. "To protect you from the hardness of the bench," he insisted in the face of Mingo's denials of need.

I'd watched the two of them from the doorway to the porch. Häberle had affectionately called him "young one," asking Mingo how it had been upriver in the time he'd been gone. How had he found his family, and someone named Estrella? Mingo looked embarrassed by the last question. I was surprised by a nerve of jealousy that jabbed through me when I realized this must be his girlfriend.

I was pondering this feeling, holding Kai's hand across the space between our two hammocks when I realized he was speaking.

"What's that?" I said.

"Thanks for being kind to me earlier."

"Was I kind?"

"Yes, you were kind. You didn't make me feel ashamed."

I swung my legs over the side of my hammock and rose to sitting.

"You were so afraid. I've never seen you like that. I always think of you as the brave one."

"Now I'm not brave, will I be thrown aside?"

"I didn't say you weren't brave. Maybe stoic is better. You never talk about the war with any kind of feeling. You never really tell me what it was like, except when I drag it from you."

"But with harsh judgments," he said. "Always."

"That's what I mean. Look at you now. Impenetrable."

"It's not easy to talk of the war, you know. Not much leeway is left to me, especially not in New York. But all of this is so strange for me. My reaction to the bombings. Meeting Häberle."

"I can see that," I said. "But it isn't easy for me either. I can't just throw away my suspicions. I try to, but they keep rising up."

Kai shifted and brought the side of the hammock down, hooking it under his chin. His face was darker than his eyebrows which had bleached golden in a week of sun.

"About me?"

"No," I said, hoping I sounded convincing. But how could a child growing up in the Third Reich, having Nazi youth groups in his school and Nazi teachers, even though he said he hated and feared both, how could he not be a little influenced by the propaganda. That's what I didn't understand. At those moments when I stopped trusting him, that was the question that arose. I thought, if he can't cop to it, some of the bad ideas must remain. The same with Häberle, no matter how much he professed to being a pacifist, he had been an adult during the war. I had to know what he had done before I could trust him completely. I was sorry, but that was the way it was.

"Everything isn't as clear-cut as you always want it to be."

"What do you mean by that?" I said, the anger seeping into my tone. "He's being very vague, as though he's fudging."

"If you had more tolerance for your own actions, you might not be so harsh on other people."

"Stop it right now."

"No. You don't think I see you making your snap judgments, but I do. Give Jorge some time. He's tired, *um Gottes Willen*, and so are you. But you're so sure there's a quick, perfectly simple explanation. You're so American in that way. It's the same as your thinking that one can take the absolutely correct action in terrible times and have it succeed. You blame yourself if it doesn't, the way you blame yourself for that child's death. The world isn't as fast a study as you'd like to think it is."

"Are you done?"

"No, actually I'm not." He took a deep breath. "At the risk of sounding pretentious, there's a quote from Kant that says, 'the starry sky above, the moral law within.' It's a very beautiful saying, but I've always thought it was a bit simplistic and righteous. Personal moral imperative is much too ambiguous a concept for a philosopher to equate it with God or the fixedness of the stars."

"Like righteous American girls do, you mean."

"You said it, Annie, I didn't. I don't mean to be harsh in return, but I think a notion of the perfect moral imperative is wrong even when it's on the good guys' side."

"You sound just like my father," I said.

"Maybe he and I have more in common that it seemed at first glance."

I had to laugh then. My father had taken me aside outside the restaurant the night he met Kai. He had such a tortured look on his face I thought he'd gotten sick on the food, when he said, "Honey, as hard as I try I can't understand what this new boyfriend of yours is saying." "Is it his accent?" I asked. "I guess that's it," he said. "We really don't seem to be talking the same language." Translated it meant to me that Kai didn't talk about politics and organizing. My father must have known my ship had set sail.

"Not to belabor the point, but I think you'd like to know that Georg Häberle didn't come here for the first time after the war," Kai said.

"How do you know?" I said, holding back any note of hostility in my voice. I was trying.

"He told me he moved here ten years before the war after working three years as a merchant seaman. He wanted to get away from Augsburg. He found it too stifling."

"Maybe you can understand that," I said, smiling tentatively. But I wondered if Kai were being naive to believe Häberle's story, to take it at face value.

"Yes, maybe so," Kai said, returning the smile.

"Tell me more about him."

"I don't know very much more than that he loved it here from the start, even Guayaquil."

I laughed.

"He found it exotic. He compared its dirt and sultry atmosphere to Calcutta, where he'd docked as a seaman."

"Apt." I laughed again.

"But he much preferred the Sierra and then he fell in love with the jungle. He first settled in Puerto Napo, on a *finca* outside of town and then the war came. He got deported back to Germany. Ecuador kicked him out."

"They could do that?"

"Apparently. The Third Reich conscripted him. He didn't tell me more. Except that after the war he hightailed it back deep into the forest where nobody could easily find him again."

"And his brother? Max."

"That's the end of my report. Your shower wasn't long enough."

"You weren't talking about that when I came in."

"Yes, Annie, you're right as usual." He was irritated again. "He stopped talking on his own. I suppose he didn't want to go into the gory details to a near stranger." He let the side of the hammock rise. I could see him through the loose weave, staring up at the ceiling.

"I didn't mean anything."

"You never do."

"Kai, don't accuse me."

"Don't you accuse me. Don't always assume the worst."

"I rather liked him."

"I hear you. Now, please, I need a nap."

"Talk to me."

"For the time being, I'm talked out, Annie. I'm exhausted."

I lay down but I didn't sleep. I wondered instead at how very difficult it was to be married. It was so much easier to be on my own, deciding each step, not being confused by warring emotions. But then I thought of Kai's warmth and kindness. When I'd expressed my distress over my experience here, my father had told me to stop devaluing myself and then said, "That's the way it goes, chicken. That's the role some of us must play, taking others' trouble on our shoulders." Kai cared about me as a person, not as a role or a political offering. I had to remember that. I got up and stood over him, looking down.

"You're pretending to be asleep," I said. "I can tell."

He opened his eyes and stared up at me.

"I'm very fond of you," I said. "We have a lot to get through in the next few days. I think it would be easier if we do it as friends."

He said nothing, but reached up and pulled me down.

"I hope this hammock is as strong as you are," I said.

He didn't answer, but kept on holding me close and let the movement of the hammock lull us to sleep.

Chapter Eighteen

"*Fräulein* Anna, don't be disappointed that your tape-recorder is broken. There are other ways to get the information out of here. Don't they say in English that a picture is worth a thousand words?" Georg Häberle said as he stood ladling the evening supper of soup into our bowls. He wore a workman's white undershirt and short shorts, the kind used for wandering in the Alps. The outfit showed off his slim brown chest and well-formed muscular legs. Well-preserved for a man in his fifties, I thought.

We all sat around the big table, Kai on one side, Mingo and I on the other, and Häberle and María on the third. It was dark now beyond the eaves of the house and raining slightly, bringing in the smell of damp earth and vegetation, but also the stench of wet charred wood and chemicals. The room was brightly lighted and buzzing with four hanging Coleman lamps.

"Also, you know that I don't speak English. What would your listeners have made of an old German speaking in German or even Spanish for that matter?" He chortled.

He was right. Our listener-sponsors were not tolerant of Germans.

"Maybe they'd have to learn to accept it," I said.

Kai's smile said thank you.

"Let us eat," Häberle said, settling himself in his seat. "Let us partake of *doña* María's delicious food." He raised his glass of the wine that he'd taken out especially for our arrival, explaining that he occasionally received a package from Germany. His mother still lived in the family-run Bookbinder Häberle house in Augsburg. "You must visit her the next time you are in Germany," he said to Kai. "And give my greetings, and María's as well, to my *Mutti*."

"Wonderful soup, *Señora* María," I said.

She nodded, wiping her forehead with a handkerchief she extracted from the bosom of her black dress. White against black, white against the brown of her skin. Her face was deeply sad, but she allowed a hint of a smile in my direction.

"It must be difficult in all this commotion," I said.

Mingo murmured assent beside me. Häberle went on eating.

"Life must continue," María said. "Life sometimes brings hardships. You may have heard that my brother is dead. He died a time ago in Esmeraldas. I've only now heard of it."

"Yes, " I said. "*Don* Jorge informed us. I'm very sorry."

"*Gracias, señorita.* It's God's way."

When we had finished eating, María cleared the dishes, disappeared behind the curtain, and didn't return. Häberle rose after some time and followed her. Shortly, María entered with the coffee, and Häberle followed with a bottle of Armagnac, the twin of the one the friar had poured from.

"We recognize the bottle," Kai said. "*Padre* Báez."

"Ah, yes, *Padre* Báez. I gave him one. So what more do you have to report about the man?" Häberle sighed.

"We have nothing to tell, only supposition. It felt as though he was up to something, not wanting us to come here, talking badly about you," I said.

"And what did the good religious man have to say about me?"

I realized that I'd boxed myself into some difficult territory. "Only that he thought if you weren't out here with the Indians, they wouldn't have any trouble."

"You mean if I weren't out here, the forest people wouldn't be being bombed? What do you think of that, Mingo? Do you think these Nazis wouldn't be using napalm on the natives if I weren't here? I ask you, *Señorita* Schmidt, are there Germans in your Vietnam? Is that why they are using napalm on the civilian population there?"

"The friar is not correct in that, *señora*," Mingo said, before I could find an answer to Häberle's question. "The Roani come to *don* Jorge for protection, not the opposite. *Don* Jorge is more generous with the *padre* than he should be."

Häberle cleared his throat. His blue eyes turned fierce as he looked across at Mingo. Then he grinned as though trying to drive his anger away. He laughed, but it was a hollow sound.

"The Roani are not violent people. They don't even have the command form in their language, that is how gentle they are. The same holds for you, Mingo Mincha. You are a mild young man by nature. You would do nothing to harm another human being. Nor would you destroy an animal unless you needed food. I know that about you." He pointed his thick forefinger at Mingo.

María sat looking down, mopping her chest and her upper lip.

Beside me, Mingo shrugged. "I'm not as perfect a man as you are, *don* Jorge. Remember, I'm a trader by nature. I believe there can be trade even in violence."

"Such as an eye for an eye," Häberle said, his voice hoarse with contempt.

"Let us say, I learned my lessons from the Salesians. They taught me their brand of Christianity."

"*Dios*," María breathed.

"And it couldn't be the lessons of your own particular tribal heritage?" Häberle said. "The Shuar are known for being a warring tribe, my son." Häberle's mouth was tight as he spoke, but I detected a note of repartee, as though this exchange was a well-established song and not as bitter as the first notes had indicated.

"I am just young enough and old enough to have witnessed what these religious men can do, how they can pave the way for what's called civilization, *señor*. Who has our friar been sent by?" Mingo shrugged. "Can we know his part exactly? We do know the oil men want to exploit this virgin area. From what my eye sees, and what stench my nose picks up, they will stop at nothing."

Häberle cleared his throat extravagantly this time. "I think *Frau* Schmidt will find Mingo's and my continuing argument on this matter very interesting, in light of her occupation and background.

"Let us present both our sides in this matter. First mine. I am here by the grace of my own will and desire. I came here for peace, feeling these were the farthest reaches of the universe and that evil couldn't penetrate here. Well, *mein Herren*, as you can see I was wrong. Genocide, greed, and the lust for power are in 1969 making their inroads into the Rio Napo and Rio Curaray territory, into the Roani reserve. But what can I alone do, more than try to protect these people from harm? More than that I'm not capable of." He sighed and leaned back against the bench, placing his palms on the table.

"This has gone on for close to two years now. First the friar came around, new to the region, as friendly as could be, saying the government had asked him to help make the Indian's transition easier. When I said I wanted no part in any sort of transition, he sent Mingo to try to convince me to get the Roani to allow the oil men in peacefully. I said to Mingo, 'What do you think, I have power over these primitive peoples? That they would do what I tell them to do? That with a snap of the finger or a Heil Hitler all would be taken care of?' I believe that's when Mingo and I began our friendship. The Roani know what they want. From me it is certain foods, medicine, some western knowledge. It was bad enough to contain them in a reserve, but then to presume to tell them to let the oil men come into the territory and take down their forest. How absurd. So I sent the friar some Armagnac by way of Mingo, but with my refusal to cooperate. Of course the friar came back on his own for one of his cordial visits, with some Chilean wine, saying that he only thought it better for the indigenous, that progress was coming anyway, and though he didn't agree, he felt we must protect them, to make certain no violence was done to them. I repeat, 'to make certain no violence was done to them!'" Häberle stopped and nodded, sitting forward. "Yes, that's what he said. Sounds like your Mafia, no? What do they call it in the states, selling protection? Shortly after that there was an incident. Two Roani were shot with bullets, and they came here to die."

"*Es la verdad*," María said, nodding. "We tried to save them, but they died, one boy and one old man. Barbarians, those that shot them, not deserving to walk this earth."

Häberle raised one hand from the table and placed it over her dark fist.

"But the story came back through the Evangelists that the Roani had speared one man who had come to survey for oil." Häberle removed his hand from María's and put it alongside his other on the table. He sat for a few moments examining them.

Above our heads on the thatched roof, I could hear that the rain had picked up. If only it had come a few hours earlier in the afternoon, then the destruction would have been less.

"I know the Roani," Häberle continued soberly. "As I said before, they are gentle despite their ferocious demeanor. Yes, they participate in spearing raids, but the raids are retaliatory and according to their own customs. If they aren't bothered, they won't bother back. There are other Roani family groups living in the Evangelists' settlements who are already indoctrinated, but our friends here want no part of the Christians. Perhaps that is why they find themselves in such grave trouble."

"But was there any evidence that they harmed the oil surveyors?" Kai asked.

Häberle's shoulders rose. "How am I to know? I have to rely on what I hear through others. The missionaries? They said they heard that one *blanco* had been mortally wounded with a spear and that his comrade had escaped with a flesh wound. The Roani? They deny that they did anything, but instead tell a tale of coming across these fellows and turning and fleeing, being frightened of white men, especially when they saw their guns. *Gott sei Dank*, that some of them mercifully escaped."

"And *Padre* Báez?" I asked. "What did he say when you asked him?"

"You suppose that I asked him, don't you, *Frau* Schmidt?"

"Yes, I would think so."

"Well, I didn't. Nor did I go to him. He came to me, *muy bravo*—you know what *bravo* is, crazy with anger. He asked me what I had in mind by not helping the Roani to accommodate themselves to this new form of civilization. That change had to come. That there was no choice and that my role as an educated white man was to prepare them for it. That whatever harm came to them was on my soul. He speaks of souls. Ach, what *Dreck. Schrecklich*. Like Hitler and his henchmen. Let the inferior people make way for the master race. *Sieg Heil!*"

Kai physically shrank back. The Nazi greeting must have unnerved him as much as it had me.

"You'll excuse *don* Jorge," María said to Kai. "He speaks with his heart. *Don* Jorge has only one heart. Not two or three like the *padre*."

"*Corazón*, you are my heart." Häberle took her hand to his chest. "My only heart."

The downpour had become torrential. It pounded on the thatch, like hands on a drum. The moist vapor intruded into the room, cooling the air.

"Then the bombings began." He patted María's hand that remained beneath his. "The initial strikes were five hours walk to the east of here. To clear for an airstrip, they said. The problem was that the airstrip was two kilometers from a Roani settlement. No one was hurt, but everyone was mighty scared. I was naive and got information of it to the government. They sent a man out here to investigate. Ha! He arrived. He looked. He left. The protectorate means nothing more than a piece of paper now that oil has been discovered. It is the government's contract with the

Evangelists, and those mighty Christians have not yet seen fit to complain of the oil company's infringement. The word came back through town, through Mingo that I was a troublemaker. That I was like all the others, meddling in what was not my business. That I was holding up progress in a country not my own. You want the truth? First, the government wants the money from oil enough to look the other way. They need the technology and capital from the international oil companies to extract their resource. Second, there *are* many meddlers. And they *are* part of the problem. There are the missionaries, the anthropologists, and excuse me, the Peace Corps. Everyone wishes their little piece. The missionaries want the souls. They are translating the Bible into Roani to win those souls. They don't want these populations dispersed before they are won over. So they go to Quito to negotiate for time, privilege, and permission to be the guardians of the Roani. They are awarded their protectorate, which they now don't want to jeopardize by antagonizing the government. There are the anthropologists who want the tribes left intact. They are in here studying and scribbling and they don't want the populations dispersed until they have it all down in their books and on their tapes. After that, who knows? Do they care for the future of the tribes? I cannot answer for them." He frowned as though trying to understand.

"Why do they bomb?" I asked. "Only to defoliate?"

When he looked at me again it was as though he had come back from a place far away. "Why? That's a good question. The sort I've never known the answer to, why men do such things. Because the weapons are available? Or they don't want to get their hands dirty? Or because it is easier and cheaper in the long run. Or because of their limited notion of the long run. Time for them is counted in weeks and months. Not millennia."

"Why would it be cheaper?" I wished so badly that I had a functioning tape-recorder and that he spoke English. I wasn't writing any of this down. I hoped Kai was listening well, and would help me recall what I forgot. "Planes cost money. And bombs certainly do."

Häberle laughed, viciously. "There is probably plenty of surplus napalm around. No, to answer a serious question seriously, it is very expensive and time-consuming to sit down with all the groups who are vying for a piece, as well as dangerous. Because in negotiation there is a chance one might lose and that the international press will get curious. No, it is better to come in here and do the job quickly. Once a portion of the forest is destroyed with no chance of reclamation, everyone lifts their arms in hopelessness and walks away. But as a hedge against recriminations, this government sets up a phony land distribution operation to seem as though they are trying their best. So they have a project, a *padre*, and a Peace Corps volunteer to point to. That is where I believe our friar comes in. At the very least he is a pawn in this. And then they can bomb, bomb, bomb. In the beginning they dropped men into the forest from helicopters by rope ladder to cut and move the trees. But it proved more efficient to defoliate from on high. For an airstrip, for a road to Brazil, and, as a side benefit, the eradication of the populations so the companies won't lose workers to slings and arrows. Davids can be a terrible nuisance to the Goliaths. Wiser and cheaper in the end to destroy them."

"And the friar," I asked, "you think is not a partner in this violence, or not knowingly so."

"I don't trust the *padre*, not this much." Mingo put his thumb and forefinger together. He sat back splaying his legs beneath the table. His thigh touched mine. I didn't know if it was intentional, but he didn't move it away.

"And," Häberle said, making a beckoning motion to Mingo to keep going.

"*Pues*, I think he is not what he looks to be."

"You mean not a man of the cloth?" I asked, using the moment to shift my leg from his.

"You learn here on the river and in the forest that things are many times the opposite of what they seem.

That's how it has been ever since *los colonos* began to come in here."

"It's always that way whenever money and power are involved," Kai said.

"But here power and money come in ragged clothing, masquerading in what looks to be *bobería*, foolishness. I believe it comes disguised to catch us innocents. To get us in their talons like a vulture an unseeing animal, but we would know a vulture. We don't recognize these silly people."

"Like the friar in his dirty clothes, his noisy outspokenness," I said.

"That is exactly what I mean, *señora*. I believe he's sent to tempt us, as the Christian brothers taught us the devil was sent to tempt Jesus."

"So you think the friar is the devil?" I said, a little disappointed in his line of argument.

"I believe he is evil. I believe he should be banished."

"Tell her what you really believe, Mingo. How far you would go, son," Häberle said.

Mingo smiled. "No, not that far, *don* Jorge. It was only a game I was playing."

"Not a game, I don't think. And if so, you shouldn't play with such notions. *No juegas asi, chico, sin intención.*"

"He thinks I mean to harm the friar," Mingo turned and smiled at me over his shoulder. He fidgeted with the beads at his neck. He shook his head, still smiling, though now it was frozen on. "Báez isn't worth harming. No. What I think is that the indigenous people should be organized to resist these incursions into our lands."

"Oh, ho, the boy is Che Guevara. Do you know who Che Guevara is, *señorita*? The kin of Castro, killed in the mountains of Bolivia recently. Living with an East German girl, I hear. He wanted to organize and arm the Indians. *Dummkopf*. Romantic hogwash. Where did it get them? Nowhere at all."

Mingo sat stiffly, with the half-smile still on his face. Was this embarrassment or controlled anger?

"Go on, son." Häberle pushed air with the back of his hand.

"What form of organizing would you do, Mingo?" I asked.

He leaned his elbows on the table, his shoulders hunching up. He shook his hair back. "It shouldn't be permitted that these oil people come into our forest at all, *ever*. The forest doesn't belong to them, but to the people who have lived here over the centuries, who have cared for the forest, who have not harmed it. There are thousands of us who will die if the oil companies, the cattle ranchers, the gold miners enter. Our forest spirits will die. The Roani, Shuar, Runa are not strangers to this destruction, to these 'civilizing' techniques. Eighty years ago our tribes were ravaged during the rubber boom by the *caucheros*. In the 1930s Royal Dutch Shell Oil built the Baños to Puyo road through refuge zones. We spoke with quiet voices until now, but I believe we can speak more loudly and as one voice." He stopped, his face serious and then, as though by plan, he put a smile on. His salesman's smile.

"Yes, but by what means would you organize?" I asked. "Who would do the organizing? And to what end, exactly?"

I noted that Häberle nodded approval, but María inspected me suspiciously.

"There is a group forming in Sucúa, an organization of indigenous peoples. The first goal is to make us proud of our heritage by preserving customs in writing, in Quichua and then our other languages, and also to inform the children who never lived in a traditional manner in the forest, to know their elders' ways. To hold onto the language of their fathers."

It sounded very mild to me, not at all like something that could disturb Georg Häberle.

"What he doesn't tell you," Häberle said, pointing at Mingo, "is that they are given housing for their organization in the offices of the Salesians in Sucúa."

"What?" I said. "I'm confused."

"You despise the Salesians," Kai said. "What is this, Mingo? How can that be?"

"That's right," Häberle said. "That is the contradiction."

Mingo hadn't even flushed when this had been exposed. And his thigh had touched mine yet again and remained. He looked at me, and it was then that I saw the place behind his eyes that told me something else was going on. As he had said before, all is not as it seems out here. I wondered what my father would have caught. "There is another agenda," he would have said. "Look for the other agenda, chicken. Don't be fooled."

"So it's convenient to use the Salesians in this way," I said. "Sometimes one must make a compromise on the way to accomplishing goals."

I saw a flicker of recognition as he glanced at me and away. His leg remained. I moved.

"Sometimes, yes," he said. "We can't always be pure in the way we work. I agree with you, *señora*." He spoke then to Kai across the table, sending his most charming beam at him. "Your *señora* is a smart woman. She seems to know how the world is made."

"Thanks for your good words, Mingo," I said. "But I don't see exactly where you and *don* Jorge part company. What would you do that he wouldn't, and what is it about his ways that doesn't make you entirely happy?"

A look passed from María to Mingo, as though to warn him to go no farther.

I was sure of it when María abruptly stood and said she was exhausted and had to go to her bed.

"You too, *viejito*," she said to Häberle, touching his shoulder. "We can talk again tomorrow after the work is done."

"Yes, my friends," Häberle said. "I'd forgotten in the energy of this discussion that we have a difficult day before us, repairing the damage those monsters did. I hope you are willing to help?" He looked to Kai.

"*Bitte, mit Vernügen.* Though I'm not much of a carpenter."

"No carpentry, *mein Landsmann*. We're not that sophisticated. Slashing and lashing, we call it here." Häberle laughed, nodding to Mingo. "Isn't that right, Mingo, son? No nails and hammers here, even though you'd be glad to introduce them."

"No, *don* Jorge." Mingo held his hands up in surrender. "That I wouldn't try to introduce. I know traditional building. I would never interfere with what is best for here."

That night we slept on the porch on straw mats. The rain had stopped but it remained overcast. It was cold enough for our sleeping bags and completely black. Mingo slept in the same spot on the bench.

"What are you thinking?" I whispered.

"That this is awful," Kai said.

"What do you think about what Mingo said?"

"He's not telling all. That much I know."

"You think so too."

"I do," he said.

"I saw a look pass between María and Mingo. She didn't want him to go on. I saw that much. I think it might be about Mingo wanting to take more aggressive action. As a pacifist, Häberle wouldn't approve."

"Remember, Annie, there's a big difference between aggression and violence. If that's where your suspicious mind is taking you." He tapped me on the head.

"Don't worry, I know the difference," I said, feeling comforted by his playful pats.

It was so different, too, I thought, not going through this alone. During the last months of my tour of duty, I had to overcome enormous anxiety just to leave my apartment. Fear of that degree is such a lonely place. Each time I stepped out my door I expected to be pelted with words or stones. When it wasn't trepidation that consumed me, it was rage. A teenage boy who regularly taunted me made the mistake one morning of brazenly blocking the center door as I opened it for classes. We were alone and I grabbed him by his tattered shirt, catching him off balance, and threw him against the metal door, his head whipping back and then forward with the impact. The appalling thonk didn't satisfy my anger. I punched him twice in the face before catching myself. I left him without apology, but I lived with the horror of my action for weeks. How could *I* have done such violence when I'd been tutored by my father since childhood that physical aggression was never a solution to disagreement? My guilt at punching that teenager in front of the community center only compounded my loneliness.

"Kai?"

"*Ja.*"

"Don't get mad at me, but I'd like to ask you a question."

"*Und?*"

"Remember when Häberle said Steinhardt the Jew, that your father took over for him, I wondered what you felt when he said that?" I waited, barely daring to breathe.

Kai slipped his arm around me and pulled me closer to him until my head was in the hollow of his shoulder. I'd just about decided I wouldn't get an answer to my question when he spoke.

"You know my father ran a Jewish man's business, Annie. I've told you that. He became a Nazi so he could run *Herr* Steinhardt's business and take care of our family. Otto Steinhardt fled to France and never came back to Germany. He never trusted his country again. Otto Steinhardt despised Germans, *all* Germans, after the holocaust."

"How do you know that?" I was afraid my question would stop him, but it didn't.

"I know it, believe me, I know it. Don't push me, this is hard enough. After the war Otto said that Gerhardt as his eldest could take over the business if he wished to stay in Germany. The problem was Gerhardt never got to the university to learn chemistry. He was concealed in cellars all through the war. And, of course, early on it was prohibited by the Nazis for Jews to attend."

"But Gerhardt runs the company now, and gives your mother a good pension." Hope grew in me. I had a fantasy of finally learning that Kai's father was a hero, and he was somehow being rewarded through the pension that was given to Gertrude. But why hadn't Kai told me this? What a thing to hide.

"After the war my father taught Gerhardt chemistry and the business. Gerhardt worked under my father for a time and then he took over as director."

"When your father died?"

"Annie, no. Please don't try to paint a pretty picture of this. I can feel what you're trying to do. No, the Occupation forces made my father give the company back to Gerhardt. Just as the Nazis gave my father a Jewish business, the Americans ordered him to give it back."

"And your mother's pension?"

"Neither love nor gratitude got her that pension. My father was a good businessman. He struck some sort of a bargain with Gerhardt. I have no idea what it was." I heard him take a deep breath. "There are some things that one can never know."

After a time Kai wrapped his other arm around me and brought me to him. "Please, Annie, can we lay this to rest? You must just accept me for myself. There is nothing I can do about my past but work to not repeat it. Please try to believe in me."

If love and compassion and empathy have a source, it has to be purely sexual, because that's what I felt in that moment, in every portion of my body, a melting, a flow, a delicious desire to have all of him inside, filling me, and equally to know that I surrounded, absorbed, and protected this man.

"I need you," I barely whispered. "I promise not to wake up the house."

CHAPTER NINETEEN

I woke before dawn to the din of birds and lay in the gray light of our mist-shrouded porch. My sleeping bag was wet on the surface so I snuggled farther in, bringing my arms into the dry warmth. Beside me Kai breathed deeply, contentedly. The light changed from gray to green until it infused the mist with a glorious golden apricot. Traces of chemical fumes and water-soaked scorched earth reached me as I tried to move my limbs. My entire body was stiff and sore.

I lay there remembering the April day when the baby Ladito was born. I'd walked down from my apartment, passing Eladio and Gala's door on my way to the community center, when Eladio stuck his head out. His eyes were bleary, but not from drink this time. He'd been up the whole night with Gala.

"*Un varón*, Ana. God has finally given us a boy."

He pulled me by the arm into their tiny, dark living area. Gala was in the alcove in bed, with the five girls around her. Her black hair was spread out on the white muslin pillow. When she saw me standing by the bed, looking down, she smiled and her dimples dug in deep and black on each round cheek.

"Look, *mi negrito*, Ana, how calmly he sleeps."

The sadness I felt remembering was unbearable. It struck in the center of my chest and moved down into my stomach with a fierceness that turned to sharp pain. I doubled over. Breathe deeply, I told myself. I thought of Mrs. Siciliano, our housekeeper when my father and I moved to upstate New York, saying to me when I felt faint at the onset of puberty, "Put your head between your knees, sweetie, and breathe deep. Get that blood back in. It's on account of you're getting the curse. Same happened to my girls when they got theirs." It disgusted me to have her mention my period aloud, but I sat obediently with my head down, and my dizziness did pass. As now, the pain in my stomach abated as well. When I could breathe normally again, I felt the emptiness and guilt I always felt when I thought of the baby Ladito. Then I pictured Angel slipping over the wall, saw his tawny thin hands, and the glint of his spectacles as they disappeared for the last time. The battered Chevy drove down the street. He must have been in that car. Was he alive or dead? Why hadn't I persevered in looking for him? Why hadn't I answered Rina's letters?

I watched the mist burn away and the trees begin to emerge out of the fog, green and heavy with water, lush, dramatic. Suddenly I understood. Angel's disappearance was where my will and my responsibility began. Volition and duty. Two qualities I'd always prided myself on upholding. The baby's death was like the mist that now burned away, a scrim of dense sorrow protecting me from another harder knowledge of myself. Kai told me I was expecting too much to think I could save an impoverished infant from death in a Third World country with my limited training. But Kai knew nothing of that day when Angel disappeared and its aftermath. I had all the moral training needed for finding and saving Angel. It was with Angel that I had truly failed, was guilty. Then I had a thought. Was my failure to act on Angel's disappearance somehow connected to my years of hiding from the world that I was a half Jew? As though Angel was a part of me and to look out for him was to expose myself to mortal peril. In childhood, and later, to stand up and identify myself as a Jew felt equivalent to following the Rosenbergs to the electric chair. To demand justice for Angel must have signified analogous risk for me, in a place deep within.

"*Morgen,*" came from behind me.

I turned to see Kai smiling and sleepy eyed.

"*Guten Morgen,*" I said and went directly to him, into the pungent, thick morning smell of him.

At our breakfast of milk-coffee and fried fish, Häberle, who had been up for hours, described the plan for the day.

"Kai, *Señor* Mingo, and I will work with the men to restore the eating house," he said sipping the hot coffee from a white enameled tin cup. He wore his tiny bikini and a pair of rubber tire sandals that reminded me of the friar.

I wondered if the friar would consider following us here. Certainly he would have conjectured by now where and with whom we had gone. A horrible new worry arose. What if the bombing yesterday had to do with us?

We were in the kitchen area on the porch. A puffy faced Mingo sat across the small oil cloth covered table from me. He, too, was shirtless, though he still wore his beads around his neck. He stared into his tin plate and ate. Could he answer my question?

"María," Häberle called to his wife, who was frying fish at the charcoal stove against the wall. "Can this young lady assist you and the women?"

"If she wishes," she said without turning to acknowledge me.

"You are lucky, my friends," Häberle said. "Today you will be participating in the work of an ancient hunting and gathering society. Not many people have that opportunity."

"I forgot to ask you something last night, *don* Jorge," I said, trying to sound casual. "It's been bothering me."

"Yes, my dear." He waited expectantly.

"Why do you think they bombed here? They've never done it before."

"Why? I don't understand, *Fräulein.*"

"Why here? Why now?"

"Perhaps they're getting ready to put a road through my house," he laughed. With a twig he picked at his discolored teeth and prodded his gums.

"Is that so? Are there plans?"

He sobered. "No, there are not, from what I know. I would guess they are upping the ante, as gamblers say. Maybe they've lost all patience with me."

María had come to stand behind him. Her face was bloated with fatigue, her eyes watery and veined.

"Is that a possibility?" I continued. "Have you done anything to make them especially impatient?"

Häberle gave an angry glance Mingo's way. "Not that I know of," he said, pointedly.

Mingo, his head down, kept shoveling food into his mouth.

"Are you afraid?" I asked.

At that María shook her head as though irritated and Mingo looked up from his meal.

"You are persistent, my dear," Häberle said. "So I will answer you. There are two sorts of people in the world: those who have gone through a war and come out more timid, and those who come out knowing it's a waste of precious time to fear. Which one do you suppose I am?"

"I would guess the latter," I answered.

"So, María, *mi esposa*," he craned his head back. "What do you say we get on with our day? Kai Schmidt! Your wife is quite some little interviewer."

When the men left, I offered to wash the dishes. "You must have some other work," I said.

"*Chica*, why do you ask so many questions?" María stood by the stove, hands on her hips, scrutinizing me.

"Maybe we wouldn't have come if we'd known everything. But now that we're here, we should know the worst, don't you agree?"

"The worst?" She laughed with bitterness, her hands dropping to her sides. "There is always worse to know. Only God knows what is to come, how it will all end. Perhaps you should ask your questions of Him instead of my husband."

She told me where to get the water from the tin drum under the porch. I went down the front stairs with one of the buckets from the day before. The drum was overflowing, filled during the night along a split-bamboo trough that angled down from the roof. The clearing lay before me, a wasteland, a blackened pool of mud. Whatever had held the earth in place was destroyed completely. On the far side, Häberle, Mingo and Kai stood with a group of Indian men in loinclothes. Häberle's bikini—like his marriage to the fiercely loyal María—was a lucky cross-cultural match. I was curious on what subterranean level he and María connected. Despite her chastisement of my questioning, I decided to find out.

In the kitchen I ladled water into a blackened pot on the stove and into the wash basin on a wooden stand. María had already scraped the dishes. "For the pigs," she said.

"*Jabón?*"

"*Aquí,*" she said, handing me a lump of homemade yellow soap.

As I washed, the sunlight touched the dishpan and the building suds. The soap smelled of tallow and the rainwater was pure.

"How long have you lived out here?" I asked, hoping my new line of inquiry was innocuous enough so that I could, as my father had taught, get her accustomed to my presence.

"Fifteen years," she said, soberly.

"In this exact spot?"

"No, no. *Cuidado, niña.*" She motioned me away from the washstand as she carried the steaming pot over and poured clear water into a second white enameled pan.

I dunked the soapy dishes individually into the rinse water.

"*Poco a poco* we came to this place, as the civilization moved closer. *Don Jorge* is not in love with civilized man, you understand."

"And you, *señora?*"

"María can be happy in any place, with a good man." she said, examining me as though in challenge. "*Don* Jorge Häberle is a good man."

"Mingo says you're from Esmeraldas."

With that she brightened. "Do you know it?"

"No, but I lived on the *costa* for two years. In Guayaquil. There must be some similarities."

"Guayaquil." She clucked her tongue. "I know that city. It's a dangerous place."

"Not so bad," I said, "once you get used to it."

"Ah, yes. Like most things in life, with time one accustoms oneself."

María and I skirted the clearing on the side closest to her house. She walked a step before me with her head down, carrying a large empty, crudely woven basket.

"Do you have children?" she asked.

"No, we only just married,' I said. "Eleven days."

"Eleven days. My goodness." She smiled. The morning light exposed how smooth her skin was. "Will you have children, *niña?*"

I was surprised at her phrasing. The assumption was in this country that one would have many children.

"Who can know that?" I said. "Do you have children?"

When she smiled this time, I observed a note of irony. "We have none."

"I'm sorry," I said.

"Not sorry, child. *Don* Jorge wanted no children. I'm barren. A perfect match. That's why I went with him, why I consented to marry him. I was a mother many times over, caring for my brothers and sisters. We were ten. Eight who lived. I was the oldest. My mother needed me."

"You cared for them all?" I asked.

When she didn't answer, I asked, "From when you were a child?"

Again she didn't reply, but walked faster, taking the lead until, at the corner of the clearing when she turned left toward the standing house, I saw her face and realized she was thinking of her dead brother.

We entered the long house by a door in the near end and stepped into a twenty-by-thirty-foot, earth-floored open space. There were a number of split-bamboo platforms built along the thatched walls and some simple palm fiber hammocks strung from wooden wall supports to posts in the center of the room. The room was windowless, but the roof was at least fifteen feet high at the center, lending airiness. At the far end of the house was a chicken coop. There were six young women in the room when we entered, and ten children. Infants suckled on two of the women, and a circle of small children played down at the end near the chicken coop. No one wore clothes.

María called out in an unfamiliar language which I took to be the Roanis'. It sounded nasal and harsh.

One of the women nursing a baby, lying in a hammock, looked at us. She raised a large hand and let it drop. She didn't smile, nor did any of the others—not even the children. As we walked over to the women, I was reminded that Häberle had said these were gentle people, that they only appeared fierce. Which they most certainly did. The women and the children scrutinized me with scowls on their faces. They were not pretty people. Their skin color was a gray-brown with a slightly yellowish tinge, and their features were blunt and flat, their bodies husky. The holes in their earlobes were stretched large, but no one wore the decorative balsa plugs. Where the men had hair cut in a bowl shape that indicated regular care, the women's was long, straggly and not particularly clean looking. As María spoke they responded with a sullen lethargy.

Gradually they stopped inspecting me and turned their full attention to María. As a give and take developed between María and the others, I let my eyes survey the room. What was most impressive about it was its neatness, the packed earth having been recently swept, and the lack of any objects lying around. Only a black ceramic bowl here, and a water carrier there, a pink plastic broom, a pile of thin blankets on one platform and on another, a tiny pile of fabric, perhaps contemporary clothes. But that was it. Homes in the *barrio* had scanty possessions, but they didn't come close to this. It was said that forest Indians had almost nothing, but I had imagined a different sort of nothing. This was absolute. No wonder Mingo thought he could corner the market in these parts.

My mother used to say, "We're like Okies only we're traveling in the wrong direction," as we drove from west to east in a car that held all our possessions. She felt sorely deprived. But this long house would have looked like the general store in Puerto Napo, if furnished with what we'd packed into our Plymouth.

One of the women—hers was the angriest face— beckoned to me in the Latin manner, her cupped fingers turned toward the ground. She sat on the hammock with one knee locked over the other, apparently to protect herself from my scrutiny. Her baby wore a double strand of beads around his neck. The nipples of the woman's huge breasts were covered with thick manioc paste. Perhaps the child got his solid food that way.

I walked over and stood about two feet from her.

"*Hola*," I said.

She said something back to me. She reached out and grabbed my arm, pulling me closer; then she stroked my arm.

"She asked where you come from," María said. "Say someplace in Ecuador, please. She would not understand the United States."

"I come from Puerto Napo," I said.

María translated.

The woman conferred with the three other women who had gathered around. They nodded and stared at me. They also stroked my arms. It was so mechanical a gesture that I guessed this was a sort of greeting.

"She said they have seen your man and he has bird - feather hair like those who come from Puerto Napo, so she knew anyway."

"Then why did she ask?"

"To see if you would lie, of course, *chica*."

"Thank you," I said to María. To the Indian women I said what a pleasure it was to have the honor of visiting their home. I said I hoped I could help them with today's work. Whatever they wished, I would be willing.

María nodded approval and translated. There was much discussion among the women. They pointed out beyond the house, and then they pointed to me and began to speak agitatedly and at length to María.

"What is it?" I asked as they continued.

"They want to know if it is your time. Only women who are not bleeding are allowed in the garden gathering the manioc. And how can they know your condition when you are all covered up. I've told them you're a truthful person, and if you say you aren't bleeding, then you aren't."

"I'm not," I said.

After María translated my reply, there was much discussion, punctuated by pauses and scrutiny of me.

"They say they would like to see."

"See?"

"Yes, they would like to inspect you."

I smiled at the women, trying to ingratiate myself. Perhaps they wouldn't insist if they saw how friendly I was. They didn't smile back.

"What do I do?" I asked María.

She shrugged, putting her hands in the air. "Pull down your panties, what else, *chica*?" She laughed.

Wearing a skirt made the physical task easier, but when I pulled down my underpants to show there was no blood on them, I was embarrassed to find them filthy with urine. These women who wore no clothes, though they did give off a fairly strong body odor, had no way of exposing their personal dirt. The woman on the hammock got up and the other women came forward. They had appeared large to me because of their dense, fleshy naked bodies, but when they huddled in close I was surprised to find that they only came to my shoulder. They carefully examined my pants and then one of them stuck her finger up me and took it out, inspecting it much as one checks the oil in a car. They all talked at once and then turned and went over to the hammock.

"You can put your panties back on," María grinned. "You can help in the garden."

"And you?"

"Oh, *chica*, I'm too old. I dried up long ago. I can do the work of men or women the way I am now." She patted down the front of her black dress.

The garden was at the back of the house a few hundred feet into the forest. The trees were gigantic about the edges, their fans of leaves distant against the blue sky. In deeper, the lianas hung down, and the light and shadow played through, but out in the garden it was all blasting light. Why hadn't they chosen this area with its low, green covered mounds for the air strike? They would surely know that this was the source of food for the small community living here. I worried that this confirmed that the purpose of the task was to warn us off.

The women—I counted seven—stopped working when we approached, one of them coming forward to speak with María. Again the same angry looks which I was becoming inured to. In fact I found it a relief not to have to smile in greeting all the time, or make charming jokes to endear myself to them as I would have in the past. The women wore toga-like garments of rough muslin, tied at the waist with crudely woven jute belts. This garb must had been put on for working outside where they might encounter the new white visitors and other strangers.

María and I worked as a team. She knelt in the damp, rich, brown-red soil. Following her lead, I plunged my hands into the earth's coolness. She pulled out a long, dirt-coated root as thick as a child's thigh. Looking around she called out, "Yayae," to one of the women, who answered by bringing over a machete. María chopped off the stalk of the plant, and placed it back in the hole, piling the soil again into a mound.

"What are you doing?"

"You always replant when you harvest," she said. "You do it immediately. In ten months there will be another crop. These people waste nothing. Jorge says that the white people could learn from them." She looked at me, our faces a foot apart. "We *negritos* could learn as well."

When our basket was filled, we followed the women to the river by way of the burned field. It was worse in the baking noon sun, glistening black and angry, sending up chemical fumes. María brought her handkerchief from the bodice of her dress to her nose.

"Cover your face," she commanded. "It causes flu."

I dutifully pulled my blouse from my skirt and put its hem over my nose, reminded of Gala and her belief that bananas made the worms the children always had, and the diarrhea that Ladito had died of. Bananas and God. Those were the two culprits.

The Indian women didn't protect themselves as they walked with the baskets on their heads, backs straight, and legs short and muscular beneath them. Beautiful they might not be, but there was a handsomeness in their self-possession.

We approached the river on the same path we'd run back and forth on hauling water. We waded downstream single file through calf deep, cool clear water with María in the lead. At the second bend we spotted the elusive Max before he took notice of us. His back was to us and the gurgling of the stream must have camouflaged our sloshing footsteps and the women's chatter. He wore thigh high boots over pants held up by suspenders, and an alpine hat with fishing flies attached. He could have been fishing in Bavarian waters. In a sleeveless undershirt his exposed burned shoulders sloped down in plumpness, making him seem vulnerable, even innocent.

María proceeded alone to warn him of our presence. Just then his line pulled, and he began to reel in, leaning back as the line stretched and strained. María stopped, waiting, allowing him his catch.

"*Komm, komm, mein Lieber,*" he crooned, until the fish was in the air, flapping silvery in the sun. He put down his pole and kneeling, disengaged the large fish. He stood then, raising the fish high into the air. "*Sei frei, mein Lieber, mein Freund,*" he yelled, and tossed it back into the stream.

"Max," María called out to him. He turned, his eyes large and blue in his oval face. He saw us behind her. Without saying a word to her, he grabbed his fishing kit from the bank in his free hand and ran, slipping and sliding, now up to his thighs, farther downstream.

María gave no explanation of what had occurred, nor any apology when she suggested that we stay in his spot. "It is deep enough and clear," she said. "A good place to wash the manioc."

María settled herself on a large rock close to the bank, placed her basket on the shore within reach, and commenced to scrub the roots. The Indian women remained standing as they washed, depositing the cleaned tubers in bark cloth slings worn across their breasts. They began in their dresses, but one by one, they removed them, depositing this cumbersome clothing in a string bag which was hooked around the leg of the pregnant girl I remembered from the day before. This ingenious washing machine darted and bobbed in and out of the current.

I tried standing as they did, bending at the waist to dunk the muddy roots, scrubbing the mud away, then dipping them again. Soon my back and thighs stiffened and ached and I had to slosh over to join María on the boulder.

"They are more accustomed to this," María pointed with her chin toward the women. "Don't worry. But keep washing."

My hands already felt rubbed raw by the action against the rough root-covered skin of the tubers.

"Does your brother-in-law always throw the fish back?" I asked after a while.

Again the ironic look. "He has always come home without fish."

"He must always throw them back then," I said.

"Yes, he must," she said.

During her pointed silence, I thought of this strange man calling to the fish as he flung it into the water, "Be free, my love, my friend."

"How old are you, *señorita*?" María asked.

"Twenty-seven," I said.

"Ah, like my brother was." She became silent again.

I would have liked to comfort her, but didn't know how. So I continued washing. The water lapped and splashed over my knees and up into my face, cooling me. The light played and shifted as the river's rhythms were reflected onto the trunks of the trees. It was a wonderful place. For the first time since arriving at the settlement, I was happy we'd come. I put aside my worry about the possibility of the friar aiming an attack at us.

"Twenty-seven is late to marry," she said.

"Yes. Here it's about ten years too late."

She just looked at me and then went back to the washing.

"But in the United States, it's only a little late. Maybe three or five years. *Pues*, I had things to do before I married," I said, deciding to answer her as close to the truth as possible. I wasn't here to organize the community. I could reveal myself. A lightness came over me, a peace, a relief, to simply say the truth and not try to find what would be correct in the circumstance.

"God was kind to you, *niña*. María married at fifteen, with great anguish."

"To *don* Jorge?"

"Oh no, *Dios mio*." She shook her hand, slapping her forefinger against the rest. "No. One of my own. *Un negrito de Esmeraldas*. But he was a boy and I was a girl and we had no idea. No idea. I didn't make any children and he left. Chin Chin, he was called. He was black but had the eyes of the *chino*. We had many Chinese in Esmeraldas. Chin Chin left the Black María. *La negra María*. Chin Chin found himself a real *China*." She laughed. "Who could make babies with those slanted *ojitos*. Chin Chin was happy and so was María. I had my things to do, too, *Señorita* Ana." She scrubbed particularly hard on a recalcitrant tuber. When she lifted it from the water she pushed it through the air suggestively. "As a girl I didn't like the business of being a wife." She thrust the root downstream to where the Indian women worked, calling to them, so that they looked up and caught it.

"But with the German, *don* Jorge Häberle, I liked it." She smiled at me, her green-brown eyes coming alive with mischief. "*Los indios* know how to plant and preserve the forest and the Germans know how to plant and preserve the woman, no?"

My face flushed hot. "Yes," I said stiffly, trying to recoup from my sudden prudishness. "At least the one I am familiar with certainly does."

"Oh, *chica*." She pinched my cheek. "You're younger than your twenty-seven years."

"Perhaps in some ways I am," I said. "But in others I'm not."

"And how are you old, *chica*?" She continued to chide.

"Old in washing tubers in the river," I said. "I've grown old from the arduousness of the task."

She laughed. "*Bien dicho, niña*, well said."

When we returned to the long house to gather food to take to the men in the forest, the women were still lounging on the hammocks while the children ran between and around them. There were extra hammocks now, so that every woman had one, strung around to form an irregular circle with the foot of each touching in the center, radiating out like spokes of a wheel. By turning and twisting their heads they could converse with ease. A haunting feeling overcame me as I observed their aimless, lackadaisical way of whiling away the hours together. It seemed so womanly, whereas I was unpracticed in such simple give and take. My only experience of this sort of female interchange was on those evenings I'd spent with Gala on the stairs of the *barrio* as the sun set, and we gossiped about our neighbors who passed by and greeted us while the sky turned to mango, and she would let loose my hair from the barrette and comb it, caressing its length down my back as though I were another of her daughters.

CHAPTER TWENTY

We gathered the baskets of fried plantains and manioc cakes. I was given a small jug of *chicha*, or *tepae* as it was called in Roani. The larger *jarras* were hoisted by the women onto their backs, held in place with long jute headband slings.

"Remember, it's strong," María said, making the drinking motion, tipping her flared thumb and fingers back and forth before her mouth. "Warn your husband to *tener cuidado* or he will find himself drunk." She slapped her forehead. "I forgot. This is a German we are speaking of. They know how to drink."

"And plant their tubers," I said. "Don't forget that."

"*Chica, chica, chica.*" She hugged me around the waist.

We walked along a well-trod path. María said it was where the men start out for the hunt and the women to gather wood. This group had only been living here for six months. They had run from other fires deeper in, had come to Häberle because they heard he would protect them. When I asked how they had heard, she shook her head in such a way that I saw I wasn't to ask any more.

We heard the men long before we arrived at the site. Their shouting and the din of a tree crashing echoed and shuddered through the forest, a roar horribly reminiscent of the long house collapsing in the fire.

"*Hombres*, we come," María called out when silence returned.

"*Komm, komm, meine süsse*," the unmistakable voice of Häberle floated like Siegfried's through the still jungle. "*Komm, komm, Liebchen.*"

In the freshly cut clearing, the men examined the tree they'd just felled. Even on its side it stood taller than they and its length was half a city block.

"Aha, the women," Häberle turned and greeted us.

"Why that tree?" María said. "You don't need anything that tall. Why do you waste a tree?"

"Awae thought we could use a canoe while we were at it," Häberle stood leaning against his axe. He spoke to a stocky young Indian man standing beside him. This Awae, who had a gentle face and red *achiote* stained in zigzag designs on his shoulders and back, said something to María. She seemed contented with his answer.

"Awae is amazing," Kai said. He'd come over and given me a sweaty hug. "He can see birds I barely find with my glasses. As though he has three-dimensional vision. Eyesight must develop differently in people who grow up in the jungle. He says there are macaws in the area and guans, manakins, and even the harpy eagle. It hasn't been heavily hunted. Contrary to what the friar says, they still use blowguns, not rifles. If things stay calm they plan to take me farther in."

"Let's hope for all of us they do," I said.

There were nine men in all: Kai, Mingo, six Indians, and Georg Häberle. None of the Indian men looked me in the face but kept their gazes toward the ground. We stood in awkward silence. Trying to take in their red-and-black tribal markings, nakedness, narrow cotton waistbands, beaded necklaces, and balsa wood earplugs without appearing to stare, I wondered what curiosities they were noticing about me. My gold wedding ring? The small gold hoops in my ears? My height and my curly brown hair?

We were interrupted by a monkey's loud shrieking.

Awae turned abruptly, speaking hurriedly to the group of men.

"It's a howler," Kai said, running over to a log for his binoculars.

The Indian men grabbed string bags and one man slung a blowgun over his back. Then they moved smoothly, stealthily into the forest. The women weren't following, nor was Häberle. For a moment I was torn, but then decided, no matter what the customs were, I was going. I ran to catch up with Kai, who was following Mingo into the forest.

Twenty yards in we stopped. Mingo and the men stood scanning the heights. Kai lifted his glasses, his arms jutting like wings at shoulder level.

"Sssst," Kai said. "Awae, sssst." Kai pointed straight above them.

The men, alerted, followed his hand, their faces straining. A naked man with gray hair on both head and pubic area saw it first. He made a yelping sound and reached back for his blowgun. Awae took an arrow from a sheath at his side so quietly there was barely a breath of sound. I touched Kai lightly to show him what was going on. His eyes left the glasses for a moment, and then went back. Awae opened a tiny pouch at his side and dipped the point in. The old man had the blowgun already at his lips, aiming it. Awae moved without a sound over to the old man and slipped the twig thin arrow into the top of the gun. When the old man signaled him, Awae cried out in a screech which rose up to the monkey, and the monkey called back, a cry of alarm, and leapt out into the open across from his branch to another, but when he was in midflight, with the tiniest "wheeetz," the old man blew into the gun and the arrow flew and struck the flash of red fur. The monkey didn't fall, but completed his trajectory to another branch. The men yelped and ran closer to the trees to stand in a tight group, their heads bent straight back, their faces lifted, maneuvering from side to side to get a better look.

"They got him good," Kai said. "He's dying. He's just hanging on." He handed me the glasses.

The monkey was looped over the branch, the arrow sticking straight out of his side.

Mingo gestured to me that he'd like to see the glasses.

"The *mono* is dead, but he won't fall," I said to him.

"They know," he said, looking up through the binoculars. "But they'll wait a little longer."

Soon the old man had handed over his blowgun to Awae and was cutting down vines which he crudely and quickly braided together. He held one end and reached the vine around the trunk of the tree, catching it with his other hand, and then, with amazing dexterity and speed, he scrambled up the tree with his bare feet, holding himself on each ascension with the brace of liana. In no time he was even with the branch where the monkey clung. He reached over and pulled it free. Calling a warning, he threw the monkey down to land with a crash a few yards away from us. Awae ran to get it. Two men with Mingo's help began to strip green supple vines from the trees. Awae tied one end of vine around the monkey's long furry tail and looped the other end around the animal's neck. When he was finished, the tail had become a strap which he hitched over the old man's shoulder so that he carried the body as though it were a handbag.

"*Exito*, success! This is a wonderful occasion!" Häberle greeted us when we arrived back and then continued in the guttural language of the Indians.

Mingo squatted to have a look at the monkey once it was on the ground. We all gathered around.

"Did the kill bother you?" I asked, taking Kai's hand. It remained slack in mine.

"Of course," he said. His eyes looked tired. "But people have to live. And a blowgun is a pretty even match against a howler. As even as they come."

The animal was beautiful at this close range, with tawny red glistening fur and the same large, black, humanlike face I'd seen through the binoculars. Its shoulders were powerful and its haunches disproportionately small. When the women were called over and a long knife appeared, I turned away. I could accept the hunt, but I didn't want to witness the skinning of this still-warm body.

Kai and I found a shady place to sit out of viewing range on some timber that had already been chopped into long logs.

"This is a rough life," I said.

Kai burst out laughing. "You can say that again."

"This is a rough life."

"Stop, please." He laughed harder, his eyes squeezed shut.

"Not man enough for this life, eh?" I teased.

"Annie, please. I can't stop. Have pity."

"I had the easy job. I dug tubers with my bare hands, scrubbed them in the river with the same tender hands, and lugged them to María's house, trying to keep pace with her. Nothing to it."

"Oh, *Donnerwetter*," he moaned and reached for me and pulled me to him. "I thought I was tough. But that old German is like nothing you've ever seen. He and these men are relentless. Look what we've done in four hours."

Six trees, in addition to the giant one, were lying on their sides. Beyond that was a six-foot-high pile of palm leaves.

"Time to eat, my friends," Häberle called from the seat he'd found for himself beside a small creek that ran by.

The plantains were dry and tasteless, as was the manioc, and the *tepae* was thick, sour, and strong. I tried to forget how it was made as I drank it down. But when it had done its job on me, the food became delicious.

We lay around, sleepy and half-drunk after we'd finished. The Roani women lolled against their men, and María sat rather primly back to back with Häberle. She rolled a pebble around and around in her palm. Mingo sat on a log some distance from us with his chin in his hands, staring out. Awae lay on his back watching the tops of trees through Kai's binoculars.

"Did you live through the war, *mein Freund?*" Häberle said to Kai.

"Yes," Kai said.

Kai was sitting up. I was lying back against the log.

"In Augsburg?"

"*Ja*," Kai answered. "Except when they sent us to the country, during the worst bombings."

"In forty four."

"*Ja*," Kai answered. "And you, *don* Jorge?"

"*Ja*, I was in Poland, not the best place."

"With the army?"

"*Ja ja*, with the army." He cracked a palm stem, piece by piece between his fingers, slowly working his way up the stalk. "I saw boys and girls in Poland playing with dead bodies. I saw them put flowers on dead Russians and make mock funerals. Catholic funerals. I found them standing giggling over a ticking bomb one day. I had to shoo them away, these little children. And they hunted in the ruins for shrapnel. Scavenging. Ordinary children playing with the refuse of war." He snapped the last bit of palm and threw it away. "And you?" He looked at Kai. "Did you play with dead bodies?" His face was gray and slick with perspiration. Deep lines dug in around his mouth.

"No," Kai said in a clear voice. "We played Olympics in the street during the day, and went to bomb shelters at night. But in the day, when we still lived in the city, we too dug in the ruins for shrapnel. We collected the shrapnel like stamps. The blackened pieces were the most valuable. And the complete shells. They could be traded. But the little flattened ones were my favorites. We would spend all day in the ruins looking for them. I had a whole collection." He laughed softly. "We didn't appear to be bothered by any of it, but I think we were. No dead bodies, but bombs aren't the nicest companions for the night. My sister would sleepwalk and when we tried to get her back into the house, when we found her on the street in her bare feet with leaves stuck on them, she just stared at us and didn't move."

Häberle was silent, as was I. I'd never heard Kai speak with such matter-of-fact bleakness.

"You say your family left when they began those last heavy night bombings of our city, son?"

Kai pulled his knees up and wrapped his arms around his legs. "My mother and sisters and I were evacuated to a small farm village. They sent the women and children away." He glanced back at me. "That's where I was when the Americans arrived. I remember how the farmers hung anything white they could find—pillows, sheets, underwear—from their windows to greet the American troops marching through the village. I remember the day clearly. Even as a boy I believe I sensed everyone's relief."

"Ah yes, to be an American soldier on those final days had to be splendid." Häberle smiled wryly. "To be the liberator, on the side of sanctified freedom."

Though I loved that he'd elicited these stories from Kai, the caustic undertone of Häberle's response fed my wariness. He continued to be an enigma for me.

CHAPTER TWENTY-ONE

I was dreaming that Gala and I were on a subway. We sat on one long seat with a tiny white coffin between us. The train rumbled softly, almost comfortingly, and then it became louder. I covered my ears. Even so I heard the din of a hundred calling birds over the racket of the train. Suddenly the birds quieted and the train took over.

Kai sat straight up out of his sleep.

"*Der Bomber*," he said.

I struggled to the surface to find him staring down at me. "We must wake the others," he said in German.

He was answered by a shout from Mingo from inside the house. "*¡Señor, señora!* They are coming back!"

I'd worn my tee shirt to bed, and I grabbed my skirt and slipped it on. I ran into the house carrying my shoes. Kai was already there. Mingo was pulling on his pants.

"Wake *don* Jorge and María. Go!" Mingo shouted at me.

I crossed the room and lifted the blue cloth without knocking. Häberle and María slept soundly, his tanned body curled around her black-brown flesh, his hands cupping her breasts.

I rapped hard on the wall. "*Don* Jorge. *doña* María."

They both sat up directly out of sleep. Her face looked young and open, until she heard the motor. Without saying a word, they reached for their clothes.

I found Mingo and Kai on the porch in front, Kai scanning the sky with his binoculars.

"They changed direction," Kai said, cupping his ear. "Over there." He pointed to our right.

Mingo struck his fist on the railing. "They're going to the settlement. They've found it."

"So I heard." Häberle's voice was thick with sleep as he came up behind us. He was dressed in long pants and a long sleeved, patched, blue shirt. "Then we go there, too," he said in a resigned voice. "We have no choice, my boy.

We had better take medical supplies. They must mean to do harm, coming back a second time and going to the settlement. Well, friends, do you join us and give a hand? *Señor* Kai. *Frau* Schmidt? Do you think you have the stomach for it? I'm afraid you have another little war to contend with." He looked pointedly at Mingo. "Isn't that right, *chico*? Isn't that correct what I say?"

Mingo didn't answer him, but went over to where María was lifting the lids off the benches around the table.

"I'll go," Kai said in a low voice.

"I'll go too," I said.

Kai frowned.

"Kai, if you go, I'll go, and that's that."

Mingo scrutinized us through the open door. He seemed jittery, continually running his hands through his hair. They shook as he buttoned his shirt.

María pulled out day packs from the hollows of the benches. She unzipped one: it contained first aid kits, fire extinguishers, and ancient looking gas masks. Two larger bags were dragged out. Häberle hoisted one on his back. Kai said he was accustomed to carrying heavy packs. Without hesitation, Häberle helped him on with it. Mingo didn't put up an argument, but instead took one of the smaller carriers and with nervous jerky movements put it on and buckled it around his waist. Four of the Indian men from the day before appeared on the porch. Häberle quickly loaded them up, and María and I took what was left.

A few words were exchanged between the Roani and Häberle.

"What is it?" Mingo asked sharply. He was becoming more agitated.

"They say that Awae and the others have gone ahead. The women are remaining here. If there are any problems, the women know how to protect themselves." Häberle's eyes narrowed as he looked at Mingo and he shook his head, his lip curling in disgust, before he walked out to the porch. He seemed a very solitary man as he stood, his back to us, his arm around a supporting pole.

What had he meant, know how to protect themselves? Again I sensed a subterranean current that I couldn't read.

"Good," Mingo said, grimacing. "*Vámonos.* Let's go."

"And Max?" María went out to her husband.

He put his arm over her shoulder. "Don't worry, my love," I heard him say. "Max knows what to do in time of war."

The Indians led the way through the forest, sometimes wielding their machetes when we got close to the river and had to fight through the underbrush. Otherwise it was clear going. As we ran, the plane would periodically circle close to us and then move off. We proceeded, accompanied by its threat, for over an hour. Suddenly it became silent. I was stunned by the change. Where one minute there had been the roar of the plane fading into the distance followed by rising forest noises, now there were no screeching monkeys, no birds, nothing cracking and crackling around us. It was as though we were suspended, not breathing, not touching anything, listening only for the plane's motor. But now that was muted, barely more than an insect's buzz, almost as though it was hanging, waiting, leaving. Then came the whistling. The whining. The explosion.

"Aiiiee!" María called out in front of me as her hands shot skyward.

We stopped. Kai's arm went around my shoulder. Mingo stood to one side, his chest rising and falling. The Indians were like statues, poised, in the green ahead. Another explosion. Another. Another.

"Come," Häberle shouted angrily, beginning to move. "Mingo, *chico.* María. We cannot stand here like babies crying for our mothers. They need us."

We ran even faster, green flying by like water. Time collapsed. But the moment came when I knew we were almost there. I knew by the horrid lung blasting fumes.

Black smoke poured toward us, obliterating our view of trees, blocking out sunlight, burning our eyes, searing soft membranes. Screams consumed what air was left.

"The masks. Everyone get your masks." Häberle put his pack down, knelt, opened it and lifted out World War One gas masks. "Use them yourselves. There are five extra." He started to cough. "Use the extras only on those who are not too burned. Be merciless. Triage. Remember triage."

Then from the swells of smoke, a shrieking child emerged covered with flames. I gagged and choked from the smell of him as he passed. I started after him. Someone grabbed me back. It was María.

She lifted her mask. "Don't go, *señora*. Put your mask on. The child is going to die. Too much fire. His body is too small."

Gagging, I bent forward. Nothing came out, only dry heaves. This time Mingo and Kai came to me.

"Annie," Kai said. "Annie."

"Calm yourself, *señora*," Mingo ordered.

"Don't get sick, *chica*," María said in a harsh voice. "We have no time for your sickness. Your mask, *chica*. Your mask is what is needed."

I knelt down, opened my bag, and attached the mask over my face.

I looked up at Kai. His blue eyes stared at me in horror through the glass covered circles protecting them.

The entire settlement was only one hundred by one hundred meters, with some thirty people living there. Four extended families, Häberle told us. We couldn't enter the clearing because the smoke was too thick. It spilled out, black and toxic, pushing us back. We could only skirt the edges, hoping to find those who ran out, on fire and screaming. I got to a woman first. Her hair was one long flame, shooting up red and white into the air. The stench of burning flesh and hair penetrated my mask. I ran after her, spraying the dry substance from the extinguisher onto her hair, onto her back where the hair stuck and burned into her skin. Onto her legs where the hair fell burning. She threw herself to the ground and rolled in the soil. "Arrrh, arrrh," she screamed. I tried to tell her not to roll, that I would spray her, but I couldn't be heard through the mask. I was afraid to remove it. Häberle had said it was too dangerous. She finally stopped and just lay there. Her eyes were wide-open, staring. Her hair had been burned completely off, leaving black charred skin over her head. She was still breathing so I put an extra mask over her face. Her eyes stared at me as Kai's had. But hers were black and beyond fear.

Another woman ran toward us. She was moving around the outside of the fire zone. She ran holding her arm high like a torch. She screamed warning. She fell a few feet from me. I ripped off my mask. I yelled, "Don't put your arm in the soil. I'm coming." But I realized she had no idea what I was saying. I felt the fumes enter my mouth, my throat, my lungs. A tearing burning. I was going to die. I put the mask back on. It felt as though I were going to suffocate. Again I saw the woman with the burning arm. It was flaming. Even rubbing it in earth hadn't helped. She made a horrifying, hoarse, braying sound. I crawled over, aiming at her with the extinguisher. She moved her arm away. I climbed on top of her and pinned her to the ground. She bucked me. She was strong. I smelled her burning flesh. I grabbed her upper arm with one hand, trying to keep out of the way of the flailing, burning part. I aimed the extinguisher with one hand. I succeeded this time. I sprayed and sprayed as she tried to buck me off. She hit me in the breast. I sprayed until the fire went out.

The smoke was subsiding so I tried to enter the clearing, but it was covered with a slick coating of black oil. I slipped and fell, my hands catching me. My flesh burned where the oil touched me. I tried frantically to wipe the lethal slime off.

"Annie." It was Kai. "Come out. Don't stay in there."

"Help me." I cried. My voice emerged all muffled inside the mask. But he grabbed me, yanking me to my feet, half-carrying me out of the slime. I cried, feeling his body next to mine. I cried as he wiped at my hands with the tail of his shirt. I could hear him repeating, "I have to get this off. I have to get this off."

A huge explosion threw us apart and onto the ground. It was followed by the pounding of smaller detonations reverberating under the surface of the earth, and a roar of fire. Smoke rose again, this time with a yellowish tinge, and smelling of sulfur, reminding me of the acid yellow of Kai's nightmare skies. "Don't cry, sweetie," I crooned, scrambling over like a land crab to cradle him.

He lifted his mask. His face was a pink circle outlined with encrusted black soot. "I'm okay, Annie. Let's take care of your hands and then get back to the others."

I soon forgot the pain of my hands as we spent the next hour spraying our extinguishers on the shrieking people. The easiest ones to put out were those who were furthest gone. They didn't run. They just lay writhing on the ground, their skin peeling like cellophane off a pack of cigarettes. Like the bark of a birch tree in spring. Like dying leaves.

We fashioned stretchers out of chonta palm leaves and lianas and branches. We all worked: Häberle and María and Mingo and Kai and I and the four Indian men who'd come with us and three others including Awae and five other Indian adults from this settlement who hadn't been burned or were burned only slightly. I teamed up with an Indian man, and he and I twined the vines around the branches. He had the usual stocky body, short strong arms and legs, and thick black short hair. His penis hung long and thin between his legs. His face and arms were painted with dashes and darts. Communicating with our movements, we concentrated only on saving as many lives as we could.

When we had finished the stretchers, we lifted the wailing people onto them. We held them by parts of their bodies that were not charred or blistering. Their burned skin bled. What hair was left on their heads was in tiny islands. The smell of them was unbearable, foul, more as though they'd rotted than burned.

While we were putting out the burning flesh, others had been getting water from the river and extinguishing the brush fires. But the screams continued. The weeping and wailing. There was no extinguishing that. Mercifully, one of the communal houses had been saved. It was twenty feet long, with open sides and a thatched roof. It was the cooking house and worked well as the hospital. There was a fireplace in the center to boil water. There were hooks to hang the intravenous glucose bags that Häberle and Kai had carried in their large packs. As best we could, we transferred the people once again to gauze covered mats. Though when we picked them up off the stretchers, much of their skin remained stuck to the palm leaves.

Sometimes I worked beside Kai. I was impressed with how brave he was. He never faltered. He carried when he had to carry. He comforted when he could. I saw him, at one point, kiss a wailing man on the forehead. The man's piercing screams subsided for a moment, but then he began again.

There were ten people in the hospital, four children, four men and two women. Two of the children and one of the men were burned over eighty per cent of their bodies. That's what Häberle said. He said that there was nothing we could do for them. They would be dead soon. "No medicine can save these children. Not even a miracle."

A young woman was writhing on the stretcher to which she was bound with strips of bandages. She had a wet bandanna across her nose and mouth. She must have been seventeen, no more. Even in her agony she didn't look older. Another woman, who also wore a cloth mask, was sitting beside her applying mud packs to her arm. Steam rose from the pack each time it was applied. The mud went on wet and sloppy and in minutes it was dry and smoking.

Mingo saw me looking and came over. In a low voice, he said, "It's white phosphorus. When it explodes, the shrapnel goes deep inside the skin. It makes a flame that can't be put out. It burns and burns. That's why it dries the mud. I've seen it burn for days in a person's body." I stared at him in disbelief. He brushed his hand across my lips. "The woman wears a mask not to be poisoned by the fumes.

Here are your killing fumes. It's better if you don't stand too near." He led me away.

The others had less serious burns, if you call an entire back not so serious. Or both legs. Or an arm. They looked as though they had been spattered with fire. Brown leathery spots and translucent areas of various sizes were beginning to form on their skin. "Napalm," Häberle said. "The gasoline jelly splatters when the bomb explodes and attaches to the flesh."

Once we got them inside under the roof, out of the sun, resting on sterilized gauze with liquids dripping into them, Häberle said there wasn't much more we could do. We couldn't pick the dirt out. We had very little antibiotic medicine. He had had a small supply of morphine in the packs, but he had used it up in one set of dosages. "The women are gathering pain-killing herbs, a forest remedy that works moderately well," he said.

We left Awae and the woman who applied the mud packs to watch over the patients. The rest of us walked a hundred feet back behind the longhouse to sit under living trees, waiting for the less injured Indians from the settlement to join us. A woman with both arms bandaged suckled a seven-year-old boy, a child who hadn't been breast-fed in years. A mother who presumably had no milk but could still give the comfort of her breast. She rocked back and forth, humming tunelessly. A white-haired woman cradled a young girl, who might have been ten, against her wizened, flat, hanging breasts, rocking and intoning as the other woman did. With her free hand, the old woman hit against the protruding bones of her chest. The children whimpered, and some babies, too, even with breasts in their mouths, sobbed and curled in closer, their fingers in tight little fists.

I sat with my back against a tree, with my legs straight out in front of me. The Indian men hunkered down, their long penises touching the ground. Their flat, brown faces were smeared with dirt and blood and carbon soot. Häberle was stripped again to his bikini. Only Mingo and María and I were fully dressed, Mingo in a once-yellow tee shirt that was now smeared black. María's black mourning dress was torn, burned and gray with ash dust. She'd lost her headscarf. Her face was streaked, as all of ours were, with tears, sweat, and filth. Kai was without a shirt. His full length pants had been torn off above the knees. He looked so skinny to me. He must have lost ten pounds in the past three days. The bones of his upper chest stuck out like those of the old woman.

I examined my hands. The palm of my right hand was swollen and beginning to blister. I had trouble closing it, but curiously it hardly hurt. My nails were broken and encrusted with black. The skin on the backs of my hands was dark-brown. They looked old and tired, the way I felt.

Häberle squatted on his haunches as the Indian men did, with his elbows on his knees. He clasped his hands and looked down on them in the same way I'd been looking at mine. After a few minutes he spoke.

"We need more medical supplies if these people are to live," he said in a slow, deliberate Spanish. A man named Kemonka from Häberle and María's settlement was designated to translate into the language of these Indians. Häberle waited as the staccato, nasal sounds were passed on. Cries from the hospital punctuated the man's words. A look of pain crossed over Häberle's face. "This immediate treatment is surprisingly not that important, but after twenty-four hours it's essential we have more antibiotic ointment or infections will develop. Someone must go to the Church of Jesus Christ missionaries downriver." The man translated. I watched the other Indians. Their faces didn't change expression. Nothing. No reaction. "It won't be easy." He spoke with controlled rage.

Mingo broke in before Kemonka could begin his next translation. "It's not worth it!" he yelled. "They'll do nothing. Only make more trouble. This is what they're waiting for."

"*Señor*," Häberle shouted back at him. "We have no choice. These people will die if someone doesn't go. I can't. That man of God won't speak to me. He won't have me on his property. You must."

"It's the same for me," Mingo said, his face turned sullen.

"*Señor.*" Häberle once again employed his controlled voice. "They have to help if they are to continue calling themselves Christians. That must be communicated to him."

"You know they won't listen to me. I'm the Jívaro boy who carries them down the river. When they learn what I need the medicine for, they'll put the two of us together. The Jívaro is the messenger boy of the German, they'll say. Pssshh." He let his hand trail through the air like a bomb's arc.

"Then take someone with you who will shame them into action." Häberle looked at me. "*Señora* Schmidt, you speak both languages. These people are North Americans. They hardly speak Spanish, only the indigenous tongues, to better convert the heathens." He stopped. He regained his composure. "If your husband will allow it, I would ask you to accompany Mingo to the missionaries and work your female American charms to convince them that we need their humanitarian aid." He looked to Kai for an answer.

Kai said in German, "Annie answers for herself." And then to me, "What do you say, Annie? Do you think you can?"

Everyone was watching me.

"If there's a problem with these people, I believe I can make them understand," I said to Häberle. At least I hope so, I thought. Back before the trouble in the *barrio*, I wouldn't have had any inner doubts. I would have believed completely in my power to succeed, would have felt the exhilaration of my omnipotence. But it wasn't the same today. Today, I only hoped I wouldn't fail.

Chapter Twenty-Two

We were to travel back to Häberle's settlement by way of the stream. It was a little longer, but we needed the respite of its coolness and the possibility of drinking water. One of the Roani men accompanied us. He was to explain to the women what had happened and to return with one of them with enough food for everyone. All the others remained to care for people, especially in case of another attack.

Before we left, Kai took me aside and said, "Try not to confuse the past with the present. Leave that behind, okay? Remember who you are, how strong you are. Remember how brave you were today. Go take care of us, okay?"

I kissed him, thinking, how strange it is that we tell others what we most want to hear ourselves.

As I walked behind the Roani and Mingo, I thought about the bombs and the black smoke, and the crying that never let up. Why would anyone ever, ever do such a thing? What could ever bring them to harm these people? Did we all have such a propensity for evil in us? What must it feel like to be on fire, I wondered, or to have the white phosphorus endlessly burning under your skin, to see smoke rising from your own arm.

I fell to my knees on the bank of the river and began to heave. The vomit came out as water and slime. I continued to vomit even though I had almost nothing in me. I retched and heaved, my whole body rising and falling with the violence of it. When it stopped, I tried to stand but almost blacked out. I crawled away, up the bank. Mingo's scuffed and damaged shoes were beside me, following my route.

"What can I do," he asked softly.

"I can't stand."

"Then lie down and rest."

"I can't lie down. I can't move."

I stayed on my hands and knees, like an animal, ashamed but beyond shame, for a long, long time. When I could lift my head without feeling as though gravity were pulling my body into the center of the earth, I sat up. It surprised me that there was such peace about us. The sun filtered through the rubber plants and palms and fig trees. The Roani man sat on his haunches twenty feet away, staring into the river. Small birds fluttered from branch to branch. A hummingbird hung over a long red tubular flower, its beak deep inside finding the nectar, its wings a whirring blur. The stream whispered by. I looked up and was startled to see Angel Castro's body looming over me like a lover's, Angel's serious face staring down at me. Then I heard Kai's voice, 'don't mix the past with the present.' But I wanted it to be Angel, wanted to be his lover, wanted him to take me in his arms and tell me where he'd been, tell me that I'd redeemed myself with how brave I was today.

"Can you rise, señora?" Mingo asked. "If you are able to, I can take you back and I'll go alone."

"No." I stood. I felt weak but I knew I could go on. "I'll be fine now. The poison is out."

He put his hand on my shoulder. He looked closely into my face. He wasn't Angel Castro but he had a nice face. It carried no aura of memory.

"We'll do what we can then," he said. "But we must get going."

We reached the Häberle settlement in under an hour and stood in front of the long house while the Roani conveyed what had happened. He made hand movements that indicated he was speaking of women and children, showing how high the children stood, or how many babies there were. The women who listened held their children either in their arms nursing, or called them near, the little ones resisting, laughing, running off. The women nodded stoically, revealing no look of special sadness or concern on their broad, brown, already somber faces.

We sat on the ground in a lean-to whose haphazard construction spoke to its having being thrown together that morning to serve as a temporary cookhouse. The women gave us a thin soup with manioc and some mild *tepae* to drink. When we'd finished, one of the women who had inspected me the day before brought fried fish on wooden dishes, which we ate with our fingers.

An older woman pantomimed that we must be careful with the bones. She made a picking motion with her thick brown fingers. She choked and grabbed her throat. The other women standing by, nodded gravely. She was right to be careful. The fish was a form of carp and full of the tiniest slivers. As Kai would say, it was a fish that lacked organization.

Mingo finished and pushed his plate aside. He stood. "The time is going," he said. I noted the same agitation he'd shown this morning. The same undercurrent of anger.

We reached the Napo by late afternoon. I was glad we'd eaten even though it had taken precious time. It had given me strength on the trail. The dugout was where we had left it two days before. It seemed impossible that it had only been two days since we arrived. Mingo untied the boat and we pushed it into the water, up to our calves in muddy silt. I climbed in first, steadying myself in the center of the boat. He followed. He paddled out into the river before he pulled the motor string, and we started traveling at full speed farther into the interior.

I had a few moments of imagining that the airplane would return and strafe our tiny dugout. But then the beauty transported me out of fear. The sun was behind us now, transforming the water into a hundred greens and golds. The sky was a flat blue to the east, directly before us, with sulfur yellow and white and copper clouds. We stayed close to the shore on our right side. The air lacked the heaviness of two days before. A breeze came up and sprinkled water over my face and arms. I leaned over the side and let my hands trail in the water. It was only then that I realized how painful the burns had become.

After a while I could feel Mingo watching me. I thought of what we'd been through: death, terror, and tremendous physical work. It was more than what Angel Castro and I had experienced together, climbing the hill, convincing people to come to meetings, feeling such pride when the community responded. I felt Angel's finger run down the side of my face. "I'll work with you," he'd said. "If there's anything to be gained, I want to use it." I saw him leave the apartment. I saw him disappear over the wall.

I turned to look at Mingo. Our eyes met and held. I wished I had resisted my desire to look at him. And yet, I don't think I could have. His face told of the same intense yearning that reverberated through me.

He smiled and spoke softly. "Perhaps you should lie down in the boat and sleep."

"But what if you need me?" I spoke softly, too. It's a wonder we could hear each other across the length of the boat. Over the noise of the motor.

"I can wake you if I need you."

He reached under his bench and pulled out an old blanket.

"To make you comfortable. Here." He tossed it to me.

I bundled it into a pillow. When I put my head down on it, I smelled the gasoline. The fabric scratched my cheek as I self-consciously stretched my body out along the floor of the boat. My bare feet were so close to Mingo's that if I let myself slide a little farther down, I could accidentally touch his. It took every power in me not to do that, not to sit up and say, Mingo, I need you right now. It won't matter. No one will know.

I made myself avoid his eyes, made myself stare up into the blue sky and the few amethyst clouds moving across. I told myself that this was all about the past. But, even though the motor hummed, it wasn't louder than the blood in my ears. I didn't sleep.

It was black night when we arrived at our destination. The moon wasn't yet up and only the trillions of stars above gave off any illumination. I was the first to see the light of the settlement on the right bank. It was a tiny blur of white in the distance. Mingo aimed toward the shore and cut the motor by half. The silence of the night rose up around us.

"*Hola, hola.*" We heard the call come across the water. "Over this way. Over here we have a dock."

"The flashlight, *señora*, here."

I took the flashlight from Mingo and shone the beam around on the shore until I found the man who had called. He was pointing to his left. I moved the light, and it landed on the rickety pier that jutted into the water.

This is it, I told myself. You'd better know what you're doing.

As Mingo pulled up beside the pier, the man was already there. He reached for the rope I threw to him and tied it to a post.

"*Buenas noches.*" I could hear the flatness of his American accent. He took my elbow and guided me onto the shaky cane walkway.

"*Buenas noches,*" I answered, putting the light to my face and then pointing it toward Mingo so the man could see who he was talking to.

"*¿Habla inglés?*" he asked.

"Yes, I speak English."

"Oh, good, good. You sound like an American. Is that so?"

"I am," I said. "Mingo Mincha is from here."

"I know Mingo. Isn't that so, Mingo. *Nos conocemos, no?*"

"*Sí, señor.*" Mingo climbed out of the boat and stood a little way from us.

I wanted to ask Mingo to come closer. To help me by just standing near.

"Nice lad," the man said.

I let my light pass over him as though by accident as I bent to slip my shoes on, wanting to see what kind of man would say "nice lad" about Mingo. He was near sixty.

Brown thinning hair. Bermuda shorts. Plaid. A paunch. Skinny legs.

"I heard your motor. For about fifteen minutes we heard you coming," the man laughed. "I said to my wife, 'I think we've got more visitors. This place is getting like Grand Central Station.' We go six months with nobody but our beloved Indians and then we get descended upon, literally. Nice to have you. Ted Albertson here." He grabbed my hand. I almost cried out from the pain when he squeezed.

At the same time a spasm of fear went through me. What had he meant about being descended upon? Had the friar come looking? Were the visitors the people who'd done the bombing?

"Annie Schmidt," I said. "I'm sorry, are there others here? I don't want to be a bother. We aren't planning to stay."

"Oh, no, no—only one person is left. We have plenty of room. He's already retired for the night. Come along. You must be starving. Please don't take my remarks as being inhospitable. Just disuse of civilized interchange." He laughed again. "I want you to meet my wife."

We followed Ted Albertson up a steep bank. Steps had been carved into the earth. He rattled on in English as we made our way.

I fell back a bit. He didn't seem to need any response to his chatter. I spoke to Mingo in a low whisper, telling him what the man had said about the guests.

"¿Quién? Did he tell you who?" Mingo said, clearly upset.

"No, he said only one man remains."

"Find out who."

"I'll try."

"Come along, children." The man was standing just above us. He reached out his hand.

I avoided giving him my injured hand. The pain was now radiating up my right arm.

There was a loud humming coming from behind the house he was leading us toward.

"It's the generator for our hospital," the man said.

"Yes, I heard you have a hospital here."

"From whom, may I ask?" His voice rose in pleasure, as though he were famous someplace and spoken of.

"*Don* Jorge, the German." I decided only as I said his name that my strategy would be one of forthrightness. It would be too hard to invent and to keep a subterfuge going. I only hoped that he would honor a request from another American. I would have to emphasize that fact if it got difficult.

"Oh," he paused. The oh had come out of him with far less joy than the question. "You've met George Häberle already."

We were at the house. It was brightly lit with the flickering whiteness of Coleman lamps. Around the porch were tall hibiscus bushes. Large red flowers hung over the stairs, their tongues reaching out as though to lick us as we passed. I thought of the flames devouring everything in sight, full trees, human flesh, communal homes.

"Yes," I said, beginning to weigh each word. "It's George Häberle who has sent us."

"Oh my." The man sighed.

The room inside was so bright from the lamps that I had to squint as we entered. The place was spotless, with shining hardwood floors. The furniture looked as though it had come from a Sears and Roebuck catalogue, with its blond wooden chair arms and a rural American scene on the slipcovers. I checked my right hand. It was twice the size of my left and red and peeling.

A woman entered through a door at the back of the room. She had white hair pulled away from her tanned round face. She was handsome in a refined New England way. Her light-blue seersucker dress accentuated the dark-blue of her eyes. Her smile, on seeing us, turned to alarm.

"This is my wife, Sally Albertson. Sally, Anne Schmidt, and Mingo, the lad with the dugout. They come from George Häberle, they say." He looked toward me and seemed to see me for the first time. "Oh, my, will you look at the two of you. Whatever has happened?"

In the bright light I saw that Mingo's clothes were ripped and caked with soot and mud. He'd washed his face, but the grime remained around his hairline and in all the crevices of his ears and nose. He appeared so small, so poor, so not belonging in this room. I looked down at my skirt and blouse. I was filthy.

"And your hand, dear?" Sally Albertson took my hand in hers, turning it palm up.

"It's not as bad as it looks. It's stiff, but it hardly hurts," I lied.

"My lord. Look at this, Ted."

Mingo put out his hand to mine and then as though realizing how such familiarity would look to these people, he let his drop.

"*No me duele tanto,*" I said to Mingo. It doesn't hurt too much. I felt an intense intimacy with him in that moment. Whether it was his gesture, or the sense of us against them, I don't know. But it made me feel both stronger and, at the same time, in need of help for what I had to accomplish.

"*A mí me parece que sí,*" Mingo said. To me it seems that it does.

"This is nothing compared to what has happened to the tribe out behind *don* Jorge's, George's settlement," I said to the Albertsons. "They've been bombed from the air, this morning, to devastating effect. Incendiary bombs, white phosphorus tracers, and napalm. My husband is a chemist and he confirms the latter."

Ted Albertson shook his head as he walked over to one of the chairs with the rural American design. "Please sit down, both of you." He directed us to the sofa.

"We're filthy," I said.

"Sit." Sally Albertson said. "After what you've been through." To her husband she said, "I'm going to get Alice. She must take a look at this girl's hand." She walked briskly out the door to the porch.

Mingo and I sat on the soft cushions of the sofa as directed. Ted Albertson was opposite us. His face was a mixture of sympathy and disdainful irritation. No doubt about the latter.

"Go on with your story, Miss Schmidt. I will attempt to listen with an open mind, though I will have to say from the outset that...no, no, just proceed. Please."

I told him about the fire bombing two days before, when we had arrived at *don* Jorge's and María's settlement, and how we'd spent the next day repairing the damage, and then how we'd wakened the following morning to the sound of the plane once again. From there, I described in as stark terms as I could what we had experienced, what people had suffered, how my injury had come from slipping in the oily residue from the bombs. That, I said, and Häberle's showing us how it splattered and clung to human flesh had convinced my husband it was napalm. At this point, Ted Albertson asked me not to go into such graphic detail.

"I have enough of an imagination, Miss Schmidt. I believe I can extrapolate from what you're saying. I'm afraid I may be less of a person than you are when it comes to witnessing suffering, of course that is if all that you say is true."

This last hung in the air, transforming my horror at the events I'd recounted to a sudden rage. But no, I said to myself. No. Righteous anger will not help. You don't care if this man believes you. All you want from him is the medicine.

Sally Albertson returned with a young woman who was a cross between the two of them with Sally's deep blue eyes and patrician carriage and Ted Albertson's pale rounded features. She was introduced by Sally Albertson as their daughter, Alice.

"Do go on, Miss Schmidt," Sally said, sounding kind. "Don't let us interrupt what you were telling Ted."

Alice sat down in the companion chair to her father's. Sally remained standing just behind her.

"One woman had white phosphorus embedded in her arm," I continued, determined to give one more try at making Ted Albertson absorb the brutality of what we'd been through. "We kept putting mud packs on the wound, but it continued to burn and was so hot it dried the mud instantly."

"Please, Miss Schmidt." He fluttered his hand. "This is becoming preposterous. I feel as though this is some rude game you're playing with us, something dreamed up by George Häberle to support his great cause."

"But it's true," I said, working to keep hysteria at bay. "I had to use a fire extinguisher to put out burning flesh. I don't lie, Mr. Albertson. I'm here on a vacation. A honeymoon, to be exact. I don't get satisfaction from this."

I began to cry. Quietly, but there was no denying I was crying. Why was I letting this happen? I couldn't look at anyone. I sat with my head down so no one could see my mouth quiver, breathing deeply, telling myself that I had to stop. We remained in silence for some time. Then the younger woman spoke.

"My father has some disagreement with Mr. Häberle, Miss Schmidt." She spoke in high reedy, constricted tones. "But it doesn't mean we're not going to help. Does it, Daddy?"

"No, it doesn't mean that at all," Ted Albertson said, sounding tired and defeated. "Alice is right. Of course we'll help you. You seem a nice young woman, not a prevaricator. I apologize for impugning your honesty. It's simply that this is not an issue of today or yesterday. I don't know what Häberle thinks he is doing. He has aggravated a situation that he should have left well enough alone. He has so provoked those in charge that it seems—and I can only take what you say on faith—that a war is being waged against defenseless people, and it's on his conscience. He will have God to answer to for this."

"Daddy!"

"I mean it, Alice. I've reached my limit. I'm furious with this man, this demagogue. He's probably told you that it's the oil company, Somaxo. Has he?"

"There's been mention of it," I said, my voice sticking in my throat. "But I'm not certain if it came from him or others." I knew I had to remain evasive. I couldn't confront him directly with a political argument. I also was beginning to feel slightly shaky. What if this man were correct and Häberle really had exacerbated the situation?

I glanced at Mingo. I wished I could tell him what was being said. He could assuage the doubts forming in my mind.

"Of course it came from him. Who else could come up with such rubbish, this lad here?" He gestured toward Mingo. "Unless George has indoctrinated him as well. No, of course it's not the oil company. The Americans would never operate in such a manner. This is an internal affair. If there are any atrocities, they are carried out by the government here. I'm not making apologies for this government, God knows, but I believe they've been driven to whatever methods they're employing by this new acquaintance of yours, the great *don* Jorge. At a crucial time he refused to pull back, to accommodate differences of opinion. As guests in these sorts of countries, one must always compromise. It is arrogant, foolish, and dangerous to do otherwise. And certainly not God's will."

Sally Albertson's expression was indecipherable, but her daughter's was not. She was furious. Alice clearly disagreed with her father.

"*Yo he dicho a don Jorge que esto no valdría la pena,*" Mingo said, furious now.

"Tell the lad that we're going to help, even though I disagree."

"He said he's going to help," I said to Mingo. "We will get what we came here for." As before, Mingo seemed dwarfed in this room, half the person he'd been on the river, in the forest. Had I been deluded by him, by Häberle, by María? Had I been taken in by the adventurousness of their lives? Had I mistakenly imagined them to be humanitarians? But no, I had seen what I'd seen. No matter that Häberle could be somewhat at fault, it never, ever excused what had been done to those people. Kai was a witness too.

"I hope so, *señora*. I hope we aren't being fooled," Mingo said.

"Tell him I am not fooling him," Ted Albertson said. "I will do what has to be done. I'm a man of God and an American after all."

I remembered our last man of God and decided not to translate that for Mingo. Also, I thought, if you understand so well, Mr. Albertson, Mr. High and Mighty, American man of God, why don't you tell him yourself?

"He knows that, Mr. Albertson. And Mingo has a high regard for you. You'll have to excuse us though—we're terribly concerned about getting back tonight. There are people who are critically injured. They may not survive, but we have to try."

"Father, I can get to work right now," Alice said in a civil voice that belied the transparent anger I'd seen.

"I'll do it, Alice. I said I'd do it. But Miss Schmidt might also wish to know how serious this is. This country desperately needs the revenues from oil production for education, health care, everything. We were working things out peaceably with the indigenous people of this region. But he had to draw battle lines. He had to have perfection. His Third Reich wasn't enough for him. No, he had to come here and make a ruinous mess, another holocaust from what you tell me. You may not be aware of what is said about him, his past acts, I mean. I hear he purports to be a pacifist. Strange for a man who has brought another racial war upon an innocent people. I'm sorry. Excuse me. I shouldn't talk like this. I should keep my opinions to myself. Vile rumors have no place in this God-fearing home." He leaned toward me, his rather pallid face now in a high flush from his outburst. His rounded features battling for control. "You have to understand, Miss

Schmidt. I am as distressed as you are about this. I may sound pompous, but I am truly a man of conscience. This is a sad and terrible situation. I love these gentle people. If you'll pardon me, Miss Schmidt, I don't think you understand this country. I don't think you understand who runs it and how it's run, and that we are only here bringing light to these people because of the willingness of the folks in charge to let us be here. George Häberle is making it increasingly difficult for us to do our work."

"I do know this country somewhat, Mr. Albertson. I spent two years here as a Peace Corps volunteer. I know fairly well who runs this country, and I know what happens when a person provokes them."

This stopped him. He stared at me as though reminded of something. He went over to a sideboard behind where his daughter sat and wife stood. As he took a pipe from a holder, Alice met my eye, telling me to hold on for a few minutes. Ted Albertson walked back into the center of the room, rummaging in the pockets of his Bermuda shorts. He found the lighter he was searching for, found the packet of tobacco, poured some in, tamped it down with the bottom of the lighter, and lit the pipe. I could feel Mingo straining beside me, though he didn't actually move a muscle. But I knew he was impatient, as I was, to get our medical supplies and move out of there. Had I somehow said something wrong? Had I made Albertson think twice? Had someone told him about me? That couldn't be, not out here, unless of course he had a short-wave radio. I waited.

"Well, then," he said finally. "I'm very pleased. I've had generally good relations with the Peace Corps. So, Alice. You're certain you can do this at this late hour?"

"Yes," she said, standing. She smiled at me and Mingo. "I believe I can, especially if you're willing to help," she said to us.

Chapter Twenty-Three

Alice spoke first in fluent Spanish with Mingo, and then in fluent Quichua. She didn't wear a wedding ring and she appeared to be at least thirty. It had to be a lonely existence out here with her parents. Even pitying her I felt some jealousy watching the two of them talking with great animation as they left the house for the dispensary. But I was too tired and agitated to bother about their incipient flirtation. I was relieved when Sally Albertson offered me use of the bathroom.

"Please feel free to use our shower," Sally said, leading me into a screened-in kitchen. I was shocked by what I saw. The room I stood in was uncannily reminiscent of the rudimentary kitchen in our apartment in Winooski where my mother had hanged herself. From the simple plumbing fixtures to the linoleum floor and the waist-high unpainted wainscoting. There was even an old wringer washing machine standing in the corner, fired by a gas motor, just like the one my mother had used for her last load of laundry. I spun around, certain I smelled Borax soap.

"Miss Schmidt, is something wrong? There are towels in the bathroom," Sally said.

"No, I'm sorry, I was just reminded of something. It's nothing, really." Once again, the past was colliding with the present.

The bathroom was off the kitchen and contained a toilet with a bucket for flushing and a wooden sink backed by a large polished stainless-steel mirror. Closing the door behind me, I leaned against the cool wall. On a night in winter when I'd come home from college for semester break, my father and I had sat at the kitchen table. We'd taken to staying up nights talking and getting drunk while he lectured me on organizing techniques, testing my agility in political discussions. That night, his eyes reddened and his speech slurred, he stopped mid-sentence and ruffled his hand through his thinning hair. "We've never spoken of your mother's death," he said. "Leah..." His voice broke on her name, and he began to cry.

"Daddy." I put my hand over his, surprised at how soft and vulnerable his flesh was. I told him he didn't have to continue, but he insisted, the tears streaming down his cheeks.

He said he hadn't seen her, had decided he couldn't bear to view her dead, to see how she had suffered in the last throes of life. He wept silently for some time and then, looking at me with his oak-brown eyes, he said, "I always worried about you without a mother. I worried too about your feelings of being Jewish and my never doing anything about it. I always wondered if it was a problem for you."

"Oh, Daddy, no. It's not a problem for me, I promise," I lied.

He stared at me intently.

I met his penetrating gaze.

"Thank God for that," he said. "At least I don't have that on my conscience." Then he went on to explain in theoretical terms how they had decided to renounce all religion when they'd married, because they were atheists and because they didn't want it to be a rift between them. His explanation felt both well-thought-out and foolish and unbearably boring in his recitation.

But didn't he understand that those principled stands of his were what destroyed her, I thought now, pleading silently to the corrugated tin ceiling and beyond. How could she disagree with the perfect man? How could she express personal pain and fury to a man who was making sacrifices for his beliefs, even going to prison for them, but at the same time refusing to fight the enemy who slaughtered her own people? How could she contain such anger without it eventually hurting someone? "What did you expect of her?" I whispered aloud, looking down at my filthy skirt, my scraped legs. I had to smile. How difficult it continued to be to face the pain of my mother's life. Even after her death, he had found it easier to struggle in the outside world than to acknowledge the suffering inside his own four walls.

To bend Mingo's phrase, I thought, harmful deeds come in many disguises.

The shower was out-of-doors, behind the house. It seemed too great an effort and too frightening to step out alone into the night. I settled for removing my blouse and scrubbing down at the sink.

I dried myself before the stainless-steel mirror, barely able to recognize the skinny, burned, too-serious person reflected back. Whoever this person was, though, she had not failed this time. She had done the job asked of her. She was not her mother; she was not her father.

Standing there with a newfound clarity of vision, I wondered whether Georg Häberle suffered from the same ailment I did. Maybe he confused the past with the present and was luring another people into a holocaust, trying in some twisted way to undo the crimes the Nazis had committed—crimes that he had perpetrated, or his brother had. In his role as pacifist, was he unconsciously allowing people to be critically harmed so he could play the hero to himself, each time rescuing them from the fire? Or the most frightening possibility: did he unconsciously want to reenact the war by bringing these people to final harm? After all, we still didn't know what Georg Häberle had done during the war in Europe.

I let the water into the sink and scrubbed my face again.

As I walked through the kitchen into the living room, I heard men's voices. I stopped. It was undeniable whose voice it was. Even speaking in a barely accented English.

I stood at the door looking in on the friar, in his dirty robes, and Ted Albertson, facing one another. The friar caught sight of me in his peripheral vision.

"*Señorita*, so we meet again." He spoke in English.

"Yes," I said. "So we do."

"I hear you know each other," Ted Albertson said, sounding affable. He didn't seem to grasp the animosity passing in both directions between the friar and me.

"Yes. We met in Puerto Napo," I said.

"A very pleasant evening, as I recall." Roberto Báez Chamino now grinned.

"Yes," I said. "Quite pleasant." I began to walk toward the front door. I wanted only to be out of there. I was very frightened. I didn't want any dealings with this man who now spoke the king's English. I felt unprotected, at his mercy, in need of Mingo at the very least.

"I think we should talk, *Señora* Schmidt—if you don't mind, Ted. It's a little business we have to take care of."

"I don't want to," I said, continuing to walk, now terrified.

"*De veras, señora, no voy a hacerle daño. Siempre se puede gritar. ¡Socorro!*" He laughed in the same manner that he had in Puerto Napo and his settlement, immediately transforming himself into the buffoonish simple friar. He had said he wasn't going to hurt me, that I could always yell for help.

I realized he was right. I weighed the possibilities and quickly decided it was better to talk with him than to make a scene. Better than running out of here.

"Are you all right, Miss Schmidt?" Ted Albertson asked. "I don't think there's any problem with Roberto here. I've known him for years. He's spent hours alone with my wife and daughter. He's an honorable man. He's from Chile. Really quite an honorable man." He nodded to Roberto Báez. "Yes?" he asked me.

"Yes," I said.

"Please make yourselves comfortable," Ted Albertson said. "I'll go find Alice and the boy." He left through the porch door.

"Sit, *señorita*, sit." Roberto Báez maintained his jovial, friar like manner.

"Cut it out," I said.

"*Señorita?*"

"Just be yourself and tell me what you want of me."

"Will you sit?" He became serious. Somehow the friar's outfit suited him better when he wasn't being silly. Perhaps he really was a man of the cloth. But a very dirty cloth, both physically and metaphorically.

"No, I'd rather stand."

"In that case, we can begin. I won't beat around the bush as you Americans like to say." His accent became fainter as he continued. I began to hear the distinct sound of someone trained in the United States. The flattened a's, the swallowed r's. Fernando Calderón had spoken in the same way, and he had gone to school in Miami.

"Do you know anything more about your friend Mingo Mincha than when we last met?"

I shook my head.

"Do you know what he really trades back here?" He walked around so that he was facing me. I'd turned away slightly so as to not have to look at him.

I forced my eyes to meet his. "In shaman darts, of course. As you told me. I had a talk with him about it. He told me it was necessary and that he had been schooled in some of the shaman duties and that he was blessed by the shamans of his community to do the trading. A special dispensation, you might call it." Contempt for this man fueled my words, my imagination.

"You're lying, *señorita*." Even with his unruly beard, I could see his mouth was tight. His pale gray-blue eyes like steel in a white light.

"*You* lied, *señor* friar."

"Aha!" He threw his head back and let out a forced laugh. Just as abruptly all remnant of laughter disappeared. "I did it for your own good, Miss Saunders. To protect you, to try to get you out of here before you found yourself in a good deal of trouble. Your friend deals in guns, Miss Saunders, munitions. He's arming the Indians to fight the exploration of oil, to fight any peaceful accommodation."

With a jolt of recognition, I thought of the explosion at the bombing site. The huge explosion and the smaller detonations. Had they been storing guns there? Had a stockpile gone off in the fire? Was that not a settlement, but some sort of a guerrilla camp?

"I see that you're upset by this." Roberto Báez examined my face.

"I don't believe you," I said.

"You have to believe me, and you have to get out of here. We want you out of here, Miss Saunders."

"Who is we? I've asked you this before. Who is *nosotros*? Who are you working for? Who are you really? You're clearly not a friar."

He smiled, the skin crinkling up around his eyes. He looked almost benevolent. "I am a friar. I've been a friar for ten years, three of them out here. But I help the people who care about this country. Care that it doesn't go down some economic sinkhole. Care that it doesn't get taken over by communists. We want progress to come peacefully. We want to work with people, hand in hand. But the tensions have been exacerbated by that fanatical German and that..." He paused, rethought what he was about to say. "That Indian trader."

"So you've been forced to resort to using napalm and white phosphorus." I turned and walked toward the front door.

"Hold up, young lady. My fine Miss Saunders. You've stumbled into something where you don't belong. This can be short and sweet. We want you out of here. You won't get hurt. The *inocentes* won't get hurt. But we want you and your husband out. I know you wouldn't want the people, *el pueblo*, being harmed because of your actions. I know you are particularly sensitive to that sort of thing. I would hate to see you suffering once again from the consequences of your actions—if you know what I mean, Miss Saunders."

I had stopped just outside the living room, on the porch with the fire-red hibiscus. Calderón. Báez had checked up on me. That's how he now knew my maiden name. I hadn't given it much thought because I'd just changed from Saunders for the trip and wasn't even certain if I'd give it

up. But down here I'd only used Schmidt. He had talked to
Calderón in Guayaquil.

"So you've talked to Fernando."

"Fernando?" His eyebrows went up. He was all
innocence.

"Fernando Calderón. In Guayaquil. He runs a
businessmen's association, a Kiwanis Club chapter. He also
doesn't like communists."

He looked as though he were searching his mind for the
connection. "No, I'm afraid I don't know him, *Señorita*
Saunders. Annie Saunders. What a nice name. For such a
righteous young woman. It fits somehow. But what we learn
in our religious training is the notion of fallibility. Only
God and, by extension, the Pope are infallible, *Señorita*
Annie Saunders. The rest of us do better to have a little
humility. Especially when we are involved in things we
know nothing about."

All I wanted was to be out of this house, away from this
man. I didn't care what I had to say to do it. I felt all the
power of his ability to gain information about me, the
extent of our inequality out here. He was the absolute
ruler. I was at his mercy.

"Do you come by your righteousness honestly, Miss
Saunders? Is your father a righteous man also? Does he too
act on his beliefs?"

I thought with a new-found irony of how my father was
in great agony while I waited for word on my Peace Corps
application. He told me he was afraid the government
might reject me because of his past, both his imprisonment
and his political work. "No, no, Daddy," I'd said to him.
"You've always lived by your principles. They have to
admire that." He'd given me such a strange look, but not
said a word. Instead, he'd come over to me and put his arms
around me, hugging me tighter than he ever had before.

"I do come by it rightfully. My father is a man of very
high principles. Now if you'll excuse me, I think I'd better
go and see about Mingo. If I'm to get out of here as you'd
like, I really better be on my way." I smiled as best I could

and even re-entered the room and shook his hand with my left. "You speak great English, Friar Báez. I'd almost not know you for a Chilean. I might even take you for an American."

"Thank you, Miss Saunders." He kept hold of my hand and gave me his best smile, showing those elegant straight teeth and crinkling his pale blue eyes. "I'm so glad you won't come to any harm. And perhaps I might let you know that it's wise to forget all of what you've seen once you return to the States. There have been some unfortunate incidents of people trying to meddle after they leave. It upsets me terribly when people come to harm. Especially such a nice woman, such a principled young woman as yourself."

Mingo and Alice had already finished packing the boxes and were carrying them to the dock.

"We have all we could wish for, Señorita Ana. This Alice has great sympathy," Mingo said as he dropped two cartons from his shoulders onto the dock. The moon had come out, and in the light, I examined the boxes with their Church of Jesus Christ logo, and then Mingo's face. Had this man betrayed us? Had he exacerbated the situation for his own gain, or was he a true revolutionary and, if he was, what the hell did I think of that?

"What is it, señora? Is something wrong?"

"Nothing. Let's finish this and get out of here quickly."

"¿Cómo no, señora. Cómo no?" he said with unusual cheer.

As I was about to step into the boat, Alice called to me. She stood on the beach holding a lantern. I could see her father at her side, but no one else. I didn't want to have to encounter Roberto Báez Chamino again, nor did I want Mingo to know that he was here.

"Your hand. We must do something about your hand," Alice said, walking out on the dock toward me.

As she gently applied some salve to my palm, I watched over her shoulder and saw her mother come down to join her father on the shore. Still no Báez.

"You have a box of Gentamycin and another of aloe vera," Alice said. "And I've packed morphine and extra glucose sacks. Be careful, Annie." She looked up at me. Her eyes were dark and mournful in the moonlight, her face a white oval. "Be very careful. I didn't tell Mingo, but Roberto Báez arrived by helicopter. He piloted it himself. My father doesn't know about his activities, but I've heard very bad things." She leaned forward then to kiss me goodbye, and whispered, "They say he's dangerous, that Roberto Báez stops at nothing. Nor does this government."

I embraced her. "How do you know?"

"I have friends among the Jesuits in Quito that my father isn't aware of. They know of Báez's activities in Peru and Bolivia. Believe me and take care. Blessings on you."

As we pulled away from the dock, I heard her voice calling out to us, "If we can help with anything..."

Mingo got the motor up to full revolution, and the rest of their words were gone as he and I roared out into the middle of the river once again.

CHAPTER TWENTY-FOUR

The current moving against us was so strong that I had to paddle to augment the motor and keep the boat on course. If it didn't get easier, it would take us twice the time to get back. But we were lucky in the moon. Its white beam showed us the way like a giant flashlight. After a while, the current lessened and Mingo told me I could rest, even sleep if I liked.

"I have no need to," I said.

"As you wish, *Señorita* Ana."

The water before me moved like mercury fallen from a broken thermometer, slipping and sliding on a surface. No structure. No way of catching it, of putting it back in.

I understood for the first time what Kai had meant when he said, "Romanticism is a dangerous trait in us Germans. It's not something we can afford to be anymore." That sense of the heroic, the vision of a world transcending the everyday, coupled with a tendency to throw over the traces, to rebel against the old order, to follow the new rule to the very end. Those were the traits that could lead to stubborn belief in a cause, or to genocide. Add to that naiveté. If what Alice intimated was true, then the depths of power working against Georg Häberle and his Indians were unmatchable—and the result of his intractability, catastrophic.

Mingo sat high on the back ridge of the boat, his hand on the throttle. His face was relaxed and handsome in the moonlight. He had regained his self. He belonged here on the river, I thought, not in some missionary's house, in its distorted notion of civilization.

"I have a question to ask you," I said.

"*Sí.*" His smile contained a suggestion of flirting.

"Do you ever doubt *don* Jorge? Do you ever question the rightness of what he's doing?"

His smile left. His eyes went into shadow.

"We disagree on some things. But I have great admiration for him, and gratitude."

"But what if he would co-operate with the government. Make a deal, say. Trade territory for peace. Wouldn't that possibly be better at this time? To stop losing lives. Isn't it inevitable that people will have to make room for oil exploration?"

He shifted down to the seat, getting the sound of the motor behind him, and leaned forward.

"No, *Señorita* Ana. There is no compromise possible with the oil company or with the government. Nothing to trade. They come in and destroy the forest. Destroy what our people live on. Destroy our way of life. And the religious men help them in the destruction. The religious ones are their best salesmen. They make my people believe that white men are to be trusted. They set us up. No. Compromise means complete loss for us and complete gain for them."

I recalled how Angel had implied the same about the Peace Corps. "Did you come to subdue us, Ana?" he had asked. "Is it a new kind of power over us?" And he'd been right: we were the secular missionaries, our country's best sales force. Sent to stabilize and pacify the population, we paved the way. I was told not to interfere in the politics of the country when we wanted to march to the *municipio*. Jon, the volunteer, was out there parceling out the land. It was becoming all too clear to me.

"The friar was back there at the mission tonight," I said. "He got there by helicopter."

"What do you say?"

"When I came out from bathing he was in the living room talking to *Señor* Albertson in perfect English."

"Those pigs of missionaries. It's as I said, *Señorita* Ana. You see now?"

"I don't think they're involved," I said.

He spat. His mouth broke into the grimace, the one that looked more a threat than a smile.

"The friar told me to get out of here and not to speak of what I've seen once I get home."

"Son of a whore."

"And he told me something about you." My body was taut with anticipation.

"What did the holy man say about the Indian, the Jívaro?" The moon was now full on his face, revealing features hardened by pure hatred.

"That you trade in guns with the Roani and the other tribe, the Cofán." I added the last, recalling the exchange of money at the first settlement. "That they buy them to fight the oil men and the government. When the friar said it, I remembered the explosion yesterday long after the bomber had left, and I thought that it must have been a stock pile of munitions that went up. Is that right? Is that why you were so nervous about everything yesterday morning?"

He didn't answer. He looked out over the water and shook his shaggy hair in that self-conscious way that made him seem not completely sincere and made me wonder fleetingly if he were making a profit off those guns.

"Tell me, Mingo Mincha, is it true what he says? Tell me why you do it, so I won't start thinking the worst."

"What could be worse than what you saw yesterday? This is serious business, niña gringa. We don't play children's games of adventure back here. You've seen it for yourself."

"I am not a child," I said. "Not some niña gringa. I know enough to see that guns can't protect those people. What power do guns have against planes and bombs?"

"Like leading the lambs to slaughter? Is that what you would say? I thought you would have a better understanding of politics, Señorita Ana. I thought you understood the role of the vanguard."

Che Guevara, I thought: "The role of the vanguard is to hasten the course of events." I heard Häberle's derisive joke about Mingo falling for the "romantic hogwash" of Che, while Mingo had sat there not smiling, not reacting.

But this time it seemed the course of events had outpaced the vanguard. The odds against success were already too high.

"Maybe so," I said, feeling ashamed and confused, like the American child he had called me. "Maybe I do think you're leading innocent people to be killed. And to what end? They'll only be trampled on more."

"More than they are now? How stupid of you. Where will we be if we don't start? Farther into the burned down forest, fighting between ourselves over less and less land? You don't think that they will kill us anyway? Go home, *nena*. Do as the friar says—go home and don't speak of this. You can only hurt us." He sneered, pushing the back of his hand toward me.

"Don't you dismiss me. Don't you dare." I lunged toward him, sending the canoe skidding precariously to one side. I grabbed his hand and began to bend it backward. I wanted to hurt him, to crush him, to quiet him. His other arm came around me. We began to turn in the current. For a second I thought, he doesn't have control of the boat, but then my rage overwhelmed me again and I pressed my entire weight against his hand, wanting to bend it back so far that I would break his wrist. He held me tighter against him, until I lost my angle on his hand and he pulled it away from me. Then his hand was over mine. Warm. Pulsing.

"Ssst, sssst, ssst," he was hissing in my ear. Otherwise there was only silence. And my own breathing. And the pressure of his hands on me. The boat turned and turned, rocking us gently. "Sssst, Ana, ssssst." His breath was soft on my wet face. He smelled of smoke, sweat, and dried blood. Where did I know that smell from? It was someone else who'd been close enough for me to smell the strong intimacy of freshly dried blood. Rina. Rina when she'd curled herself inside my arms in my hot, closed-up apartment after the riot. After Angel had been taken away. Angel would have been able to accept what Mingo had just told me. He would have been strong enough, certain enough in what he believed. Wouldn't have had to retreat or run away when things got too serious. Angel would never have abandoned any of us.

The moon appeared and reappeared, appeared and disappeared as the boat turned. Shadow and light. Day and night. Mingo kissed my hair. My eyes. My mouth.

"You must believe, Ana. Some things a person must only believe in and be willing to die for." He touched my breasts.

All sense of time and place went from me. I felt only his presence around me. He became Angel. His hands on me were Angel's. Angel's finger running down my cheek, to my collar-bone, into my shirt. Wanting him. Wanting Angel. What he could give me.

I pulled away from Mingo. He held on. I yanked away again and his hold gave way. I sat on the floor of the canoe shaking my head.

"I can't do this," I said. "I can't do this to Kai. I'm sorry. But I really can't. I'm sorry if I insult you."

The canoe continued to turn. The night was exquisite, clear, star-filled, the moon shining directly down on us now.

"You can't insult me, *Señorita* Ana." His smile was twisted.

"I only just got married. Not even two weeks ago," I said. "I would be very unhappy with myself."

"*Pues*, then we each don't understand the other's big principles. At least we are equal in that, *Señorita* Ana, beautiful Ana."

"Please stop."

"I'll stop." He wasn't smiling.

"Thank you," I managed to say.

Without answering, he started the motor. The boat bumped and bounded through the water, working its way against the current, which had begun to pick up.

"Do you need my assistance?" I asked reaching for the paddle.

He stared at me. The moon, bright as daylight, exposed everything in that moment, all desires, hurts, our mutual feelings of shame.

"Not yet," he said.

"I can't help it, Mingo. I could never believe as strongly as you. I would always doubt myself. Always be afraid that I was making a worse mess for people than I was making it safer."

"There isn't a choice, Ana." He sat very still now. "It isn't a choice between danger and safety for our people. It is doing what must be done and going on from there. I want to tell you a story."

I nodded, okay.

"It is a story about there being no idea of leaders in our culture. We believe that each person must take justice into his own hands. If we lived in the forest as in the old days, and you committed adultery with me, your husband could take my scalp." He grinned. "Perhaps we are lucky that you are loyal to your husband."

"Perhaps you are," I said. "My principles saved your good looks."

Mingo became serious again.

"My father drove the schoolbus for those Shuar children who didn't go to the Salesian school but had to travel over the river into Macas. He didn't have trouble learning to drive. My father is so able a man that they gave him a driver's license without his having to read or speak Spanish. He rose from bed on time, and he picked the children up on time, and he carried them safely across the hanging bridge, but what he couldn't understand was someone who thought himself better or who had more power, shouting at and bossing another person around. My father only understood to fight back, to retaliate. That was the way it was done in the forest. One day a Latina, whose rich husband had come to build a cow ranch, told my mother to clean the outhouses of the men workers. My mother fainted from the filth and couldn't finish. The woman wouldn't pay my mother her day's wage and

shouted ugly names at her. My mother went home and told
my father. All my father understood was to go and slash
the man, her husband, in payment for the insult to his
wife. My father was sent to jail for three years, even though
he had only scratched the rancher. What my father did
was wrong in your society. If he lives here, he must follow
the rules of this culture. But why did my father live here?
That's what I ask. Why couldn't he have stayed in his
forest where he belonged, where he understood the ways?
He didn't want to leave. He followed his son, who had
been stolen from him to be civilized. You see, Ana, they
want us to live by their rules, and when we resist, when we
live by our own rules, we are punished by theirs. But they
never live by *our* rules when they come to our land." He
shrugged. "I try to think how it would be reversed, if we
conquered Quito or Guayaquil. But I can't imagine.
Whenever I go to Quito or Guayaquil, *I* feel less. You—
white people—have too many things. You travel too fast.
You have many inventions to make life easier. It is
impossible for me to see you as inferior to me, to my earlier
life in the forest. You are too many, too loud, too powerful.
But the times I feel superior to you are when I see your
stupidity, your cruelty."

"I try not to be cruel," I said.

"*You* is white people and Latinos of this country in
general, Ana. Not María. Not your husband. I can see a
good man there. Not *don* Jorge, though at times his
stupidity shows."

"Everyone is stupid at one time or another."

He ignored this and went on. "Just as you think I am
responsible for the actions of my people, that I shouldn't
give them guns, I blame you for what your people do. Your
people are more stupid and cruel when it comes to us, to
the forest. All the white man sees is money and dirty
Indians. That's why I give guns to the Indians. To feel
some power against that cruelty and stupidity. Even if we
lose, we can maybe win some dignity."

"But you said you were organizing. I assumed peacefully. At *don* Jorge's you said there was an association of indigenous."

He laughed. "That's what I tell *don* Jorge. To make him feel better. He doesn't approve of the guns, but he does like the idea of Indians organizing and petitioning the government for our own land, for our own idea of our land." He laughed again. "Did you ever petition the government in this country as an *indio*? Alone. Without the paternal arm of the *evangelistas*. With no money, no land according to Latino laws? As a people who cannot vote." He held up his hand. "*No, perdóneme*. That is what the indigenous association is fighting for, acquiring the rights of the Indian to vote. A fine goal. But one that could take twenty years to achieve. All the forest could be destroyed by then. No, *Señorita* Ana. Guns will be of more assistance in this battle than organizing for the vote. You also remember, don't you, what I told you, that the association is originally the idea of the Salesians? How fast do you suppose that the Salesians truly wish to move?" Again the grimace. His white teeth large and brilliant in the moonlight.

"And *don* Jorge?"

"Some days he knows of it. Other days he closes his eyes to it. Some days he makes up his own story of why and how. *Don* Jorge wishes the best for us. He is as good a man as I've told you. But he lives sometimes in his own world. There are times I think he is as strange as his brother," he said with finality.

After a while, Mingo began to sing. Steadily. Monotonously. Like an incantation. I moved up to the bow of the boat. The song was Indian, one that I'd never heard, but its flatness and dissonance were familiar. It droned on and on, sometimes melding with the sound of the motor, sometimes rising over it in a melancholy arc.

My mother sang when we drove across the country after the war, after my father had been released from prison. I was barely four, but I remembered when the man came with the telegram, and she told me we were going to be with a person named Daddy, and that we were meeting him in a place called Ohio. We packed up the car, loading the roof, the trunk, the back seat, and set off from Sacramento, my mother driving night and day, only taking catnaps on the side of the road. We had no money for motels. In the middle of the night she sang to keep herself awake. Beside her in the front seat I worked to stop my head from wobbling on my four-year-old neck, feeling responsible for keeping her awake. "My best little companion," she called me on that trip. It was wonderful having her call me that. It was a time to remember, to cherish. She sang "Oh Susannah," and "She'll Be Coming 'Round the Mountain." We went straight across the plains on a highway that stretched much like this river, with our headlights scaring up rabbits and prairie dogs and my mother throwing her head back and singing at the top of her lungs. My mother was full of anticipation on that trip, and happy.

It was later, when we were living in the first small town in Ohio, that my mother's overwhelming sadness began. What a life it must have been for her, hopping from one tiny apartment to another, with our scratched and scuffed belongings. We lived in communities where she could easily be ostracized for being an intellectual, for wanting to work outside her home, and for being Jewish, all the qualities that made my mother who she was. She had grown up in an intellectual Jewish family. Even her mother had earned a doctorate in biology. But my mother went where my father led, hid her Jewishness behind his name, and her ambitions behind the doors of our apartments, all so he could find work in this treacherously foreign territory. For his sake she followed the rules of the new culture until the day she no longer could.

As the boat bounded through the water, Mingo sang on.

I fell asleep and dreamed of Gala pushing the baby Ladito in the hammock as she and I sat talking through the night.

A silence brought me awake. I opened my eyes to find Mingo smiling down at me.

"Well, we are here, Ana. Our trip together is nearly at its end." He reached out his hand and I took it, aware of his fingers tightening around mine. He pulled me to standing. He was very close and in the predawn light his face looked thin and drawn.

I examined my injured right hand. The swelling had subsided, leaving the skin rough and like an over-large covering on a smaller frame. It was stiff, but there was almost no pain.

"I'm glad you rested," Mingo said, touching my palm. "We have a hard work before us."

The supplies had been packed into three cartons. Each was terribly heavy. We were standing in the first reaches of forest, with the brush pressing in around us. Mingo helped to place a carton on my head, like a Shuar carrying water. I held my head straight under the weight, my neck stiff, shifting slightly to find the center of balance. I reached up and clasped the box, touching Mingo's hand as I did. "I've got it."

After a moment's hesitation he removed his hand. "Sí, Ana. Very good."

I walked through the tangled green, following Mingo, as though it were my own woods. I thought of Friar Báez and his threats. Mingo was right, there was no compromise in this situation. Any negotiation meant certain destruction of the forest. There would never be a compromise toward preservation, toward honoring what was, toward taking what knowledge the Indians had garnered over the centuries and learning from it. No, the only plan was to impose an outside notion of progress, a concept of incremental eradication.

Mingo stopped suddenly in front of me. I almost bumped into him. We stood silently, listening.

"Did you hear anything?" he whispered.

"No."

We stood so close that I could smell his sweat, strong and pungently sweet, like over ripe mangoes. It came through the back of his soiled shirt, the cloth sticking to his skin. His arm was up balancing the cartons as was mine. I could see the fine line of his muscle where the sleeve fell back. His hair glistened with moisture. He lifted the boxes off his head and set them down on the ground. Then he removed mine from my head. Without saying anything he put his arms around me and put his mouth to mine. His body was hard against me and I felt myself sinking into the intensity of the embrace. I allowed the thought that I was a Shuar girl, that this was an innocent first kiss and that I had no need to resist. Then I felt his hand lifting my skirt and finding its way into my pants. I wanted him as terribly as I'd wanted César in the hallway of my apartment. But then I had been a girl, responsible to no one but myself.

I wrenched away. His face was dark with desiring me, mirroring the way I felt. It would be so easy, I thought, trying to control my breathing, trying to douse the feelings that pounded through me.

"It's not fair," I said. "What you say about us imposing our culture and ways on you." I stopped to catch my breath. "You can't get retribution by making me do your bidding. Don't use me the way my people use you. Don't do that to me."

"It doesn't look as though I would be using you." He brazenly rearranged himself in his pants. He was still hard. "It seems as though it would be equal. As though the feelings are the same across two cultures."

He was right. I couldn't shed these feelings like unwanted skin, just as I'd not been able to rid myself of my memories. Just as my connection to this country wasn't a minor infatuation. Just as my sorrow wasn't a passing sympathy, nor my desire to do right. It all was embedded in me, in the same way that I attached to people at their roots and didn't let go, in the same way that my father believed he could make change and Mingo would go to any lengths to fight for his people and his forest. Maybe I wasn't as different from them as I had thought.

"Mingo, don't be cruel to me. I'll try not to be cruel to you. Yes, I want you. But I'm not going to do it. I don't care what you think."

"Tell me, *señora*, do you fit so well into your own country? Do you speak as fine English as you do Spanish? Are you so lovely there? Can you live in every world so well?"

"Not so well," I whispered.

"I think you can. Not like me. You saw how I would be in your country, with rich *gringos* all speaking English. You saw my poor clothes and different manners. I look good out here, but there...no, no, I would not be good enough for Ana."

"That's not why, and you know it," I said. "I told you, I don't want to hurt Kai. It's crazy. I can't start a marriage with an affair with another man."

"But it is why, *señora gringa*. I cannot last a minute with you outside of this forest." He knelt and picked up the carton I'd been carrying and placed it on my head a second time, but this time his hand didn't linger.

I wanted to tell him that it was cheap to make the two equivalent, but I realized that in a way he was right. It did have to do with how difficult, how impossible it would be for him to cross over into my culture or me into his. If it was hard enough for me with Kai, and if the difficulties had been unresolvable for my parents, then it was impossible for two people like Mingo and me.

"Let's go," I said. "People need these things."

CHAPTER TWENTY-FIVE

We arrived at the settlement by mid-afternoon and went immediately to leave the cartons under the house where it was cooler as well as dark and damp. Was Kai here? Though I'd done nothing wrong, I did feel shaken and didn't want to see him immediately, not until I'd calmed down. Mingo left his boxes and walked out and up the stairs without speaking. I followed him along the encircling veranda, glancing in through the main door as I passed. There was no one there. The room seemed changed; it was like returning to a childhood home after having grown up. It was more meager somehow, not as fine and substantial as I'd recalled. The mats on the living room floor were fraying. The floor was scratched and a little dirty.

We rounded the corner, and I saw María standing at the charcoal stove.

"So you're here." She turned from frying fish. Her face was somber.

At the far end, where the porch took its turn to the back of the house, the pregnant girl sat splay-legged, scraping maize from cobs, while the older woman who had given me water the first day crushed the kernels in a mortar. They looked up at us, stared, then returned to their work.

"Hello, María. It's good to see your black face again." Mingo went to her and put his arm around her shoulder.

She looked back at me and then averted her eyes.

"Is *don* Jorge here?" he asked, keeping his cheek close to hers. She didn't seem to mind, seemed accustomed to this familiarity from him. I remembered how they had walked to the house that first day, their heads together.

"No, he remained with the injured. So did the *señorita's* husband and the Roani men. I returned with the women who brought the food." To say this last seemed a tremendous effort for her. It looked as though she could cry at any moment, as though her face was bruising from withheld pain. "Did you get the supplies? They are needing the medicine."

"We did our best, Señora María." Mingo took a fried fish with his hand from a plate on the table next to the stove. He kept his arm around her. "Ask the señora gringa how it went. She's the one who did all the work."

María looked around him at me. His contemptuous tone and reference to me cut deeply. I stood like an awkward child, the corners of my mouth threatening to turn down from shame, from being left out. I could see that María had heard the tone in his voice.

"It was difficult," I said, struggling to maintain my composure. "But we got the antibiotics, morphine, and glucose. The man, Ted Albertson, is stubborn and is very angry at don Jorge. He blames him for this." I suddenly didn't care about protecting her or Mingo. They could hear what I had heard.

María spat on the floor. "They're stupid people," she said, "white idiots." She flipped the fish with vehemence, sending the oil sputtering and crackling.

"You're right, Señora María. They are so white. They are like the flour they try to give us. They are like the milk of a mother's breast, they are so white." Mingo waved the fish in the air, glancing menacingly over at me. "Do they still drink from the mother's breast? Is that what causes them to be so white?"

A smile started on María's face.

"They are baby white," he continued, punctuating with flourishes of his fish, moving back and forth behind María as though performing some repetitive dance. "Not like don Jorge. We have darkened him up a little. But white, white, white, like lice. So white you see the blue of their veins against their skin. Oweeeywa, so ugly, they are so white." He bent over in a half-bow, half-retch.

María's hand went to her mouth and she turned her back to me.

"They are so white." He wasn't going to stop. "They turn bright pink the minute the sun touches them, not beautiful bronze like me, or chocolate brown like you, or a nut-and -earth color like these ladies here." He bowed again, this time to the Indian women. He righted himself and ate another bite of fish.

I waited until his soliloquy had ended, rigid with the same rage and humiliation I'd felt when the people of the *barrio* had taunted me and thrown stones. Then I walked to the far end of the porch and stood against the banister, looking out. Mingo was like the boys who only wanted to get back at me because of whom I represented. I felt the blows I'd landed on the boy's face at the center's gate reverberating once again in my arms and fists, and I remembered my deep satisfaction at finally having hurt one of them.

There was silence behind me on the porch. I didn't give in to it by speaking.

"But the *Señora* Ana knows how to talk to these people." Mingo's voice, though still containing an edge of provocation, was somewhat conciliatory. "She did very well with them. She got us what we needed. I could see that the *señora* knows well how to get what is needed from people. I admire that. We can use that."

I thought, this is a man who has set himself up to do life-and-death work but allows his racial fury to be distracted and dissipated over a flirtation that wasn't consummated.

"Ah, foolish boy. Those men came here, threatening me, saying that you had to leave or more harm would be done to all of us." As María spoke I heard her slap fish onto a platter.

I spun around. "Who came?

"Who was here, *Señora* María?" Mingo asked, taking hold of her forearm.

She shook her arm loose from his and began to put fresh fish into the frying pan. The grease sizzled.

"Was it the *padre?*" I asked, moving back into the kitchen area. Had he flown in?

"No, no, no, not the stinking *Padre* Báez." She looked at me, tears welling. "It was the men who do the dirty work. It was Latinos from *la costa*. My people. Filth. I know those men for all my life. Those are the men I escaped. I hate those men." Her face broke into exhausted pieces. The oil from the fish pan spat high into the air. She stood with her long arms at her sides, weeping silently, ignoring the fish that had begun to burn.

"Here, let me." I took the spatula from her hand. She didn't resist.

"*Señora* María," Mingo said gently. "Tell me what happened to you. Did these men hurt you?" He didn't touch her but stood close.

She shook her head slowly from side to side, her tears running in rivulets down her cheeks. I flipped the fish and thought of the men in the obscure light of the *tienda* in Puerto Napo talking to the friar and those sitting around outside, drinking beer.

"Tell me, María," Mingo said. "It's important that I know."

"Aaiiiee, my little brother, my German, these Indian people! Why does God punish us? What has María done to God? She has a good heart. Why should she have to suffer so?"

"What did they do to *don* Jorge? María, did they hurt *don* Jorge?" Mingo shouted over her wailing cries.

"*Nada, nada, nada.*" She backed away from us, swaying her body.

"Why do you cry then?" He bent toward her, holding his hands outstretched before him.

"Because they said they will harm him if he doesn't stop. They will come here to kill him. They will kill you, also, and the *gringos*. They said the *gringos* must leave and *don* Jorge must stop and that Mingo Mincha must get out of here."

"They said the word murder?" I looked from Mingo to her. Roberto Báez had only insinuated as much to me.

"*Sí, señora.*" Her eyes flashed green. "*Sí, sí, sí.* Don't you understand yet. These men are killers. They kill from the air. They kill from the ground. They don't care. I said to them, 'You already kill innocent people and you want to harm more?' They said, 'We kill no one.' I said, 'You lie. On top of killing, you are liars. They are suffering in the forest from your fires that come from your airplanes.' A fat one who smelled of perfume said, 'You are foolish, María, old black one. We are trying to protect people, to make certain no harm comes to these innocent people. It is your husband, and the Jívaro and the *gringos* that bring harm to them. You foolish, blinded old black woman.'" Her eyes opened wide in rage. "I ...am...not...blind." She struck her fist against her chest with each word. "I see with my eyes and my heart. I feel with my body."

For a moment there were only her deeply drawn breaths. The Roani women had stopped working and were watching from their corner. I wondered if they understood much of this.

"When did they come and where are they now?" I asked. "How did they get here?"

"They came in the night and they left in the night," she answered in a hollow voice, staring at me. "Where did they go? How am I to know that, *señorita*? Under the earth where all worms go. They went away on foot. Perhaps to Puerto Napo. To their air strip. To Guayaquil. All I care is that they're not in my house. That I don't need to see their faces. I don't care what God says, I hate these men." She doubled over. "Aaaieee," she sobbed. "Aaaiiee, *mis corazones, mi hermanito, mi alemán, mis indiositos.*"

I dropped the spatula. The pregnant girl rose and rushed over to the fire, picking up the spatula from the floor as I went to María and put my arms around her. Her body was strong and muscular and shaking with sobs.

"Come, *Señora María.* Let me take you to your room," I said, looking up to Mingo.

He nodded and mouthed *Sí.*

To my surprise, she let me guide her back into the main house and into the room where I had seen her the morning before, peacefully asleep in *don* Jorge's arms. The bed was made and I opened it with one hand while holding her with the other.

She moaned as she sank to the bed. I took off her plastic shoes and carefully helped her lay her head on the blue muslin covered pillow. Her knees rose to her chest when I got her down.

"Lie straight, please let your legs go loose. It will be better for you if you can relax your legs, *Señora* María."

"*No puedo, no puedo, no puedo,*" I cannot, she mumbled over and over.

Her body was rigid with resistance. It took great force to push her legs down, but as soon as I did, her entire body went slack.

She lay for some time not crying, only breathing deeply. She seemed almost at peace, until another spasm shook her and her body writhed horribly. I sat beside her, holding onto her, thinking she must have been waiting until we came back to let go with her grief and fear. I wondered where Mingo was now. What was he doing? But who I really wanted was Kai. I wanted him to be here to help, to tell me what to do. What if those men came back? What could I do to protect María, to protect myself? Then I thought of Mingo's guns. But I could never use a gun.

The light had found its way through the screened windows set high in the wall up under the eaves, and shifting, spotlighted María's black-and-brown figure on the blue sheets. She must have felt its sudden warmth, because her eyes opened.

"Why does this have to come to us?" she asked. "We harm no one. We only want peace."

"I don't know, *Señora* María. If I could have the power, I wouldn't allow you to feel pain. You are too good a woman and work too hard for others to have such cruelty done to you, to have such loss."

"I'm no longer a Christian," she said as though confessing a wrong. Her eyes pleaded. "I spoke to God before, but I don't deserve to. I have lost my faith."

"That doesn't matter," I said. "You live more like a Christian than *Padre* Báez or the man at the mission, from what I can see."

The stream of light was now directly on her face and she moved to one side squinting, unable to entirely escape it.

"My brother was a good boy. He was never bad. Those *indios* are good. They are God's true children. *Don* Jorge says they don't even harm the forest. My brother did no one any harm. My brother was only a baby. He was young like you, *niña*. Tell me *americana*, why did they kill my brother?"

"I don't know, *señora*."

"Why don't they kill those milk-white missionaries? Why don't they kill that lying *padre*, that Roberto Báez Chamino with his filthy ways? Why did they kill my little innocent brother?"

I had no answer for her.

"He had nothing, my little brother. He was as poor as these people. As poor as I was before I met my kind German who took me in."

On the dresser, the one piece of furniture in the room besides the bed, was a photograph of the two of them. She was in a flower print dress and a wide-brimmed hat. Häberle was in a *guayabera*, light pants and a Panama, the kind they made in Jipijapa on the coast. He was smiling proudly out at the photographer. Her dark face was lost in the shadow of the hat.

I reached over and picked the photograph off the top of the bureau. She took it from me and looked at it for a long time. With her finger she wiped at the image of her face.

"You see that?" she said. "You see how a black face doesn't show? That's how I felt when I met him. As though a black face didn't show next to his. But he didn't let me feel that way. He said I had my own beauty. He said my strength was my beauty." She clasped the picture to her breast as tears washed over her cheeks and fell onto the pillow. "But this time I can't be strong. My brother was to come live with us. He was to be our child. I sent him money. I fear that they killed him for the money. I have great fear that he took the money to the bar and boasted of it and bought drinks for people and that's why they killed him, to get the rest of the money I sent him."

"I don't think so," I said. "He probably left it at home. Wasn't he a smart young man?" I wanted to take her in my arms and tell her, no, María, you are not responsible for your brother's death. Some things in this world are well beyond your control. You are not guilty of the ills of the world, the viciousness in this world.

"Oh yes, he was a smart boy, *muy inteligente*. He wouldn't have taken the money to the bar. You're right. Oh, I hope against the God I no longer believe in, that he didn't carry my money to the bar."

After that she didn't say anything. She just lay staring into space. I remained on the bed beside her. I put my hand on her arm and caressed the softest skin I had ever touched. This must be why people have families, I thought, to touch such skin whenever they wish. The shaft of light moved slowly across the wall, passing the crucifix, as, finally, María slept.

After a while I sensed a presence at the door. It was Mingo standing with the older woman.

"She's sleeping," I whispered.

His expression was benign, even kindly.

"I'm leaving," he said. "We must get food and medicine out to the settlement before dark."

"You'll need my help," I said.

He shook his head. "No, Ana, you stay with María. She must sleep and she can't be here alone. Max is around, but she needs a woman. I can go with Yayae, here." He indicated the Indian woman who hung back from us, looking at the floor. "She will carry the food and I can take the medical supplies."

"You can't take everything," I said, finding myself not wanting him to go.

"No. *Pues*, we can get the rest tomorrow. They can't use all of it in one day." He stood with his hands in his pockets looking tentative, almost shy.

"I could go with you. One of the other women could care for her."

"That would give me pleasure." He grinned. "But I believe you can use the rest also. And it's better maybe that we don't go together? What do you think?" He touched my arm.

With that touch I immediately longed to move through the forest with him in the dusky night.

"That's right. I am very, very tired."

"Ana?"

"Yes."

"I wasn't kind to you."

"No."

"*Discúlpame, por favor.*" His hand was still on my arm.

I nodded, not trusting my voice. But as I looked at him, I saw that he was just a guy, even with all he was involved in. He could act as badly or as well as any young man when it came to matters of infatuation. As could I.

"One other thing," he said. "Please can I trust you not to speak to María of what the friar has said of the guns?"

"She doesn't know?"

"She knows. But she doesn't speak of it with Jorge. It wouldn't be good to add this to her burden." His hand dropped from my arm. I felt its loss.

"It's crazy, Mingo. You've got to talk directly to him about this. It's divisive otherwise. Anyway, how can he not know? You may think he's strange, but he isn't an idiot."

"Ssst," Mingo said. "Don't talk so loud. You're going to wake María." He beckoned me fiercely from the doorway out through the living room to the front area of the porch. He spoke sharply to the Indian woman, and she didn't follow us but stayed just behind María's cloth covered door.

On the porch, Mingo pointed down the stairs. The man called Kemonka stood at the bottom, cradling a rifle.

In a voice flattened by fury, with his fingers pinching into my arm, Mingo said, "That is what *don* Jorge will never allow. He would send Kemonka away, or make him throw his gun into the river. I have great admiration for *don* Jorge, but it stops there, with that idea. If he had allowed the Roani to be armed from the beginning, none of this would have happened."

"I don't know about that," I said. I wanted to say, you are foolish, Mingo Mincha. It would only have escalated the situation earlier. You cannot win with these people. The same would have happened as in Vietnam. They would have sent in more and more fire power, and trampled you to the ground and ruined more of the beautiful forest. But what did he want to hear from me, a white *gringa* on her honeymoon.

We faced off silently, until I said. "You're hurting my arm, Mingo Mincha. Please let go."

He released his hold.

"I'm sorry, *señora*."

"Thank you." I rubbed the place he'd been squeezing.

"I want you to know, *señora*, that even though I act the *burro*, I know what good work you've done for us."

"*Gracias.*"

"*De nada, señora.*"

He called for Yayae and she came from the room. They spoke in sign and pigeon language. They started down the stairs. Almost at the bottom, Mingo turned.

"Don't worry, *señora*. Those men are cowards. They would never kill a *gringa*."

"What a comfort."

"*De veras, señora*. And also, I take your fear with me so you can sleep softly tonight without it. *Adiós, chica*. Care well for my friend María."

"If it's so safe, why is Kemonka armed?" My eyes met Kemonka's. I knew he understood what I'd said.

"Because Kemonka is no pacifist." He trotted down the rest of the stairs and disappeared around the corner of the house before I could say more.

"*Señora*," Kemonka said. His Spanish was as guttural as his own language.

" *¿Sí, señor?*"

"The men. They don't come. Cowards. Don't come two times."

Though I said it made me feel better to know and thanked him, I wasn't at all reassured.

Chapter Twenty-Six

After Mingo left, I sat on the side porch where Kai and I had slept, watching the afternoon light deepen until it became a vibrant red pouring like water through the tiny spaces between the green leaves. Even as I reveled in it, it disappeared suddenly with almost no afterglow and I found myself in darkness. I lit the lantern and left it on the table inside, but I stayed on the dark porch, straining to hear human sounds over the frogs, cicadas, and last rustling of birds. How was I going to get through this night?

I was startled out of a reverie by footsteps in the big room. I slipped from my chair and hunched down in the darkness, my heart ricocheting around my chest. I tried to listen, but I could barely hear for all the noise going on inside of me.

"María," I heard myself call before I'd consciously decided to say it.

"Sí."

"Oh, thank God. I'm out here on the porch."

"Ah," she laughed. "I hear fear in your voice." Her shadow fell onto the floor.

I stood to see her figure in the door. "You scared me."

"Where is Mingo?" I heard from the solidity of her voice tinged with humor that the old María had returned.

"He went with the food and medicine. He took Yayae."

"He said for you to stay? To protect me?" She laughed again.

"He thought I needed the rest."

"I know Mingo. He thinks the María is not able to care for herself these days."

"You were very upset."

She was backlit by the lantern in the living room, so that I couldn't see her face. But I could tell she was scrutinizing me.

"Come," she said. "I'll make dinner for you." But instead of passing back through the living room to the other side, she came out onto the darkened porch. She went over to the railing and leaned against it looking out.

I joined her and we stood side by side listening to the night noises. Now, with her company, they sounded benign.

"Tell me, do you like it here, *chica*?" she asked.

"Yes," I said. In the evening air, I could smell faint traces of chemicals. "The forest is magnificent, and your house is very fine. If not for the horror of the bombings, I would be happy here."

"Ssst, ssst, sst," she agreed. I could just make out her profile as it slowly emerged from the darkness. "I miss Esmeraldas in times like these. I miss the *alegría*, the many people, walking in the square at night, walking down the road and saying *buenas noches* to the *gente* who pass by. There are no roads here. The river is our road. You can't walk down a river. And do you know something, *gringa*, even without this, without the bombers coming from the sky, there is something lacking here. There is never the same kind of liveliness that María knows. These are good people, but they are different from me. When they dance it is different. And they laugh at different jokes."

"Do they laugh?" I asked.

"Oh, yes, they sometimes laugh," she sighed. "But María shouldn't be complaining. She has the German. The German makes up for not having people. Did I tell you he is very kind to me? Did I tell you that? Because he is."

"I can see he is very nice to you."

She turned to look at me. I could make out her sad smile. "That's good. I like that you see, *niña*."

We cooked what was left of the fish and María boiled some yucca. Sitting at the little table on the porch in the kitchen area in the light of a kerosene lamp, we picked over the fish, using our hands. María was very clever with her long brown fingers, finding bone after bone, barely disturbing the flesh. I ate, but without gusto. I kept

worrying, what if they were out there training their guns
on us? Kemonka's protection would be a moot point if they
shot at us and ran. Which was exactly the problem with
Mingo's political notions. It was like some horrible joke,
the Indians first fighting with their stone-age weapons
against fire arms, and, as soon as they had modern fire
power, the invaders escalating to bombs. A never ending
escalation.

I heard a sound in the interior of the house and rose
abruptly from the table.

"*Chica.*" María put her hand out to me. "Calm yourself.
It's nothing but the brother of *don* Jorge returning. This is
his hour of return. In the dark. Long after the sun has gone
down."

I was shaking. My legs wouldn't hold me, and I had to sit
down.

"*Niña, niña*, does the María have to care for you?"

"No, I'll be all right." I went back to picking at my food,
prodding around in the fish, wishing I hadn't revealed
myself as such a coward. Wishing Kai would come back.

María looked at me for a long minute as though gauging
the depth of my fear and then stood and went into the
house.

"Max, *compadre* Max," I heard her call.

"*Ja.*"

So he spoke after all. Curiosity at least succeeded in
calming my body. The shakes vanished.

"So you are here, *compadre*?"

"*Ja...ich...bin...hier.*" His words came out slowly and
haltingly, as though he lacked practice in putting together
a fluid sentence.

"Good. Something is safe then in this world."

"*Ja...ja.*"

"Do you wish some food, *compadre*?"

"*Ein bisschen... bitte.*"

She returned to the porch smiling to herself. "He is
here. Don't be frightened, *niña* Ana." She came over to me
and sat again at the table. She pulled her chair around so

that she was close beside me and she took one of my hands in hers. "That is a man who is frightened. Forever he will be like that. It isn't good. You don't want to become like Max. *Sin remedio*."

"I thought he didn't speak," I said, imitating her hushed tones.

"He speaks to some people." She caressed my hand. "To me. To his brother. But not very much. It's sad. *Muy triste*. There are times he becomes like an animal. He makes animal sounds and he tears things apart. And then he tears at himself. He scratches at himself and, if we don't catch him in time when he's like that, he has long bleeding cuts down his body, which we must tend to, not to let them get infected in the jungle heat and wet." Her hand stopped on mine. "It causes us very much trouble when he's here. And Jorge has sadness then that closes him away from me." She patted my hand and stood. "Let me get his food ready."

"Will he eat out here?"

"No, no, no, *chica*. Max must eat alone. In his room. Or sometimes with Jorge or me. But almost never. One time he told me that with people he becomes very lonely. By himself he feels as though he can live. He's afraid people will give him *mal de ojo*." She touched her face just below the eye. "That they will harm him with their thoughts and wishes. But I don't understand. I say to Jorge, 'How does he do his work? He works in a brewery in Quito when he's not with us. There are other people in the brewery.' Jorge thinks that if he doesn't have to speak with them beyond what is necessary to do the work, he is able to. But any other way of being with people is too frightening for him." She lifted her hands in the air. "How can a person understand such things? I can only do what I can do. Feed him. Wash his clothes. Give him a roof and a bed and talk to him on the days he has no fear of me."

"And the bombing? Mingo said the bombing makes him worse."

She thought for a moment. "*Pues*, perhaps. But no, not truly. Maybe Mingo heard him on a day when he was like an animal, and maybe it happened after a bombing. The truth, niña? María doesn't believe it has anything to do with that. María believes it is only about what lives inside of him, in his heart and thoughts. It is a memory of something that comes back like a ghost to him on any day. It is something governed from another world. Not from this one. Not from bombs falling today or tomorrow from the sky."

I sat finishing my meal, daring myself to remain alone until María returned. I heard her murmuring in the other room. I thought of what she had said about his harming himself. What could this be in punishment for? Had he always been like this, or was it caused by what he had done in the war? Yet another person for whom the lines between past and present were blurred. But why should I care? If he had committed heinous acts, why shouldn't he suffer for the rest of his life? It was all too strange, these two brothers here in the forest. The one not speaking, and spending his leisure days fishing from dawn to dark, throwing his caught fish back, and maiming himself. And Georg Häberle, setting himself up as some sort of savior of innocent people. I thought of María, living out here, cut off from the world she came from and for which she seemed to have affection. All out of love for this man. All because he thought her fine and beautiful as a black woman. What did that serve? I had to smile to myself. But he plants well, she had said. Those German men do plant well.

Even though I planned to stay awake all night, watching out, in case someone was lurking in the forest waiting for his chance to attack, I still got into the hammock. It felt safer with the fiber fabric wrapped around me. I had a pillow and a soft flannel blanket. I remembered Gala's Ladito, how she had wrapped him tightly in swaddling clothes in the hammock strung across their room. I had thought at the time that it was cruel to do that to a child. Later I learned that babies prefer to be tightly wrapped. They feel safer not to have too much freedom to wave their arms and legs. Now I desired that

same security of having my arms bound to my sides by soft
material. I imagined how it would be as I lay staring wide-
eyed into the complete blackness of the night. I forced my
eyes yet wider, trying to both see and hear with them. I
thought I heard an ominous rustling below. I strained to
listen, begging that I be allowed to see the morning, that
Kai be allowed to come back to me. I needed him. There
could be no denying it anymore. Once on the beach on
Long Island, in the early fall, about a year after I'd met
him, Kai had gone for a jog down the shore. I had never
been with anyone longer than a few months, and I was
doubting my feelings for him. I found him too stodgy, too
unpolitical. Maybe he wasn't even handsome. Maybe I
didn't even like to make love to him. Why had I picked a
German? Was it out of my own anti-Semitism, and on and
on. As I sat on the empty beach a fog came in off the bay
and enfolded me in its damp chill. I wrapped the blanket
around me to keep warm. An hour went by and he didn't
return and I began to shake with fear. Please, I pleaded.
Please don't leave me. Please, I will do anything if you
don't leave me. Abruptly my mood changed, and I thought,
I don't need you. I don't want you. I hope you never come
back. But I didn't get up. And I didn't stop shaking. A half
hour later he appeared through the fog, his face red, his
breathing labored. He fell down on the sand beside me.

"I got lost. I couldn't find you. I think I must have gone
past this spot ten times."

I didn't say anything, just continued to shake.

"What is it?" He sat up and looked at me.

"Nothing."

"You were afraid I'd left you."

I found myself trembling more uncontrollably.

He put his arms around me. "Don't you know," he said.
"I have to work all the time to keep you from running away
from me. Twenty, thirty times in this year you would have
left me. I don't know, I'm crazy maybe, but I won't ever let
you go."

I slipped out of the hammock and made my way unseeing, feeling along the outer wall of the building. I no longer cared if anyone was out there. I had to find Kai's backpack. I felt along the floor. There it was. I unzipped the outside pocket, found what I wanted, and groped my way back to the hammock. I climbed in, wrapped the sides up so they closed over my head like the sheets my mother hung out to dry on washday in the backyards and on the landings wherever we lived. Before that terrible day in winter, I had loved hiding among the sheets. I loved their fresh smell, how they embraced me when the breeze blew, and the way the sun glowed through. I lay softly crying and twining my injured hand in Kai's cotton neckerchief, bringing it to my nose to smell his scent.

CHAPTER TWENTY-SEVEN

"*Hola, Hola.*"

I started awake and flipped out of the hammock at the sound of Georg Häberle's voice calling from below. Checking my watch, I found it was already nine. I slipped into my clothes, watching as he, Kai, and two Indian men trudged across the clearing in the bright morning light. Kai and Häberle were as brown as the Indian men and practically as exposed, Häberle in his bikini and Kai wearing only his ragged, ripped pants. They had rough beards, Häberle's a white skim and Kai's a deep red. The Indian men's faces were as smooth as boys'. All four men carried large woven hunting sacks suspended from their heads, so that they couldn't easily look up with the pressure of their heavy loads. They stopped at the midway point and spoke with each other, clasping upper arms, before the Indians turned to walk to the long house.

I came around to the landing just as Kai and Häberle were climbing the stairs. When Häberle reached the top, he looked at me out of a ravaged face. He produced a faint smile for my benefit, but it was a supreme effort. "How happy I am to see you, my dear," he said, taking my hand absently, and then he was past me, laboring like an old man.

I helped Kai down with his bag which was too heavy to hold onto. I had to let it drop to the floor. The next I knew, Kai's arms were around me and mine around him and I felt a body as thin as a boy's, so slight as to be made of bird bones filled with air. His familiar odor of sun, acrid sweat, and a sweetness akin to milk came through the stench of old smoke. This is Kai, I repeated to myself. My Kai. I held on tightly, whereas his grasp was featherlike, as though he had no strength left for more.

"How good this feels," he said into my hair. "How I need this. I'm so tired. We haven't slept at all."

We kept holding on. I felt the sunshine and a soft breeze on my back. From somewhere far off came the sound of a woman singing.

"It's so peaceful here," Kai murmured. "It's like arriving in heaven after having been in hell."

I didn't say anything.

"It's war, Annie, but not the side I saw. Not from a bunker or biking through the streets. It's the horrible aftermath I knew nothing of. Horrible."

"Worse than what I saw?"

"To watch such suffering over time and to be unable to do anything about it was the worst for all of us. We lost the man and children." He shuddered. "I wish the others could die. Death would be better than the pain they're in. The morphine that Mingo came with last night doesn't even penetrate. And the disfiguring results of those burns are going to be grotesque. They can't possibly heal properly with the treatment we've given them," he paused. "I feel weak. I'm going to be sick." He sank through my arms to the step. He slumped over with his arms on his knees, his head on his arms.

I rubbed the back of his neck, not speaking, kneading my fingers into the tendons and tight muscles.

His hand closed over mine. "I'm okay now," he said. "It's passed." He looked up at me, his eyes dark-blue and unblinking. "I'm not as brave as I'd like to be."

"I think this isn't anything to be brave about. We just do the best we can do," I said, putting my hand to his bearded cheek.

Kemonka appeared at the bottom of the stairs. He didn't have his gun anymore. He'd come with Awae. They saw us on the top step and continued walking around the house, talking and gesturing to each other. They sounded angry, but perhaps that was just due to the tonal quality of their language. From their gestures I guessed they were speaking of the injuries, Awae pointing to places where arms had been incinerated, where faces were scorched, deformed.

"Awae never rested, never complained. He kept working and working. We had to build a shelter for those who weren't sick. They couldn't stay in the hospital. It was too awful in the hospital." Kai stopped talking and looked at my hands. "How are they?" he asked, examining them.

"Not bad. A woman at the mission put some salve on and the pain stopped."

"Yes, we heard about the mission from Mingo. Jorge says you and I have to leave. He doesn't want us here anymore. It's too dangerous." He combed his fingers through my hair. "If anything had happened to you, I don't know what I'd do, Annie." He kissed me on the lips, his beard scratching. It was a rough kiss as though confirming that we still existed. "I must tell you something else. Last night after we'd built the makeshift house, Mingo insisted that we go to the landing strip. Mingo and Jorge had a bad fight which I couldn't understand much of but in the end we all went. Mingo got three of the Indian men and..." Kai shuddered.

"What is it?"

"You know about the guns?"

"Yes, he told me. Or rather the friar did."

"Well, he had more hidden away, buried in the forest, that didn't get blown up and he gave them to the Indians. He wanted me to carry one, but I refused. Jorge would hear nothing of it. He was furious."

It's a little late for fury, I thought. He should have stopped Mingo a long time ago if he didn't approve.

"And?"

"We went. It must have been midnight, but the moonlight was filtering through. It was so beautiful." Kai shook his head. "Mingo had us running for three hours and then there it was. *Scheisse*. Two planes standing in the moonlight on a grassy runway. Two army-issue pup tents nearby." Kai put his fists to his temples and began to rock.

"Kai, tell me," I whispered, knowing what had transpired, seeing in my mind's eye the shots fired into the tents, ripping through the fabric, and the men's screams. "Who did it, Kai? Who fired?"

He pulled on his hair, shaking his head from side to side so violently that for a moment I thought perhaps he had. "I don't know," squeezed out of him. "I don't know who fired. I couldn't take it. When I saw what Mingo had in mind, I froze. I couldn't call out and I couldn't stop him. I just wanted to get the fuck out of there. I should have realized what was going to happen. But when it did, all I could think of was to run away. I was afraid I'd be killed. My whole body was shaking from the inside. I just walked away, Annie. I just backed off, thinking I don't want to be out here if somebody shoots. I didn't care about anyone else. My only thought was, 'I must lie down behind a tree. I don't want a bullet in my body.' Nobody said anything to me afterward. I don't even care what they think of me—it's what I think of myself. I know now I'd save myself before I'd protect another person. Possibly even you."

"I don't believe that. You always care about others first."

"This isn't hypothetical, Annie. I saw how I acted on the battlefield."

"Was there shooting?" I asked, feeling my breath grow short. Kai's fear had finally penetrated and it became my own. This was more dangerous than saving people after they'd been bombed.

"Yes."

"Did anyone get hit?"

"Yes."

"Who?"

"Annie, one or two of them. Please, I can't go on."

At our meal with Kai, María, and me, Häberle explained what he wished us to do. He didn't think it was safe for any of us to stay here, and he had to return with the extra medicine. He wanted us all to accompany him to the bomb site, and once there, Kai and I would leave by another route with Mingo, making our way back to Mingo's boat, and from there we would travel up the Napo in the night. We had to go directly to Quito and leave on the first flight to any point in the United States. Häberle didn't want us in the country. He didn't want to be responsible for us. And furthermore, he said, it was more important to get the information out about what was happening.

"And Max?" María asked. She had been sitting with us, not eating or speaking. She had served our usual food of fish and rice and then had sat pensively with her eyes down all the time Häberle was speaking.

"Max must come," Häberle said. "No one is safe here under the circumstances, María-le."

"He left for the day," she said. "How will you find him?"

"My brother, my brother." He stood and walked around the room. He still wore a bikini, now with sandals. He had showered and shaved. "I can't leave him here. What if they come? They'll certainly think he is me."

"He'll hide from them, you've said so yourself. He knows what to do," María said. She folded her hands in her lap. She sat erect. "I know your brother. He will refuse to go with us. He's better here, *don* Jorge, doing for himself. There is no way to protect him."

"Are you hard? Have you become a hard woman?" Häberle shouted, coming over to the table and leaning forward, bracing himself with his hands on its top. "He's my little brother. He's not a complete adult."

I reached out to Kai who was sitting beside me.

"You say he fought in a war. He didn't die, *viejo*. He found his way through. He'll survive," María said.

Häberle's eyes squinted almost closed, but I could see the blue of his pupils flitting from us to María and back.

"He is simple in the head from the war, you know that, *Señora* María. You know he would be like a child before them if they caught him."

"Then he'll run away," she said. Her face had hardened, was giving nothing.

I didn't know exactly what was going on. Was this some sort of twist on her grief for her own brother?

"You understand nothing," he yelled.

I jumped. Kai kept hold of me.

María began to slide along the bench.

"You know nothing of war. They will shoot him in the back if he runs from these Nazis. They will think nothing of shooting him in the back. Just as your friend Mingo shot those men in their sleep."

As María walked past him, he clutched the side of the table.

"María, he should not have shot those men. I don't believe in killing. I will not allow killing. I have seen too much killing in my life."

"So have I, *señor*. So have I." She turned at the door and stood framed against the blue of the curtain. "They kill from the skies already. What do you say to that? Should there be no punishment? Should we allow them to go unpunished?"

"They will be punished. We will find a way, *mi amor*," he said, his voice gravelly with remorse.

"Pssst. You don't know this country as I thought you did, my love," she said. She waved her finger in front of her face. "The poor never win *en mi tierra. Y los indios*? You think the Indians have as much chance as the poor? Oh, dear *don* Jorge, no, no, no. You may have lived through a war, but you don't understand. You don't see that nothing can be done without killing. If one side kills, the other must as well. There is no choice."

She lifted the curtain, but didn't go through. "I'll be ready to leave in an hour. I'll tell the others to be prepared. I will try to find your brother, but if I don't see him, I'll still be ready to leave in one hour." The curtain closed behind her.

Häberle remained with his fists on the table top, his long stringy muscles straining. Even with his shower and shave, there were dark lines of dirt in the deep crevices of his face, across his forehead, down his cheeks, in the spidery age lines of his upper lip.

"My wife doesn't know what true war is," he said, hoarsely. "Mingo and she don't know how bad it can become. Here we have only the beginnings of a modern genocidal war. They have been killing Indians for centuries in the Americas, but now it will get worse, mark my word, now that they have the technology, the way we Germans had the technology, Mingo's *scheisse* guns will be like that." He snapped his fingers, sneering. "He'll be stepped on like the cockroaches these people think the Indians are. The Indians are a nuisance to the government and the oil companies. Get the *indigenas* out of the way, clean things up. Then we can live as we wish. Then we can be the best, the richest, then no one can push us around. Oh my God." He tapped his knuckles against the table. "It's like your Vietnam, *señorita*, in more ways than the napalm. They first aim to pacify these people with land and goods. To keep them dependent and vulnerable. Our dear friend Mingo feeds directly into their plans in more ways than he can even imagine." Häberle moved stiffly to the side of the table opposite us. He slowly let himself down and sat with the palms of his hands flat on the table's surface. "Let me explain something that you may not understand. You know now that Mingo trades in guns and western goods. What you may not know is that such trading, even in its simplest form, the bartering and selling of tee shirts to the tribes, gives him great power, shamanist powers to be exact."

Remembering the friar's early accusation, I felt the shock of what Häberle was saying about Mingo.

"Don't look so frightened, *Fräulein*. This fact does not implicate our friend in evil doings. The most powerful men of the Shuar and other communities obtain and maintain their power through such trading of western goods. Nonetheless, it is dangerous because it prepares the tribes for the Evangelists. And to some extent the Salesians. They too lure these forest people with goods. The religious colonists' strategy is to make the Indians economically dependent, and once they have them where they want them, they go for their souls like an arrow for the target. That is my argument with Mingo. Such trading eats away at the fabric of tradition where he should be working to strengthen it. Oh, he says he achieves this work through his Salesian-run Federation of Shuar Centers, but he knows better than that. As soon as the government pushes a little harder the religious hypocrites fold and pay obeisance, just as the Evangelists did with this Roani reserve when the government wanted to explore for oil. They will do whatever the government asks to keep themselves within grabbing distance of their prey.

"Mingo should have focused his attention on resisting the proselytizers. He knows better than anyone what destruction they do. He knows how they work hand in hand with the exploiters. Within the reserve all power is granted through the missionaries. These tribes can only gain real political power by a true indigenous coming together, not with Mingo's foolish gun-running. His guns come from weakness," Häberle went on, his eyes burning with belief. "I needed Mingo's help in promulgating these notions when talk started about the oil companies. I thought he was willing when he recognized what *Padre* Báez was doing. But then he got this misguided notion of bringing guns in. I needed a tribal man to work co-operatively, peacefully, rationally. To help the Roani speak for themselves. Without his partnership, I was only some German with an obsession about how it should be. An ex-Nazi, a megalomaniac they said, from whom the Indians needed to be protected. Protected from me. When it is the government these Indians must be protected from. Now with Mingo's guns the government has the excuse to move in and eradicate them. Because to the officials the Roani and Runa are nothing. *Nada. Nichts.* Indians are valued less than animals by them. At least animals you can get hides from or birds their feathers. They don't even have gold teeth, no gold teeth like we got from the Jews. No more..."

"Maybe we should stop here, *Herr* Häberle," Kai interrupted.

Georg Häberle smiled. "You too, you think I'm a Nazi. You think I want to kill your wife, maybe, because she is a Jew?"

"Please, sir, this is going too far," Kai said. "We're all upset by what's happened. Please don't go on."

"I may have certain points of view," Häberle continued as though driven by some perversity of will. "Certain peculiarities. Certain secrets in my past."

Neither of us answered him.

Then Georg Häberle got up from his side of the table and came around to mine. I shrank away.

Kai stood. "Please sir."

"Please sir, yourself." Georg Häberle embraced me, pulling me gently to him. Inside I resisted, but I allowed him to hold me. He smelled of fish and garlic and María's homemade soap. "Don't suspect me so, my little *Frau*. Please don't suspect me so. I could see it in your eyes that you think I'm evil." I shook my head. His hand came to my cheek stopping me. "No, I saw it. Listen to me. The government here sent me back to my country when the war started. They sent all Germans of fighting age. I knew nothing. I believed in my country even though I'd chosen not to live there. I felt sorry for my country, so torn apart. I thought maybe it was a good thing that someone was trying to bring it back together. I didn't know who this Hitler was until I got to Germany. Please believe me. But once there, I couldn't stand up against the forces. Please believe me, my sweet young woman, that I did only what was necessary to get by. I quickly saw what monsters they were. But I am not innocent. I am as guilty as those who did worse. This man has no illusions about his own goodness. I try to make up for my transgressions, in my way. I do my best, little *Frau*. We all do our best in this house." He still held me clenched to his body. He leaned down, putting his sweaty face to mine, his odors filling me. When he spoke again it was in a whisper. "My brother Max was only a boy. I didn't know him until the end of the war. He was nineteen. I'd left when he was two years old. I never knew him as a whole man. I have no idea of his morality. I know that he was a sensitive enough boy to have to go to a mental hospital after the war. Is he evil? Does he have a conscience? I don't know that, my lovely *Frau*. I only know he rarely speaks. I know he trusts no one. I brought him here after the war. Please try to understand. He is my little brother."

Kai and I packed in silence on the side porch. We had to take all our belongings with us to the bombing site if we were to leave from there. The last item I put in was my defunct tape-recorder. What would I have gotten if I'd interviewed Häberle? Would the story have been less ambiguous in a running narrative? Would a hero have emerged?

"I'll carry the camera," Kai said. "Do you want me to take the tape-recorder, too?"

I shook my head. "No, I'll take the recorder."

"Maybe I can get some shots at the camp," he said in a flat voice.

"Oh, Kai, what does it matter?" I tied the cord of my pack and buckled the flap. I dragged it over to the wall and left it leaning there.

"Come here," he said. He was sitting swinging in the hammock, pushing off the floor with his foot. "I said come here."

I sat beside him, falling down in the hollow, so we were one.

"We should get going," I said.

"We have a good half-hour."

We swung in silence.

"Are you ready for what's next?" he asked.

"I've decided not to think of that," I said. "How can I possibly be ready. How could we ever have been prepared for what we've seen?"

"And who we've met here?"

"What do you mean?"

"Häberle."

"I don't want to talk about him." A wave of nauseous dizziness came over me, as though factions were warring in my head. "Can we stop before it turns vicious?" I tried to get out of the hammock, but Kai held me back.

"Maybe I want to talk about it."

"What good is it, Kai? He's culpable."

"You don't give him any credit for talking to you about it, for admitting it? Most people I know pretend it didn't happen, pretend their innocence, even forget, have real amnesia about it."

Like your own family, I thought.

"No matter how much he wants to make up, tries to absolve himself with his so-called pacifism, he committed crimes against my people."

"Your people?"

"Yes, my people. Jews. He and his evil, crazy brother."

"Sometimes I think you stayed with me to prove your Jewishness to yourself," he said with a sigh.

With that, a rage whipped through me like a firebomb blast. I grabbed his shirt and yanked it, ripping it down the front. I sank my fingernails into his bare arm, feeling a surge of pleasure at the vulnerability of flesh. He pushed me away with his sharp elbow.

"You stop that, fucking stop that," he growled. "Stop trying to hurt me."

"Don't you ever insult me like that," I seethed, grabbing his other arm. "Don't you ever open your filthy mouth to me again."

"You hate *my* people, Annie. You hate my language. You hate my country so much you must hate me too. You chose me so you'd have somebody to hate and hate and hate. I'm not going to let you honor your mother any more by hating me. I'm tired of it. Tired of being hurt by you."

My fingers went slack. No, I love you, I thought. I chose you to prove that love exists, that sadness and evil don't run in the blood; I wanted to prove that beneath history and politics, even beneath personality and psychology, is where we connect. Yes, beneath all our differences is the place we first found love for each other. Where words, and wars, and cultures don't matter.

"What is it?" His voice was chilly with suspicion.

"It's too hard to explain," I whispered.

He let go of my wrist. "My stomach aches."

"No, no." I touched his belly lightly. "I heard what you were telling me."

"I shouldn't have said those things. I don't know where they came from. I have shooting pains in my stomach. I hope it's nothing we ate. I love you, Annie. So damn much."

"I know. I heard that, too. I was even more vicious than you."

"I think maybe I'm beginning to feel better now," he said.

"That's good." My face was against his bare chest.

"I'm going to try to talk more about how it was, Annie. But it's not so easy because I don't know that much. Believe me, people who may remember really don't talk about the war. It's very hard to broach the subject."

I recalled that one theory about the amnesia of the Germans was that they had a moral conscience and that acknowledging the atrocities was too great a challenge to that morality. I offered as much to Kai.

"I don't know about that. It sounds too good, if you know what I mean. More likely it's about not wanting to blow open the myth of our superiority. I really don't know, Annie. I'll tell you my private stories, but I'm not so good on social theory. I do have one memory, though, that might interest you. You want to hear before we go?"

"Of course."

"During Occupation we got kicked out of our house because it was the best in the neighborhood. They gave it over to an American officer named Kaplan. When he left he asked if he could keep a recording of ours he'd come to love but couldn't buy in the postwar, Munich stores. It was Mozart's piano concerto, Köchel listing number 580. My mother, of course, gave it to him. It wasn't until I came to

America that I realized he must have been Jewish. But what I want to tell you is that when we had to move out of the house our family was separated, my sisters going with my mother and I with my father. My father and I lived in a room up over an automotive garage. It must have been around when he was being de-Nazified by the Occupation army, the Americans. My father was a very quiet man, so it's difficult to say if there was anything different in his demeanor at that time. Try as I may, I can't perceive if there was meanness in the man. All I know is that he remained kind to me. During that spring and summer I often would be in the room alone after school. American troops were bivouacked in the garage yard below. I watched them, usually half-hidden by the curtain. But once a soldier caught me looking. He called something to me and then tossed up a bar of chocolate which I had never tasted and a fruit I had never seen. I saved the strange round fruit for when my father came home. My father told me it was an orange and showed me how to open it and break apart the juicy sweet sections. Then he left the orange peel on the window sill. After a few days, when it had dried, he chopped it into tiny slivers which he took to my mother who baked them into a cake. My first week in America I walked into a supermarket and was overcome by the aroma of Occupation, that indelible mixture of chocolate and oranges. I remember thinking that if America had been totalitarian, considering the might and influence of the country, the whole world could have smelled of chocolate and oranges."

When he had finished, I examined the inside of his upper arm and saw how blood had broken through in little crescent shaped cuts. I kissed and rubbed my cheek against them.

"Your tears smart," he said.

"The better to ward off infection," I said.

Perhaps there would always be unspoken thoughts and suspicions in this area between us. Maybe that was how it was between most married couples, even those who didn't have to reach across so much history, but it didn't mean we couldn't love each other and feel compassion for the other's reservoir of memory. As blasphemous as this might seem to my father, there had to be safe houses of privacy and human ambiguity where the rules of politics weren't allowed.

María and Häberle were not in the house. I went around to the kitchen. The woman Yayae was packing a three foot high basket with a head holder attached, like the ones Kai and Häberle had carried.

"María?" I asked. "Don Jorge?"

She understood and pointed in the direction of the river.

I started back around the porch to tell Kai, when I heard a man's and a woman's voice from the direction of the river. They were both yelling.

"I think that's María and Jorge," I said, when I reached Kai. "Maybe it has to do with Max. Should we go?"

We ran down the stairs and along the path to the river. When we got there I at first saw nothing. Then farther down, almost at the same place we'd seen Max the other day, Kai spotted María and Häberle beckoning to someone. As we drew closer we saw Max. The man stood hunched over, dressed in his hip high boots and overalls and undershirt. He was without his hat, and his gray hair stood out around his flushed face. He looked both the old man and the boy as he huddled there, waving them away with the back of his hand. "Váyase, váyase. Auf gehts. Auf gehts." He called in a mixture of Spanish and German.

"Come, brother Max, please, mein Bruder. Du kannst nicht hier bleiben. It is too dangerous." Häberle called to him, stepping now into the water and beginning to wade across. The river reached the middle of his bare thighs. The current was strong, and he braced himself with each step.

Max, still bent over, backed his way along the bank. He left his belongings as he moved away.

"María," I called over the sound of the river. "Can we help?"

She turned and raised her hands helplessly into the air. The skirt of her black dress was soaked as was half the bodice, as though she'd slipped and fallen into the water.

"There's nothing to be done. He won't come. Jorge won't give up." She took the black scarf from her head and bent down, dipping it in the river. She mopped her face as she walked toward Kai and me. "We have begged him and chased him from there to there to there and back again, since lunchtime. Why can't *don* Jorge stop? *¡Viejito!*" she yelled out, with her hand cupped to her mouth. "*Viejito*, come back. Leave your brother in peace!" She turned to Kai. "Go do something with that German. Maybe you can talk to him. He is grieving already for his brother's death. Tell him his brother will be safer here than where we are going."

She linked her arm in mine and began to walk determinedly along the bank.

"He thinks because I've lost a brother, he will too. He is more superstitious than María. Uneducated María. Oh *chica, chica*. We have all gone *loco* with this. We are all now as crazy as that brother of his. Poor soul. Poor little animal."

As for myself, I was glad he wouldn't be accompanying us.

We stumbled along arm in arm. Her skin was like satin against mine and her muscles and tendons like the toughest gristle. I thought of how Rina always linked her arm in mine and how initially it had embarrassed me until I'd learned this was the way of Latin women. I clenched María's arm tighter against my side and concentrated on her strength and the comfort I found in her closeness.

"You heard about what Mingo did," she said when we'd reached the path to the house and stopped to look a last time downriver.

Kai and Häberle were struggling to get out of the water on our side of the river. Max was nowhere in sight. The light indicated that it was past noon. I knew we had to get started immediately if we were going to reach the settlement and have a few hours of light left to work.

"Yes, I heard from Kai."

She glanced up at me, but didn't ask the next question of whether or not I approved. I guessed that she took Mingo's side in this. I didn't answer her unasked question, because I didn't yet know whether I supported Mingo or not.

"It's going to make things very dangerous," she said. "I hope you understand that, *chica?*"

"Yes, I do," I said.

"Ah, good. Your husband has talked *don* Jorge into giving up. Thank God you came along. I would never have gotten the old man to stop trying."

I glanced over in time to catch her expression of love and deep concern, before it changed to the bravado of disgust.

"*Loco*, the German has gone *loco* like his brother."

CHAPTER TWENTY-EIGHT

We moved swiftly along the path through the high trees, low palms, and grass. It had been traveled so often in the last days that a well-trodden swath was cut into the vegetation. I was in the middle of our large group and Kai had taken up the rear at Häberle's request. Häberle, with Kemonka and Awae, led the march. María was just ahead of me, her dark figure carrying one of the head-slung root baskets. From time to time one of the naked children ran beside her, and then fell back to me and fell farther back to one of the Indian women, and then with darting spurts ran fast and gracefully up to the men in the lead. They had been told to be silent as we all were, and only the sound of their bare feet on earth could be heard. I did my best to place my sneakers carefully down, but even so, they fell with thuds that seemed to resound through the forest.

Our entire settlement, with the exception of the runaway brother, Max, had come with us. Häberle in his agitated state had insisted. I'd seen him talking furiously with Kemonka under the house when I'd carried down my pack. Kemonka appeared to want to stay on guard with his gun. But Häberle had prevailed, and here we all were: seven Indian women, five Indian men, four children old enough to walk and run, and three infants carried on the women's hips, and one in a cloth across the pregnant girl's naked torso.

The sun was slanting through the trees when we got on the trail, but it remained cool on the forest floor. We didn't rest once during the two hour trip. Even the children who had to urinate paused on their own and squatted or sent streams from tiny penises and then ran to catch up. I knew we were close to the settlement when the stench of chemicals and charred earth and the foul smell of day-old burst animal carcasses greeted us.

When we reached the clearing, we found it devoid of all life. There was nothing more than a huge, empty expanse of black, oil-slicked ground with devastated trees, limbless and twisted, fallen giants lying dead on the slimy floor. Or the others, still standing, forlorn, stripped of all life, waiting for a faint wind to topple them. But there was no movement. No shadows. No sounds of birds or animals. No human enterprise. Only the relentless sun, temperatures ten degrees hotter than in the forest, and craters dug wide and deep in the blackened earth.

"Go back," Häberle whispered to our stunned group. He motioned wildly. "Go back into the forest. Quickly. Something has gone wrong." Then he spoke in the Roani's language, equally urgently.

We turned and ran down the path and then cut over into dense underbrush. We scrambled through, balancing, not to be toppled by swinging branches and our top-heavy packs. We grabbed children by the arms, pushed others through on their buttocks. Kai picked up the smallest boy and carried him in his arms. The forest floor opened again, but still María and Kemonka motioned us farther on until we came to a stand of trees growing in a circle. Words passed between Kemonka and María, and she stopped and told us to get down.

We sat, we squatted, we hunched over. We had formed our own irregular circle within the trees' circle, with the children in the center. I looked around. I looked behind us. No Häberle.

"Where is *don* Jorge?" I whispered to María, who knelt beside me.

"*Ya se fue,*" she said through closed lips.

"He shouldn't have gone alone," Kai, squatting on my other side, said in English.

I looked behind me again. "I think Awae went with him. But why did they leave? Why did Jorge send us away?"

"Because everyone has gone," Kai said. "The shelter we built was demolished. Something must have happened. Some sort of retaliation. Please have it not be that."

María grabbed my shoulder and shook her head vehemently to silence us.

I linked my arm in Kai's and we sat there for about ten minutes, waiting, breathing shallowly, all of us. The Indian men and women had fear in their eyes, too. They would scan the ceiling of the forest and back down to the ground and up to the canopy again. I found eyes skimming my face. It was the first time any one of them had looked directly at me. Even Kemonka, who squatted with a rifle across his lap, looked at me and his eyes softened as though in recognition of another human caught in fear. I thought, they are as unaccustomed to this sort of war as I am, to these enemies who come from the air and drop fire to the earth to destroy everything. We waited and waited. My legs went from aching to numbness.

"*Chica,*" María leaned toward me, grasping my arm. "I need a favor, please."

The tension of the silence by now had become unbearable. Even her speaking in a whisper lessened it somewhat.

"*¿Sí, cómo no?*"

"A favor, *chica*. Speak to God for María. For *la negra María*. I cannot." She put her free hand to her heart.

"María, I don't..."

"Please, *niña*, tell God, if He brings my Jorge and Mingo and the others, the Awae, the others, if he brings them back I will believe in Him. If He makes it all good again. I will forgive Him for the loss of my brother." Her fingers dug into my arm. She came close, her face touching mine. "Please, *chica*, *niña*, I count on you to speak to Him. He won't hear me. You must help the old black one."

Without further question, I began. "*Nuestro Señor, por favor, nos escucha, por favor, ayúdanos, ayuda a la Señora María, la buena Señora María, la negra Señora María. Por favor, traiga el don Jorge otra vez a nuestro lado. Por favor, nuestro Señor, traiga el don Jorge, Mingo, Awae, y todos los otros, los indios, todos por favor, tráigalos todos a nuestros lados, sanos y vivos. Gracias, Señor, gracias por todo su ayuda, gracias por escucharnos aquí en la selva."*

I went on, my litany repeating itself over and over. I thought of the rhythms and the words I'd heard the few times I'd visited a Catholic church with Mrs. Siciliano, our housekeeper, and I tried to copy them. As I did, two voices spoke in me. One aloud for María, and the second silently for myself. I thought of Gala and Ladito, Rina and Angel, and I asked forgiveness, for having ill-served them, for having left them behind.

Before I opened my eyes, I could feel that the prayer had helped, that the group had calmed. I felt their breathing become slower, deeper, quieter. Kai's arm in mine relaxed. When I stopped speaking, there was silence again. María had let go of my arm and had her head down. She made a sign of the cross and kissed her hands. She crossed herself again and started to murmur a prayer of her own, the words of which I couldn't make out.

Kemonka watched me, but the other Indians stared across our group into the forest. The children began to look exhausted, their eyelids growing heavy, as they were caressed by the adults, both men and women. Whatever happened now, would happen, I thought. I gazed around at the green as the others did, at the lianas hanging from high branches, at the geometric patterns of the palms, at the misty air caught in the upper reaches of the trees, and I thought, it wouldn't be so bad to die here in this beautiful place with these people. Though I was no closer to belief as a result of the prayer, for the first time I felt an acceptance of death. That it was a human occurrence, an earthly possibility, and that there would be another sort of existence within it, in its process. There could be a swooning and a peace, and an embrace. It could be done with other people. I didn't close my eyes, but kept them wide open. I wanted to remain in that reverie, take it in, never to be without it.

A crashing came through the forest, the sound of many feet breaking through. Simultaneously, we all clasped hands around our circle, the Indian men and women, María, Kai, me. The children sat up in terror, whimpering, crawling into the laps of the adults. The crashing came closer and closer. They were a few feet from us, obviously following the path our own feet had made as we'd rushed here, away from danger. "Please," I whispered. Suddenly a face appeared across the group from me, over Kemonka's head. An Indian face. Awae's face. It was like seeing a dear old friend. Awae.

He shouted in the Roanis' language. The men rose, shouting back. Kai leapt up and ran to Awae embracing him. Awae stroked Kai's upper arm and shook it, hopping up and down. As this went on, three other men appeared out of the forest. I recognized them from the bombing. Their arms, shoulders, and legs were wrapped in gauze. Otherwise they wore nothing. With them was the old man from the monkey hunt.

"Jorge?" María asked. She had risen slowly and walked over to where Awae stood with Kai and the others.

When they answered her, their words raced, all of them talking together, hands flying and pointing. The old man made a gun with his arm. Then took Kemonka's gun from him. He made shooting noises, pointing it at Awae. Awae fell to the ground clutching his chest.

"¡Aiie! ¡Dios!" María collapsed to sitting.

"María." I scrambled on my hands and knees to get to her. "María, what is it?"

"Aaiee!"

"Is it Jorge?"

"No. But those men, the ones who came for me the other night, they went into the hospital." She rocked back and forth holding herself. "They shot at my Indians. They killed more. A child." She rocked. I didn't touch her.

"They're going to kill him, I know they're going to kill Jorge. They are devils. I damn those devils," she screamed.

"María," I said. "María, you must listen to me. Remember how you told me not to give in to my fear the day of the bombing? You told me there was no time for it.

You must do the same. *Don* Jorge is still alive. Please, you are the only person who can speak to the men without Kemonka translating. Stop this hysteria and speak with them. We must know what to do."

She didn't move. She didn't respond to me.

"What is it exactly?" Kai said.

I told him as I watched for some reaction from María.

"I knew they would retaliate. They couldn't let it stop at that. Mingo was a fool to have done this. It only gives them an excuse for more barbarity. Jorge is right on this."

I nodded. Mingo was an amateur against professionals, against mercenaries really. He had no idea what he was getting into, nor who was paying them, nor how much power and money was riding on their success. All his guns and traditional beads and stories of his father's shame and Che Guevara theory and racial rage wasn't going to win this one. It was the same as me going up against Fernando Calderón and whoever had backed him. But Häberle's dream was equally unrealistic. The indigenous population, no matter how peaceful and well-organized, could never prevail against the force of western thought and money.

María stood. With her arms wrapped around her waist, her eyes to the ground, she talked with the men in a subdued voice. I listened to the darkness of the language.

She looked down at me where I still sat. "*Chica*, the story is this. Of the three men who invaded the camp and killed our *inocentes*, the Aucas mortally shot the fat one. I remember *el gordo*, stinking of perfume. The one who put his body close to mine when he threatened me. Our men killed him with one of *compadre* Mingo's guns. His two friends didn't stay to collect their man, but went running like cowards into the forest." She crossed herself. "God forgive me, but I'm glad we had the guns."

"Have you always been glad to have them?" I asked quietly.

For a moment she stared at me, assessing what her answer should be. "Yes, *chica*. I have always agreed with Mingo on this. There is no other way to fight this filth."

"And Mingo and *don* Jorge?" Kai asked, squatting down beside me. "Where are they now?"

"Mingo went after the two who ran. Awae and these men stayed to try to bring their dead to life." She rubbed her breasts as though they pained her. "When Mingo returned, he said everyone had to move on. But before leaving they found a good place for the dead in the forest and covered them with palm leaves. They carried the injured who couldn't walk to the new camp Jorge was setting up." Then she indicated the three men standing with Awae. "Awae said it is important that you know these men worked very hard." She looked pointedly at me.

As Kai and I nodded our appreciation to the three men and Awae, all I could think of was whether Mingo had shot the remaining two intruders. There wasn't a way to ask Awae who stood, not moving, his face grave. I decided to ask María.

"Did Mingo kill the other two, *Señora* María?"

"Don't ask questions that mustn't be answered. I trust he did what was right." She bent to pick up the basket she had been carrying.

I helped her lift the heavy burden and set the support strap properly on her forehead. "I don't want you to know, *chica*. It's better that you don't know everything.

We followed the Indian men through the forest to the new settlement. There was no trail, no faint path that I could see. Two of them had machetes which they wielded high, whacking and slashing through an area thick with low trees and undergrowth. We stepped over fallen branches and leaves, palms and breadfruit trees and elephant ears. The air was hotter here. When we had traveled some way, we heard the caracara's warning screech.

"This must have been a settlement," Kai said, coming up beside me.

"Yes," I said, wiping sweat from my face, out of my eyes. "Judging by the low growth."

He stayed beside me. "Are you okay?"

"I hope so. Are you?"

"Did I hear what I think I did back there. Did they kill three men?"

I met his gaze momentarily, trying to telegraph that yes, I thought they had said that.

"Oh, Annie, I'll be so glad to be out of here." And with that he dropped back.

I imagined an extended family peacefully living in the clearing for a year or two. Then when the soil had given out, moving deeper in, finding another place, slashing and burning and beginning again. But they took up so little space. So little destruction. Why couldn't they just be left alone? As soon as the thought entered my consciousness, I heard my own obstinate naiveté. I knew it would never be that easy again.

We trudged on through the hot, still air. It recalled the oven-like summer days when as a child I'd sit on the curb in whatever midwestern or New England town we lived in, with my new best friend, and we'd be too hot for more than making up stories based on our favorite cowboy movies or Errol Flynn swashbucklers. We'd compete for who was the bravest, who could ride the horse straight through the canyon knowing there was a possibility of an ambush, or who could walk the plank for her beliefs. It was I who instigated these games of the imagination, secretly believing I would be the most valorous, the unspoken assumption always being that I was on the side of good. How different reality was.

I thought of the radio station and our bravado in reporting the latest prison uprising, or the riots at the Democratic convention of the summer before, or interviewing Vietnam Vets Against the War who committed daring acts of disobedience. We were brave in the security of our studios or even in the streets, but always with microphones before us, between ourselves and the action. We reported on the use of napalm in Vietnam, on the escalating violence in demonstrations and the bombings by the left underground in the States. We would pledge proudly to get the story from both sides, but really we were egging people on to further confrontation, exhilarated by each escalation of violence. I spoke big words and marched where and when it was safe. I now saw the difference between what I did and what my father had done. Both my father and Mingo—even taking into account their human frailty—had made mindful, binding choices. Both had agreed to accept the consequences of their decisions, whereas I swung out in blind rage at an Ecuadorian teenager and wasn't able to demand information about my friend Angel. I blamed Kai for being a child to whom war had seemed normal and elevated his reluctance to talk about it to a state crime. I condemned George Häberle who had been thrust forcibly into a war he didn't understand until it was too late. All this while I, their accuser, had barely glimpsed the power of fascism. What I'd learned in these few days was that a little thoughtful humility went further in understanding the ways of the world than my usual righteousness. Something my own country could stand to learn as well.

It was late afternoon when we arrived at the location they'd chosen for the hiding place. We were brought into the area by an Indian man who'd been standing guard with another. They both carried guns. The area was overgrown.

"We didn't clear it," Mingo explained after we exchanged greetings and María stopped the crying that had sprung from her on seeing Häberle. "We can't take the chance of being discovered from the air or the ground."

Mingo carried a gun. He wore no shirt, only long dark pants and sneakers. The necklace of tiny red, white, and turquoise beads was still around his neck. He smiled and bowed slightly. "Señora," was all he said directly to me.

There was tension between Mingo and Häberle. It was nothing in what they said, but in their manner to each other. They were formal, yet on more equal footing. Mingo didn't obviously defer to the older man. Häberle didn't watch over him.

"*Du musst gehen heute Abend*," Häberle said to Kai. You must go this evening.

Kai was so tired he could hardly speak. "How far is it to the boat?" he asked Häberle. "I've not slept in two days. I hope I can hold up."

"To get to the river won't take long from here," Häberle explained. "In an hour on foot continuing north, you'll be at a tributary that intersects with the Napo. A small canoe moored there will take you to the spot on the Napo where you left Mingo's boat, and from there, you can sleep in the dugout. The motor can do the job. Isn't that right, *Señor* Mingo?"

Mingo didn't answer, but glared at Häberle. He didn't want to take us back, didn't want to leave here with the job unfinished. But Häberle was determined to get us out of here, and despite the tension between them, he still prevailed.

Häberle didn't continue with this discussion. Instead he asked Kai to make some photos before leaving. "You must bring the proof back."

As Kai knelt and clumsily worked at unclasping and untying his backpack, I asked about what had happened at the other site.

"We lost some men," was all that Häberle would say, his face sagging with either fatigue or despair.

"And children too, from what I heard," I said.

"Yes, *Fräulein*, and children." He glanced over at Mingo with near hatred in his eyes. "We have made foolish mistakes out here in the past few days. And we have paid the consequences."

Mingo turned and walked away.

The lean-tos they'd covered with palm leaves were strung to standing trees, well-camouflaged from the ground and from the air as Mingo had said. As I approached them with Häberle, Kai, and María, the stench of rotting, festering flesh all but overwhelmed me. The wounded lay on mats, asleep it appeared, with their heads fallen to one side. Intravenous bags hung from the edge of the slanted structure. Liquids dripped into their arms. Their bandages were soaked through with blood and pus, and where the bandages hadn't been applied, flies were landing on the open wounds and sucking up the ruined cells. One child remained. I couldn't see how she could be living. Her flesh was chewed up and covered with flies. The woman who sat at her feet kept fanning them away.

"They don't heal in this environment," Häberle said, clutching the top of the structure as we looked in. "The wounds are festering faster than the antibiotics can fight the bacteria."

"The others?" I asked, counting five bodies including the child.

"That's it. *Todo. Alles*," he said. Then, "It's a blessing to be dead. We have those storm troopers to thank for that."

Kai walked away and sat under a tree. I couldn't move.

"Come." Häberle took my hand. "Come please, we mustn't look any longer."

I followed María over to another tree and we sat beneath it. Kai was stretched out across from us, his eyes closed. Mingo had come back and was talking intensely but quietly to Häberle. María put her arm around me and pulled me close. She urged my head onto her breast. She soothed my cheek with her hand.

"This is why I lost my faith in God, *chica*. To see people suffer makes me doubt His goodness. It is because of this." She leaned forward and kissed my forehead, whispering. "And why I believe Mingo is right in the use of force."

Swiveling to look up, I found that her eyes were closed. "No more questions," she said. "No more answers from María."

Mingo and Häberle went over to Kai. They sat down on their haunches and talked with him for a few minutes, then Kai, picking up his camera, stood, groaning from the effort. I watched as he hesitated and then strode over to the lean-to with the most serious cases and began taking photos. His skinny shoulders hunched with each shot. He shook himself at one point as though to exorcise what he

was taking in. When he had finished, the three of them
spoke some more, and Kai turned and began shooting the
clearing, including the women who sat under the tree
peeling the manioc they had carried here. The children
sat watching the women, transfixed, too exhausted to play.
I imagined that the pictures would show how beautiful
these people look here, how well they fit in. At Häberle's
place, I'd found their appearance slightly disagreeable,
pugnacious, too crude. But here, in the untouched green,
where their skin was the color of tree bark and earth, and
their black hair like the darkest shadows, and their features
gentle when set against the green, more than beautiful,
completely in harmony with their environment. Where
they had looked awkward both with and without clothes at
Häberle's, here their skin and hair were the finest, most
luxurious coverings.

"You'll send me something from America to remember
you by?" María asked.

How I once hated that question! When it felt as though
my total value was determined by what I could send from
America.

"What do you want?" I asked.

"Perhaps one of those photos," she said. "Of the *indios*, or
of you and me. I could put it by my bureau beside the photo
of *don* Jorge and María."

"I'd like that," I said. "I'll make a second copy and put it
on my bureau. But are you going back to your house? Is it
safe for you there?"

She shrugged. "*Don* Jorge will decide that."

Kai took the last pictures, first of Häberle and María for
Häberle's mother in Augsburg, then of Mingo and me,
then of all of four of us, followed by a group shot with all
the Indians, Kemonka and Awae kneeling in front with
their weapons. Kemonka had his gun and Awae his
blowgun. As Kai was about to put the camera on automatic
so he could be in the group photograph, we heard a
rumbling in the distance.

"It's not the plane," Kai said. "I'd know the sound of that plane anywhere." Then his eyes narrowed and he looked at me. "It's the helicopter. They can land with that."

Without another word, we all began to run to where the women had laid out the food. Each of us grabbed something and raced toward the deeper forest. Kai and Mingo stayed behind moving the grass so that no one could tell it had been matted down. I stopped and turned back.

"Please hurry," I called, fearful that the friar was piloting the helicopter, remembering what Alice Albertson had warned, 'Roberto Báez is dangerous. They say he stops at nothing.' The rumbling had become a roar, though it must have been a mile away.

They both came running toward me. Kai kept going, but Mingo stopped. He had his gun raised.

"Idiot," I yelled.

"I am not an idiot, señora."

"If you fire that gun, we could all be killed."

Häberle came up behind us. "Mingo, by my honor, by everything we have had between us, don't fire on that machine." He shouted, beseeching through the motor's clamor. "Please. You don't know what they're carrying. For God's sake, let them fly by. We must get these gringos out of here. They must get back home and tell this story. Don't jeopardize that. Please, son. Do this one thing for me."

Mingo shook his hair back. He stood. "You're right," he shouted. "It would be a very foolish thing to do."

I took Mingo's arm. "You're not an idiot," I yelled as we broke into a trot, running to where the others hid beneath the trees. The noise of the helicopter was close to deafening. "I'll admire you always for that."

Though he looked at me, he didn't smile.

We moved far into the wood, deep into the cool darkness before stopping. The helicopter was directly over the spot where the lean-tos were. They could never see us in here, but could they spot the lean-tos? The rotary blades were louder than a bomb explosion. We sat huddled together with our ears covered and our eyes upward. The tops of the trees swayed from the wind generated by the helicopter. I imagined the grass Kai and Mingo had carefully moved being swept this way and that. Would the lean-tos withstand that wind? We didn't have to worry that anyone would call out. They were too weak and no one could possibly hear them through the soul splitting din. Beside me a woman sat cross-legged, whimpering. Was the copter leaving? I gave a questioning look to Kai. He lifted his hands from his ears and listened. He nodded. It was rising above the treetops, still circling. It wheeled yet higher and then it moved off, its roar receding for a good fifteen minutes before there was complete silence in the forest.

CHAPTER TWENTY-NINE

The parting wasn't easy for any of us. Häberle kept wanting to be assured that we would get the photos developed and send them to reporters for papers and magazines. I promised that we would, though I didn't tell him that I had my doubts about how much coverage it would get. The straight press, as we called it then, was reluctant to publish anything so provocative without government confirmation. But I promised I would do something on my radio station.

Häberle said that as soon as they could move the injured they would return to his house. I was relieved to hear him say that he thought the Roani should move on. But before they could, they had to gather their manioc roots to plant in their new home. He and María would go to Quito where he wanted to approach the German embassy. They might be receptive, he said, once he had the photos from us in hand. "You must send them as soon as they are developed. *Pronto, pronto, pronto.* Do your hear?"

During these last interchanges we all tried our best to keep the mood light. Even Mingo and Häberle parted on relatively amicable terms, though Mingo was more taciturn about his plans. He would go to Macas, he said, to visit his father and get some merchandise.

Kai embraced Awae vigorously, causing the Roani to laugh uproariously, setting even Kemonka off on a round of high shrieks. I went to the Indian women I knew and formally bid them *adiós*. They seemed pleased.

And María. I couldn't let go of her nor she me. Finally Kai said in a low voice that we had to leave.

"Awae has to take us in the dugout to Mingo's canoe and get back here to help, Annie."

I held María, felt her soft full breasts against mine as I whispered, "you take care."

"Go with God. He'll protect you," she answered.

When we reached Mingo's boat we shoved off immediately. It had taken us two hours in Awae's canoe, an hour longer than we anticipated. We traveled into the setting sun, back toward the west. Kai collapsed onto the floor of the dugout, covered by his plastic poncho and within moments he was breathing deeply. I faced into the intensely red sky, and thought of my mother saying on our trips across country, "Red sky at night, sailor's delight, red sky in the morning, sailor take warning." I remembered the red sunrise on the morning, not a week ago, when the sun had risen gigantic, shimmering red out of the water. My mother had been right.

When darkness came, I sat so that I was facing Mingo, but we didn't speak. I was exhausted, but felt I should try to stay awake through the night, to watch for trouble, to see if any plane or helicopter was advancing from behind us. He could watch the sky in the direction we were headed. The water was easy here and I didn't need to help by paddling. I settled in and watched the stars appear. That night the Milky Way was a wide solid white streak the length of the river.

The next day was overcast. Kai stayed awake so I could nap. I was feeling increasingly unwell. My stomach had started to grow queasy. Dozing didn't help. It only made my head reel more to lie at the bottom of the canoe and feel the roll of the water beneath me. Mingo stared silently out over the water. Kai watched some birds, but then put away his glasses saying he'd lost his enthusiasm. A dull depression seemed to have descended on us.

We camped that night on the far shore. "I can't go on without sleep," Mingo told us. But when we got there and started a fire, he brought out a jug of *tepae* the Roani women had given us, and he and Kai began to drink and talk. I lay down in my sleeping bag, too tired and woozy to sit up. I watched the two in the firelight, Mingo facing me with the red flames deepening the color of his skin. He laughed as they talked of the birds Kai had seen and wanted to see. Kai had his back to me. His hair was lighted to copper by the flames. I drifted off as they spoke of "the next time," when Mingo would take him to see the harpy eagle and the manakins.

The next morning I woke choking on sour burning bile that had risen in my throat and started down my windpipe. I tried to release myself from my sleeping bag, but couldn't and instead rolled over and vomited on the ground beside me. I lost everything, the tinned sardines, the crackers, the *tepae*. When I did extricate myself from the bag, every inch of my legs was covered with flea bites, and all the way up, beneath my underpants to my waist. I threw up again. By now the two men were awake and watching me through sleep-glazed eyes.

"Let's just go!" I cried. "There's no help for me now. It can't be worse on the river."

That day it poured. A torrential tropical downpour. We had to use our ponchos to cover the boat, not to become flooded. I sat in the bow, with my clothes and hair plastered to my body, vomiting and eventually dry-heaving into the rushing water. There were times I had to help with the paddling, as weak as I was, and I would look into the brown and gray murk before us, wondering if we would ever be out of there. We couldn't see the shore on either side. How the hell did Mingo know where he was going, I wondered. By late afternoon, everything transmuted to gold and silver when the sun found a break in the unrelenting rain. I watched, entranced, as silver raindrops fell on my skin. It was a miracle of nature, I thought deliriously, just before being overcome by another spasm.

But the true miracle happened when we pulled up on the Misahuallí beach to find the bus there, standing as though waiting for us in the once again bombarding rain.

We boarded, and the three of us sat side by side on the wooden seat. It was dark in the almost empty bus with the canvas side flaps pulled and battened down. I fell asleep.

In Puerto Napo Kai and I descended from the bus while Mingo handed us our bags. The bus began to rev its motor.

"Mingo, get off," Kai cried. "They're leaving."

"No, *señor*, I stay." He was sitting on the side with the canvas resting on his shoulders like a coronation collar. "I'm going to Baeza."

"But you said Macas," I said. "You have to get off to go to Macas."

"No, *señora*, I'm afraid you were mistaken. I'm going to Baeza to visit friends. *Adiós*. Until we see each other."

The bus grumbled to a start, its wheels spitting up mud behind. Mingo reached his hand down and I grabbed it. His flesh was warm in the cold stinging rain. "*Adiós*, *señorita. Adiós, Señor Kai.*"

Kai grabbed on, too, so that we were all three holding each other and then the bus bounded forward and Mingo slipped away. We stood in the rain watching as the bus turned the corner and drove out the road heading toward Baeza and points west. We watched until it had disappeared.

I threw up again onto the muddy street. We were standing by the building that held the general store. It began to rain harder, almost toppling me.

"Let's stand under here," Kai said, indicating the overhang of the porch. "We can't cross the river in this."

Kai helped me drag my bag along the muddy boardwalk. Once beneath the protection of the porch I sat down on it. Kai sat beside me. "Do you want to stay overnight in the Jaguar?" he asked.

"I want to get out of here," I said. "I'm afraid. I'm cold and sick and afraid and I'm not ashamed to say it."

"Not ashamed to say what, *Señora* Schmidt?" A voice spoke behind us.

I turned to see the friar like an apparition in the doorway of the *tienda*. He wore his dark robes, the ones that didn't show the filth as much. He spoke unabashedly in English.

"Please," I said. "We're going. Leave us alone."

"Just get out of here, you bastard." Kai stood.

I was too weak to stand.

The friar didn't smile. "I'm not here to harm you two. You needn't worry."

"But are your henchmen around the corner?" Kai said.

"I beg your pardon. I don't believe I have henchmen. I believe it's the other way around. I believe your hired killer just left on the last bus."

At that moment Jon, the Peace Corps volunteer, came out of the *tienda*. At first, I don't think he recognized us. We must have looked like beggars.

I stood. I started to speak and my mouth filled with the sour taste that forewarned another episode of vomiting. I tried to swallow it down, but it erupted out of me. It was only bile, but I doubled over with the intensity of the attack.

When I recovered enough to look up I saw that Jon had realized who we were. I reached for my bag.

"Kai, let's get out of here," I whispered.

"I want to kill him," Kai said, as he reached for his own pack.

"Well, we can't."

"*Señorita.*" The friar dug into the pocket of his garment.

"Don't," I said, frozen with fear, imagining his pulling a knife and killing us outright on the street.

"Take these, my dear. They'll help you with your stomach trouble. I wish you well on the remainder of your journey. I trust you're leaving for the States. I'm glad to find you out of harm's way. But do try these, *señora*. In truth, they will be good for you."

I took the tinfoil package that he was thrusting toward me. It was easier to take it than to put up a fight. As I dutifully put it in my pack, I heard Kai say in a quiet and controlled voice, "You are a guilty man, Báez. It's you who have the lives of these people on your soul."

Even though it was still pouring, the ferry was operating, and in minutes we had each made our journey across the turbulent river, swinging through the sharp, stinging drops to land on the dock we had lifted off from only five days earlier.

In Baños the next morning, the sun came out as we
rumbled into the town square. Kai stood and forced our
window open, letting fresh air into the stinking bus. The
minute he did I scrambled over him and vomited onto the
street.

When we stopped for refreshments at a *tienda* on the far
side of town, Kai made me get out, holding me up as he
did. He propped me against the side of the bus while he
went inside. When he returned I saw him through a haze
walking toward me with a bottle of Coca Cola.

"Here," he said. "I want you to drink this and take one of
the pills the friar gave you. I checked them and they're
charcoal. They'll do the job in an hour."

"I don't want anything he gave me," I said, starting to
slide down to a squat. The sun felt too hot. I wanted to be
out of my body, away from my raw and wounded stomach
and my uncontrollably reeling head.

Kai pulled me to standing. "Annie, come off your horse
and take these pills. I spent my life's bank account on this
soda out of a brand-new bottle. You'd better drink it."

I started to laugh and cry at the same time.

"What's the matter?" he said, a sly smile creeping onto
his too thin face.

"Your high horse," I gasped. "Off your high horse. Not
just any old horse." I couldn't go on to explain the second
malapropism as I dutifully swallowed and choked with
laughter on the sweet, peppery coke. Two in one, I thought,
a new record.

The bus broke down on a road above a small village. I
had been sleeping. The pill had worked and my stomach
had settled into place. I woke when Kai jiggled me.

"Something happened. We have to get off."

Hills rose up above our dusty road. And on those hills
were the tiny patchwork fields that signified highland
Indian cultivation. Each little patch was bordered by gray-
green agaves, and the large quilt they made was bordered
by the darker green of eucalyptus. Everything was dusted

with gray dry earth. There was no sight like this anywhere else in the world.

"One hour, no more," the bus driver said.

At that, everyone—most of the passengers were Indians—dispersed. They knew an hour could mean half a day. I heard the sibilant conversations of the Indians saying there was a market in the town below. But I didn't feel up to it. Instead I walked higher up the hill with Kai. We found a place for me to sit on a stone fence at a crossroads looking down toward the village. Kai proceeded on up the road with his binoculars.

"Call me if you need me," he said, already engrossed in a new hummingbird he'd spotted.

"I will," I said.

I sat as the Andean sunlight blasted periodically out from behind giant gray cumulus clouds. People were walking up the agave lined road toward me, pulling resistant pigs, cows and baby calves behind them. Indian women walked in their wide skirts, burdened with piles of wood or sacks of grain on their backs. A group of ruddy-faced Indian schoolgirls climbed toward me in their vibrant blue-and-red plaid uniforms and red sweaters. As I sat, I heard the songs Rina would sing, the songs of sadness, *tristeza*, and I thought of how she remained loyal to the Andes, to the home of her mother. I began to cry. I thought of Lucy found in her own excrement and of Jody weeping inconsolably on the bathroom floor that Christmas day. We had stepped off the plane in Quito, that first day six years before, onto the stairs rolled up for us, out into the blinding sun and the insistent droning of funeral dirges. I had walked down the stairs to the tarmac with the mountains rising dizzyingly before me. I saw that girl and I knew why I was weeping. She and all the others with her who descended those stairs in 1963, three weeks after the death of their president, still believed they had the power to make it a better world.

I looked up the road and saw Kai standing with his arms raised, holding his glasses to his eyes, seeing his world through them, the world he'd created for his own safety, a world he could control when all else had failed him, and I knew why I loved him. Because who else could understand my disillusionment but someone else who had experienced it earlier and even more profoundly? I had returned home from the Peace Corps and found that no one heard me. No one wanted to know what had died in me, not even my father. But Kai had known without my saying it. Kai had known what I hadn't known myself.

I sat watching a young Indian boy ride a donkey up the road toward me. It was a white and gray donkey laden with greens. The boy was dressed all in brown and gray. The town behind him was of mud houses, some white, others in pastel pinks and greens, all with red tile roofs. Beyond the town was the Pan American highway, reaching from south to north, stretching the entirety of the lower half of the continent. Past that were mountains. And all around me those foothills of gray-green patchwork that I loved so much.

Yes, this time I would speak of what I'd seen even if it was only on the air of my own small radio station. I would do what I could do. All that I could do. I would report on María, Häberle, Mingo and the Indians of the forest. Perhaps I would even finally search for Angel.

Yes, I was certain I would.

A truck full of Indians drove along a road parallel to mine, going up into the hills. The Indians were wearing the same deep reds and blues of the schoolgirls, their heads topped with dark green serge hats. I watched them travel up to their villages that I knew to be poorer and drier the higher they journeyed. And it was already so poor and dry right there where I sat.

Curbstone Press, Inc.

is a non-profit publishing house dedicated to
literature that reflects a commitment to social change,
with an emphasis on contemporary writing from Latin America
and Latino communities in the United States. Curbstone presents
writers who give voice to the unheard in a language that goes
beyond denunciation to celebrate, honor and teach. Curbstone
builds bridges between its writers and the public – from inner-city
to rural areas, colleges to community centers, children to adults.

This mission requires more than just producing books.
It requires ensuring that as many people as possible know about
these books and read them. To achieve this, a large portion of
Curbstone's schedule is dedicated to arranging tours and programs
for authors, working with public school and university teachers to
enrich curricula, reaching out to underserved audiences by
donating books and conducting readings and community programs,
and promoting discussion in the media. It is only through these
combined efforts that literature can truly
make a difference.

Curbstone Press, like all non-profit presses, depends on the support
of individuals, foundations, and government agencies to bring you,
the reader, works of literary merit and social significance which
might not find a place in profit-driven publishing channels. Our
sincere thanks to the many individuals who support this endeavor
and to the following foundations and government agencies:
ADCO Foundation, J. Walton Bissell Foundation, Inc., Connecticut
Commission on the Arts, Connecticut Arts Endowment Fund,
Lannan Foundation, LEF Foundation, Lila Wallace-Reader's Digest
Fund, Andrew W. Mellon Foundation, National Endowment for the
Arts, and The Plumsock Fund.

Please support Curbstone's efforts to present
diverse voices and views that make our culture richer.
Tax-deductible donations can be made to:
Curbstone Press, 321 Jackson Street, Willimantic, CT 06226